Day by day Dolores worked herself into a panic over the coming child, but it was a panic without energy, a feeling that she could hardly move and that soon she wouldn't be able to move at all or even speak. There were days she pulled herself out of the blackness—she would hustle her daughter Tessa out of the door, and they would go shopping together—and she would see the look in Tessa's eyes. They were anxious and filled with love, questioning why it couldn't happen every day. It broke Dolores's heart, but she felt there was nothing she could do.

When she had told Tessa the new baby was coming, she had seen such conflicting emotions in Tessa's eyes—excitement and fear—and she had known that it was an important time to be there for Tessa, but she'd had a headache and spent most of that day in bed. . . .

TO THE FOURTH GENERATION

Nell Kincaid

BALLANTINE BOOKS • NEW YORK

Copyright © 1992 by Nell Kincaid

All rights reserved under International and Pan-American Copyright Conventions. Published in the United States of America by Ballantine Books, a division of Random House, Inc., New York, and simultaneously in Canada by Random House of Canada Limited, Toronto.

Library of Congress Catalog Card Number: 91-93141

ISBN 0-345-36715-4

Manufactured in the United States of America

First Edition: May 1992

BOOK ONE

1

As Amelia Flaherty drove up to her daughter's house, she felt the same pang of dismay that always hit her whenever she got to Pollard Street. Dolores and Eddie's house was tall and dark green, at the exact center of a long row of other tall, broken-down houses, all of which had once been owned by Lane Mills Incorporated, and all of which, in a long-ago attempt to bolster employee enthusiasm, had been painted the colors of the sheets and blankets the mill produced. At the time, the houses had added brightness and color to a town that was otherwise mostly soot-blackened brick or weathered-gray clapboard, but now that the colors had faded and chipped, the buildings looked as forgotten and dilapidated as the rest of Lodenton and countless other towns in Western Pennsylvania.

Wisely, the mill had decided to sell the buildings rather than try to keep them habitable—many had fallen into such serious disrepair that the town was threatening condemnation. They had sold them to real estate speculators, mostly to one company, which had in turn rented them out to people like Eddie—all, from what Amelia could see, lowlifes who took no pride in where they lived and even less in themselves.

The front yard, which was a narrow strip of earth covered with weeds and a broken sidewalk, was strewn with broken toys that Amelia thought had probably belonged to the children of the previous tenant—Tessa was too young still to play with toys outside, and Matthew hadn't even lived long enough to sit out on the lawn.

"Dolores?" she called in through the screen door.

"In here," Dolores called out, in a slack, flat voice that let Amelia picture her exactly: she would be reading the newspaper at the kitchen table with a sink full of dishes and a filthy floor, probably with the radio and TV on at the same time so that she wouldn't miss any news reports. Or she would be reading one of her scrapbooks, "The Days of Jack and Jacqueline," and crying.

Amelia had worried initially when her daughter had decided she was the spitting image of Jacqueline Kennedy, then merely the wife of a hopeful, attractive senator. It was true that Dolores bore to her a remarkable resemblance, not that Amelia had ever confirmed this to Dolores's face; she hadn't wanted to feed what she felt was an unhealthy and futile fantasy life. What difference would it make in her daughter's life even if she did look remarkably like the first lady? She was still married to an angry and dishonest man who couldn't hold a job for more than two months at a time; she had still lost her baby son under what Amelia would always feel were mysterious circumstances.

But now here it was, December 1963, and now that Kennedy had been assassinated, Dolores acted as if her life had personally been ruined forever by the event—*no one* could understand how upsetting it was.

When Amelia walked in, she saw that her mental picture had been right—Dolores was reading the newspaper at the kitchen table, no doubt scouring it for pictures of JFK or Jacqueline. And Tessa was screaming her head off from the crib in the corner.

Amelia went right over and pulled her granddaughter out.

"What's the matter with you?" she said to Dolores, who was watching as if she were a pet rather than a person—a cat blinking and watching, but uninvolved. "She's soaking wet."

"She must have just wet, then," Dolores said, stubbing out her cigarette. "I changed her five minutes ago."

Amelia didn't say anything. Tessa's diapers were soaked and stained, and when Amelia took them off, she saw the worst case of diaper rash she had ever seen. Tessa's bottom looked as if it had been seared. "My God," Amelia said. "This diaper rash is completely out of control."

Dolores pushed past her. "I know that," she said. "And I already took her to the doctor, so don't give me that look. I change her all the time, but it's never enough. I've never *seen* anyone who goes to the bathroom as much as she does."

Amelia knew what that meant—that Matthew had been different. She knew that it was as painful for Dolores to talk about him as it was for Amelia to think about him—her first grandchild, her only grandson. And she knew that Dolores had loved him.

"I want you to consider coming back to live with us," she said. There. She had said it. The words were out, she had set the ball in motion. She pinned the last pin into the diaper and settled into a chair with a happier, quieter Tessa in her arms.

Dolores blinked, and her eyes were hard as she said, "Why would I want to do that?"

Amelia sighed. "Because I know you're having a hard time. Because I know that you don't have enough money to care for Tessa properly, much as you might want to. Because it would give you time to rest and think about things without any pressures. I could take care of Tessa all day every day. Even your father is desperate to have you back if you think it will help."

Dolores lit another cigarette and looked up at the ceiling. At that moment, she looked so much like the former first lady that Amelia was almost tempted to say something. Sometimes she wanted to, just to see if her daughter would smile—something Amelia hadn't seen in months. But then she thought of the unhealthy underside of the truth: no doubt, Dolores looked so remarkably like her idol at that moment because she had studied the pose in a mirror; Amelia suspected that this was often true, that when Dolores was supposed to be changing her daughter's diapers, she was turning her head just so in front of the mirror, adopting as regal a pose as she could.

"I realize you don't think Eddie is the greatest husband in the world," Dolores said. "God knows I don't, and anyone who's even breathing would be able to see that he's a little on the moody side. But why you would think that would mean I'd want to move back home—"

"It could be absolutely temporary," Amelia said, feeling that her voice sounded too desperate, too accommodating. She looked down at Tessa, and Tessa was looking up at her with those adoring blue eyes that Amelia saw in her mind every night before she went to sleep. Would they be there the next day?

"Oh God, I don't know anything anymore," Dolores suddenly said, running a harried hand through her hair. She looked up at the ceiling again and took a long, slow drag on her cigarette. "Sometimes I think that I really should leave Tessa with you—go out and get some sort of job so that we would have some more money. Sometimes I wonder why I'm even staying with Eddie when I'm so miserable and he obviously is, too. Or maybe he doesn't even care. I don't know. But I just . . ." She looked into Amelia's eyes, and Amelia was careful not to interrupt; it was the longest string of sentences Dolores had spoken to her in years. "I really can't face living back home; that's all. I just can't face it. Maybe I leapt out of the frying pan and into the fire when I left with Eddie, but at least it was my fire, something I had chosen for myself.''

"But now you have a child," Amelia said. "You have to be sure that you're choosing the best place for her to grow up. You can't just think of yourself anymore." She couldn't help thinking of Matthew right then; if she had said these very same words to Dolores back then, would he still be alive today?

Dolores stubbed out her cigarette and put her head in her hands, and Amelia looked down at Tessa. Bright, beautiful blue eyes, and Amelia couldn't help thinking they looked so knowing. She rocked her softly and slowly and watched as her eyes closed. Poor baby had to be exhausted if what Dolores said was true, that she cried three fourths of the night because of the colic. Maybe Dolores never got any sleep, but that meant Tessa never did either.

Amelia hadn't quite told the truth about Dolores's coming home. Mack didn't particularly want her to; he would tolerate it, she knew, if Dolores decided to come home, but that was all. As far as he was concerned, Dolores had "made her own bed," and now she had to lie in it. "We didn't hold a gun and ask her to marry that bum," he had said more times than Amelia wanted to acknowledge. "She has something to complain about, she should have thought of it before she went and married the bum." As if he had the perfect marriage, and as if people weren't allowed to change their minds if conditions grew serious enough.

Amelia looked across the table at Dolores, who was smoking a new cigarette and looking sulkily off into space.

"That's one thing you would have to stop if you moved back in with us," she said.

"I'm not moving back in with you, so forget it," Dolores said without looking at her. She had the same expression—stubborn yet somehow without any will at all, that Amelia noticed all too often these days—the same willful set of her jaw Amelia had first noticed after Matthew had died. It was one day, a spring day when she had come down to Pollard Street to take Dolores shopping—as usual, there was only one car for Dolores and Eddie to "share"—and Dolores had been sitting at the kitchen table with the Acton paper spread out in front of her, obviously reading the story Amelia had read with horror that morning: a neighbor, Wanda Hopheimer, a young woman with two small children, had climbed over the bridge down by the mill and jumped into the Lodenton River.

"Oh, did you read that?" Amelia could remember saying to her daughter. "Isn't that just terrible? With those two young children?"

And she would never forget the look in her daughter's eyes as Dolores had looked up at her—utterly without hope, dull and gray and dead. "My questions are different," she had said. "I just wonder how she got the nerve to actually do it."

Amelia had been chilled by her words. "How can you say that? I know that this is a terribly difficult time in your life with Matthew gone—"

"You don't know anything," Dolores had said.

And indeed, Amelia had discovered that her daughter was right. She had never known, and indeed suspected that she still didn't know, the emotional depths to which her daughter could sink.

She knew that, in a sense, Mack was right: their daughter had chosen a certain route, marrying a man who would never be anything but trouble. Perhaps Dolores would never be able to pull out of the situation she had created for herself. But what about her daughter and any other children she might have?

Amelia looked down at her baby granddaughter and wished she could make everything better for her—if only she could just take her home and treat her as her own child!—and she wondered if she would ever be able to.

"Anybody home?"

Dolores's mother had left, and Dolores was sitting at the kitchen table in a shaft of gray, late-winter sun.

The man was pounding on the door, not knocking like a polite person would, and Dolores knew he was another collector. Sometimes they pretended to be polite—she would never forget the one who seemed so nice, he was so apologetic, he said his car had broken down right outside their door and could she just call his office for him? He wouldn't even ask to come in because he was a stranger, but if she could just call . . . and then the minute she had opened the door to see his car, he had touched her with the legal papers and said, "You're served."

She tiptoed back to the kitchen so she could get to the baby before she started to cry.

"Hello! Anybody home?" the voice yelled.

Dolores had just reached the baby. She was just about to pick her up when Tessa began to wail, and then the man pounded at the door again.

"Hello? You're going to have to open the door sometime," he called out.

Dolores sighed and set Tessa down. The man was wrong, she felt like telling him, because she *didn't* have to open the door sometime. She could wait inside longer than he could wait outside, and where could she even go without a car, anyway?

"Mrs. Madrewski?"

Dolores lit a cigarette and tried to shush the baby, and she looked across the room at the TV and hoped more than anything that that wasn't why the man was here. If she lost the TV, honestly, she thought she'd die. It was almost her only link . . .

"Get me a beer," Eddie said, putting his feet up on the coffee table.

Dolores half wished the man *had* taken the TV today, so that at least Eddie wouldn't get to watch it first thing when he came home from work.

She brought the beer back from the kitchen and hoped Eddie would keep the volume down so it wouldn't wake Tessa up.

"A collector was here today," she said.

He flipped open the top and took a long sip. She could tell what he was doing—pretending it didn't bother him, pretending he wasn't "phased," his favorite new word. But she could tell he was upset, just from the way he was holding his beer and the way his eyes were almost half-closed, blue eyes that had seemed like the greatest eyes in the world when she had first met him. Elvis Presley with blue eyes, with light brown hair that had the same one big wave as Elvis's, and with the sexiest walk she had ever seen.

"What'd he say?" he finally asked, setting the can down. From the sound she could tell he had drunk half.

"I didn't open the door," she said. "I thought that's what you told me to do."

He took a long, slow deep breath. "I did," he said, looking at her in a way she didn't understand. Sometimes she hated herself for being so afraid.

"He had a blue car, a blue station wagon," she said. "Does that tell you anything?"

He blinked, and she knew she had made a mistake. "How would I know anything about who he is from his car?" He looked angry and confused, the same way he had looked when she had first met him: angry at the deli store owner back then because they wouldn't take his check, storming out into the parking lot and then looking at her and saying, "Do they know you in there?"

She had liked that because she had been sixteen and he looked to be at least twenty-two or twenty-three, and he was talking to her as if she counted. And he looked like Elvis, of course, except with even nicer eyes. Not quite so soft.

"That's my best friend's dad that owns the store," she had said.

She could remember the exact car he had been driving back then, a light blue Mustang that looked kind of beat up but still had style, and he leaned back against it as if he wanted to talk to her for a while. "You live around here?"

She nodded. "Forever."

He smiled. "Sounds like a long time," he said, and he pulled out a pack of Camels. She liked his arms, she could remember back then how they had looked so strong and muscular.

"It is," she said, looking around. She was hoping someone would see her talking to this handsome man, a man no one even knew, but there was no one around. It was late afternoon and the mine had already closed, but the factory was still on shift, and it was one of those dead times in Lodenton that always made her feel she was going to go crazy someday.

"What are you looking for?" he asked. "Worried about a boyfriend seeing you talking to me?"

She shook her head. "I don't have one," she had said, which was true.

He had smiled, secretly, or so she had thought back then. So much was just a habit with Eddie, a way of looking great, but nothing more. "Ever been to Lakeville to the drive-in?"

She hadn't, she had always gone to the Lodenton drive-in because it was so much closer.

"Why don't you hop in, then, and you can get a little taste of the outside world. You look like you could use it."

He had seemed like the most exotic, exciting person she had ever met. He was twenty-four, and he worked over at a bottling plant in Mills Falls, a town she later discovered was just like Lodenton, but at the time it had sounded like Paris. He was from Ohio originally, and he was planning to be rich someday, and he told her she was the prettiest girl he had ever seen in all of Pennsylvania.

And next came the part that she still couldn't remember clearly: had she honestly felt that if she left home and ran off with Eddie Madrewski that she would lead the life she had always dreamed of? She had been beautiful back then, and she had secretly dreamed of going to New York or Hollywood and being discovered by some powerful man. Had she really thought Eddie was that man?

She could remember that she had loved being held by Eddie, even more perhaps than making love with him. He felt strong and solid, and she felt secure with him. When she was with him, she didn't feel what she called the cloak dropping down. She didn't feel the despair that sometimes came over her. He was a future.

Dolores heard the leg of Eddie's chair squeak, and she looked over out of the corner of her eye. A few moments later, he had come back from the kitchen, carrying another can of beer and a bag of potato chips.

Dolores felt her heart skip a beat when she saw the potato chips, because the bag was almost empty. Eddie would be screaming at her any minute now. She had meant to buy more, but she had gotten thrown off because her mother had come this morning and yelled, and then the collector had come. And she hadn't been able to go to the A&P because by the time the man left, it was almost time to get dinner ready, and all she had done was go to the corner deli. But now she was realizing all the things she had forgotten: more potato chips, more tomato juice, even beer if Eddie was in a mood and finished the eight that were still in the fridge.

Ed Sullivan came on and Dolores stood up and walked out of the living room. Eddie would keep watching to see if Topo Gigio was on, if she was really lucky—she had discovered at the beginning of their relationship that he was less likely to think of things to fight about if she was physically away from him, even just in another room.

Dolores could hear Tessa crying upstairs, the quiet whimpering that meant she was going to start screaming pretty soon, and she walked to the top of the stairs and listened.

Silence, at least for a minute. She tried not to think the thought—what if it was like Matthew?—and went into her bedroom. She hadn't looked at her project all day, and she needed to at least for a few minutes, to show that there was another world outside the one she was living in.

She took out Volume Five from under the bottom shelf in the closet, but as soon as she brought it up onto the bed and opened it, she felt the hopelessness that enveloped her now whenever she looked at the pictures, ever since the assassination.

Her mother had been criticizing her even more since then—making it worse—saying that *of course* the nation had changed and everyone was devastated, but it was time to get on with her life; everyone had to "get back to normal," she kept saying. Dolores had a new baby, and the baby was more important than anything else, she would say, and she kept saying it in a voice that made Dolores know what she was thinking: look at what had happened to Matthew . . . and would the same thing happen to Tessa?

What frightened her was that she knew she had loved Matthew more than she loved her new baby, someone who still remained nameless in her mind. A stranger who happened to be her baby. And even though she had loved Matthew so much—she'd never forget that feeling when he would look into her eyes and she would realize she meant everything in the world to him, it was as if she was being blessed by some sort of magic when she looked at him—even though she had loved him so much, he had died, and in her care.

And it wasn't Tessa's fault that she had come into the world at the wrong time. Dolores knew that. But there was something about the timing—when she got pregnant again, her neighbor Mrs. Felting had said, "When the new one comes along, it will help you forget all about Matthew," and in that moment, something terrible had happened, Dolores felt. She had awaited the birth with a combination of dread and fear. She resented the new baby because somehow, she felt, it had stolen Matt's life away. It had pushed him away so it could come into the world and have her all to itself, and that was how she had thought of Tessa before she was born: as an it, as a nonperson.

She heard Eddie clumping around in the living room and she quickly put the scrapbooks away. She could hear he was drunk from the way he was coming up the stairs. Drunk and, she hoped, tired, although she couldn't tell if he was planning to go to bed or just come up to use the bathroom, because the TV was blaring—"Gunsmoke," which she yearned to watch so she could see Amanda Blake. She was so beautiful.

Eddie stomped into the bathroom and slammed the door, and Tessa began to cry softly.

Dolores raced over to the crib and picked the baby up.

Her eyes were such an intense dark blue. It made Dolores nervous sometimes, because she had the feeling babies knew a lot more than people gave them credit for. What if they knew what you were thinking? What if they remembered it forever after, or they remembered how you had treated them after they were all grown up?

She looked down at the baby and said her name. "Tessa," she whispered. Tessa was Dolores's grandmother's name, and Eddie had liked the idea because it meant they would get more money when she was born.

"Tessa," she whispered again. Sometimes, secretly and only in her mind, she called her Jacqueline, because she wondered if maybe, if they had named her that instead, she would feel differently. "Tessa," she whispered. "Try to be quiet just for tonight, okay?"

"Goddamnit," Eddie said, coming out of the bathroom. He was storming toward her, Dolores could tell, and when she turned around, he was only inches away. His face was purple with anger. "You'd think I could come home and have a beer and take a goddamn shit around here without a problem," he said, and she realized with horror another thing she had forgotten at the store: toilet paper.

"Shut up," he said, glancing at the baby in Dolores's arms. Tessa had begun to cry, and Dolores was bouncing her gently, but it wasn't helping.

"Shut *up*," he said, and Dolores backed away instinctively. "Goddamnit, I'm talking to you," he said, and as he raised his hand, it almost seemed to be in slow motion as he brought it down hard on Tessa's face.

There was a silence. Dolores felt as if she were dying. Tessa began to scream then, and Dolores acted more quickly than she had in years, moving with a purpose she had never before felt in her life. She pushed past Eddie—she could see the purple splotch growing on Tessa's cheek.

"I'm sorry," Eddie said, and Dolores could feel his hands on her shoulders. "Is she all right? Let me see."

"Get away from me," she said.

He had moved around to the front, but she moved past him. "Get *away* from me," she said.

She didn't say anything more. She went downstairs and she picked up her purse, and she took Tessa out to the car. She saw Eddie running out of the house, and she prayed the car would start—of all times, now she needed the car to start.

"Dolores!" he called out.

She gunned the engine and pulled out.

In the rearview mirror, she could see Eddie in the moonlight, standing at the end of the driveway with his hands at his waist.

She knew he'd know where to find her—where else did she have to go but her parents' house?

But at least she'd be safe. She'd probably be bored and angry and feel trapped, but at least she'd be safe.

2

"Are there more pictures?" Tessa asked.

Amelia closed the photo album and set it back on the coffee table. "I imagine there are pictures of you in every room in the house," Amelia said. "But you know that: up on the bathroom wall, in my and Mack's bedroom, up on the kitchen wall. . . ."

Tessa's eyes were huge and clear and questioning. Too many events had followed one another too quickly, Amelia felt, for someone only four years old.

Amelia never would have thought Dolores would marry again; it was an action that, in Amelia's mind, required more energy than her daughter possessed. But what she hadn't realized until recently was that her daughter's moods swung to two vastly different extremes; once Dolores had left Eddie and begun living under their roof, Amelia was able to see what she had never seen before—weeks during which her daughter would do nothing but lie on the couch and stare vacantly and unseeingly at the television set, followed by days or even weeks during which she would be a flurry of activity, cleaning the house from top to bottom and talking almost nonstop.

"I think our daughter is a manic depressive," she had said to Mack one day. She had read about the condition in the newspaper and in a *Reader's Digest* article, and it was her understanding that it was a condition that could be treated.

"Is that what they're calling it these days?" he had said, barely glancing up from the fly he was tying. "If you ask me, that's kind of like calling a manure pile a waste management system. You can call it what you like, but it's still a pile of shit. And *she* can call it what she likes, but what she ought to do is get herself a job."

"She doesn't know anything about it," Amelia had said with irritation. "I'm the one that's been reading about it."

"A job or a good man would straighten out all them kinks. Get her headed in the right direction."

It had been a typically frustrating conversation—had Mack even heard half of what she had said?—but surprisingly, on her own, Dolores had indeed gone out and gotten a job, as a clerk at Lundgren's Hardware Store, and to Amelia's even greater surprise, had ended up marrying Gerald Lundgren, the son of the owner, last June.

"Grandma?"

"Yes, honey."

"Do you have pictures of anyone else?" Tessa asked.

Amelia knew who "anyone else" meant to her granddaughter. "Do you mean pictures of your father?"

Tessa's cheeks darkened. Amelia had never seen anyone so young blush before, and she felt it couldn't be a sign of anything good in the girl's life. "Do you have any?" Tessa asked again.

"Honey, I honestly don't think I do." She didn't want to tell Tessa the truth—that after Dolores had left Eddie, she had gone through the house and torn up every picture that he was in. "I can tell you what he looked like."

Tessa screwed up her face. "But do you remember were there any pictures ever?"

"Well, sure, honey. I'm sure there were. But pictures get lost all the time."

"But in the pictures did he hold me like a doll?"

"Do you mean did he hold you in his arms?" Amelia asked, cradling Tessa in her own. "Of course he did, Tess. All the time." It was a lie, but she supposed one of the ones you had to tell during your lifetime. What would be the point of telling Tessa the truth about her father? Although Amelia didn't agree with Dolores's approach, which was to say nothing. Wasn't it natural that the child would grow more curious the older she got?

"Can I look in your top drawer again?" Tessa asked.

"Of course, dear. Just be careful of the perfume." She watched Tessa run out of the room, and she tried to think if there possibly could be any pictures of Tessa's father in the house. It was now two weeks since Dolores had finally told Tessa that she would soon have a baby sister or brother, and it seemed as if Tessa needed the reassurance that came from seeing her own baby pictures: her mother had loved her and held her, too, back then; she had been loved. "Mommy's stomach is like a ball because there's a little baby inside," Tessa had said to Amelia when she had first found out. And the look in Tessa's eyes had broken Amelia's heart. It was clear that Tessa thought she was supposed to be happy—there was a false, hopeful smile on her face—but that actually she felt frightened and insecure.

"Grandma?"

"Yes, honey."

Tessa had come back into the living room with a small lap blanket and an empty glass jar. "Could you wrap me up like a baby and give me milk?"

"Oh, honey. Come here," she said, and she held out her arms. Tessa climbed into her lap and laid her head against her shoulder and let the blanket slide. "You don't want to be a *baby* again. That would be going backward. Would you like it if everything started to go backward? If you had to walk across the street backward, and if I talked backward, and if you had to look at me upside down?" Amelia twisted so she was looking at Tessa upside down, and Tessa began to laugh. "And anyway, you have all the advantages in being older," Amelia said. "Your baby sister or brother will have to lie in a crib all day and wonder what's going on, and you'll be able to do all kinds of things that the baby won't be able to do. He'll look at you talking but not have any idea what you're saying, or if you're telling me secrets—"

"Or if *you're* telling *me* secrets!" Tessa said, suddenly excited about the idea.

"That's right. And another thing the baby won't be able to do for a while is help Grandma with her shopping, which is what you're going to do this afternoon with me. Or make cookies, which is another thing we have to do, for Grandpa's dessert. Do you think he'd like that?"

"He'd love it," Tessa said, rubbing her hand on her stomach. "And me, too."

Amelia smiled and patted Tessa's behind. "Up you go, and let's get all that shopping done, then, and we can have all the cookies done by the time we take you home."

"But I don't want to go home," Tessa said, looking up at her as Amelia gathered Tessa's shoes and socks. "I want to stay here with you and Grandpa."

They went through this too often, in Amelia's opinion. It wasn't right that a girl should dread going home. But she couldn't say she blamed her granddaughter for the way she felt: from what she had seen, her stepfather barely acknowledged Tessa's existence unless he was disciplining her for something that usually, in Amelia's view, at least, was nothing more than a four-year-old's perfectly normal behavior.

"Maybe this weekend you can spend the whole weekend with us. I'm sure your mom would say yes if we asked her in just the right way."

Tessa narrowed her eyes. "You mean tippytoeing and saying it when she's sleeping with her eyelids shut?"

Amelia smiled. "We'll see. Something like that."

They went into the kitchen, and Amelia left a note for Mack—cold meatloaf in the fridge, and they'd be back by early afternoon. He was working so hard these days, putting on a new porch for a woman who lived across town. In fact, he seemed to be working harder, Amelia felt, than before he had "retired." But she supposed she was lucky. She often heard about men who retired and then proceeded to do nothing but moon about the house all day, supposedly puttering, but in reality driving their wives out of their minds.

But she also worried about him. He wasn't as young as he thought. She had made the mistake of telling him that the other day, and you would have thought she had told him he was about to die. He had gotten furious, and later on, she had seen him studying his face in the mirror like a young girl. He was still a good-looking man, certainly. At fifty-eight, he looked more like a man ten years younger, with pale blue eyes and a ruddy, healthy-looking complexion. What Amelia felt aged her most—her gray hair—merely looked distinguished on Mack. But whether he liked it or not, the truth was he was getting older.

"Grandma, Mommy brang home that dress in that store," Tessa said, pointing to a dress shop on the other side of the street.

Amelia glanced over, but she was concentrating on finding a parking space. Honestly, one would think that in the middle of a working day in a town where almost everybody worked at the mill or in the mine, one would be able to find a parking space!

"Did you see it?" Tessa asked as Amelia pulled into the space. "Mommy says she looks just like Jacqueline when she wears it."

"Oh, really?" Amelia glanced again at the store, but the window seemed to be a jumble of dresses. Then she saw one in maroon, Dolores's favorite color, and she had the feeling that had to be the one. She imagined Dolores standing in front of the mirror with her jaw set just so, holding her head just so, telling her four-year-old daughter she looked just like the former first lady, and didn't Tessa think so, too?

Amelia took Tessa's hand and led her up the street, and for a few moments she imagined that the small hand holding hers was Dolores's at that age, and she tried to remember: had she done something so wrong, either one terrible incident or a series of inexcusable mistakes, that had turned her daughter into the woman she was today? What she remembered of her marriage and Dolores's childhood years was that until Dolores had turned into a teenager, it had all been like a sunny, amazing dream. Amelia had married her childhood sweetheart, she had loved him with all her heart, and they had created a beautiful little girl, finally, ten years after they had married. And even though she hadn't been able to have any more children, she had felt fine. One was enough when she was such a joy.

Amelia sometimes had the sinking, guilty feeling that the reason she took such almost delirious pleasure in being with Tessa, just as she had with Dolores at that age, was that sunny, beautiful, happy little girls were all she was equipped to deal with. When Dolores had become a teenager, it seemed as if overnight, her door was suddenly shut all the time and she was always angry, always dissatisfied. Nothing that her mother said pleased her, and worse, most of the time, it embarrassed her. Even worse still, she didn't seem to care about things one way or the other, unless they related to her or the way she looked. Amelia had felt utterly betrayed, as if someone had come in during the middle of the night and exchanged her daughter for someone else's. What had happened to the little girl who had looked up at her with those dreamy eyes full of love?

She had read often enough that teenagers were extremely difficult; she certainly wasn't naive enough to have expected anything different. Yet, nevertheless, she had felt betrayed, and later, when Dolores had stayed as moody as a teenager, Amelia had wondered if perhaps it all stemmed from something she had done wrong.

"Grandpa!" Tessa said, and she tugged at Amelia's hand and then stopped.

Mack was sitting in the window of a restaurant with Lauralee Wicks, the woman he was building the porch for. They were both laughing, and Amelia took in the picture as if in a freeze frame before looking away and holding Tessa's hand all the tighter. Lauralee Wicks had on all sorts of makeup—she had just moved to Lodenton from someplace in Connecticut, and Amelia knew she was connected with Main's Department Store, something to do with fashion. And she looked like a fashion model, like one of the mature ones they were starting to show lately—lustrous brown hair with a streak of gray, not a hair out of place, matching fingernails and lipstick. And Mack laughing and looking into her eyes with an enthusiasm Amelia wished she hadn't seen.

"There's the door," Tessa was saying, tugging at her grandmother's hand. "I want to see Grandpa."

"Not right now, honey. He's having a business meeting," Amelia said. She glanced back—she didn't want to, but she couldn't help herself. Mack was still laughing, and Lauralee Wicks's eyes were shining brightly.

"I'm turning into one of those things," Dolores said. "You know what I mean—that thing that blew up?"

Gerald lowered the paper and looked across the table at her. "What are you talking about?" His voice was both angry and uninterested at the same time.

"Those things. Dirigerels or somethings."

"Are you talking about blimps?"

Blimps. Of course. She had forgotten the easy word. She looked down at her stomach and then back at Gerald. "I guess that's the word I meant," she said quietly.

He shrugged. "What do you expect? You're having a baby. You look the way you're supposed to look."

She wanted to scream. She couldn't bear the way her body looked, and she couldn't bear what had happened to her life. At first, she had thought Gerald would be the perfect husband: he was polite and he was even tempered, and she knew he would never hit her or drink too much. In fact, at first she had felt that she was marrying into something like a miniature First Family. In Lodenton and even a bit in Acton, the nearest large town, the Lundgrens were a prominent, respectable family. Didn't everyone go to Lundgren's Hardware? Didn't Gerald look a bit like a senator or even a president (though not, of course, like JFK), with his light brown hair and square, even features? Of course, she had the feeling senators weren't allowed to have beards, but Gerald's was always neat and closely trimmed. And other than the beard, she felt he could easily have been a national politician; Gerald's father had been supervisor of Lodenton for almost twenty years. But Dolores now saw that the Lundgren family's steadfastness and respectability had added a luster in her eyes that had blinded her when she agreed to marry Gerald.

She was beginning to feel she was losing her mind again, sinking into the badness that had led her to Eddie, that feeling that made her need major ups and major downs in her life. Her daily routine with Gerald was relaxed and astonishing to Dolores; she realized that most people lived in this organized, crisis-free way, but she had never experienced it as an adult. They ate breakfast together in the beautiful house Gerald had built with his own hands; Gerald was cheerful and sober in the morning and always on his way to work by seven, after having spent at least two hours each morning working on the new wing for the baby. Dolores would leave at eight, taking Tessa to her parents' house and then driving to the hardware store to start the day. She would pick Tessa up, go home, and make dinner. Gerald would come home and eat, and then he would work some more on the new wing, and then they would all go to bed. No screaming, no fighting, no hanging up on collectors or hiding in the dark.

But he didn't know her; he barely spoke to her. He was never outwardly mean, and he was always looking forward to his day at work and coming home to a good dinner in the evening, always talking with great enthusiasm about whatever part of the house he would work on that evening. But he couldn't talk about anything else; he wasn't interested. And the truth was that it terrified her the way he talked about the new baby. Everything had to be perfect, every inch of flooring, every stick of furniture, every second of the baby's future life. And it frightened her for herself and for Tessa. Didn't anyone else matter but the new baby?

Plus she had never told him the truth about Matthew. She hadn't planned on ever mentioning Matthew ever, at all—it hurt even to say his name aloud—except that Gerald had insisted on coming with her to the gynecologist after she had discovered she was pregnant, and when the doctor had said, "So this is your second pregnancy, Mrs. Lundgren?" she had felt compelled to say no. But instead of telling the whole truth, she had said—all the while feeling Gerald staring intently at her from off to the side—"My first child was stillborn," and almost burst into tears.

She had betrayed Matthew with that one sentence, and she hated herself for having done it, and she feared for the future in ways she couldn't express even to herself.

* * *

"Let me have that section when you're done?" Dolores said, keeping her voice as calm as she could. Gerald no longer encouraged her in her scrapbook work—he gave her a glassy-eyed, blank look when she mentioned Jacqueline or JFK, and she had sensed it would be better to pretend she had lost interest. But she had spotted a picture of Jacqueline in the paper he was reading, and it was hard for her to pretend that she was calm.

She felt almost breathless with excitement: it had been weeks since she had had something to cut out!

When Gerald put the paper down, she couldn't help herself; she pounced on it like a starving cat on a mouse, and she could feel him looking at her. She tore the page in half and was just standing up to get the scissors when she checked the other side of the page, and she sat back down. There it was in the police blotter, in black and white. Eddie Madrewski, in jail for breaking and entering, drunken driving, resisting arrest.

And unaccountably, she suddenly missed him. She wasn't sorry she had left him, and when she thought about the violence, she was more sure than ever. But Eddie had known who she was; Eddie had known the truth about her, and he hadn't expected anything of her. Gerald was expecting her to be a happy, normal mother to his child, and she was terrified.

"I guess now is as good a time as any to say what I have to say," Gerald suddenly said, pushing his chair back from the table with a squeak.

She looked up at him. She wanted to trim down the picture of Jacqueline, to paste it into the book while it was still fresh and exciting. "What's the matter?" she asked. Tessa was sitting at the table, too, eating quietly and wordlessly, the way Gerald liked. But now she was looking up at him with her huge blue eyes, looking frightened.

"I want you to stop working at the store," he said.

"Why?"

"Because your proper place is at home," Gerald said. "You're having a baby, Dolores. That's a job in itself. When you're in your eighth and ninth months, you'll be wanting to rest, but until then, as I see it, you have a job at home with the new wing."

"What are you talking about?"

"I didn't build it so it could be empty," he said. "I built it so you could decorate it for the baby."

"How long can it take to decorate two bedrooms and a bathroom?'' she asked. She felt itchy to work with the clipping and her scrapbook, angry and uncomfortable about the conversation.

He looked down and squared off the placemat so it was parallel to the edge of the table. ''The point isn't how long it can take if you're rushing. I want the new wing to be special. I want the baby to love it and be happy in it—''

''What about Tessa? It's not just going to be for the new baby,'' she said. She glanced over at Tessa, who was looking down at her plate. She seemed to be blushing, a dark-haired little girl with pale blue eyes and a scarlet flush of self-consciousness across her cheeks.

''Tessa, too,'' he said. ''Obviously. You're going to have to choose wallpaper and supervise the men who'll hang it. You're going to have to choose furniture, carpeting, drapes, lighting fixtures—it can't be done in a week, Dolores.''

She got up and cleared the dishes from the table. She was afraid of not working, but she didn't want to tell him because she knew he wouldn't understand. She knew how she would feel if she was alone all day: she would have too much time to think and brood—she would have too much time to think about Matthew and worry about the new baby. She would sink into an abyss. ''I know most women stay home when they're expecting, but I can't,'' she said.

He looked confused and irritated. ''What do you mean; you can't? You don't go to work, and that's that.''

''You don't understand,'' she said.

Tessa hopped off her chair and started for the living room.

''Hup,'' Gerald called out. ''Get back here.''

Tessa tiptoed back in and looked up at him.

''What do you say?''

''Um, can I be excused?''

''That's right. Yes, you may be excused.'' She started to run out but Gerald called out ''Hup!'' again, and Tessa stopped as if she had been trained to stop on a dime. Dolores looked away. ''That's the third time this week,'' Gerald said in a harsh voice she never heard him use at the hardware store.

''The third time for what?'' Tessa piped up.

''Huh. Don't play dumb with *me*, Tessa. You know exactly it's the third time you tried to leave the table before you were excused. So I'll tell you what. The next time you try it—and someday you'll thank me because I'm the only one around here who's teaching you any manners whatsoever—the next time you try to leave the table without being excused, you can eat your meals in your room for a week."

"Gerald," Dolores said.

"Don't interrupt me here, Dolores. I know what I'm doing," he said without looking at her. "So we understand each other, Tessa?"

"Yes," she said quietly.

"Yes? Yes what? Just yes?"

"Yes sir," she said.

He jerked his head. "All right, then you can go. But remember what I said: one more time, and you eat in your room for a week."

Tessa ran out, and Dolores felt as if a blanket of shame were settling over her shoulders and head. Why couldn't she say anything in defense of her daughter to Gerald?

He was standing up. "All right, now it's your turn," he said. "Tell me what I don't understand."

She came away from the sink and watched as he moved closer, but she felt as if he were a stranger. "I can't be home alone," she said. "I know myself well enough to know that, Gerald, and I'm telling you that."

"Well, I'm telling you you're not going to be working at the store."

She stared at him. "You're firing me?"

"I'm going to lay you off indefinitely, Dolores, and if you go out and find another job anywhere in town, you can be assured I'll have them lay you off, too."

She felt helpless with anger and frustration. She knew he was telling the truth; his word carried weight in Lodenton, and she probably wouldn't find another job she could keep. But she didn't even know if she'd be able to look, even if his threat weren't hanging over her. Working at Lundgren's had become so comfortable; she wasn't ready to set out on strange new turf.

Day by day she worked herself into a panic over the coming child, but it was a panic without energy, a feeling that she could hardly move and that soon she wouldn't be able to move at all or even speak. Despite Gerald's disapproval, she continued to take Tessa over to her mother's almost every day, or else Tessa's grandmother came to pick her up. There were days she pulled herself out of the blackness—she would hustle Tessa out the door, and they would go shopping together—and she would see the look in Tessa's eyes. They were anxious and filled with love, questioning why it couldn't happen every day. How come sometimes they had fun together, and the other times she would come into the room and her mother couldn't get out of bed? It broke Dolores's heart, but she felt there was nothing she could do.

When she had told Tessa the new baby was coming, she had seen such conflicting emotions in Tessa's eyes—excitement and fear—and she had known that it was an important time to be there for Tessa, but she'd had a headache and had spent most of that day in bed. And then Tessa had come in the next day in tears and said she had heard Gerald talking on the phone, and was it true her real dad was in jail?

"Oh, honey, come here," she had said, holding out her arms and hugging Tessa as she climbed into bed with her.

"Is it true?" Tessa had asked, putting her thumb in her mouth and leaning against Dolores's shoulder.

"It's true, but it has nothing to do with you," Dolores had said, stroking Tessa's hair and shoulder. "Your life and your future have nothing to do with your father."

"But was it like on TV?" Tessa asked. "Did he have a gun and go into a house?"

Dolores hadn't known what to say. In fact, Eddie and Charlie had used a gun and robbed a 7-Eleven, or tried to. But why did Tessa have to know? "I'm not quite sure what he did," she lied, feeling inadequate. "But I love you and that's what counts, Tessa. It's the only thing that counts in this world. Your father wasn't the greatest person in the world, and it's better if you forget all about him."

"But why?" Tessa asked. "Did he love me?"

At least Dolores had been able to smile, she remembered that. "Oh, he loved you a lot," she had said, and she was sure that it had been clear she was telling the truth. "He loved you an awful lot, Tessa. But you probably won't ever see him again."

She had looked down and seen tears streaming down Tessa's face, and she had gathered her up in her arms and held her for what seemed like hours, and she had known then that this was what it was supposed to be like—they were supposed to have talks like this all the time, and she was supposed to hold Tessa in her arms all the time—but there was something that stopped her from feeling and acting the way she knew she should.

She was filled with fear because she knew that love wasn't enough. She had loved Matthew more than she had ever loved anyone in her life. She had tried to take care of him . . . she had loved the smell and feel and sound of him, and she had felt that life wouldn't be worth living without him. He was everything. And yet, she had lost him forever.

She could remember exactly how she had felt when she and Eddie had gone out that night, and she knew it was because she had been so young. Defiant, because Matthew had been crying and coughing all day, and now he was quiet at last. She had done her job, and Eddie was being nice to her; he wanted to show her off because she had lost the weight from the baby, and at the back of her mind, a voice had said, *You can't leave the baby alone!*

She knew it. She knew that it was the absolute wrong thing to do, but she also knew that she felt trapped being at home all the time, that when Eddie wanted to go out, you went out, and she wanted to go out and have fun. It would be so quick, it would take such a short time. And Eddie was in such a great mood, telling her how beautiful she looked and how she had her shape back so fast. Everything would be fine.

Don't leave the baby alone, the voice had said, but she didn't listen. Eddie took her to McSweeney's Roadhouse, where there was a kind of amateur semistrip show, and she had felt good because he wanted her to get up there and show herself off. She didn't want to because she knew it was lower-class and cheap, but she felt good that he thought she was so pretty, and she was drinking as fast as he was.

She could remember exactly how they had progressed; it was a matter of starting with beers and then switching to Scotch somewhere along the way, and she remembered how free she felt thinking it didn't matter what she drank, what went into her breast milk, because she could take one night off, just one.

Some of Eddie's friends she didn't know too well came and sat at the table with them, and she was able to speak without Eddie telling her to shut up.

By the time they left the bar, she was so drunk she was seeing double and holding on to Eddie. She could remember she had fallen once on the way out and for a blinding moment thought Eddie would get mad at her, but he had only picked her up, hugged her, and told her she sure was pretty when she was drunk. They had laughed at that on the way out—it had sounded unaccountably funny, even though now she couldn't remember why—and driven home with Eddie at the wheel probably as drunk as she was.

Dolores could remember the car careening into the driveway, and only then was she aware that they had been out for hours.

Hours and *hours*. The neighbors' outdoor light went on, and Eddie had held up his middle finger. "Goddamn nosy-ass neighbors," he had shouted into the night, and it was then that Dolores had had the terrible feeling. It really *had* been hours and hours. She looked at her watch and squinted to see. They had been gone for six hours.

The house was quiet and dark—had they really forgotten to put any lights on?—and Dolores ran upstairs to the baby's room. She turned on the lights, and she knew, right then, even though she was seeing double and she was standing ten feet away. His face was contorted, and there was fluid coming out of his mouth, stuck there, but you could tell where it had come from. She held out her hand and his forehead was warm, and for a moment her heart had leapt; she had been wrong—she was drunk, and she had been wrong.

She scooped him up in her arms and he felt different, and she cried out because she knew.

She heard Eddie clumping around downstairs and the crash of a glass, then Eddie cursing. Tears were streaming down her face, and she pressed her cheek against Matthew's; she sank against the wall to the floor and held his skin against hers, and she wished more than anything that she had died instead of him.

And she knew what she had read was true: losing a child was the worst thing that could happen on earth. And now here she was, and she wished there was someone she could talk to about all of it, but there wasn't anyone in the world she felt close enough to.

3

"We'll have a pink cake and pink decorations all around the house, don't you think?" Dolores said.

Tessa nodded and wrote "pink cake" down on their list. She was afraid to be so happy, but she couldn't help it. She and her mom had been talking for three days about the birthday she was going to have—it was going to be her ninth. It was going to be all girls, Tessa had the feeling, except every day she changed her mind. Some of the other girls in her class had had boy-girl parties, but she didn't really know any of the boys, and the most popular girl had had a sleepover with just girls, so Tessa felt that the safest thing would be to do what Cindy Carmello had done.

There was one part about the party that felt terrible, that her grandmother wouldn't be able to come because she was in the hospital. Whenever Tessa thought about what was going to happen, she felt as if she was going to go crazy, and she knew there was no one she could talk to about it because the only one she could ever talk to about anything was her grandmother. And there she was, in an all-white bed with nurses and doctors all over the place, and they said there was a lump in her breast and that no one knew what that meant. And Tessa could tell that her grandma was scared because she looked all gray—gray hair and eyes and even her mouth was pale without lipstick—and Tessa had heard her say "I'm scared" to Mack in a small voice Tessa had never heard before.

But she had made Tessa promise she'd be excited about the party no matter what. "I've always told you that you can make all kinds of friends if you're not too shy to invite them over. If you invite some girls over and they have a good time, they'll invite you to their houses, too."

Tessa doubted her words because she just didn't see how they could be true. What she knew was that when she walked through the halls at school, she felt invisible. There were always girls in twos and threes and they were always talking about something and laughing, and she was never part of it. Sometimes, on certain days when she had more courage and she told herself she didn't care, she would go over to the popular girls' table in the lunchroom and say, "Is this seat taken?" or sometimes even just sit down.

But the same thing always happened. There'd be a little bit of silence, as if they were all sending secret messages to each other, and then they'd start talking as if she weren't even there. And she never knew what to say to make them like her.

Tessa felt she'd give anything in the world to know why it happened and what she could do to change things. She still knew a lot of fairy tales because she would hear Gerald reading to Louann, and whenever she heard about three wishes a person got to make, she always knew what her wishes would be: that she could live with her grandparents, that her mom never would get so sad again that she had to go back to the hospital for weeks or sometimes even months, and that she would be popular.

Plus (and she knew this was bad) she wished that her little sister had never started to play the piano. It seemed like forever ago that it had happened, except that it was almost exactly a year, on Tessa's eighth birthday. Her grandmother was there playing "Happy Birthday to You" on the piano; and Louann, three years old and she could hardly even climb onto the piano bench, had come and climbed up and started to play. And from that day on, Tessa was always "the sister of that one who plays the piano." The prodigy with the thing called perfect pitch.

But at the party, Louann wasn't going to play the piano even once—Tessa's grandmother had promised she would talk to Tessa's mom about it—and it was going to be all outdoors, a barbecue and then swimming in the aboveground pool, and then a sleepover in the den that night. Tessa had gone to the library and taken out two books of ghost stories, and what she hoped so much was that they would all sit around and she would read them, and everyone would be screaming and having the greatest time.

"What do you think about the time?" her mom said. "Do you think two o'clock would be good? Or maybe three."

Tessa bit her lip. She had no idea. She didn't know when the normal time was because she had only ever gone to three birthday parties for kids at school. "Um, maybe three," she said, because what if the party wasn't going well? She didn't want it to last forever.

Her mom smiled. "Then three it is."

She looked beautiful right then, and Tessa felt a pull of love for her. Sometimes when her mom was feeling bad, she got so skinny and sometimes even old-looking—especially when they were going to take her to the hospital so she could feel less sad—but right then she looked beautiful and glamorous.

"I know that Jacqueline has always had special parties for her children," her mom suddenly said. "In fact, I'm sure of it." She stood up. "I think I have an article in one of my scrapbooks."

"I don't have to see," Tessa said, but her mom had already left the room.

Tessa looked down at the list and tried not to think about what she had once heard her grandmother say over the phone, that the way Tessa's mom was so interested in the Kennedys was crazy. And she tried not to think about what if her mom went into one of her bad periods again before the party, then what would happen? She looked down at the list and read the words out loud like you would in school: crepe paper, hamburgers, hot dogs, rolls, salads, pink cake. Plus her mom had promised that for her present, they'd go to Main's together and pick out some clothes. "It's so important at this age for you to be happy with what you're wearing," her mom had said, and Tessa had felt so relieved that she wasn't going to get something like a teddy bear or dolls for her present. She wanted to dress exactly like Cindy Carmello and the other girls who were popular.

Her mom came back into the room with one of her scrapbooks, the one with the red cover, and Tessa felt her stomach jump. The one with the red cover was the one she had spilled the wax on when she and Louann were melting down crayons one day, when she was showing Louann how to make shapes out of wax. She had looked down and right there on the page, right on a picture of the whole Kennedy family, were all these blobs of purple and red she and Louann had just mixed together. She had ripped out the pages with their cellophane and put them into her schoolbag and then thrown them out at school, and then she had hoped that her mom would never notice.

But now, she could tell, just from watching the way her mom was turning the pages, quickly as if she was confused and suspicious, that her mom already knew. "There are pages missing from this book," she said. She sank down slowly into her chair and laid the book on her lap, and she was staring straight ahead as if she didn't even know where she was.

"Really?" Tessa said. She wished she knew how to change the subject, because she was sure she was going to let the truth pop out like a mouse. Plus what if Gerald came in? Her mom would maybe even get in trouble then, because he was always yelling when he saw the scrapbook. Once she had even heard him say, "If I had had any idea about all this crap, Dolores, you can be sure I wouldn't have gotten into all of this." And she had felt that he meant the marriage by "all of this."

"I don't understand this *at all*," her mom said, flipping the pages. "I can't imagine how pages could just drop out of an album." She looked up at Tessa, and her jaw was hanging there like a rag. She looked confused and angry and like she was about to cry, and Tessa felt her stomach starting to burn.

Tessa tried to look casual. "Maybe you just forgot which album the pictures are in."

Her mom shook her head like a kid. "Absolutely not. I would never forget. I know these albums better than I know my own house," she said. She flipped the pages again but more quickly this time. "And I know exactly which pictures are missing." When she looked up, her lips were stretched out in a thin line. "I wonder if Gerald took them."

Tessa was starting to feel sick. "Gerald?"

"He absolutely hates these albums, you know. Every man I've ever been with has hated these albums. Your father—" She stopped.

"My father what?" Tessa asked. She was amazed her mom was even mentioning him because it was always as if he had never even existed except when Tessa brought him up.

Her mom shrugged. "Oh, it was so long ago. But I kept the albums secret from him for the longest time. I had to —"

"Why?" Tessa asked. She knew she shouldn't jump too quickly with questions, but it had just popped out.

"He would have stolen them," she said.

"Why?" Tessa asked again, because who would steal someone's scrapbook? Who would even want it unless they were "fascinated" too, because that was the way her mom always described it—"I have a fascination with that family," she would say.

Her mom set her lips in a thin line again, and that was when she really did look a lot like Jacqueline. "Your father was in the habit of stealing anything that was valuable," she said. "Whenever he saw what he thought of as an opportunity, he took it. And I was always afraid he would steal the albums—I only had two of them then—so I kept them secret until one night when he discovered them."

"And then what?" Tessa was glad because she wanted to know, but also because her mom wasn't thinking about the missing pages anymore.

"He found them when he was getting ready to go to a new job. He was always scared in that kind of a situation. He pretended to be so tough, but he was really just a scared little boy. And when he found them, he was furious." She stopped to pull her cigarettes out of her purse and light one, and Tessa couldn't get over how normal the afternoon suddenly felt. This was what most girls probably did with their moms, sit with them and talk, instead of tiptoeing around them while they were lying on the couch.

"He never did want to admit how much I looked like you know who," she said. "That was one of the things I loved about Gerald so much right away. It was almost the first thing he said to me, and he didn't see it as a threat, as if I'd use it to leave him or find a better life. But Eddie always resented the resemblance. He always seemed nervous when I talked about it, as if I was better than he was just because I looked like Jacqueline. But anyway, the night he found them, he blew up and accused me of spending my time making the scrapbooks instead of doing housework. He tried to tear the cover off one," she said, and she started to smile in a funny way. "I can still remember how mad he was, because it was the first one, the leather-bound one, and of course, those are almost impossible to tear."

Tessa was starting to get nervous. She had been silly to think her mom would change the subject away from the scrapbook; it was all she was going to talk about until she found out what had happened.

Her mom's smile faded and she looked down at the red cover again. "I still don't understand how anyone could feel threatened by a hobby. Even Gerald . . . he's changed so much." She looked past Tessa to the doorway that led to Gerald's workshop. "I just wonder if he did something to those pages."

"Mom, I really don't think he would," Tessa said. She shrugged. "Anyway, if it's just a few pages—"

"Just a few pages? This is a keepsake, Tessa. You don't destroy someone's keepsake. And I wanted to show you the picture of that party.''

"But I don't need to see a picture," Tessa said. "That was their party, and this one will be mine." Suddenly she felt she sounded more like her grandmother than herself. Sometimes that happened when she was talking to her mother.

"But it has to be wonderful," her mom said. "It has to be the best party you've ever had. Maybe we should have some sort of theme," her mother said, talking like a fast motor all of a sudden. "I read an article once about a party where the mother gave all the girls makeovers, and it was a huge hit."

Tessa was shocked. For her mom to say "I read an article once" and have it not be about the Kennedys seemed to Tessa like having Gerald suddenly start speaking French.

"Do you think that's a bad idea?" her mom asked. "Don't forget I worked in a beauty parlor, and I took enough cosmetics courses in high school to last a lifetime.''

Tessa felt as if she couldn't breathe. The truth was it sounded wonderful, but she was afraid to believe in it because it sounded too wonderful. Who was this person making all these normal-sounding suggestions? What about the mom who had spent almost all last month lying on the couch staring into space?

Her mother snapped the album shut and stood up. "It's up to you, Tess. Whatever you want to do on that day, we'll do. But I think you should decide by this afternoon so I can get all the supplies we'll need.''

Tessa felt so strange—her mom was acting the way Tessa had always wanted her to act, all her life, and she half couldn't quite believe it and half felt scared. It was too different.

"I don't know. My nose has been running for three days," Mack said. "Do you think it's the flu?"

Amelia looked past him out the window. They had given her a wonderful room—Dr. Wanamaker was a firm believer that one's mood played a major role in one's health, and he had told Amelia he always put all his patients on the south side of the hospital, especially in spring. But she wished he had made an exception in her case. For some reason she found the sight of the dogwoods in bloom to be achingly sad.

"Do you?" Mack said.

She let her gaze slide in his direction. Mack's face looked fuzzy and undefined except for his eyes—those pale blue eyes, almost colorless, that evidently cut through even the morphine-spiked haze she was in. "Did you take any aspirin?" she asked. Suddenly she felt desperate for sleep.

"Aspirin is for headaches," he said. He stood up and pulled back the curtain as he looked out the window. Then he started to pace. "I need something that will cure me, Amelia, not just kill a headache. They always talk about inventing a cure for the common cold, but I'd like to know when they're going to do it."

She tried not to think about the word *cure*. What was it, exactly, that the doctor had said yesterday? "We talk about 'cures' for breast cancer in terms of a five-year time span. If the patient has no symptoms for a five-year period following surgery, we say that that patient is cured. Of course, that's no guarantee that another cancer won't form. But in terms of what we've removed, we can say we've been successful."

Five years. It seemed like an eternity to wait.

"Are you all right?" Mack asked. "Do you want me to call the nurse?"

She shook her head. "I'm fine," she said.

"The other thing is I feel a little queasy," he said, holding his stomach for a moment like a young boy. "That meatloaf you made. I don't know. Maybe I should have thrown it out."

- She squinted to make his face more clear. "I made that a week ago. I would have thought you'd have finished it by now."

"I meant to," he said, suddenly sounding, too, like a young boy. "I forgot about it, and then I was hungry and I saw it, and I ate the whole thing. Now I don't know."

Amelia thought about the night before last, when she had called him to remind him to bring along her other bathrobe, the blue one that was so much more comfortable than the hospital robe. She had called and called, and then Dolores had called and called, and there hadn't been any answer.

And Amelia had made a terrible mistake, revealed something she had sworn she would never reveal to her daughter. "Do you think he's on his way?" Dolores had asked. "Although God knows why it would take him two hours to get here."

"He's not on his way," Amelia had said, feeling woozy but also sharp as a needle. "I had forgotten tonight is Tuesday."

"Tuesday?"

"Tuesdays are for Lauralee Wicks," she had said. When she had said the words, she had felt both relieved and ashamed. She had never said them to anyone, and she felt as if a pressure had been lifted from her insides. But to her own daughter!

She wished immediately that she could take the words back,

but then something strange happened. Dolores said that she already knew, that she hadn't ever wanted to say anything but that she had seen Mack more than once with the woman. "I knew he had finished that stupid porch of hers a long time ago," she said. "I've seen them all over the place. He doesn't even bother to hide it, does he?"

Now, she looked at Mack, rubbing his stomach and evidently wondering where his next meal was going to come from, and she wished for the courage to tell him that she knew, to confront him and hash it all out.

She had thought, when she had first discovered the affair, that she would tell him that she knew. She would tell him and that she wanted him to leave, that he could go live with Lauralee Wicks or whoever else he might want to live with.

But she didn't tell him. She didn't ask him anything, and she found that she held on to her secret knowledge almost as a weapon: he might think he was fooling her, but she knew better.

But ever since the doctor had said those few stark words—"You have a lump in your left breast, Amelia,"—what she wanted wasn't to hurt Mack, or to let her secret knowledge tumble out at him. What she wanted was to be held and to be made unafraid.

He was looking at his watch. "Do you think that gift shop is still open downstairs? They probably have Rolaids or Tums, don't you think? Do you think they'd make me feel any better?"

She was achingly tired. "You know their hours better than I do," she said, resting a hand on her stomach. Would they find something in her abdomen next? With Mrs. Rachins down the street, they found a mass in her stomach, and she was dead not four months later.

"Ah, maybe I'll see if it blows over," he said, and he looked at his watch again. "I guess . . . I could go downstairs and get some Tums and then come back," he said, but she could tell from his voice what he wanted. He wanted her to say that she had had enough of a visit, that it would be easier for her if he left. And, in fact, the words would be true; it was such a strain watching him try to make conversation, pacing and looking at his watch without realizing he was doing either one. And painfully, she always ended up realizing that even if Lauralee Wicks didn't exist, Mack wasn't the type of man who would want to sit with her all day and keep her company.

"Would you like that?" he asked. "I could pick up another paper for you and some Tums for myself."

So halfhearted. It was at times like this when she wondered what other men were like. She had married Mack so young; he had been her high school sweetheart, her first and only love. In the hallways after the operation, as she would shuffle along on the arm of Dolores or Mack, she had looked into the other rooms and seen so many different types of husbands. There was one who read to his wife from Dickens every day: Amelia had been surprised to hear him say "Pray tell" until she realized he was holding a book in his lap. And there was one who sat and read silently, to himself, all day, but held his wife's hand in his and every so often stroked her forehead. Many looked like Mack from what she could see from the hallway—shuffling and uncomfortable—and she supposed that Mack was just typical, a man who was frightened of the setting and uncomfortable about having to face his wife and have a conversation for an extended period of time.

"Grandma!"

"No, me first!"

Amelia heard a scuffling out in the hall and watched Mack's face as the girls came running into the room. He adored them both, of course—he was always making them wooden toys and toy boxes and little puzzle sets—but lately she felt he was favoring Louann.

"Easy when you get close to that bed," he said after he had hugged them both. "Don't go jostling it, you two."

"Grandma, look!" Louann said, paying no attention to her grandfather. She had started to jump on the bed, but Tessa held her back.

"Don't jump on the bed," Tessa said. "Grandpa just said."

"You girls settle down," Dolores called, coming into the room. Amelia was shocked at how tired her daughter looked—there were dark circles under her eyes, and her skin had the gray pallor of someone who hadn't been outside in weeks. "Mother, how are you?" she asked, kissing her gently on the cheek. Her hair smelled of cigarette smoke, and Amelia had an image of Dolores lying on the couch with the television on, sound off (the way she liked it these days), and a cigarette dangling from her hand. Asleep, ready to set the couch on fire. "You look better," Dolores said.

"I just want to get out of here," Amelia said, smiling because the girls were suddenly both holding out small bouquets for her.

"Mine's bigger," Louann said, pushing hers forward. "Grandma, smell. It's daffodils and violets."

Tessa hung back and then laid hers on the sheet.

"They're beautiful, both of them," Amelia said, scooping up Tessa's flowers into her hands. "These ferns are lovely, Tessa."

Tessa beamed, but a moment later Amelia watched her smile crumble as Louann climbed into Mack's arms, already full of some story she just had to tell him that second.

"We're pretty much ready for the party," Dolores said, pulling up a chair. "What else do we have left to buy, Tess?"

"Um, I don't know," Tessa said. She was still hanging back, open-mouthed and envious, as Louann chattered at Mack and regaled him with her silly tale about her piano teacher.

"Well, we still have to get the cake, of course," Dolores said. "We thought pink and white, with pink candles." She sighed. "I just wish I had been able to find those pictures."

"What pictures?" Amelia asked. Her incision was throbbing, and she wished she could be alone. Louann had jumped off Mack's lap and come skipping across to the bed, and Amelia felt herself wince involuntarily when she thought Louann would leap onto the bed.

"Daddy took pictures of me playing the piano," Louann said.

"Not those pictures," Dolores said, with an edge in her voice. "The pictures of the birthday party Jacqueline had for Caroline that year. I know they were in one of my albums. I don't make mistakes about things like that, and I know they were in the album with the red cover. I just can't understand—"

Amelia saw Louann's hand fly to her mouth. She held it there and looked at Tessa with huge, saucer-wide eyes.

"What?" Dolores said. "What is it, Louann?"

Louann bit her lip and kept looking at Tessa. "It's a secret," she said quietly.

"A secret? About my album? What kind of a secret?" Dolores asked. Her voice had cracked as she said "album." "What kind of secret?" she said again.

Amelia suddenly saw that Tessa's face had turned crimson. "We spilled wax on the album," Tessa said. "We were making crayons into those little pots and pans for Louann's dollhouse, and the wax spilled on the pages, and I tore them out."

Dolores's eyes were filling with tears. "I can't believe it," she said. "Why didn't you tell me? Why did you let me think Gerald had done it, or that I was losing my mind?"

"Oh, honestly, Dolores," Amelia said, "try to get a hold of

yourself. It was a few pages of an album, and Tessa said it was an accident.''

"It wasn't on purpose," Tessa said in a small, hopeful voice.

But Dolores had begun to cry. Tears fell down those high cheekbones, and Amelia could hardly bear to look at her grand-daughters, both horrified that they had done something to make their mother cry like that. She motioned to both of them to come to her, and she put her arms around them, but she could tell they wanted to be held by their mother right at that moment.

"Dolores, just stop," Amelia said. "They were pictures. You have hundreds.''

"We made Mommy cry," Louann said quietly.

The day of the party Tessa woke up half wishing the party was a dream and that the day would be like any other day. The sun was slanting through to the place on the floor that she knew meant it was eight o'clock, and she thought, seven more hours. It felt as if she had seven more hours to live.

She went over to the window to see if Gerald's truck was still there—he was leaving on a camping trip that morning with his fishing buddies—and luckily, it was gone already. "I'm not stay-ing in this house with seventeen screaming girls, I can tell you that much," she had heard him say to her mom the day before yesterday, and her mom had flipped on the washing machine right when she had answered him. All Tessa could hear was a pleading tone, and she had walked away and felt sick.

But it was just as well that he'd be gone. What she wished was that her grandmother could be at the party, or even just there in the morning so she could tell Tessa how to act. "Just be yourself" was what she had said in the hospital. But Tessa didn't see how that could be true. When she tried to be herself, nobody liked her or even noticed her. And when she tried to be like the popular kids, they acted as if they hated her. One day, after she had convinced her mother to buy the same skirt for her that she had seen on Cindy, she was amazed because they ended up wearing it on the same day. She had worked up the nerve to go up to Cindy and had forced herself to smile and say, "I like your skirt!" And Cindy and her friends had looked at her as if she were nothing, and she had seen one of them roll her eyes.

She heard a sound downstairs, and she went down to the living room. Sometime in the night or in the morning, her mother had put up all the decorations. There was "Happy Birthday" strung across the ceiling in big pink letters, and pink crepe paper twirled with white. It looked great, but it also made Tessa nervous. The party was really going to happen.

"Happy birthday," her mom said, coming in from the kitchen with a steaming cup of coffee. Tessa could smell it all the way across the room.

Her stomach lurched. "Thanks. So Gerald's gone?"

Her mom nodded. "Since four this morning. I've been up since then."

That sounded wrong, even though Tessa couldn't figure out why.

Tessa followed her mother back to the kitchen and looked in the refrigerator. Everything was still there, in exactly the same positions they had been in the night before—the cake, the meat, the hot dogs. She pictured Cindy Carmello biting into a hamburger that was too rare and saying "Eww," and the ends of her fingers started to go numb.

"When are you going to start the grill?" she asked.

Her mother had the hunched-up look she sometimes got before she went into her bad periods. She was always hunched up and looked small whenever she was being taken to the hospital.

"Mom?"

Her mother ran a hand through her hair.

"Mom?"

"Uh, around four, wouldn't you think?" she finally said.

Tessa had a bad feeling that was getting worse. She tried to picture her mom at the grill, flipping hamburgers the way most people's dads did on TV, like on "The Brady Bunch," and she couldn't.

"Mom? It's two-twenty," Tessa said.

Two hours ago, her mother had said she needed to take a nap, and she was still in her bedroom with the door closed.

Tessa knocked and opened it, something she had been afraid to do till then. She hadn't wanted to see what she was now looking at: her mother on the bed with the covers pulled up almost to the top of her head, and all the shades down at the windows.

"Mom, it's almost two-*thirty*."

"I don't feel well," her mother said. She pulled the sheet down so Tessa could see her face. It looked like she had been crying, with mascara or something black all under her eyes and down her cheeks. "You'd better call your friends and tell them not to come."

"It's almost *time*. I *can't* tell them not to come." She heard Louann come running up the stairs.

Louann came into the room and jumped on the bed as if she were doing a cannonball into a pool. "I see a car," Louann cried out, and she started bouncing up and down. "There's a girl getting out, and she's got a present for you, Tess!"

Tessa looked at the clock by her mom's bed and felt weak with dread. "Mom, come on."

Her mother slowly pushed back the sheet and sat up. At least she was dressed.

Someone was knocking at the door downstairs and calling "hello?" and Tessa held out her hand for her mother. "Come on. Okay? Please? You feel fine, I know you do."

Her mother followed her as if she were a dog at the end of a leash, and they went downstairs. The girl at the door was named Millie Grunwald, and luckily she was down at the bottom of the list in terms of popularity, one of the ones Tessa had invited as padding, in a way, because she had known she'd come.

"Hi," Tessa said. "Come on in." Out in the street she saw Millie's mom in the car, who honked and waved and called out "Happy Birthday" as she pulled away.

Millie came in and pushed the present at Tessa in that nervous way Tessa always did herself at the few parties she had been to. "Here," she said. "Happy birthday."

"Thanks," Tessa said.

Millie looked past Tessa and seemed kind of shocked, and Tessa turned around.

Her mom had sat down on the living room couch and had put her head in her hands. Louann was perched like some kind of little animal right next to her, burrowing her head against her shoulder, but it didn't even look like their mother noticed Louann was there.

"She isn't feeling too well," Tessa heard herself say. She also felt as if she could hear the blood in her veins, as if she could feel her heart beating and pushing the blood around her body.

Girls started arriving in twos and threes, and Tessa's mother went upstairs and shut the door to her room. Every time anyone was dropped off, Tessa thought of asking one of the mothers to help her, but she couldn't get the words to come out. And what the mothers saw looked totally normal: a bunch of girls talking in the living room and looking at the makeup Tessa's mom had set up on the table, and probably a mother in the kitchen getting everything else all set up.

Tessa went outside to look at the barbecue, and she started pouring the charcoal in until she realized it wasn't such a great idea to do the barbecue by herself. What if she set the yard on fire? She had never paid all that much attention to what Gerald did when he made a barbecue, and he was always saying that he was completely in charge.

"Tess, they're all hungry in there," Louann said, running out of the house and letting the screen door slam shut. "Plus they're all into the makeup, they're already trying everything *on*."

Tessa followed Louann back in to the house. There was a cluster of girls around the makeup. They hadn't actually opened any of the packages, but Cindy Carmello had a little circular container of eyeshadow in one hand and a brush in the other. "When's the makeup artist coming?" she asked.

All the talking had stopped, just the way it always did in school: when Cindy opened her mouth, everyone wanted to hear what she was saying, even the unpopular kids.

"Yeah," another girl said. "We want to get started."

"The makeup artist is my mother, and she isn't feeling well," Tessa said.

There was a silence, and Tessa could hardly stand to look at Cindy, but she also couldn't resist: Cindy's reaction would determine everyone else's. "Your mother?" Cindy said, giving a little laugh. "I don't want to be made up by your *mother*. I thought a real *makeup artist* was coming. I wanted to have a real *makeup* session."

"Make-*out* session," one of the girls said—Tessa couldn't see who.

A few of them laughed, and Tessa was relieved for half a second, but only half a second.

"So this is it?" Cindy said. "We're not having a makeup session?"

"We could make ourselves up," Tessa said. "Or we could make each other up. I've done it a bunch of times, and—"

"I could have done that at home," Cindy said in a snappish, horrible voice.

"You could try," Louann piped up. "Our mom bought all kinds of makeup you probably don't even have."

For a second, Cindy looked down at Louann, and Tessa wondered whether she was softening, maybe. Maybe Louann's suggestion, because it had come from a five-year-old, would mean something. But Cindy looked straight into Tessa's eyes and said, "If I'd've wanted to put makeup on with my little sister, Tessa, I could have done it at home."

Tessa heard a sound and she turned around. Her mother was at the bottom of the stairs in her nightgown, holding her bathrobe tight around her waist. She looked a hundred years old, and she looked like she had been crying.

"That's her mother," she heard someone say.

"*I* don't think she looks like Jackie Kennedy."

Tessa pushed past the girls and her mother and ran upstairs.

4

"Not unless you get an *A* in English, I can tell you that much," Gerald said. "Eighth grade is when these things start to count, Tessa, and I can promise you nobody is going to be looking at you much in the way of college if you keep going the way you're going."

Louann was practicing scales in the living room, endless, repetitive exercises that Tessa felt must have been designed as a kind of musical Chinese water torture. Up and then down, up a bit and then two notes down, over and over until Tessa couldn't think. "And let me ask you something as long as we're having this little talk here, Tessa." She hated the way he said her name; he always said it as if it were a bad word. "Let's say you were running a store, just like I run the store downtown. I don't think you would be running a hardware store, but let's say a dress shop, or a store where they sell those gourmet foods like that one down on Tyler Street." Tessa felt as if her brain were hardening while he spoke. "Now, if you had an employee who wasn't doing her job—she was taking long lunch hours and not helping the customers the way they needed to be helped—at the end of the week, would you just pay her the way you paid the other employees?"

She despised the way he was always making people agree with him even when they didn't. Her mother always had a terrible time holding up her end of an argument, and Tessa was always horrified at how her mother would go emotionally limp in order to try to end one. And then Gerald would keep hammering away anyway, stroking his beard and fixing those dark brown eyes on her until she had completely reversed herself.

"Would you?" he asked, tipping his chair back for a mo-

41

ment. He let it fall to the floor again, she was sure for effect.
"You know you wouldn't," he answered for her. "At least if
you were a good manager. You can't treat the good ones and the
bad ones the same, Tessa. And I can't say to you, as my step-
daughter, 'You haven't kept your grades up or kept up with your
chores, but I'm going to buy you that dress for the dance anyway.' As a responsible man, I can't do it."

She wondered if she could run away. She had thought of it
countless times and had begged her grandmother to let her live
there, even if it was only for six months or even three.

"You see why I can't do it, and you have to agree with me,
don't you?" he said. "I can see it in your eyes, the way you
don't want to look at me."

She looked him straight in the eyes then. "I don't agree with
you," she said, although her voice hadn't come out as strongly
as she had meant for it to. "My grades are *B* minus and *C*. I
don't think that's so terrible."

He shook his head. "It isn't near good enough, and you know
it. Louann gets straight *A*s and look at all else she does, with
the piano and the gymnastics."

"Louann is in third grade. It's a little bit easier to get *A*s when
you're in third grade, Gerald." She had known she shouldn't
say it, but the words had slipped out.

Gerald's face had turned dark purple—all you had to do to
see it change color was to insult Louann—and Tessa could see
that he was holding himself back, trying to be what he considered "a fair man," something he prided himself on almost constantly. "I told you before and I'll tell you again. If you get an
A in English—let's just say if you get an *A* on that project you
were talking about at dinner—then you can get that dress you
want so much. I think that's as fair a deal as you could find from
anyone in town."

She knew it was as good an offer as she was going to get from
him, but she felt trapped and angry. Didn't he understand how
important clothes were? Probably he did, she realized, but he
didn't care, because it didn't have to do with Louann. The only
one who understood, surprisingly, was her mother, but how
often could she raise an objection to anything Gerald said? He
counted every penny as if they were about to go into bankruptcy,
and he knew every outfit Tessa owned. Once when her grandmother had bought her a sweater on one of their afternoon out-
ings, Gerald had spotted it like an eagle the moment she had
walked in to the kitchen. "Where's that sweater from? Who

authorized you to write out a check?'' (to Tessa's mom). ''Don't you know we have to pay for Louann's trip to Philadelphia this month?''

''Tessa, you look beautiful in that dress. Just beautiful.'' Tessa could feel herself blushing, and she looked away from Mrs. Bartlett. At the beginning of the eighth-grade school year, Tessa had made friends with another unpopular girl, Annette Bartlett, who had just moved to Lodenton. At first Tessa hadn't wanted to be friendly—why tie a lead weight around herself by associating with someone else who had no friends? Plus Annette was plain-looking, with almost colorless light brown hair and pale, unnoticeable features. In Tessa's mind, the kind of girl who could never hope to be popular. But Annette and her family had gradually worn Tessa down. Tessa was so much happier going to Annette's house after school than going home to her own; Annette's family was ''normal'' in the way Tessa had always dreamed her own family could be; her father was a doctor, and her mother was a reading tutor, and her little sister wasn't a prodigy at anything.

But lately, an envy had formed at the edge of her feelings, and she could feel it eating away at her affection for the Bartlett family. Annette's mother's compliments made her feel self-conscious and angry that the woman was so sane compared with her own mother: when she said that Tessa looked beautiful or had done well at something, she never compared Tessa to herself or to the Kennedy family.

''Are you going to get it? Did your mother give you a check?''

Tessa shook her head and felt herself blushing again. ''She said maybe next week,'' she said quietly.

Annette came out of her dressing room wearing the same dress in a different color—a long, cotton India Imports dress that skimmed her waist and fell softly to her ankles. The dress was flattering, and Tessa wanted one for herself more than ever.

''That looks wonderful,'' Mrs. Bartlett said. ''I think you should get this one and the green.''

Annette was beaming, and Tessa felt the beginnings of panic: this was the fourth week in a row that Annette had bought something new, and Tessa could see that her friend was slowly being transformed by her clothes. Soon Tessa would be the only one who had to wear her backward-looking shoes and those ridiculous Peter Pan–collared blouses.

''Tess, would you like me to call your mom and tell her how

wonderful you look in the dress?'' Mrs. Bartlett asked. "I'm sure that if she knew—''

"No,'' Tessa said quickly. She knew that the two mothers had spoken a few times on the phone, and that so far, her mother hadn't sounded bizarre or crazy to Mrs. Bartlett. But Tessa knew that it was only a matter of time; and also, she had said a few things about her mother that didn't happen to be true, and she knew she would be embarrassed if Mrs. Bartlett found out.

She didn't even know how the lies had begun, actually; the first lie had popped out the first time she had gone to Annette's house, and Mrs. Bartlett had asked about her family. She had heard of Louann, of course—everyone in town knew who Louann Lundgren was—and Tessa supposed, looking back, that what she had wanted to do was make someone else in the family look interesting, and she hadn't known how to do that with herself. "My mother is an artist,'' she had said, surprised at the words as they came out of her mouth. "I think she actually would have been pretty famous if she hadn't married my stepfather.''

"Really,'' Mrs. Bartlett had said. "What sort of art does she do?''

"She's a painter,'' Tessa had said. She could still remember how she had felt as if she were falling through a tunnel, but that it had almost been pleasant; it was another life she was creating. "She's had several exhibits in New York, actually.''

And from there, the stories had sprung up freely and unexpectedly—and unnecessarily, too, Tessa felt, in some cases: that her real father had been a painter, too, and had moved to New York to pursue his career; that her uncle had died at sea; that Gerald had an identical twin who was in a mental institution.

She worried often about being found out, but as the weeks passed, nothing happened, and she imagined that she knew the reason why; her mother would be too self-absorbed in any of her phone conversations with Mrs. Bartlett to ask any questions or allow the conversation to deviate from the course she had set.

"Tessa? Do you want to look at anything else before we go?'' Mrs. Bartlett asked.

Tessa looked at her reflection again in the mirror. The dress was exactly the same as the one Cindy Carmello had worn the other day, except that it was a slightly darker shade of purple. She knew that she was pretty—her mother and grandmother told her so all the time. And though she wouldn't necessarily have believed her mother's words ("Your looks are what's going to allow you to leave Lodenton,'' she would say to Tessa almost every day), she could see it for herself: light blue eyes much like her grandfather's, high cheekbones, dark brown hair that fell thick and straight to her shoulders. And this was what she couldn't understand: did the other kids at school not like her because she was *too* pretty? She felt that they probably didn't even notice her much; who would give her a second glance in the clothes Gerald forced her mom to buy for her?

''I think I want to try on that one other dress,'' Tessa suddenly said, ''just in case my mom ever changes her mind.'' She felt the way she did when she was about to tell one of her lies about her mother. It was a feeling of anticipation and excitement and unexpectedness, a catching of her breath that she both dreaded and loved. She went back into the dressing room and took off the dress and laid it on the bench. She tried on the pink one, but she had known even before she put it on that she was just stalling to work up her nerve; she looked at herself in the mirror and said ''the purple one is better,'' softly to herself, and then she rolled it up and put it in her purse and covered it with her wallet and makeup case.

She was excited and frightened and happy as she left the dressing room, and she felt good holding her purse tight against her side as she followed Mrs. Bartlett and Annette to the cashier. She knew she wouldn't get caught; Chasen's was a dinky little store that would never have anything sophisticated like people spying at you from behind the mirrors, and the attendants went back to the dressing rooms only a couple of times an hour.

From that afternoon on, it was as if a whole new world had opened up to Tessa. Her need felt physical and would hit her like a pang of hunger at the end of almost each school day. She could get a blouse or a dress or lacy pantyhose; the only thing she couldn't figure out was how to take a pair of shoes. But she felt transformed. Within two weeks, she had almost gotten a real wardrobe together. Each day, she would pack the clothes she wanted to wear into her schoolbag, and she would change in the girls' bathroom as soon as she got to school. Her only problem was that she had no way of having the clothes cleaned without being discovered. So they lay in a heap at the bottom of her closet, and Tessa hoped vaguely that an answer to the problem would come to her at some point.

Annette noticed what was going on right away—''I thought you hadn't bought that dress,'' she said—and Tessa had told her the secret; it was so easy, and it was even fun. Annette was shocked and frightened—"You'll get caught, you're sure to get caught," she kept saying—and also seemed, beneath the fear, to be disapproving as well. But Tessa didn't care; the act of lifting the clothes—because that was how she thought of it, almost as if she were liberating the dresses and shirts and scarves from the store—gave her a feeling of power she had never experienced in her life. Maybe her sister was the best pianist in Lodenton, the one with perfect pitch who was going to be famous someday. But she had something, too, and it was a secret, and it was hers.

"Attention, shoppers. We're offering a forty percent discount on all ladies' underwear in the red-tagged racks on the first floor. That's a forty percent discount, ladies . . ."

Tessa moved off the escalator and surveyed the second floor. Sweaters and dresses, all in junior sizes. She had been to Main's only once before because it was all the way in Acton. But now with her grandmother needing that special bra, the trip was necessary.

It was the one part she didn't want to think about, that her grandmother had had one breast taken off and now there was trouble in the other one. When Tessa thought about it, she felt like screaming, and then she tried to shut herself down or think about something else.

"Ladies, this sale will only last until five P.M. today. That's five P.M. . . ."

Tessa moved over to some sweaters that looked beautiful from a distance—bright blues and purples and reds, and she wanted them all. She felt as if she were floating rather than walking, a sleek, smooth shark parting the waters with its fin.

There didn't seem to be any guards on the floor at all. When she had seen the one on the first floor, she had been shocked, because it was the first guard she had ever seen in a store in real life—uniformed, with a walkie-talkie. But she supposed that the first floor was where most of the shoplifters would concentrate, since all the bins of clothes were there, and it would probably be a bigger temptation.

The sweaters were cashmere, and they were as soft as Louann's rabbit, lush and expensive looking, and Tessa could just picture the red one with her black skirt. What she didn't like to think about sometimes was that even though she had been wearing her nice clothes for a few weeks, she still hadn't gotten to be popular—something she admitted she had thought would happen overnight. But it did seem to be starting; just yesterday, hadn't Cindy Carmello come up to her and asked where she had gotten her plaid skirt? It was something that never would have happened the year before.

Tessa pulled three sweaters from the rack and took them toward the dressing room, but she was stopped as she began to walk into one of the cubicles.

"I need to give you a tag," a woman's voice called out.

Tessa turned around. "Oh, sorry. I didn't see you there." She had never had to be tagged before in either of the stores she had lifted from.

The woman, a bored-looking white-haired lady who made Tessa think how much prettier her grandmother was, handed her a little blue plastic "3" and waved her in.

Tessa felt a confusion ruining her floaty feeling. She felt as if she were walking rather than moving through ice-blue water. She was holding three sweaters that they knew she had!

She tried one on but felt bored and angry. She knew that what she should do was just go back downstairs to meet her grandmother, but now that she was looking at herself in the mirror, she felt she had to have the purple sweater. Purple was going to be her color—it made the blue of her eyes look bluer, and she loved the idea that people at school might associate her with a color the way everyone associated Cindy Carmello with red.

She took the sweater off and got dressed again and handed the three sweaters back to the woman outside the dressing room, and as she walked back to the rack, she felt the ends of her fingers go numb. If she did it quickly and smoothly, no one would see. She had practiced it a thousand times in her mind, and they said that if you did that, the way tennis stars sometimes did, you could achieve almost anything.

She glanced around once and pulled one of the purple sweaters in her size off the rack, and then she glided over to a corner (she felt as if she were moving through water now) and slipped it under her coat. Her heart skipped one beat and then another, and she looked around again—maybe she hadn't been careful enough!—but no one had seen her.

There. It was done. It had been scary doing it this new way, but she had done it.

She went to the ladies' room and stuffed the sweater into her purse and then went down the escalator to find her grandmother.

She was still by the bra counter, but at least she was paying. Tessa glanced at the bra—she could see that one cup was totally padded—and she looked away. *Don't think about it, and don't*

*think about how Grandma suddenly looked as if she had aged
ten years.* Because no one knew yet if she was really sick. Sometimes Tessa would start to think about what her life would be
like without this rock-solid wonderful person she adored, what
it would be like if she couldn't look into those calm gray eyes
and move close and smell the vanilla and rosewater her grandmother always smelled of. And she would have to turn off her
thoughts, just shut them down. She tried to do it right then; she
had a wonderful new sweater that she knew Cindy Carmello
would love. That was what she would concentrate on.

"Grandma?"

Her grandmother turned to her and smiled, and then she
looked confused. She looked past Tessa, and Tessa saw her
mouth open and then felt a hand on her arm.

"Excuse me," a man's voice said.

She turned around, and it was a man in uniform. "Would
you give me your purse, please?"

"What?"

Out of the corner of her eye, Tessa could see her grandmother
move forward. "Leave her alone. What do you mean, give you
her purse?"

"Is this your daughter, ma'am?"

"She's my granddaughter. Who are you?"

"Main's Security," he said, touching his hat. "Your granddaughter was observed putting a sweater into her purse." He
looked at Tessa. "If you'd just hand it over, miss."

"This is absurd," Amelia said. "There's obviously been some
sort of mistake."

"If you don't mind," he said, and he pulled the purse off
Tessa's shoulder. The movement was gentle and unexpected,
and she didn't have time to stop him. He unsnapped the top, and
there it was—purple cashmere—never to be worn to school.

Tessa looked for one moment into her grandmother's eyes.
She had never thought she would feel bad about what she had
been doing, but right then she wished that she could take it all
back; she would have worn a burlap sack to school not to see
the disappointment and shock in her grandmother's eyes.

"I told you before," Amelia said. Tessa could hear the tension in her voice, and she moved closer to the door so she could
hear more. "They're not going to press charges because I made
it quite clear it had never happened before."

"Do you know that's true?" Mack said. "How do you even

know that's true? I remember hauling Tessa back to the Malenkys' when she took that Malenky girl's doll home under her
shirt. Not once but twice."

"That was a long time ago."

"That's exactly what I mean," he said. Tessa felt her face
growing hot. "That girl has a streak, and you know it. Always
wanting what isn't hers, always wanting to have the most. How
about the time I made them both those dolls, the red and the
yellow, and first she made Louann trade and then she pulled the
legs and arms off the one Louann ended up with? She's got a
streak, Amelia, and I don't know that keeping this a secret from
her folks is such a great idea. That's all I'm saying."

There was a silence, and Tessa jumped back from the door
in case her grandmother was coming out. But then she heard her
say, "If it were just Dolores, it would be one thing. I think she
would treat the incident for what it was—something that a lot of
young girls do as an adventure. Something that has to be stopped,
but that isn't a capital offense. With Gerald, Tessa would never
hear the end of it. He's far too strict with her already. You know
as well as I do that he treats her like a second-class citizen."

"All I'm saying—"

"I know what you're saying, and I won't have it, Mack. I
cannot spend the next few days worrying about my health and
about whether Gerald is making too much of this with Tessa. I
can't do it. I'll be alone in that hospital—"

"What do you mean, alone? I visited you every day last
time."

Another silence. Tessa stepped back from the door and started
backing up toward the kitchen, and the dining room door opened
and her grandmother came out.

"Honey, I want to talk to you," she said, and she put her arm
around Tessa's shoulder and led her back to the kitchen. "We
can start getting supper ready while we talk, all right?"

Tessa nodded. She loved the feel of her grandmother's hand
on her shoulder. It was something she could never admit to
someone like Annette—when they talked about boys and what
it would feel like to be kissed, Tessa knew that that kind of
touching was what was supposed to feel the best. But sometimes
she wondered if a boy would ever make her feel as secure as
she felt with her grandmother.

"I want to ask you something, and I want you to tell me the
truth," Amelia said. She handed Tessa a potato peeler, and
Tessa picked up a potato. She didn't want to look at her grand-

mother because she was afraid. "I want you to tell me if this is the first time you've ever done this."

Tessa wished she could disappear forever. She looked down at the peels, and it seemed as if they were moving the way her stomach felt like it was moving inside of her. "Um, once—or twice, actually—when I was little, I took a doll from Sally Malenky," she said.

She looked up at her grandmother then—she felt as if she were lifting a shade to peek out from underneath—and her grandmother nodded and looked relieved. "And those were the only times."

Tessa nodded, and she felt as if something had shifted inside. She had told a lie to the person she loved most in the whole world, and nothing had happened.

"Good," her grandmother said, and Tessa was shocked; wasn't she going to ask whether she was sure, or was she certain there was nothing she had forgotten? How could her grandmother be so naive? "Because if I felt that this was a problem, I would have to tell Dolores and Gerald. But I honestly feel that it's best for you if the incident stays within this house, Tess." She looked into Tessa's eyes. "I know how tough he can be on you sometimes. And I think that, sometimes, toughness is the best thing—but not when it isn't warranted."

Tessa felt as if she were inside a bottle and her grandmother's voice was coming to her through the glass.

"But this means you have to keep the incident a secret. You can't tell anyone about it. I'd never hear the end of it if Dolores or Gerald found out I had kept this from them."

"I wouldn't tell," Tessa said.

Her grandmother nodded and then smiled. "I'm not acting as a wonderful example, am I, honey? But I feel it's the right thing; sometimes you have to break your principles."

"I understand," Tessa said.

Her grandmother reached out and touched her cheek with the back of her hand. "And when I'm in the hospital, I want you to be good and to think about what happened."

"When are you going in?" Tessa asked. She knew that she had been told the exact day, but now she couldn't remember.

"On Thursday," her grandmother said softly.

Tessa thought about her grandmother all in white in a hospital bed, with tubes and those sacks of clear liquid. Then she looked away and tried to think about something else.

* * *

"It will just make me feel better to check," Amelia said. "I don't know why you can't understand that."

Mack signaled for a left and shook his head irritably. "Because I don't know what there is for you to see over there," he said. "You were just there yesterday."

"I'm going into the hospital," she said stiffly—sometimes she felt she could barely control her anger with Mack these days—"and I want to see them before I go in. I don't find that strange or bizarre."

"But it's always the same when Dolores is like this," Mack said, signaling for another left. The houses they were passing were bigger than in their own neighborhood—Gerald had prided himself on having bought the worst house in the best neighborhood and transformed it into the nicest—almost palatial—house. The trees in this neighborhood were all huge and well established, the lawns as wide as Mack and Amelia's entire property. "She'll be lying on the couch with the television on; Gerald will be working; and the kids—you have to face it someday, Mele—they don't even pay that much attention to us when we visit. Maybe Louann. But I can promise you Tessa isn't spending every morning just hoping her grandparents are going to show up two days in a row."

Sometimes he understood nothing. Amelia stared straight ahead and tried not to look at him, tried to say nothing because she didn't want to argue right before she was due to go in.

"You know it's true," he said, and she felt as if he had pushed her over a cliff.

"You don't understand anything," she said, facing him and seeing a brief look of surprise in his eyes. "You've categorized us as grandparents as if that means we're not important to the children; you've categorized each of your grandchildren into black and white—Tessa's always wrong in your eyes and Louann is always right. And I'm always blind, aren't I?" She hadn't meant to say the words—certainly not now—but of course it was impossible to take them back.

"What do you mean, blind?" They were pulling into Gerald and Dolores's driveway. Gerald's truck was gone, but Dolores's car was there, looking stolid and settled, as if it hadn't been moved in weeks.

Amelia opened her door and began to step out of the car. She didn't have to have the conversation if she didn't want to.

"Amelia," Mack said. He came around the front of the car and faced her. "I want to know what you mean."

She felt herself smiling. "If you only knew how transparent you are, Mack. I'm sure you have no idea that you never ask me what I mean—you barely listen to anything I say anymore—but when you know—quite well, I'm sure—exactly what I'm talking about, you act as if you're confused." She glanced up at the door to the house to make sure neither of her granddaughters was standing there or listening. "I'm talking about Lauralee Wicks and whomever else you've been seeing, and I can tell you something: if I come out of this again, and I'm well, I want you to leave the house."

He looked stunned. His pale blue eyes narrowed until they were almost closed. "What are you talking about?"

She held up her hands. "I don't want to have this discussion," she said, and she began to head into the house. "You heard what I said, and I meant it."

She could feel fear rising in her throat like bile. She hadn't meant to say the words; she certainly hadn't meant that he had to leave no matter what. In her imagined conversations with him, she had laid out the future as more of a compromise: he would stop seeing the other woman or women, and they would reforge their relationship together. "Dolores?" she called into an empty-sounding hallway. Her hands were shaking.

"Up here!" Dolores called, in a high, lively voice. Amelia looked out the hallway window and saw Mack opening the hood of the car.

"Yes, hold on just one moment, would you? My mother's here. . . . Thanks." Dolores looked like some sort of electric doll as she came out to the landing with the phone to her ear and waved at Amelia. She held up her index finger and mouthed *Just a second*, and Amelia kissed her hello and walked past her to Tessa's room.

"Yes. *Any*way," Amelia could hear Dolores saying. "It's so nice to talk to someone who's interested in my work. I had no idea Tessa would have talked about it." Amelia hesitated in the hallway. What work could Dolores possibly be talking about? "No," Dolores said. "Not paintings. It's a collection—she didn't tell you? . . . No, no. It's a photo collection about the Kennedys. Jacqueline, mostly, from when she was married to JFK. Since we've never met, you would have no way of knowing this about me, but most people see a tremendous resemblance. . . . That's right."

At the end of the hallway, Tessa's door slammed shut, and Amelia stepped back.

"Well, anytime," Dolores said into the phone. "And I'm sorry about the misunderstanding with the clothes. Maybe I just heard Tessa wrong or misunderstood. . . . That's right. . . . Me, too. Good-bye." She hung up and brushed off her hands. "Well. That was nice." She suddenly frowned. "Are you all right? I didn't know you were even coming over."

"I'm fine," Amelia said. There was a bitter taste in her mouth, and when she thought of what she had said to Mack, she felt as if she were going to faint. "What was the misunderstanding?" Amelia asked.

"Oh, that," Dolores said. She went into Louann's room and dragged the vacuum cleaner out to the landing. It was amazing, Amelia felt, how quickly her daughter's mood could shift; just yesterday she had acted as if she would never walk again. "I found a huge pile of clothes at the back of Tessa's closet. On the floor. Really nice ones," she said with great animation. "Tessa said that they were Annette's—you know, that friend of hers from school—and that Annette hadn't wanted them anymore. So I called Annette's mother to thank her."

Amelia felt her stomach souring and beginning to burn. "And she said that they weren't her daughter's."

"That's right. But she wanted to know all about my collection. Apparently Tessa told her I was an artist."

Amelia looked down the hall and saw that Tessa had opened her door a crack. She peeked out, and her eyes met Amelia's only for a moment.

Amelia wondered if the day would turn out to have been a turning point; had she lost Tessa forever the way she had once lost Dolores?

Tessa's door shut, and the lock clicked softly into position.

5

"*Sonata in E Minor for Piano*, Ludwig von Beethoven, Louann Lundgren," the program said. Louann could hardly feel the ends of her fingers. She looked around the hotel room, at Tessa unpacking and her mother sitting nervously at the edge of the bed, and her stomach felt as if it were twisted into a knot. She looked down at the program again and tried to make sense of it. "Junior Division, ages 12–15," it said, and Louann wanted to say, But I only just turned twelve. Why do I even have to be doing this? Twelve was too young to be playing in a contest in New York City. Twelve was when you were supposed to be allowed to have fun.

"This isn't very fancy," Tessa said. "I thought when you said a hotel in New York, it would be something nicer than this."

"It's where Gerald always stays when he comes here for the hardware convention," their mother said. She was lying down, with her head against the headboard, but there was an energy in her eyes that frightened Louann. All that Louann had been hearing for three weeks was that she was going to go to New York and win a "major contest with contestants from all over the United States" as her mother would say to anyone who would listen. Louann felt as if the lights in her mother's eyes depended these days on how well she could play, and that from tonight on, what would matter was how well she had performed in the contest.

"But we're not at a hardware convention," Tessa said irritably. "The only people I saw in the lobby looked like they were from *Lodenton*."

Louann saw her mother smile, and she was stunned. It was so hard to make her smile, and usually Tessa wasn't the one to do it. But her mother was practically glowing; even her skin

54

looked smooth and young and as if she had gone through some strange process of growing younger and more energetic.

"We're going to go straight over to Fifth Avenue as soon as you girls change clothes," she said, getting up from the bed, "and we're going to eat someplace very special before the concert."

Louann's stomach started to roil. "I'm not that hungry," she said.

"We'll see how you feel later. We're sure to see someone famous where we're going, and you're going to relax and forget all about the concert." Her eyes were gleaming. "That's how I planned it, to distract you so that you're perfectly relaxed."

Louann sat down on the bed and looked at her overnight bag. Her music was inside, but what was she going to play? How did she know her fingers would do anything at all? She could remember once, when she was eight and her parents had arranged to have her play at the First Pennsylvania Bank in Acton, it was the biggest audience she had ever played in front of—rows and rows of old people, plus a few kids who looked like they hated her and were bored. She had sat down to play, and it was a Bach Invention she had played thousands of times before—she would play it in her sleep and on the school bus, just using her fingers, she knew it as well as she knew her own name. But that day when she had sat down, nothing had come out. Her fingers had felt numb, and her mind was blank; when she looked at the music, it looked like Sanskrit, like something she had never seen before. Her mother had come up to the bench and sat down with her and put her fingers on the keys, but they felt like someone else's fingers. How had she ever played a piece that was as complicated as it looked on the sheet music?

"You can do it if you just relax," her mom had said. "Just close your eyes and take a deep breath and relax."

She tried to do what she always did, even though she hated it because she felt like someone trapped in a cage; she wiped her hands twice on her hips, on whatever she was wearing, and closed her eyes for two seconds. The ritual was something she had started a long time ago, because what it meant was: if you do these two things, you'll be able to play, and everything will be fine. Sometimes she felt as if a series of rituals had taken over her life; sometimes she was on the street in Lodenton, and she would say to herself, You have to get to that red car before that old man reaches it, or when you get home, your mom will be dead. She didn't fully believe the words, but she believed them enough to follow whatever they told her to do, and then she would feel crazy and helpless because they would turn out not to be true.

But that day at the bank, what happened when she closed her eyes for two seconds was that she saw herself in the backyard, lying in the grass in the shade. She didn't want to be sitting at a piano in front of two hundred old people; what she loved about playing was that it was like a dream world, the only place she understood completely. Whenever she began to play, music suddenly made more sense to her than anything else in the world. She could almost see the notes, she could feel their shapes, and she understood them better, she often felt, than she understood how to write her own name. But when she played in front of an audience it wasn't like a dream world at all.

"Honey, you know the piece so well," her mom had said. "If you just start playing . . ."

But the notes hadn't come, the movements hadn't come, and she had ended up having to walk away without playing anything at all. She could hear the lady at the bank apologizing—"I'm so sorry, ladies and gentlemen, but she *is* such a young girl"—and she had felt like saying, "I am, and that's why I don't want to do it."

"This bathroom is disgusting," Tessa called out. "There's hardly any toilet paper left."

Their mother didn't seem too concerned. "Someday you'll both look back on this hotel—Louann, you'll be staying in Paris or London or Rome, ready to perform in front of a huge audience, and Tessa, you'll be somewhere wonderful, too, doing something glamorous and exciting, maybe even modeling—and you'll both look back and laugh." She was unpacking her and Louann's suitcase, and Louann felt sick as she watched her mother pull out the dress she was supposed to wear tonight and hold it up in the air. "Look at that. You'll look like a vision."

"You will," Tessa said, coming around behind Louann and pulling her hair back into a ponytail.

Louann looked at them both in the mirror and then looked away. A plumpish girl with glasses and mousey light brown hair, and her beautiful, gorgeous sister. This year Tessa's face had developed the most amazing angles and shadings—it reminded Louann of all the models in the magazines Tessa was always studying, and almost every night, Louann wished that she could change places with her sister.

"I'll make you up if you want," Tessa said. "I know how to

do it so it won't even look as if you're wearing makeup. You'll just look really great.''

Louann felt as if her stomach were dropping out; she felt as if they were talking about a fantasy evening that would never come true. The truth was that it was still a shock she was even going to be in the concert. Her teacher, Mr. Winkler, had told her to enter something "for the state" and then a "regional competition," and she hadn't even thought about it. She didn't really know what it meant, and she had played, and she had done well.

And then suddenly she had been invited to New York, and part of her had felt a thrill because she could see how excited her parents were. "Haven't I always told you you were the most talented girl in all of Lodenton?" her father said to her when he heard she had been entered in the competition. She knew he was as proud of her as he ever had been in her life. But now, she realized that, in the back of her mind, all along she had been pretending it was unreal, that the performance would always be in the future. And yet, tonight she was going to have to play in front of hundreds of people. And when she looked at the dress her mother was holding up, she knew that she wouldn't be able to do it. She could see herself walking onto the stage in it—it was maroonish velvet, with a white lace collar and lace cuffs and a black patent leather belt, which Tessa had already said she wanted as soon as the concert was over. But she saw herself going up on that stage and then standing there like a statue.

"Mom?" She felt as if she were eight and it was that day at the bank when she couldn't go on.

"Yes, honey. Just *look* at this dress! It's elegant, but it's also eye-catching. It's expensive, but it doesn't look showy. Don't you love it?"

Louann glanced over at Tessa. She was watching their mother, looking at the dress without saying a word, in the way that Louann thought was more real than when she pretended to be so happy for her. Not that she wasn't—Louann knew that Tessa was proud when she played—but Tessa had never had anything like that. No one had ever paid attention to her in any special way, ever, except for their grandmother. Once, Louann had even said something about it. "I wish you could be the one that gets up in front of everyone and gets all the attention," she had said. "You'd be so much better at it, and I don't even like it is the truth." But Tessa had just stared at her as if she had said the stupidest thing in the world.

"Darling, don't you love it?" Her mom was by her side now, and she was still holding up the dress.

"It's beautiful," Louann said.

"What's the matter? Don't you like the color? Don't you remember? We chose this ruby red—that's what the label said, ruby red—because it's such a royal color. It's understated. I'd never want you to go out there in something cheap-looking."

Louann wanted to say right then and there that she wouldn't be able to play. If she said it right then and there in the hotel room, it wouldn't be so awful, because they could just have dinner and go back to Lodenton, and everything would be okay. She would tell Mr. Winkler, who luckily had gotten the flu or he would have come *with* them—she'd just tell him she had gotten sick, too, maybe even with his flu, and that was why she didn't go on.

"I don't really feel all that great," she said. She looked at Tessa again to see if Tessa would maybe guess what she was feeling, but Tessa still had on a frozen, glazed look, just staring at the dress as if it were the most famous or rare thing in the world.

"Well, it's natural to be nervous. It would be *un*natural if you weren't. But once you see the restaurant I'm taking you to, you'll forget about how you feel, and you'll see what it means to be talented and successful. You'll see your future, both of you. I've planned this for a very long time."

"How could you have planned it when you didn't even know Louann would win the competition?" Tessa asked, flopping onto the bed.

"I mean in *general*," their mother said, finally arranging the dress on a hanger and placing it on a hook. "I have one hope in life, and that's that both of you will leave Lodenton and make something of yourselves instead of doing what I did. With your talent, Louann, and your looks," she said, looking at Tessa, "there shouldn't be anything to stand in your way."

"You say that," Tessa said, "but then when I try to talk to Gerald about going away to college, he says there's no money and that I have to go to Acton."

"Well, Louann's lessons," she said quietly.

Louann went into the bathroom and washed her face. She had heard the argument so many times—all her life. Tessa couldn't do this or Tessa couldn't do that because *Louann* had to have her piano lessons. She couldn't even count how many times she had said, "Maybe I'll just give them up for a while." But her parents had said no, absolutely not, she couldn't even think such a thing. Now there was a chance that their grandparents could pay for Tessa's college because they were back together again, but there was a year where Grandpa Mack had gone and lived in an apartment in Acton, and then there hadn't been any extra money in the family at all.

"Louann, hurry up," her mother called, and Louann dried her face and looked at herself in the mirror. She wished more than anything that she was back in Lodenton with her friends.

"Now, the place we're going," Louann's mother said, "the Russian Tea Room, is where hundreds of famous people go. It's near a lot of theaters, so there are actors and actresses, but really everybody who's anybody."

Louann saw Tessa roll her eyes, and she felt that Tessa wasn't being fair. Their mother had a sickness, and it made her different—what their grandmother had said was that mental illness was a sickness like any other kind, that it wasn't your fault—and Louann felt that Tessa blamed their mother, as if the illness were something she could control. Maybe not for the parts where she slept a lot or cried a lot and had to go to the hospital, but what their grandmother called the extras—the parts about the Kennedys and other famous people she got interested in from time to time. But Louann really didn't see why there was anything wrong with liking famous people or reading about them.

"Oh my God," their mother suddenly said, and Louann felt a clutch on her arm like a vise. "Just stop, just wait a minute," she said, and she held them both back as if they were horses in a corral. "Look at that taxi, look who's getting in."

"Oh God," Tessa said real softly, and Louann suddenly saw: it was Jacqueline, and she looked just like her pictures. In a second she was in the taxi and gone, but Louann felt the way she had in Lodenton once when a storm came through town when they were shopping—it was a hail storm and everyone had to run for cover, and then it was over and it was bright, but it felt so different . . . as if the town had become different forever.

Her mother was gripping her so tightly it felt as if a man had grabbed her. "I can't believe it," Dolores said softly. "I just can't believe I saw her. And she saw me; she looked into my eyes, and she was surprised. Did you see that?"

"You're out of your mind," Tessa said. "She didn't look at you. She didn't even see us."

"She did so. I saw her. She looked right into my eyes, and it was as if she was looking into a mirror." Her voice was high and like a girl's, and Louann felt her stomach start to roil again.

When her mother's voice turned into a girl's, sometimes it meant she was going to go into a bad period again. "Louann, you saw it, didn't you?"

"I didn't really see her," Louann said. "I didn't even see her until she was really almost in the taxi. I just saw her back." Louann felt the way she always did in French class, as if she couldn't find the syllables or sounds to say what she really meant.

"Well, *I* saw her," Tessa said. "And she didn't even glance at us. Not once."

"I wonder where she was going," their mother said in her kid's voice.

"God, what does it *matter*?" Tessa exploded. She looked furious. "Why do you even want to *speculate*? What difference does it make to you where she was going? It has nothing to do with you, and it never did, and it never will. You don't even look like her anymore."

Louann watched as her mom's face crumbled. She had never seen it happen exactly that way, just falling apart and shifting until she looked a hundred years old and miserable, and then tears were falling from her eyes. "Well, thank you so much for your vote of confidence," she said through her tears.

"Confidence? What does confidence have to do with it? It's not a matter of whether I have confidence in your theories or beliefs or whatever they are, it's a matter of whether they have anything to do with reality. And they don't. You looked like her once but you don't anymore, and even if you did, what would it matter? Your life has nothing to do with hers, and I wish you would just stop."

Their mother was walking away. She had let go of their arms, and she was walking away, back up the street in the direction they had come.

"Mom?" Louann called out. She broke into a run—she had to because her mother was walking so quickly—and when she caught up with her, she caught her arm. "Stop," Louann said. "Aren't you going to wait for us?"

"I have to lie down," she said. "I'm going to go back to the hotel."

"But what about lunch?"

"I'm not hungry anymore. After what your sister said to me, I don't know whether I'll ever eat again."

"She didn't mean it," Louann said. Tessa had come up behind her, and Louann turned and looked at her. "You didn't mean it, right?"

Tessa sighed. "What does it matter? It's over, so we can forget it."

"I have to lie down," their mom said. "We have to get back to the hotel—"

"But it's our only day in New York," Tessa said.

"Please. I feel weak."

They spent the rest of the day in the hotel room. Tessa went outside for a few minutes to go to a McDonald's a few blocks away, and Louann spent most of the day lying down and feeling sick. She dreaded the concert, and she wished that her mom hadn't seen Jacqueline, because now it was all she could think about and all she could talk about. And she was so sad! Louann tried to think about things her grandmother had told her. "Sometimes your mother feels things very deeply, but not in the same way you would, dear. She feels very, very sad sometimes, and it isn't for any reason other than that there's a circuit or a chemical that's wrong in her brain."

Six o'clock came, which meant an hour until the concert, and Louann knew she should eat something, but she couldn't. She put her dress on and washed her face and let Tessa make her up, and then it was almost time to go—they had to leave ten or fifteen minutes to walk to the recital hall to get there on time.

But her mother was in bed with the covers up to her ears. "Are you going to come?" Louann finally said.

"I just can't," her mother said. "I want to, but I just can't. Tessa knows where the concert hall is—it's near the restaurant, near where the taxi was. Take some money from my purse so you can take a taxi home."

Tessa was over by the bed in a flash. "You're not coming? Dolores, come on," she said. It always bothered Louann when Tessa called their mom "Dolores." Louann felt that it was wrong, even though she couldn't explain why. And now, it just made Louann feel more scared: things weren't right; everything was falling apart.

Tessa started to pull the covers back, and their mother made a wail that was like the sound of a cat. "No, I can't. Just leave me alone."

"Fine," Tessa said. "We're going to go to the recital and we're going to leave you here, and Louann is going to be wonderful and you're going to miss the whole thing."

Louann felt as if she had no blood left in her fingers as she left the hotel with Tessa, and her knees were as weak as they had been that day in the bank.

"I never thought it would get this bad," Tessa said when they were outside. She was walking quickly, but Louann didn't know if it was because they were late or because she just wanted to get away. "She just can't have the focus on anyone else for even one second."

"What do you mean?" Louann asked. She had no idea what Tessa was talking about.

"Isn't it obvious? She's always telling us how she wants our lives to be so much better than hers has been, but I'm not sure it's true. You know, it's very selfish just to withdraw into yourself the way she does. It's a selfish act to fall apart, Louann. And when there's the smallest chance for some focus to be on us— look at this afternoon if you want—she falls apart. *She* wants to be up on that stage playing the piano tonight is what I think. And she can't accept the fact that this obsession she has is just a fantasy. And she's dropping you just when you need her most."

Louann didn't want to hear it. She knew it could be true, but she didn't want to hear it. She could see where she was going to play, the building with the canopy, and there was a huge crowd of people outside, kids and their parents, and there were limousines, and there were kids carrying violins and cellos, and Louann wished she were anywhere in the world except there.

"I don't think I'm going to be able to play," she said.

"Oh, you can do it," Tessa said. "Louann, you were meant to do it, and you can do it."

That was what Louann never understood. Why was she meant to do it just because she could pick a note out of the air? And if people were meant to do certain things, why wasn't there anything her sister was meant to do?

"Anyway, you have to do it, because pretty soon I'm going to be living here, and I have to have *someone* come to see me every so often, don't I?"

"What do you mean, living here?"

"I'm going to move here, to New York," Tessa said. "I can feel it."

"But what would you do?" They were getting close to the crowd, and Louann felt as if her feet had dropped off, as if she were moving through some sort of liquid.

"I think I'd find out when I got here," Tessa said. She stopped at the edge of the crowd and smiled a dazzling smile. "Who knows? Maybe I'd manage your career."

She took Louann's elbow, and they went into the hall to register, and then they were shuttled backstage to where Louann would have to wait. There was a girl Louann had seen at the last competition, a small, blond-haired girl with tiny, pearly teeth and tiny hands that played beautifully. She gave Louann a narrow, hate-filled look.

"I think I'll just leave," Louann whispered up to Tessa.

"What? Listen, I know you're nervous, but just try to relax. Breathe deeply and picture yourself playing as well as you've ever played in your life."

The concert began, and a lady came up to Louann to say she'd be on soon, and the minutes flew by. Everyone sounded perfect and the pearly-toothed girl went on and got the biggest applause of the evening, and then the lady came and touched Louann's shoulder and said, "You're next."

Louann heard applause, and for a second she thought about how her parents weren't out there—how her dad was at a convention in Arizona, and her mom was back at the hotel room, probably asleep. Her grandmother was feeling weak back home, and her grandfather wasn't the type to come by himself. She felt a push at her back—Tessa's sharp fist—and she walked out into the bright lights and saw the piano. The lights were too bright to see the audience, but she could feel them; she could hear some of them coughing.

Her knees felt like jelly, and she started walking across the stage toward the piano, and then the music slipped out of her hands and scattered to the stage floor.

She bent down and picked the sheets up, but she could see she wouldn't be able to get them back in order; she read the page numbers, but it looked like another language. Her hands started to shake, and she put the music into position on the piano—she wouldn't be able to play anyway, she wouldn't be able to do it.

She made her fingers go into position on the keys, but they were bouncing, just shaking. "Um," she said, and her voice carried because of the microphone near the piano, where she was supposed to announce what she was going to play. "Um," she said again.

Her fingers were shaking, and then her arms started shaking, and she felt as if she wasn't going to be able to breathe, her breath wasn't going to come much longer. "I'm sorry, I can't," she said, not meaning to have the words go out into the microphone, but there they had come. She got up and ran—forgetting her music—into the wings, and she ran past Tessa and down the hall.

Tessa was right behind her. "What happened? What's the matter?"

"I couldn't do it," Louann said. She felt as if a mist had lifted, though. She could feel her fingers and her feet, she could feel the floor beneath her feet, and she could breathe. "I just couldn't do it," she said. She looked into Tessa's eyes, but she couldn't read them. "I'm really sorry."

Tessa sighed. "I can't believe you did that," she said. "Were you really that scared?"

"I was numb," Louann said. She wondered what her father was going to say when he heard about it.

"What do you want to do now?" Tessa asked.

"Go back to the hotel," Louann said, because it was the truth.

The room was quiet when they unlocked the door. Right away Louann saw the flickering light of the TV screen. So her mother must have turned off the sound.

"Mm," she said from her bed. She was under the covers, and she moved, and then Louann saw the pills—an empty bottle Louann knew had been full before, because she had seen her mom take one last night back home before she had gone to sleep.

"Tessa, the pills," she said.

Tessa picked up the bottle. "There was more than one in here?"

"The whole bottle, almost. Maybe even the whole thing."

Tessa picked up the receiver and called down to the desk. Louann hardly even heard what she said, except to Louann she said, "Wake her up. Make her sit up," and that was what Louann was trying to do.

"Mom, come on," she said. She was pulling from under her mother's shoulders, and the scariest part was that her mother opened her eyes for one second, and then they rolled back into her head.

"Oh God," Louann said, and she let go.

"Wake her *up*," Tessa said. She was still on the phone; it sounded as if she was talking to the operator now.

Louann pulled again and held her mother behind the shoulders, and it reminded her through her panic and fear of when her mom had held her when she was sick and just a small child. "Wake up," she whispered. "Wake up."

6

"I just want to get out of here and start living my life," Tessa said. "Sometimes I don't even feel like finishing school."

Amelia heard the words with alarm. She looked up from her sewing to see if she could read Tessa's eyes, but of course there was nothing to see other than those dark-lashed blue eyes that let you see only what Tessa wanted you to see. "You know you have to finish school," Amelia said, threading a new needle. "Especially if you want to leave the area. You know that as well as I do."

Tessa sighed. "I know," she said. "It's just that I can't face going home anymore. Last night, I wanted to borrow that white sweater of Dolores's—you know, the one with the pink threading?—and I went into her room. She was sitting there at her dressing table just sobbing. It wasn't—well, she isn't in one of her spacey phases; she's been pretty normal lately. And she was sitting there crying, and they were the most real tears. Do you know what I mean?"

"What was she crying about?" Amelia asked. Red spots had formed at the tops of Tessa's cheeks, and Amelia felt that her granddaughter had been more upset than she knew; it was so rare for Tessa to talk about her feelings.

Tessa took a deep breath. "She had a whole stack of pictures—they were of her when she was sixteen, I guess when she met my father, and some that even had him in them." She paused for a moment, and Amelia remembered how Tessa had always yearned to see pictures of her father.

"Were they what you had expected?" she asked.

Tessa shrugged. "I refuse to think about him. I don't want to think about a man we had to leave like that. But she obviously was. And she was just in tears because she had 'lost her looks,' she said. She kept showing me each picture—I mean, she showed me the whole group two or three times—and each time, she would say, 'Look how beautiful I was. And look at me now.' It was just horrible."

"I'm sorry you had to deal with that," Amelia said. "But in a way it encourages me. What frightens me most is when she doesn't care about anything, when she's letting time pass more than anything else."

Tessa didn't say anything. She stood up and moved around the living room restlessly, the way she had been doing since she was a child—picking things up and putting them down, looking at herself in the mirror above the fireplace, looking out the window. "Do you think I'm going to be like her?" she suddenly asked. She pulled her hair back into a ponytail and came and sat down next to Amelia, and in that moment, she did look remarkably like Dolores—the same high cheekbones and wide jaw, the same handsome mane of dark hair. But now her eyes, usually so hard to read, were filled with concern.

"Like her in terms of her illness?" Amelia asked, and Tessa nodded slowly, looking for a moment like a child. "I don't think so at all, Tess. Not at all. By the time she was your age, your mother had shown all sorts of mood problems and swings. Do you worry that you might have inherited the problem? Because I don't think they're sure it's hereditary—it's a chemical imbalance and may have nothing to do with how you grew up or what genes you might have."

Tessa looked down at her hands. "I don't know," she said quietly. "Sometimes I just wonder about this whole family. I just want to get out and be different and to have come from a different place sometimes. I can remember how, when I first met my friend Annette back in eighth grade, I told her parents all kinds of lies about our family. They just popped into my head, and I let them come out, and I really felt better for it." She looked into Amelia's eyes. "The way I felt better just for a while when I was taking those clothes," she said quietly. "But sometimes I just feel cursed. I mean, I look at my mother and the men she's been with . . . I've actually been thinking about my father lately, but even Gerald. And you and Grandpa."

"What about me and Grandpa?"

"Look at what happened," Tessa said angrily. "That's not supposed to happen at your age; person gets sick, and then the marriage breaks up."

"You know that when we separated, it wasn't because of my

illness," Amelia said. She could remember the conversation with Tessa so well—Tessa's eyes absolutely furious, and her refusal to listen to any of Amelia's pronouncements that Mack was still a good man. "And Mack has changed; the experience changed him, Tessa."

"But he still did it to begin with," Tessa said. "He still cheated on you, and I'll never forgive him for that. Sometimes I wonder if there's something in our family that makes us make bad decisions about men."

"Have you made a bad decision?" Amelia asked. She felt a sheen of dread cover her as memories of Dolores and Eddie flooded back; it was impossible to control a sixteen- or seventeen-year-old girl. When they fell in love, there was no talking to them about anything. Especially if they wanted to escape from their family.

Tessa's eyes were unreadable. "A man asked me out," she said.

They were words Amelia had been expecting to hear for years; her granddaughter was beautiful in a way that Amelia knew was absolutely magnetic for men—her figure was full and shapely, a classic hourglass, and her face was truly beautiful. And certainly Amelia had hoped that Tessa would begin going out with boys from school. But those words made her remember how terribly headstrong Dolores had been when she ran off with Eddie. Now, Tessa had said the words in the same challenging tone Dolores had used back then.

"How old is he?" Amelia asked.

Tessa shrugged. "In his twenties, I guess. He delivers furniture for the store next door to where I work."

"Tess, that's much older than you; you're too young to go out with someone that age."

Tessa's cheeks darkened to purple. "It's not going to be serious, Grandma. It's just something to do this summer. Working at a dress shop is okay, but it isn't exactly something I spend my evenings thinking about."

"But a boy your age—"

"The boys my age don't pay any attention to me," Tessa said.

Amelia knew it was true. She had gone to enough plays and recitals at Tessa's school to know that her granddaughter was a girl who didn't fit in either with the boys or the girls. Tessa always stood at the sidelines while her classmates talked and joked with one another in groups of two or three. And Amelia supposed that, at this point, it was such an ingrained pattern that it was impossible for anyone—Tessa or any of her class-mates—to break it.

"You have to be careful," Amelia said. "Men in their twenties want certain things—"

"Grandma, you don't have to tell me," Tessa said. "I know all about it."

Amelia heard the unmistakable chugging of Mack's old Cadillac outside the house, and she looked past Tessa out the window. Mack was unloading the groceries into the wooden cart he had made just for that purpose—he would never admit that he needed it to carry groceries inside—"I'm thinking of putting it on the market" he would say when anyone asked him about it—and Amelia felt a rush of love as she watched her husband carefully lift each bag out of the car and place it in the cart.

She was glad she had taken him back. He had promised to change, and he had kept his promise. This was the message she wanted to convey somehow to her granddaughter: things weren't always black and white, and people could change. She didn't want Tessa to resent her grandfather for the rest of his life for something that was over and done with.

"Hello!" Mack called. "I've got deliveries for a feast here. Amelia?"

"We're in here," Amelia called. She could hear the cart moving smoothly along the wooden floors—everything that Mack made or owned ran smoothly except for his car—and out of the corner of her eye, she saw Tessa stand up and walk to the window. "I should get going," she said. "I told Louann I'd take her shopping."

"I want you to be careful," Amelia said. "Remember what I said—"

"There you are," Mack said. "Hey, Tess. How's my girl?"

Amelia watched as Tessa looked through him and then finally forced herself at least to meet his eyes. "Fine," she said tonelessly. "I have to go. Grandma, I'll see you soon." She bent down and kissed Amelia's cheek, and a moment later, she was gone.

Dolores looked in the mirror and began to cry. What was it that article had said? That they had discovered that there was something in tears of sadness that they couldn't find in tears from an allergy or an eye problem—some substance or enzyme that was supposed to make you feel better when you got rid of it. But she felt as if her crying was the wrong kind—the kind that scientists said wasn't good for much of anything except getting rid of germs.

She wanted to go back into the hospital; it was as simple as that. She wanted to go back into the hospital, and she wanted to get off the pills the doctor had given her. She felt crazy on them, and out of control.

"I'm not going to send you there again," Gerald had said to her last night when she had complained. Her chest hurt, and the tips of her fingers and toes were tingling all the time, and she felt as if her body were filled with boiling water instead of blood. It was scary and she wanted help, but Gerald wouldn't listen. "I can't live like this anymore," he said. "I swear, Dolores, this in-and-out-of-the-hospital stuff just isn't going to work. I can't take it."

"I'm not doing it because I want to," she told him. "It's not because I want to."

"You could pull yourself up by your bootstraps. *That's* what you should want to do. That's what you should motivate yourself to do, the way that tape I bought you says to do. You think of the positive, and positive things will start to come true. What you do is dwell on the negative, Dolores."

And she had almost laughed, because his description was so completely ridiculous. She didn't "dwell on the negative"; she felt *infected* by the negative. When she closed her eyes she saw horrible things; what haunted her when she was awake and asleep was like a black cloud that was completely enveloping, that was far more powerful than her will or than any pills the doctor had ever given her.

She was afraid to go to the store because she saw shapes; she felt people behind her, and when she would turn around, no one was in the aisle. When she got into the car she was afraid of what she would do; she was terrified to drive either of the girls because she felt so unsure. When she saw headlights, they seemed to be drawing her to them, as if her grip on the steering wheel were being controlled by someone else.

But she continued to go when she could, to the store and to drive Louann to her lessons, because she could do it on automatic most of the time, and facing Gerald when she couldn't was just too awful. "I won't *have* it," he would scream, and although he wouldn't hit her—he never had—he would hit the table or the wall and make a tremendous noise, a loud noise that made her feel like a rabbit in a hole. And he had gotten so big. Gerald reminded her of a huge, angry bear when he was annoyed, and his size and weight made her feel she existed less because he took up so much space in the world.

"All right, here it is," Gerald said one Monday morning when the girls were both gone. He slapped the newspaper and then threw it down in front of her onto the kitchen table. "Here it is, and you can go and get it."

She knew what he might be talking about—she was afraid to even look, because what if it was?—but even out of the corner of her eye, she could see she had been right: it was the want ads from the Acton *Herald*. "I'm not ready," she said quietly, without looking. She wouldn't look; that was all there was to it.

"Damnit, pick it up and see what I've circled," he said. He pulled out a chair and sat down next to her, which was something of a relief. When he stood over her he seemed like a giant, as if he were casting a shadow across every cell of her body.

"All right, *I'll* look at it and you can listen," he said, and he picked up the paper. "Lodenton Beauty Shop needs experienced cosmetician, light experience okay as long as applicant is personable and attractive. Hours flex, call for appointment. Back-to-work housewives okay." He threw down the paper, and she finally looked up at him. He was sitting in the chair backward, hooked onto the back like a monkey. But his eyes looked fierce. He was too interested.

She looked down into her lap. She saw a stain, and she thought of something she had read in the paper the other day, that you could get out all kinds of things with baking soda, that it did so many things. She would have to try it.

"Dolores, I asked you a question."

She looked up at him. "What?"

"Do you want me to drive you to the interview?" he said, as if he had said it a hundred times before. "If you call and they want to see you, I'll drive you. I'll go into the store late if I have to, or not at all."

"I can't," she said. She wished her voice hadn't sounded so soft, but it was all she could muster up, the most voice that could come out of a body that felt like someone else's. "They won't want to see me," she said.

"I happen to know that's not true," he said, and she felt her heart jump. He picked up the paper then and read out the number. "Five-five-five, oh-three-nine-eight. I called at eight o'clock this morning, and they said they'd be happy to see you, eleven o'clock sharp. They said you'd be perfect. They don't want to pay someone with ten years' experience, Dolores. They want someone presentable who knows a little bit and can learn a little bit—"

"But I can't. . . ."

He shook his head. "You can and you will. Dr. Elting said you're supposed to get out into the world; those pills are only good for so much. He said you could get a job if you wanted to—"

"But I don't want to—"

His hand came up and then slammed down on the table, and she felt as if he had hit her, she felt her eyes wincing and her shoulders hunching, and she heard a whimper come out of her body.

"You don't want to," he bellowed. "You don't want to be a wife and you don't want to be a mother and you don't want to go out and get a job. Well, I can tell you one thing, Dolores. If you don't want to do any of those things I mentioned, I am never going to take you to that hospital again. And I'm never going to drive you to Dr. Elting again. And I'm not going to authorize anyone to give you any medical treatment—any treatment *I* have to pay for—unless you start being at least one of the above. I don't even care which it is, Dolores, I swear I don't, but it had better be one of them, damnit."

She shut her eyes and then squeezed them shut tighter, and she thought about New York and how, for a few minutes, before she had seen Jacqueline, she had actually imagined herself and her daughters living there, without Gerald, and far, far away from Lodenton. She had imagined herself as the talented, beautiful mother of Louann, world-famous pianist, and Tessa, also a beauty and doing something wonderful and fascinating with her life.

And then she had seen Jacqueline, and Tessa had screamed at her, and the truth had come out. It would never happen; it could never happen.

"Dolores, look at me."

She was afraid. She felt his hand on her chin, and she flinched and opened her eyes.

He looked gentle this time, not like the frightening man who had hit the table so hard. "I'm sorry that I get angry sometimes. It happens because I see you wasting yourself, limiting yourself. You can go out and get this job. I know you can. And it will help you." He paused. "You're unwilling to try anything else . . . to be with me." He stopped, and she tried not to think about it—Gerald reaching for her at night, and then she would have to climb out of bed and sleep downstairs, hoping it would take longer until the next time he tried. "I know you can do it," he said gently.

He held out his hand. "Now come. If you come with me, you can do it."

She shook her head. "I can't. Not—"

"You can," he said.

She shook her head. "Not with you. That was what I was going to say. Let me go by myself."

He looked confused. "You want to go by yourself? How will you get here if you gave the car to Tessa?"

"I'll take a taxi," she said quickly. It already felt like a relief to have him listening to her instead of hectoring her. She had said the right thing, and now he would leave her alone. "I promise," she said, and in the back of her mind for a few moments, she could actually imagine herself going. What if she really did get a job? It would mean Gerald wouldn't yell at her anymore. It would mean he would leave her alone, because he said "any of the three," it didn't even matter which one. "I promise," she said, except that she couldn't remember whether she had said that before or not.

He put his hand on her shoulder and squeezed it a bit, and she felt herself flinch because she had thought, for one second, that he was going to hurt her, but he was looking down at her with great tenderness all of a sudden. "I want this," he said softly. "I want you to be better, Dolores, and this is the way to go. It's what I've read and what Dr. Elting said, and I want it. For both of us and for Tessa and Louann."

He had mentioned Tessa. It was the first time in all these years that he had mentioned Tessa as if she were equal to Louann. "I promise," she said again, and he let go of her.

He left the house, and she felt that she was going to go. If she got the job, it would mean Gerald would stop yelling at her, and Tessa and Louann would be proud of her. It would mean there was a chance she would get better, because she had heard her doctor say the same thing: "You have to get out in the world, Dolores. It might seem like an idea that's too simple, but in fact sometimes the simplest solutions are the best ones. And in my opinion, if you got out there into the world, you'd be ten steps ahead of the game."

Ten steps. She had never known why he had said "ten steps," because why not twenty or a hundred? But she knew what he meant, and she knew that everyone was right.

She looked down at the ad and looked over at the phone and she thought about calling—what she would say, what they would say. What had Gerald told her? That they wanted to see her at eleven o'clock sharp. She felt numb at her fingertips, and she didn't even know if her legs would hold her if she stood up— what if she fell in the interview? What if she crashed her car through the glass window at the front of the store? But she pushed her chair back, and she stood up, and she looked around the room.

It was the kitchen of someone who wasn't all there, that was what she had heard a neighbor say down at the Grand Union once, when the woman didn't know she was standing right down the aisle. "You should see that Lundgren house—the one where that nice fellow lives, Gerald Lundgren? I swear that woman has never cleaned the kitchen since she moved in. The husband does it some of the time, but I don't think it's right that a man does it, do you?"

There were cobwebs hanging from the ceiling, and there was grime from the cabinet doors on up to the walls, and then the crack at the ceiling. Dolores didn't know when she had last washed the floor. It was true that Gerald sometimes did it. He said it wasn't right to be living in such a dirty house; it wasn't good for Louann—and as she looked around, she had a thought: Jacqueline had never washed any floors; she was sure of it.

No, she told herself, because that part of her life was over. She wasn't related in any way to Jacqueline, and her life didn't have anything at all to do with Jacqueline's. Tessa had said it, and she had seen it for herself in New York. What she had was an eleven o'clock appointment at a beauty parlor, and if she didn't go to it, Gerald was never going to leave her alone, never, not ever.

She went upstairs, and she thought about how she had expected it would be so different with Gerald. He had started out as such a different person from the way Eddie was, but in the end, how much difference was there really? Everyone tried to make you do things you didn't want to do, and they made you live a life you didn't want to live.

She went into the bathroom and looked at herself in the mirror, trying to decide how she would get ready for the appointment. But when she looked at herself, it was as if she were seeing herself for the first time, for the first time in years, since she had been young. She saw someone who was aging and incompetent. She saw someone who was no longer beautiful or even pretty, and she looked at the pictures on the walls that she had put up of Louann and Tessa, and the picture of herself as a young woman, her favorite picture of herself, although she didn't know why. It was a picture Eddie had taken at the Wilton County Fair, and she was standing in front of a ride she had refused to go on because she had been afraid it would break. But she was laughing, and there was no sign of fear in her eyes. She had been young and beautiful, and now she couldn't even get herself to go to an appointment for a job she didn't even want.

She turned and faced the mirror again, and she pictured herself walking into the interview and all the young girls who would be there, too, and what could she say? *I used to be young and beautiful but I'm not anymore, and the truth is . . .*

She knew what the truth was. She would never be able to leave the house to go on this interview or any other. Gerald would yell at her, and then he would be tender, and the girls would be confused. She would go into the hospital, and they would put her on pills, and then they would take her off the pills to try something else, and always she'd be scared and sad because she had wasted so much, and she would keep getting older. . . .

She turned and went over to the tub and turned on the water. She had read about this, and in the back of her mind, there was a voice saying, *You're not really going to do this.* She had read that it was painless after you cut, and actually dreamy. . . .

You're not really going to do this, the voice said, except that she was. She took off her shirt and her skirt and her bra and then her underpants, and she hung them neatly over the hook on the door. She made the water the perfect temperature—it was one thing she could do, she could draw a great bath for herself. She almost started to laugh, but instead she opened the medicine chest, and she took out Gerald's box of razors, and she shook one out into the palm of her hand.

7

"It's a year and a half exactly," Louann said to Tessa.

They were at the breakfast table, and Tessa had to think for a moment what Louann meant. But then it was so obvious: a year and a half since their mother had done it.

What was odd was that on that day, Gerald had come home early. Usually he stayed at work at least until six and sometimes even until seven, but for some reason, he had come home early. Tessa could still remember how she had agreed to pick Louann up from her lesson that afternoon, so she and Louann drove up together, and Louann had said, "Dad's home! I wonder why."

Tessa didn't know why she had known it was a bad sign, but she had known. And she had known that whatever had happened had happened to her mother, because Gerald had never been sick a day in his life. When things happened, they happened to her mother.

And then they had seen the car parked down the street with the words Loden County Coroner across the side. Tessa would never forget Louann's face—she had been thirteen, old enough to know that "Coroner" meant that someone had died. "Oh my God," she said.

"Don't go in," Tessa said, getting out of the car. "Let me find out—"

Then the door opened, and Gerald stepped out, and he held out his arms, and Tessa thought he meant for her, and then in a flash Louann was past her and sobbing in his arms.

Afterward, that night, he had told them something Tessa knew was the key: he had wanted her mother to get a job, and he had set up an interview for that day.

"How could you do that?" she said. "You knew she wasn't in any shape to go out and get a job."

75

"Hindsight is always twenty-twenty," he said, and she wanted to punch him.

Mostly what she felt was a sorrow for Louann and their grandmother, for what she knew they both had to be feeling. She only felt numb. She had loved her mother, and the thought that she had chosen to die—chosen! it was staggering to her—was awful and painful. But she didn't actually feel the pain. She felt nothing except anger at Gerald and sorrow for Louann and their grandmother, and that was all.

She had graduated from Lodenton High and was now a freshman at Acton College—not the future she would have chosen for herself two years earlier, but the future she had ended up pursuing—and she still wanted more than anything else in the world to leave home.

"Did you call Grandpa and Grandma?" Louann asked.

"Nope," Tessa said.

"But they'll be upset over the anniversary," Louann said. "If I want to go over later, will you take me?"

"I don't know." Tessa *wanted* to be able to handle the responsibility—she wanted to do the right thing for Louann, to be there for her—but more in the abstract than in reality. She didn't want to chauffeur her around when Gerald or her grandparents could do it just as easily.

And she had her own plans for that night; she was going to go to a bar called the Depot, where she had heard that a lot of the more sophisticated students from Acton liked to go. Apparently they liked to see "real people" and to soak up the local atmosphere—an idea that had made Tessa seethe with resentment until she had realized that these students, mostly from New York, were sincere: they genuinely liked the area and were fascinated by people who were coal miners.

What particularly amazed her—and made her slightly uncomfortable—was that the Depot was where she had gone on her three dates with the man from the furniture store (she still didn't even like to think of his name). She could remember that on the first date, she had thought Jim Herrick was so polite. He had asked her at least twenty questions about herself, and she had thought that this showed he was sensitive and interesting. The boys at Lodenton High, when they spoke to her at all, always seemed so concerned with themselves.

And Jim Herrick seemed interested in showing her off to other people at the Depot. She had liked the idea that she might become someone's girlfriend, the girlfriend of an older man, even if he was just someone who delivered furniture. He was handsome and seemed popular, even if it was only in his own small world.

The second time they went out, he was quiet and polite. He brought her home early, he kissed her good night, and arranged for their next date, that coming Saturday night.

Looking back, Tessa knew that she had been naive. Jim Herrick had told her that they needed to stop at his apartment for just one minute and then they could be on their way. At the back of her mind, Tessa had known something would happen. A voice said, *He's not telling the truth,* and she was pleased. She would finally get to make love to a man, and she would no longer be a virgin.

But with the half-acknowledged thought, she had also assumed that Jim Herrick would be romantic and that the evening would be like a normal date.

Her first clue that she had been wrong was when he let her into his apartment and she saw that it was just a single room he had rented from someone in town—a single room with a huge double lock that he snapped shut the minute they were inside.

"I thought you had an apartment," she said, and she knew immediately that she shouldn't have said it.

He looked angry, and he came up to her and put his hands at her neck. "Why do you care?"

Suddenly she was afraid. Before, when she had wondered whether or not Jim Herrick would try something sexually, she had felt ambivalent about it. Yet she had felt adventurous and as if she were looking fate in the eye, making some sort of a dare. It had never occurred to her that he could be a dangerous man.

"I don't," she said quickly. Her voice was a whisper.

"You think you're so great, don't you, that you're above everything because of the way you look."

"I don't know what you're talking about," she said, amazed that he would be talking that way. Why was it a threat to him if he liked the way she looked?

"You're all alike, all you women who think you can get anything you want," he had said, and he had pulled her to him and then pushed her back on the bed.

Looking back, she couldn't exactly say what had happened; had she told the story to a friend, she wouldn't know whether to say she had been raped or had gone to bed with him almost willingly. She had tried to push him away, but at the same time, she had known she wouldn't succeed, that it would probably be dangerous to fight too much. And also, at the back of her mind, she had told herself that this was in fact a man she had wanted to sleep with, so did it make sense to try to fight him off?

What amazed her most was that afterward he had acted as if nothing strange had happened. She had gotten out of bed and begun to get dressed, and he had asked if he could see her again. She had said "I don't know," and left a few moments later.

She had finally told him no—she had to see him almost daily while she was working at the dress shop—but even now, when she sometimes saw him around town, he acted perfectly friendly and casual, as if they had parted on the best and most normal of terms.

But she didn't want to think about Jim Herrick and her past. The Depot was going to be a place for her to meet other kids from Acton.

"Do you think Grandma and Grandpa realize?" Louann asked.

"Realize what?"

"About the anniversary. Do you think they realize."

"I don't *know*," Tessa said. Out of the corner of her eye, she saw Gerald look up sharply from his breakfast plate. She stood up and started to clear the dishes. "Why don't you call them if you're worried?"

"Tessa," Gerald said in a warning voice.

She looked at him the way she always did these days—flatly and with hostility. She hated the sight of him. "What is it?"

"I don't want to hear that tone of voice."

She sighed. "I don't know what tone you mean. I think Louann should call Grandma and Grandpa if she's that worried that they're upset."

"Then you can say it that way, just the way you said it to me. This is a sensitive subject."

"I don't need you telling me it's a sensitive subject," she said. She slammed the plates down in the sink and turned on the water full blast. She wished so much that she had been there that day; what Gerald thought of as "offering to help her get a job" must have seemed like a terrible threat to her mother.

"You could offer to drive your sister, then, on such an important day."

She turned to face him. "The year and a half anniversary? Thank you, no. I'm in school, in case you've forgotten, and I have people to see. And Grandma and Grandpa can easily come pick Louann up if everyone wants to make some bizarre occasion out of it, and you know that.''

In fact, she had no one to see and had made no friends at Acton, but at least she had a plan, and at least she was starting a new part-time job at the college that day.

''Tess?'' She was leaving the house, but Louann had caught her at the door.

''What is it?''

''I'm sorry if I got you into trouble. I just feel weird if we don't mark the days.''

Tessa sighed. ''It doesn't mean we have to have a ceremony,'' she said.

Louann's eyes started to fill with tears, and Tessa held out her arms. ''Come here,'' she said, and Louann hugged her. ''We all have to mark these things in our own way. I'm different from you, but you shouldn't let that stop you from doing what you need to do. I'm sure if you want to do something, Mack and Amelia will take you in their car. Maybe you should go up to the cemetery.''

Louann looked up at her. ''Can't you come, too?''

Tessa shook her head. ''I don't want to do that kind of thing, Louann.'' What she wanted, desperately, was to leave home as soon as she could, no matter what she had to do to accomplish it.

''I'm sorry, Professor Beckwith isn't in,'' the woman said into the phone. ''Can I take a message?''

She had the most beautiful eyes Glenn had ever seen—pastel blue, almost turquoise—and alternately expressive and impossible to read. He had seen her working at the snack bar for a few weeks, and then she had disappeared; he had never expected her to appear in the math department office.

''I can't understand what you're saying,'' she said into the phone. She looked across the office at Glenn for a moment, but he wasn't certain that she was even seeing him. ''Can you spell that?''

She was a woman who was out of his reach, he was certain— probably one of those homecoming-queen types who only went out with football players. And those types never seemed to be interested in men like him. ''You always seem to be *reading*,'' he could remember his ex-fiancée telling him when she was trying to explain why the wedding was off. As if reading were the most heinous activity on earth.

He had wondered what this woman was doing, working at the snack bar, and he had almost been tempted to use that corniest of lines, What's a nice girl like you doing in a place like this? But all he had ever said to her was, "Let's see—I'll have a bag of pretzels and a Coke." And it was actually fairly obvious what she was doing there—all the local and ·scholarship students at Acton worked part-time at various jobs—and Glenn felt that the fact that this beautiful woman had to work to pay for her studies somehow humanized her.

"Wait a minute," she was saying into the phone. "Can you just . . . That was Z-A-R—"

Glenn stood up and walked over to her desk. "Zarenka-Killian conference," he whispered, and then he wrote it down on a sheet of message paper.

"Ah," the woman said, both into the phone and at him. It was the most luminous smile he had ever seen.

Don't even think about it, he told himself. When he thought about a woman in words like "luminous," it meant he was getting into trouble. And that was *not* what he was looking for this term.

"All right, I'll give him the message. . . . You're welcome." She slammed down the phone and shook her head. "And thanks so much for making my first day on the job that much more difficult." She looked into Glenn's eyes. "People can be so rude. Thanks, by the way."

"No problem," he said—an expression he hated. But he was incapable of thinking about word choice right at that moment.

"So what can I do for you?" she asked.

"Well, actually, I'm looking for Rich, too."

"Rich?"

"Beckwith."

"Are you a professor?" she asked.

"Nope. Grad student. Glenn Stokes."

"Hi. Well, he's not in, obviously. But I'll tell him you stopped by."

"What's your name?" he asked.

"Tessa Lundgren," she said. She had barely looked at him as she had said it.

"You used to work at the snack bar," he said. He sounded like an oaf, and he wished he could start all over again. Wasn't it obvious she had worked at the snack bar?

She rolled her eyes. "Thank God that's over. That was almost enough to make me quit completely."

"What are you studying?" he asked.

"Oh, I'm not sure yet. Something that will take me out of Loden County, I hope."

He smiled. "How does applied engineering sound?"

"What?"

"That's what I'm getting my doctorate in. The department is always looking for new undergrads."

She looked mystified, and he hoped she hadn't taken offense. "You're always acting as if you know so much more than everyone else," he could remember Cynthia telling him. "Don't you know that most people don't even care about the things you know?"

"I really don't know," Tessa Lundgren was saying. "I was thinking of going into something like marketing."

For a moment, he was disappointed. Marketing seemed like such a mercenary, soulless activity. What would interest a person in an activity like that except money? But he knew it was unfair to judge a field about which he knew almost nothing; and in any case, people were generally more complex than their careers indicated.

Glenn felt he had to seize the moment. "Well, if you'd like to talk about it sometime," he said.

"I wouldn't be interested in engineering," she said, fiddling with the message pad. Her cheeks were coloring slightly; he felt this might be a good sign.

"I didn't mean about engineering, necessarily. But your interests . . . sometimes it helps to talk to someone new."

"Oh—" She hesitated, and he could see that she was going to say no. "Well, actually, I don't think my boyfriend would be too thrilled."

"Ah," he said, trying to think. "May I ask if it's serious?"

"Serious. You mean the relationship," she said.

"That's right. I guess I'm asking if you're engaged. That sort of thing."

"Well, no," she said, looking down again. "But I'd say it's serious. He's a lawyer here in Acton. He has his own practice." She looked into his eyes as if the words were some sort of challenge, and he felt a twinge of hope.

"I thought you didn't want to live in Acton," he said, and her cheeks stained purple as quickly as a piece of litmus paper.

"We can always move," she said. "Anyway, it's not necessarily that serious. I told you we weren't engaged."

He smiled. "I don't mean to embarrass you. I'm just teasing."

She gave him a cold, level look. "I don't like to be teased."

It was time to stop; maybe he would have a chance if he came back another time, but clearly he hadn't handled himself well. "Look, I'm sorry if I've offended you. Maybe we can start fresh another time."

Another cold look. "I've already told you I'm seeing someone. Is there something else I can help you with? Did you want to leave Professor Beckwith a message?"

"Uh, yeah. Just tell him he can call me over at Radicon. I'll be there for the rest of the afternoon. That's the plant over in Wilton."

"I know," Tessa said. "All right, I'll tell him."

"It was nice meeting you," he said.

"Same," she said, with about as much conviction as a turnip, Glenn felt.

He left feeling edgy and full of regret, wishing he could take it all back. But then he told himself it was unimportant: he had pledged that this semester was one in which he would concentrate on studying—the last had been a waste after the breakup, too many nights in which he had read for three hours and then brooded for four.

Plus he didn't believe in anything as absurd as love at first sight. He was attracted to her—he had been attracted to her since the moment he had first seen her—but was that worth the feeling of raw, sharp regret that he had started off on the wrong foot with her?

"You're never going to be happy with anyone because you choose women for the wrong reasons," Cynthia had told him. "And then you don't even admit it to yourself, Glenn. You think you're so perfect—you think you're above things like falling for someone because of her looks—and that's always going to trip you up." And then: "I feel sorry for you," and then good-bye. She had accused him alternately of being too romantic and too scientific, and she resented him for both. And there were times he had to agree with her assessment, that the combination of the two outlooks could create problems. Here he was, once again, thinking about a woman he barely knew; and he'd be trapped soon enough, if she were interested in him, by his conviction that the relationship could be perfected if they both simply tried hard enough.

There is no relationship, he told himself. You barely know

the woman, and she hardly looked at you except when you were helping her out.

He turned into the parking lot at Radicon and willed himself to think about something else.

The music was blaring when Tessa opened the door—Loretta Lynn and a blast of smoky air that brought back unpleasant memories of Jim Herrick. She could remember how, when she had seen the Acton students over by the bowling machines when she was with Jim, she had hated them because she had thought that they felt superior. But at the Acton snack bar Tessa had overheard a girl who was obviously from some sophisticated East Coast city say, "I think those coal miners are the coolest guys on earth. All the people in this town seem so amazing. It's like real life, you know?"

Well, this was her turf. She ordered a beer and stood next to a small group of kids at the bar, and she listened to their conversation, trying to think of an in.

"I thought your dad was in television," a girl, not particularly good-looking, said to one of the guys.

"Nope. He represents a bunch of actors and writers, but he's not at a network or anything. He's an entertainment lawyer."

Tessa began to feel light-headed. These were the people she had been waiting her whole life to meet.

"Hey, how do you get this thing to work?" a guy in the corner asked, fiddling with the change machine by the bar.

"You have to knock it with your hip," Tessa said, remembering Jim doing that whenever he wanted to get a pack of cigarettes.

The one whose father was an entertainment lawyer looked at Tessa with interest. "Are you from around here?"

"My whole life," Tessa said. "Actually, in Lodenton, which is about thirty miles away." She smiled. "This is the big city we're in right now." He wasn't nearly as good-looking as the man she had met in the math department that day, but she didn't care. If she could get to know him, it could mean the start to so much!

"Really. Mike Strachman, by the way," he said, holding out his hand. "And this is Alice Gruen and Steve Clancy."

"Hi," she said. She felt nothing, no attraction whatsoever, when she shook Mike's hand, but she told herself that could come later. "Tessa Lundgren," she said. "Nice to meet you."

"So what do you *do* when you're growing up in a place like this?" Alice asked.

"Well, it's mostly work," Tessa said, sipping her beer. "If you're a kid you do chores—my family had all kinds of chickens and pigs and goats, and we had to feed and water them from the time we were three and four. And then if you're an adult, you either work in the mill or in the mines, and you work all the time. My father was a coal miner, and I really didn't even get to see him all that much while I was growing up, because he was gone by three-thirty every morning. And then after his shift in the mine was over, he worked some fields near our house until the sun went down. We didn't own the land—we didn't have the money—but he was kind of like a tenant farmer."

"Hey, someone should play 'Coal Miner's Daughter,' " Mike said, flipping the titles on the jukebox. "You must love that song."

"I do," Tessa said. What she loved was being the center of attention. "It's really an inspiration, hearing stories like Loretta Lynn's, because you realize that anyone can become what they want; it doesn't matter where you start out."

"I don't know about that," Mike said. "I mean, both my parents are lawyers, and it's hard for me to even *discuss* being anything other than a lawyer with them; they just flip out completely. And in the few discussions where they consider the possibility that I might end up being something else, they end up throwing every connection in the book at me. They won't let me try to make it on my own."

"But you don't take advantage of them? The connections, I mean?" Tessa asked.

He shook his head. "If I get a job at a newspaper, I want it to be because of my writing talent—not because my father knows the publisher."

"I can understand that," Alice said. "I feel the same way."

"I want to make it on my own, too," Tessa said. "But if I had connections, I would use every one I had. Every day for as long as I can remember, I've dreamed of being somebody else and somewhere else—with a father who didn't have to get up at three in the morning every day, with uncles who didn't die of black lung disease at forty, someplace where there's more to life for a woman than working at the mill making sheets and curtains."

"So *that's* what they do?" Alice said. "Mike and I were wondering. Have you ever worked there?"

"Every summer," Tessa said. "It was brutal. It was always ninety-eight degrees, and the machines are so loud you're deaf until you've been out of there for two or three hours. I have an aunt who went deaf at thirty-seven, and the doctor said there was no question about it: it was from the machines."

"What did you do there?" Mike asked.

"Oh, whatever they needed me for. That's what you have to do if you're a summer worker. You can pick it up pretty easily, though. I always did. The main thing is being glad you're not down in the mine. Now there are women down there, and it's something I've vowed never to do."

It was so odd to pretend to be the very things she had never wanted to be. But it was so easy, and she felt more comfortable discussing her false past than she would have discussing her real one.

The door opened, and a gust of cold air blew across the table. Tessa looked up at the door and immediately looked away. It was Jim Herrick.

"So tell us more about your father," Mike said. "I assume he's still alive."

Tessa nodded. "He's only forty years old, but mining is all he's ever done, and already he's an old man. He looks sixty and he moves as if he's eighty. It's so amazing thinking of the differences between that kind of life and your father's," she said. "I wonder what they'd have to say to each other if they met." Out of the corner of her eye, she could see Jim Herrick approaching. She had the feeling she had actually felt his presence before seeing him—a tall, dark force she wanted to avoid.

"Tessa," he said.

She looked up. "Oh hi," she said casually. He was standing there as if he expected her to introduce him around the group.

"How's things?" he asked.

"Fine," she said, barely looking at him.

He was standing there as if he had no intentions of leaving.

Mike was suddenly holding out his hand. "Mike Strachman," he said.

"Hey," Jim said. "Jim Herrick."

"How about a beer? We were just talking about Tessa's father."

Jim Herrick didn't say anything. He was looking at Tessa as if he were remembering that night, as if he wanted her to as well.

"Are you a miner, too?" Mike asked.

"What?" Jim asked, finally looking away from Tessa.

"Are you a coal miner?"

"Hell, no," Jim said. Then he looked at Tessa. "Your father's not a coal miner."

Tessa felt as if the room had frozen, as if everyone were motionless and silent. She felt her mouth open and close, and she meant to say something, but no words came out.

"Oh," Jim said. "You mean her father? Not her stepfather? But he wasn't a miner either."

Tessa found her voice. "Excuse me," she said. She set her beer down on the bar, and then she walked out without looking back.

"I guess one thing we have in common is the question of sibling rivalry," Glenn said, taking another sip of wine. He still found it amazing that Tessa Lundgren had finally agreed to go out with him—and more amazing still that now they were on their second date. "Of course, the situations are different because my brother and I were in exactly the same field—I think I told you he's an aerospace engineer over in Saudi Arabia."

"And you never see him?" Tessa asked.

Glenn shook his head. "He's made his life over there and rarely comes back. And we were never close. My father saw to that," he said, leaning back against the banquette. "It amazes me sometimes that families can be plagued with so many problems that seem preventable when you look at them from a logical standpoint. I look at my brother and myself, and I know that we would have been close—we could have been best friends—if our father hadn't worked as hard as he possibly could to pit us against each other. And I look back and I wonder what he thought he'd be gaining."

"Maybe it was a question of competition . . . thinking that if he egged you both on, you'd both do your best," Tessa said.

He was interested in what she was saying, but he was also transfixed by her eyes, by her voice, by the fact that he had gotten her to say yes to another date.

"I don't know," Glenn said. "Sometimes I'm not sure even *he* knew what he was doing because of all the drinking he was doing at the time. And that's what's funny, looking back, at least for me: I spent eighteen years trying to get him to notice me, and he probably wasn't noticing much of anything at all."

"He died when you were eighteen?" Tessa asked.

Glenn nodded. "In a car accident. At least no one else was

hurt, which was a miracle—his car had crossed onto the wrong side of the highway.'' Glenn took another sip of wine and turned the glass to catch the light of the candle at their table. ''Sometimes that's why I think I'm so eager to have a family,'' he said. ''I look back at all the school events he didn't come to and all the long talks we never had, and I can hardly wait to be just the opposite for my sons or daughters.'' He paused and took another sip of wine. ''So do you feel . . . um . . . I guess what I'm trying to ask is whether your mother's death made you more interested in having a family or less.''

He could see she was surprised by the question, and he hoped he wasn't moving too quickly. It wasn't that he was asking Tessa to marry him and have his children, but he had a thousand questions about her, and he wanted to know how she felt about everything and everyone.

''That's a tough one,'' Tessa said finally. ''I suppose what was hardest for me was the idea that she would be willing to leave us; I know that if I ever had kids, I'd love them so much that I would never, no matter what, willingly leave them. Particularly like that.''

''But do you *want* to have children?'' he asked.

She smiled. ''Is that a proposal?''

He knew she had meant her question as a joke, but he was embarrassed. He liked her more than he wanted to; he felt as if he were throwing away all his principles and rules, all his plans about how to pursue a relationship, with every passing second. ''I ask because women today have so many choices,'' he finally said. ''You have so many more options than our mothers and grandmothers had; that must present you with some interesting dilemmas.''

''Well, I think I'd like to, eventually,'' she said. ''I hope that whatever career I choose, I'll be able to take time away from it to have at least two. But I also know that I want to have a career,'' she said. ''Sometimes it's hard for me because I expect things to be as black and white for me as they are for my sister. But I figure that something will come along for me.'' She smiled. ''At least I *hope* so. I keep assuming that if I keep an open mind, it will all fall into place somehow. . . . You don't think I'm being naive, do you?''

He looked into her eyes and smiled. ''No, not at all. Keeping an open mind is the best way to approach anything, I've always felt,'' he said. What he believed was that he was falling in love with her.

8

"But do you love him?" Amelia asked.

Tessa's eyes were pale and unreadable. "Grandma, I've been seeing him for six months."

"But do you love him?" Amelia asked again. "Six months or six years, Tessa, the time doesn't make any difference unless you love the person."

"I love him," Tessa said, with an edge to her voice. "I don't know why you keep asking me that as if you think it's impossible."

Amelia didn't say anything. What she suspected was that Tessa *felt* that she loved Glenn, and that she *wanted* to love Glenn—but that Tessa would never love anyone, not in the true sense of the word.

Lately, she had been remembering an incident that had happened soon after Dolores had married Gerald and Louann was on the way. She had been dividing up the last of the cat food for their outdoor cat's kittens and had said, "Whoops, now there isn't enough for Chloe," their ancient indoor cat who spent her days following the spots of sun in the living room. Tessa had suddenly burst into tears. "I'm going to be like Chloe," she had said, tugging at Amelia's skirt.

"What are you talking about, honey?"

"Mommy's going to forget about me, and there's not going to be enough."

"Oh, honey, she would never, not in a million years. And enough what?"

Tessa had suddenly transformed her face into stone then— Amelia had never seen such a young child able to become unreadable—"Mommy won't love me anymore," she had said, calmly and as if she hadn't been crying just moments earlier.

Certainly it had been a natural fear on Tessa's part—didn't all siblings fear for the arrival of a new brother or sister?—but in this case, Amelia felt that Tessa had been right: there wasn't enough love in the house, even for *one* child.

"Grandma?" Tessa asked now.

"Yes, honey."

"Why do you think I shouldn't marry him?"

Amelia felt like a traitor. The truth was that she felt Tessa would ultimately make Glenn unhappy. "Help me set the table, and we can talk," she said softly. She wasn't feeling well, either, and it was something she couldn't put her finger on—not enough to call the doctor about, just a tiredness she couldn't get rid of.

"I just don't see why you would want to rush into anything," Amelia said. She took out the green linen tablecloth from the sideboard and fluffed it across the table, and for a moment she could picture Tessa at age of six or seven helping her, all eager blue eyes and that high-pitched little voice asking a million questions. Amelia felt as if it had taken place a hundred years earlier, and she felt exhausted.

"I don't think it's rushing," Tessa said. "Um, the good silver, Gram?"

"Of course. How often are we going to have a celebration dinner for your engagement?"

Tessa smiled and pulled out the top drawer of the breakfront. "I just can't believe I'm finally going to be leaving home," she said. "No more hostile looks from Gerald, no more of his nagging." Amelia heard too much of Dolores's voice in Tessa's, so excited to be leaving home to go live with Eddie. "Did I tell you Glenn got a recruitment call from a company in Westport, Connecticut? Can you imagine? That's where Paul Newman and his wife live. I'd just love to live there."

"Is he determined to leave the area?" Amelia asked.

"*He* isn't," Tessa said. "And they're pretty interested in him at Radicon. But I'll just let him know—I mean, I already have— how much I want to leave. He's gotten calls from companies all over—Phoenix was one, and one in L.A.—so I'm not worried."

"Does he want to have children right away?"

"He wants what I want," Tessa said, setting down the last spoon with a look of satisfaction. "He's always saying that marriage is a two-way street—I know it sounds corny, but Glenn always means it when he's saying these corny things—and that he thinks the key is to always be aware of what the other person wants, and to try to take that route when you can. He's developed all sorts of theories," she added.

"I don't know what you mean," Amelia said. She was trying not to think about the fact that just reaching for the plates was making her arms ache.

"Well, it's funny," Tessa said. "Glenn is a scientist, and I guess I never realized that if you're a scientist, you're going to be scientific about everything. But Glenn really is. He's studied relationships in all kinds of books, and he's read all about how long certain phases of the relationship should take—"

"How long?" Amelia asked, astounded. "Do you mean there are actually books that tell you how long a courtship—or whatever you would call it nowadays—how long an engagement should last?"

Tessa nodded as she set out the gravy boat. "Glenn says he's breaking all the rules but that he can't help himself. He said you should know each other for eighteen months before you make a commitment to each other."

Amelia couldn't help smiling. "That all sounds very scientific, but I wonder how someone who calls himself a scientist can assume that the same period of time would be necessary for everyone on earth."

Tessa hesitated, as if thinking it over. "Well, that's what Glenn says. I have no idea how many books he's read. But it's like everything else in his life—when Glenn wants to become an expert about something, he reads absolutely everything he can on the subject."

In fact, Amelia could picture Glenn at home—in the house Tessa had described as neat as a pin—earnestly reading a book about how to find one's perfect life mate, with a stack of similar books nearby. She liked him enormously—her first thought when she met him was that he was like a tall, handsome, teddy bear, very sweet and very smart. But certainly there was something naive in his approach.

"You know, he was engaged once before," Tessa said, looking around and finally picking up the cut-glass fruit bowl off the sideboard. "Do you think for the centerpiece?"

"Why not?" Amelia said. "What happened with the other engagement?"

"She broke it off at the last minute," Tessa said, turning the bowl around and then standing back to look at it. "I think he was pretty devastated by it."

"Well, naturally."

Tessa looked up at her with blank, pale blue eyes. "But if she decided she didn't want to marry him, why would he still want to marry her?"

"So it's electronics, is it?" Gerald was asking with a mouthful of turkey.

"Applied engineering," Glenn said hopefully—that was the quality Amelia hadn't been able to put her finger on; Glenn always seemed so hopeful. He was a nice-looking man—actually quite handsome with his soft brown eyes, his fine, light brown hair, and his easy smile. But Amelia felt that his hopefulness softened his good looks, somehow blunted them, and she was surprised that Tessa had fallen for such a gentle, optimistic man. "Right now I'm working over at Radicon part-time, in research and development," Glenn continued, "and—"

"Have you ever heard Louann play?" Gerald asked.

Glenn smiled politely. "I've heard *about* her playing, but I haven't had the pleasure yet."

Gerald jerked his head at Louann. "Play him that sonata you've been practicing, honey."

Louann's cheeks darkened. "Not now," she said softly. "We're in the middle of dinner."

"So? Everyone's heard of dinner music, right?" He looked around the table, but when he looked at Amelia, his eyes barely met hers. This had been the pattern since Dolores's death, and Amelia was relieved Gerald had never felt the need to win back whatever affection she had ever felt for him. She didn't blame him directly for Dolores's death—her life had led up to that moment surely and certainly—but she didn't feel he had ever helped; and Gerald knew this. "Just play enough for him to hear how good you are."

"Dad—"

"Honey," he said in a warning voice.

Louann put down her fork and walked out to the living room. Amelia felt that the silence was uncomfortable—everyone but Gerald knew how much Louann didn't want to play at that moment—but when Louann began to play, everything changed; the house was filled with the most achingly emotional notes, astonishing considering that they were coming from a sixteen-year-old's playing.

"She's unbelievable, isn't she?" Gerald said in the middle of a particularly complicated passage.

"Amazing," Glenn said quietly.

Louann finished the movement and stood up.

"Bravo," Gerald called out, clapping. "But you're not done yet, honey. Finish the piece."

"I really think people would like to eat in peace," she said. "I can finish later."

"Don't be silly. You all want to hear the rest of the sonata, don't you?"

"She doesn't want to finish it," Tessa said.

"I see," Gerald said. "And you would know, wouldn't you? It wouldn't occur to you that you could be proud of your sister, would it? Or that your fiancé—Glenn here—might be more than a little interested in hearing his future sister-in-law play. A prodigy isn't someone you come across every day." He looked at Glenn. "You know that," he said, as if it were possible that Glenn didn't.

"I think what Tessa meant—" Glenn began.

Gerald held up a hand. "Oh, I know what Tessa meant. I've lived with that girl long enough to know what she meant. *You're* the one that hasn't lived with her long enough to know."

"Look," Glenn said, setting down his fork. "I don't want to get into a family squabble, but I feel that as Tessa's fiancé, I have a right to give my interpretation here. And frankly, I don't see what the problem is. Louann is obviously tremendously talented, but she's already told you she doesn't want to play any more during the meal. So if you don't mind my asking, why is there a problem?"

Gerald set down his fork. "I think I've had about enough to eat here," he said, standing up. "Amelia, Mack, thanks for the meal. Louann, get your things."

"What? I'm not leaving."

Amelia was astonished. "Gerald, I really think—"

"She has practicing to do," he said gruffly, standing by the doorway. "Louann."

"Tessa and Glenn can take me home," Louann said. "Or Grandma and Grandpa. I haven't even eaten yet."

"We'd be happy to take her," Glenn said.

Gerald stared at him. "I'd be 'happy' if you didn't, and if you would stay out of this."

Glenn set his napkin on the table and stood up. Amelia found it surprising and appealing that color had come into his cheeks— he always seemed so calm, but clearly his emotions were coming to the surface. "Again," he said in his careful, deliberate manner. "I don't quite understand why this has become some sort of incident. Clearly your daughter wants to eat with us—it was supposed to be a celebration dinner—and I don't see why there's a problem with that.''

"Boy, you're two of a kind, I can see that much," Gerald said, flipping on his cap. "Everything for yourselves, and you don't care what anyone else might feel about anything. Well, I can sure see you chose perfectly, you two. I hope you're real, real happy.''

Amelia thought that Gerald would try again for Louann—she was sitting at the edge of her chair as if she thought he would pull her along with him—but instead he straightened his cap and walked out, and a few seconds later, Amelia heard the roar of his engine outside.

"Well," Mack said, rocking back against his chair legs.

Amelia looked over at Louann, who was on the verge of tears. But Tessa was smiling at her grandmother. "So," she said, "I guess you can see why I love this man, can't you?''

Amelia glanced over at Glenn and wondered if the marriage would even last a year.

Glenn had never been so happy in his life. Within two hours, he would be married to the woman he was more in love with than anyone he had ever known in his life.

He looked at himself in the mirror and adjusted his tie. He knew he wasn't the handsomest man on earth, but he felt he had never looked better, because he knew what happiness could do to a person's features. And he knew it was corny to say or even to think, but he felt that his life was finally getting started and that his dreams were finally coming true.

Of course, "dreams" wasn't exactly the right word; they were plans he had laid for himself, plans he had hoped would come to fruition at approximately the right point in his life. He had always wanted to meet his wife-to-be while he was still in graduate school. He felt that it was healthy for a relationship if each person got to see what the other person had to achieve and experience to get to the next phase in his or her life, and Tessa had now seen the kind of studying he had to do, along with the part-time work at Radicon, before he could call himself a scientist of any sort at all.

The intensity of his studies had been one of the areas of contention when Cynthia had broken up with him in college. "I can't take another night of staying home with these goddamn books!" she had screamed at him three weeks before they were to be married, and that fight had marked the beginning of the end. He would never forget how amazed he had been at the intensity of her anger, and how each argument led to an even more forceful argument immediately afterward. She had been seething with resentment over so many things and was angriest when he had looked at her and asked, "Then why did you say yes when I asked you to marry me?"

It frightened him sometimes that that had happened. There weren't supposed to be great depths of uncertainty in a relationship, oceans of mysterious feelings and resentments beneath the surface. That was how he always thought of the failed relationship, as a small boat that had been rocked by stormy seas; and one of the many things he loved about his relationship with Tessa was that it had been so calm. He had met her, he had fallen in love with her, and they agreed on so many things. She wanted to have two children, and so did he, although he felt certain he would want more if she did, too; she wanted to go wherever his career required him to go, but he was ready to defer to her wishes, too. Everything in the relationship had to be a two-way street as far as he was concerned.

One night, though, when he had brought Tessa home to her stepfather's house, she had gotten into a tremendous argument with Mr. Lundgren—Gerald—within seconds. It was like watching gasoline catch fire, and he had been amazed and speechless. He was ready to acknowledge to himself if not to anyone else that if there was one area of Tessa's personality that made him nervous, it was the ferociousness of her anger in some situations. Yet, with him she was like an angel, and she seemed so consistently happy.

She didn't know what she wanted to do with her life other than to marry him and have some sort of career, and he supposed that was normal for someone her age. To him, her approach seemed to be that of someone young, but then he supposed it was only in comparison to himself that he felt that way. At six he had decided to be a scientist, and he had never wavered, even when faced with the fact that his older brother was a math genius—a situation that was oddly parallel to Tessa's. But Tessa seemed open to anything and everything as a possible future for her. And he had the feeling that perhaps she would even want to have a large family, as he did. She had specified two, and naturally he would accept her decision if she felt strongly, but since she had no definite career aspirations, he had a secret hope he would keep to himself. He was always amazed to learn that some people entered into something as serious and permanent as marriage without knowing what the other partner wanted in terms of children, a place to live, all the important "details" that were in fact so fundamental.

What stunned him, though, was that he was so in love with Tessa that even had she given all the wrong answers to his questions, he would have married her as long as she had said yes. He knew it was wrong to be pleased—all the books said so, and he knew it instinctively as well—but what amazed him was that someone as beautiful as Tessa could have fallen in love with him. And he wished he knew what the components of love really were, how it was that he was in love and about to marry someone he had known for only six months.

"I do," Tessa said.

"Then by the power and authority granted me by the Commonwealth of Pennsylvania, I hereby pronounce you husband and wife."

Tessa felt as if she were falling down an abyss as Glenn raised her veil and kissed her. She was married. She had done it. She was supposed to feel soaring joy, but she felt numb.

Louann was playing the Bach Cantata she had chosen, and now it was time for Tessa and Glenn to walk back down the aisle. It was a small group in the church, but it seemed to be a sea of nameless faces as Tessa walked down the aisle—and then she saw Glenn's mother. The woman was staring at her with the most unadulterated look of hatred Tessa had ever seen.

Tessa squeezed Glenn's arm, and for a moment she felt flooded with the love she knew she was supposed to feel. He was her husband, and he was like the Rock of Gibraltar.

When they got to the Acton Arms, where they were going to have a small reception dinner before flying off to Nassau, Tessa went off to the ladies' room to check her makeup before dinner. She had just sat down in front of the mirror when she heard the door open, and she looked up. Standing behind her was Eleanor Stokes, Glenn's mother, who had opened her purse and was reapplying her lipstick.

Tessa felt uneasy, but she told herself there was no reason to. Eleanor Stokes lived in Utah, and there was nothing she could do to Tessa even if she despised her. Glenn lived in Acton now, and he was her husband.

"What did you think of the ceremony?" Tessa asked, turning to face her new mother-in-law. She didn't even like to ask the question—she didn't care what Eleanor Stokes thought about anything—but it was the first thing that had come to mind.

"It was what I expected," Eleanor Stokes said.

Tessa knew that she shouldn't ask, but she couldn't resist. "What do you mean?"

Eleanor Stokes looked down at her. "This is a small town in the middle of nowhere, and the two of you have few friends, from what Glenn has told me. Therefore it was what I expected," she said with triumph.

She had obviously been planning to say those very words, and Tessa was enraged. For a moment she could hear her mother saying, We're destined to be better than everyone else. The two of you will be more famous than you can imagine. How *dare* Eleanor Stokes insult her and Glenn?

"Well, I can see that I would have done better to follow Glenn's advice," Tessa said. "He didn't even want to invite you, but I insisted. And we realized we couldn't invite his uncle without asking you, too, but obviously we made a mistake."

Eleanor Stokes smiled a mean, thin smile. "Glenn is a very naive man, but he didn't inherit that quality from me, I can assure you." She snapped her purse shut. "I can also assure you that you're very much mistaken if you think you can take my son's future away from him. You think you've bought yourself a mighty rich ticket, and I see where you think you're going. But Glenn isn't going to stay naive for long, married to you. I give the marriage a year at most, and I'd bet money on it."

Tessa couldn't believe this was the devout, church-going mother Glenn had described. "I'll be sure to tell Glenn everything we've said to each other," Tessa said. "And then we'll see where his naiveté ends. Maybe he'll wake up sooner than you think."

Eleanor Stokes's face looked as if it had turned to stone. She opened her mouth to speak but then shut it, and she turned and walked out.

Tessa's heart was pounding. She didn't want to care what that woman thought, but it had been a disturbing incident nevertheless. Before the wedding, she had thought about what a disaster it would have been if her mother had been here and started rambling on about Jacqueline, but if her mother had been in one of her more lucid moods, she would have been able to say a lot; Tessa was going to be an important, famous person one day, and no one had any right to say otherwise.

Tessa felt an almost physical need to tell Glenn about the

incident—adrenaline was pumping through her veins—but she didn't get a chance until the reception was long over and they were on the plane for Nassau.

"I had a really unpleasant encounter with your mother at the hotel," she said after the plane had taken off.

"I know," Glenn said, not looking at her. "She already told me about it."

Tessa was shocked. Now she realized she should have assumed Eleanor Stokes would forge ahead and establish her own version of events, but she hadn't thought of that before. "What did she say?"

"She said you told her we almost didn't invite her to the wedding—"

"That's a lie," Tessa said.

He was looking straight ahead. "I don't think we should talk about it right now," he said.

"But Glenn, she was lying. I want you to know that."

He finally faced her. "I know that something unpleasant happened and that you'll never get along with my mother unless I intercede in some way. If I were ever forced to choose between you in any lasting way, then I would choose you. You're my wife, and I feel that that's inherent in the marriage contract. When we get back to Acton, I'll try to work things out."

"Work things out? There's no way you or anyone else would be able to work this out, Glenn—"

"But that can't be true," he said, smiling automatically and, Tessa felt, rather servilely as the stewardess set down their drinks. "Even if you didn't say what Mother said, there has to be a reason she claims you did. And if I can get at that reason, and talk to you about your feelings toward her, then I think we can solve the problem."

"What if we just hated each other on sight?" she asked.

He shook his head. "I don't believe in that," he said. "There has to be an underlying reason, even if a person perceives he hates another person on sight. If he feels that way, it's for a reason."

"What about love at first sight? You told me you fell in love with me the moment you first saw me."

He was silent, and for a moment, Tessa took stock of what had happened: they had been married for four hours, and they were already fighting. She didn't want it to happen.

"I can't explain it," he finally said. "But I hope to, one day. I think it's essential that we both believe we can work every problem out somehow, Tessa. I know that in our marriage, what I'm going to try to do, and what I hope you'll try to do, is always communicate, always keep the channels open. If each of us knows how the other one truly feels, I don't see how we can go wrong. It's certainly what I've seen in every book I've read about relationships.''

He certainly was naive, she felt. She couldn't believe that anyone could really think life was like a math problem, solvable as long as you had all the components of the equation.

Underneath, she felt the beginnings of rage, sharp edges that were starting to puncture her feelings for him, which she thought of as somehow soft. She found it almost limitlessly irritating that he could think that a book—any book at all—could explain the complications of relationships. But she loved him. And strangely, the very qualities that she loved in Glenn—his solidity and steadfastness, the fact that he was always completely honest in declaring his feelings—were also the sources of what she felt would become increasingly irritating. But she supposed that it didn't really matter. They weren't going to agree on everything.

And she put the whole question out of her mind as soon as they arrived in Nassau. It was the middle of the night, but she still knew she loved the island from the moment she stepped off the plane. The air was warm and humid and smelled like flowers, and it smelled and felt so different from everything she had ever known!

They took a taxi from the airport to the hotel, a huge, modern building surrounded by palm trees, with the ocean right out front, and lush, landscaped gardens that seemed to be moving in the warm, misty moonlight. At the registration desk, all the other guests looked attractive and wealthy, and Tessa had such a strong sense that her new, wonderful life was about to begin that she felt like shouting. *This* was what she had always wanted—to go to a country where she would be considered vastly wealthy in comparison to the people who lived there, to spend time doing nothing or whatever she wanted, because she was rich enough not to have to work, to lie on the beach and get tan and eat the best food in the world, and be served at all hours of the day and night.

When they made love that night, Tessa was too aware that it was her honeymoon night, that she was supposed to make the most of it and make it memorable forever. She felt a nagging, grayish anger beneath the surface, and she tried to put it out of her mind. She was married, and this was her honeymoon, and they were in Nassau, which seemed like one of the most beautiful places on earth.

The next day, they set off on a half-day trip with a dozen or so people in a glass-bottomed boat, and Tessa was ecstatic at the beginning of the trip. The ocean was turquoise, exactly the color of the sky, and the smell of the salt air was overwhelming. How much she had missed while she had been growing up! This air was nothing like the air of Lodenton; no wonder people lived along the beaches of the world. Maybe someday she and Glenn would live in the Hamptons, or even on the Riviera.

Soon after the trip began, though, Tessa's enjoyment was replaced by embarrassment and growing irritation. She hadn't known that Glenn had taken a lot of natural sciences in school; she had always assumed he had only been interested in things like math and computers, and she had never bothered to ask. But she learned, along with everyone else on the boat, that he had been fascinated with fish in high school, and he knew all about marine biology. And now he was rattling off boring-sounding details about fish and the ocean as if everyone had signed up for a class instead of a trip.

For someone like Tessa, it was impossible to understand that many of the people on the trip were not only interested but fascinated by Glenn's information. What Tessa didn't see was that more often than not, once Glenn had gotten started, he was answering people's questions rather than bringing up subjects of his own. But to Tessa, who lived in the firm belief that everyone led a more successful and interesting life than she did, it was impossible to believe. She was sure they were all actors and surgeons and executives who were bored to tears.

By the time the trip was over and they had disembarked, Tessa was so furious she could hardly see. "I hope you had a good time," she said.

"I did," he said, raising his hat and running his hand back through his hair. He looked refreshed and pleased with himself. "I thought I had forgotten all of that; I'm glad I didn't."

"That makes one of us," she said.

He looked surprised and hurt. "What's the matter?"

"You *bored* half those people to death, Glenn. They didn't take the boat so they could hear a *lecture*. Everyone went because they wanted to have fun. Hardly anyone even had a *drink*."

"I'm sorry you feel that way," he said after a moment. "I don't think you're right about it, but you should have said something."

She felt as if the blood were beating out of her veins. Why was he so *calm*? She had just insulted him, and he was so *calm*.

She had a brief, terrible thought: it had been a terrible mistake to marry him. She was going to be this irritated and annoyed with him for the rest of her life.

"Hit me," Glenn said to the blackjack dealer, and Tessa felt a glow as he hit twenty-one again. It was the fifth time in just a few minutes, and Glenn was by far the best player at the table. Normally she wouldn't have cared—she didn't feel that gambling was a skill that was particularly interesting or sophisticated—but there was a very sophisticated couple standing next to them, and each time Glenn won, the man, gray-haired and distinguished-looking, would shake his head and murmur about how good a player Glenn was. Although they were much older than she, Tessa could see they had been an extremely handsome couple years earlier. The woman had beautiful, fine features and lovely brown eyes, and the man was the type who would simply get more handsome as the years went by.

"Ah, I think I'll quit while I'm ahead," Glenn finally said.

The man laughed. "I think I'll quit while I still have my credit cards intact. Would you like to join us for drinks in the lounge?"

A few minutes later, as Tessa sipped a white wine and soda—the same drink the man's wife, Celia Wadlen, had ordered—she felt a glow of satisfaction settle over her. The man, William Wadlen, was an entertainment lawyer in New York—exactly what Mike from Acton's father had been!—and he represented some of the most famous people in the world.

Tessa thought the Wadlens' lives sounded fascinating. The wife, Celia, ran a small antiques shop on Madison Avenue, and they spent almost every summer in Europe. William Wadlen was asking Glenn all kinds of questions about his work, and he seemed to be genuinely interested.

"Tell me more about your invention," William said, leaning back against the banquette as he lit his pipe. Tessa felt that the gesture was extremely sophisticated, and she decided she was going to try to get Glenn to start smoking a pipe. "I hope it wasn't under the aegis of your work at Radicon."

Aegis. She didn't know how to spell it, but she loved the way it sounded. And she supposed it was about time she learned just what the invention was; every time Glenn had spoken about it in the past, she had tuned out almost immediately. It wasn't that she wasn't impressed—she admired him for having invented something—but it had always bored her to listen to the details.

"Well, basically, as I said, it's a component that makes re-corded sound somewhat more faithful to the original. But it was definitely part of my work at Radicon; they've already received the patent on it, and that was certainly part of my agreement with them when I signed on."

William Wadlen shook his head. "That's the greatest draw-back to signing on with a company like that, signing away all of your proprietary rights. You're part-time with them now, but you really ought to think about where you're headed before you jump into a career position with anyone. Seriously. We can talk about it more if you give me a call in New York. If you have the kind of mind that can develop patentable components at this stage of your life, don't throw it away for what you might mis-takenly perceive as security."

Tessa was thrilled. A lawyer from New York, and he was telling Glenn what a great mind he had! She felt as if she would burst with pride. Glenn was her husband, and a man like Wil-liam Wadlen was telling him he had a golden future.

Celia Wadlen turned to Tessa while the men exchanged cards. "Are you involved in the same field?" she asked.

"Oh, not exactly," Tessa said. "We met at the college Glenn is studying at—Acton, up in Pennsylvania—but science isn't one of my strong points. I'm thinking of going into retailing, actu-ally."

"Really," Celia said.

It wasn't true—Tessa had considered it only to the extent she had considered virtually every occupation at one time or an-other—but this was something Tessa didn't even fully realize herself. For her, as long as it had once been a fleeting thought, it held the same weight as if it had been a burning, lifelong obsession. What was important to her was that retailing was what Celia Wadlen did, and therefore it was acceptable and in-teresting and a field that a sophisticated person might choose to go into.

"Any particular specialty?" Celia asked.

"I was thinking of antiques," Tessa said.

There was a look in Celia's eyes—a blink, and then it was like looking at a wall. Tessa knew she had made a mistake and that Celia knew she was making things up. But Celia was too polite to acknowledge that she knew. "We must talk about it sometime," she said, but in a tone of voice that made it clear that talking about it was the last thing she wanted to do.

Later on, Tessa couldn't put the exchange out of her mind. Back in their room, she analyzed the evening over and over again to see if she could figure out what she had done wrong. How had Celia Wadlen been so quick to understand that she was lying? Was it easy for people to tell at other times? Tessa had always been confident that she could fool anyone about anything; but then, she had spent her whole life in Lodenton, where people were dull and unobservant, she could see now.

She felt as restless as a child. "I think we should ask the Wadlens to have drinks with us tomorrow night," she said, sitting up against the headboard. "Or maybe out on the beach during the day. They said they were usually by the coconut huts."

"They also said they're on their second honeymoon," Glenn said without looking up from the tour brochures he was reading. "I don't want to hound them, Tessa."

"But William likes you so much. It's so clear. Did I see him give you his card? What does it look like? I want to see it."

He sighed. "It's just a card." He reached across the pillow and touched her cheek. "And it's late," he said.

"I just want to see it," she said, getting out of bed. She went over to Glenn's wallet and pulled out the card.

William Wadlen, Crane, Exner and Wadlen, Esqs. Three-forty-two Park Avenue, New York, New York.

The letters seemed to glow off the paper. The address might have been in Paris or London or Vienna as far as the effect it had on Tessa: the promised land. The land where successful people lived and were happy.

And William Wadlen had said such wonderful things about Glenn. "I'm so proud of you," she said.

"Come here," he said, holding out his arms.

That night their lovemaking seemed particularly wonderful to Tessa—in a new place and a strange place, with a man who had been called "brilliant" by a New York lawyer. Tessa felt her life would change immediately, and that she had been brilliant to marry Glenn—she wouldn't have made a mistake in such an important area of her life.

The next day, Tessa got up early and roused Glenn so they could be downstairs by eight-thirty. "I heard William say they were early risers," Tessa said. "He said he always has breakfast meetings at around eight-thirty in New York, and he can't get out of the habit.''

''I told you I didn't want to hound them,'' Glenn said. He didn't understand why, on their honeymoon, Tessa was so interested in being with another couple. And he was still hurt about yesterday, how she had been so angry at him for talking to those people about marine life on the glass-bottomed boat. While he had been talking, he had had a fleeting thought: I'm happier than I've been in years—on my honeymoon with the woman I love, out in a boat in the Caribbean, discussing something that genuinely interests me with people who are all ears and filled with questions. He had looked over at Tessa and not understood why she looked displeased rather than relaxed and happy, but he had assumed it was because she was too hot, or uncomfortable in some way. Later, when she had told him how bored she had been, the words had cut him to the quick.

''We're not hounding them if we happen to see them at breakfast and we happen to say hello,'' she said. She was already putting the room keys in her purse and was evidently going to leave whether he came with her or not. ''And it isn't as if we weren't going to eat breakfast anyway.''

He put his wallet in his pants and followed her out of the room. He felt at a loss and uncomfortable—something was wrong with the picture—but he felt that maybe Tessa was acting high-strung and flighty because it was their honeymoon; emotions were supposed to be brimming over, and he supposed that it was natural that hers would flow in more than one direction.

Down in the dining room, Tessa spotted the Wadlens at once—irrationally, he was annoyed she had been right about the timing—and she touched his arm and started off across the room. ''There they are,'' she said excitedly.

When they were ten feet away, William Wadlen looked up from his newspaper and saw them, and Glenn was certain he could see a flicker of annoyance pass across the man's face. It was only eight-thirty, after all. ''Maybe we should wait,'' Glenn said, but Tessa was forging ahead.

''They're almost finished,'' she said. ''They won't mind.''

''What a nice surprise,'' Tessa said when she reached their table. ''We were just talking about how happy we were to have met you last night. Do you mind if we join you?''

''Well, we're just finishing up,'' William said, ''but sit down with us if you'd like. Why not?''

Glenn felt awkward—he wanted to be alone with Tessa, and

he didn't want to have to socialize so early in the morning. And after the first few moments, he could see that Tessa's confidence was dissolving. There were long silences between brief and uncomfortable bits of conversation, and she didn't seem to know how to fill them. They had talked about the glass-bottomed boat tour—William and Celia had taken it years ago and didn't think they'd do it again. They had talked about bicycling—William felt he was getting "a bit old" for it, and Celia stayed silent.

More silence, and Glenn sipped at his coffee and looked around the room. In the corner, there was a young couple he had spotted last night. The man was kissing the woman's hand, and Glenn was sure they were on their honeymoon. What did it mean if people looked at you and didn't think you were on yours when you were?

Tessa broke the silence. "Glenn and I were thinking of going downtown to look at the stores today. Maybe you two would like to join us."

"Hm," William said. "There's an interesting idea."

"I'm afraid we have other plans," Celia said quickly.

It seemed to Glenn to be an excuse, and he was embarrassed for Tessa. "Well," Tessa said quickly. "Maybe another time."

The waiter brought their food, and Tessa proceeded to try to bring up Celia's business again—antiques were so interesting. How, exactly, would a person get started if she wanted to start a store of her own?

"There's so much to know," Celia said. "It's impossible to know where to begin." She smiled a tight smile. "I suppose it's another instance in which one could say that if you have to ask, you'll never know."

"I wouldn't say that's true, darling," William said. "There was so much you didn't know back then." He looked gently at Tessa. "It's a matter of trial and error and study and passion, like anything else. I imagine your husband wouldn't have discovered half the things he's discovered if he didn't feel passionate about the very act of discovery, even the feeling of being in a laboratory. Am I right?"

Glenn nodded. What William was saying was certainly true. But he didn't understand why Tessa was so interested in the antiques business all of a sudden.

"Well, it's the same with antiques," William said. "Celia lives and breathes them, and has since we met. That's *how* we met, as a matter of fact, at an auction at Sotheby's. I imagine if you feel the same way, you could do just as well as Celia's done.

Maybe better, since you wouldn't be in New York, and you'd probably have less competition down there in Pennsylvania.''

"Well, you never know," Tessa said. "We might even live in New York someday. Right, darling?"

"I suppose it's possible," Glenn said. "If the right job came along, certainly it could happen."

William raised a finger. "I don't want to hear that word 'job' from you again, Glenn, until you think about what I've said. I don't want to call you a year from now and find that you're some drone in a dead-end job. Get out there and think while you're young, before you settle down. Before it's too late." He looked at his watch. "Speaking of late," he said. "We'd better be running along."

They stood up and said good-bye, and Glenn watched as Tessa followed them with her eyes.

"I'd like to see them again before we leave," Tessa said, still watching as they left the restaurant.

"I think we've seen enough of them," he said. "They said they're on their second honeymoon. I don't think they want to spend their entire trip with another couple. And I'm not even sure they're that crazy about us," he added, because he believed it to be the truth.

Tessa looked down at her plate for a moment, and she looked like a little girl of five or six. When she raised her eyes to him, they were despondent. "I know you're right," she said, in an odd, throaty voice. "I knew it but I couldn't admit it to myself. *He* likes *you*. That would be obvious to absolutely anyone. But she hated me—did you see that? She felt that I was a nobody— the only reason she agreed to speak to me at all was because of you, and William."

"Don't be so upset," Glenn said. "What does it matter even if it's true? We might not see them for the rest of the trip, and after it's over, we'll never see them again."

"That isn't the *point*," she hissed. "I'm *nothing*. When people meet you, they see a promising young scientist, someone who has a mind and can invent things. They look at me and they see nothing."

"I really don't think that's true," he started to say, but she lashed out so loudly the people at the next table turned around.

"Why are you being so *mild* about this?" she cried. "Doesn't it bother you that there are people who think that your wife is a nobody?"

"Tessa, calm down."

She seemed suddenly to realize that people were looking at her, and she sipped her coffee and took a deep breath. "I want to open an antiques store," she said.

He stared at her. "What?" He had heard, but he couldn't believe he had heard correctly.

"Why not? William said all it takes is passion and trial and error and something else—"

"Study," Glenn said quickly. "Which I thought you were already doing at Acton. Not to mention the fact that there wouldn't be that much of a demand for antiques where we live. Don't forget that the Wadlens' store is in New York. But that isn't even the point. You don't know anything about antiques."

"I could learn. And you could start applying to companies in all the big cities across the country, so that when you finish the program, we could move right away. Or maybe you could go out on your own the way William said, and I'd be able to open a store in a big city."

He felt that she was mildly out of control. She seemed to be near tears, more emotional than he had ever seen her before. "We can talk about it," he said, which he meant, wholeheartedly. To him, it was a wild idea, not well thought out at all, simply an emotional response to a perceived slight by a woman Tessa would never see again.

But it was important to respect and respond to Tessa's needs, he felt, no matter how inappropriate he thought those needs might be. If running an antiques store was what she wanted to do when she finished college, then it was certainly worth talking about. A good marriage was based on respect for the other person's ambitions. He would never forget the first time he and Tessa had made love, and they were lying in each other's arms. He had felt so much love for her when she had confessed her dreams. "Sometimes I just ache when I think about what happened to my mother and how much she wanted for me." Her voice had sounded small and frightened in the darkness, and he had held her more tightly as she went on: "I can't tell you what it was like—my mother thought she had somehow been robbed— she looked so much like Jackie Kennedy, and she felt that that meant something, that it meant she was due something she had never gotten. I think at some level, she always knew that was crazy. And we knew," she said quietly. "But she was still our mother. And sometimes I feel so out of control because I want so much, and I don't know if that's crazy or not."

He had kissed her then and said what he felt wholeheartedly.

"I don't think a person can ever want too much, whether they have other problems or not. It sounds corny, but life is what you make it, to a large, large extent. There's nothing wrong with wanting the best." And he could remember that, in his mind, "the best" had meant a happy home life and a satisfying career.

But now, sitting with a woman who suddenly seemed child-like and out of control, he could see that Tessa had an uncertain feel for what was possible and what was important. "We can certainly talk about it," he said again. "And when you finish college—"

"I'm not going to finish college," she said. "I think college is useless for someone like me."

"I'm sure that Celia Wadlen went to college." He didn't know why he had even said it—the words had just come out—but they had gotten her attention.

Now Tessa looked confused and concerned. "You're right. People like her have always gone to college. But that doesn't mean you can't start looking for jobs in big cities to give us a jump. Do you promise? As soon as we get back?"

"I have to finish the program at Acton," he said.

"But you've already spoken to some recruiters. I think you have to start looking early. In fact I'm sure of it."

She sounded like a child, like a small child with big, unrealistic dreams that couldn't possibly be met. But he had always planned to be open about a place to live, and he wanted to do whatever was necessary to help make her happy.

But he still felt uneasy. He didn't understand why a person would want to befriend someone who wasn't interested; he didn't understand Tessa's need to be liked by people she barely knew and whom she would never see again. He wanted to be everything to her; he wanted their life and their relationship to be rock solid. He wanted to understand her every mood, and he was already failing miserably.

9

"This is a real occasion," Gerald said, holding up his wine glass. "I'd say this is the first happy occasion we've had in, oh, I don't know how many years."

Amelia glanced over at Tessa and Glenn. It was unfortunate but true that in Gerald's eyes, their wedding two years earlier hadn't been much of an occasion at all.

"Well, hell," Mack said, sipping at his wine. "Are you going to tell us what the hell the occasion is all about, or are we going to have to guess for another whole week?"

Amelia looked away from him. She had barely been able to look at him since that morning.

"All right," Gerald was saying, still holding up his glass. "Since you insist. Let's have a toast to the most beautiful, talented girl in all of Loden County, who's headed for New York City to the Juilliard School of Music."

Tessa's face was white as a sheet, and Amelia felt her heart turn over; Tessa looked exactly as she had on that birthday so long ago when Louann had first begun to play.

"Well, congratulations," Mack was saying, holding up his glass. "That's really something."

"That's very impressive," Glenn said. "Juilliard is extremely difficult to get into."

Louann's cheeks were dark pink, and she was looking down into her lap, but Amelia could see she was smiling. And she certainly had a lot to be proud of. But Amelia wondered if she wasn't too young to be going off on her own.

"Juilliard's in New York," Gerald said, looking at Tessa.

"I know where it is," she snapped.

He was smiling. Beaming. "My little girl going off to the big city, I just pinch myself to see if it's true or not."

"What about expenses?" Mack was asking. "If it's in New York it must be an expensive school. New York is an expensive city to live in, too."

Amelia wished he wouldn't speak so she wouldn't feel she had to look at him. She still felt raw from the morning—a day on which she had been happy to wake up and do minor, mindless chores. Doing the laundry, sipping coffee, listening to the radio—and then smelling the perfume on his shirt, not even holding it up to her nostrils to check but having it waft up to her as if to announce *I'm back*. Lauralee Wicks, with that perfume you could recognize anywhere. And looking into Mack's eyes as he left the house and asking herself why he had started up again, and how long it had been going on.

"We'll manage," Gerald said, shifting in his chair. He had gained an enormous amount of weight, and each time he moved, it looked as if he were doing so with great difficulty. "Somehow. I've got a bit put away. I was hoping this day would come someday, and now it has."

Mack was shaking his head. "It's got to cost two or three hundred dollars a month just to rent an apartment there."

"More," Gerald said. "We've already looked into it. Of course, I wouldn't want Louann to live alone—it's too damn dangerous for that—but if she had a roommate, even then it would be three or four hundred a month just for the room."

"You two let us pay for it," Mack said suddenly. Just like that. As if they had all the money in the world.

"Mack," Amelia said.

He looked at her as if he had just realized she was at the table. "You know we talked about it, Amelia," he said, which was true. Once, years ago, and before they had ever separated. There was less money now, and Amelia felt more of a need for it.

"We don't need to discuss it anymore now," she said, controlling her voice. "Gerald, I'm sure you weren't counting on it, so we can think about it before we let you know."

"Sure, sure," he said, in a way that made her realize he *had* been counting on it.

"Well, all I know is we're getting on in years," said Mack, "and I'd like to see my granddaughters enjoy some of the money we've saved up while we're still around to see them have a good time. And it doesn't look like Tessa needs any help in that department, what with Glenn lined up for a big-time job in electronics."

"Glenn has all his student loans to pay back," Tessa said.

Glenn cut in quickly. "Which I wouldn't dream of having anybody but me pay back." He stared at Tessa. "What's gotten into you? I would never want your grandparents to pay for my education. Ever."

"I just thought since he *asked*," she said.

"Don't be ridiculous," Glenn said. "We can manage just fine on our own, thanks. Call me old-fashioned, but I think it's the husband's job to make sure all the finances are taken care of."

Mack was nodding with approval, and Amelia felt like slapping him. There was something so vain about his offer, she felt. He wanted to look wonderful to the world and to his family; yet what was he doing to her?

Later, when everyone was gone and she was washing the dishes, he came up behind her and kissed the back of her neck. She closed her eyes and found that tears were welling up.

"What's wrong?" he asked softly, against her shoulder now. "You were quiet as a mouse all through dinner."

"I'm tired," she said, losing her nerve.

He slid his hands around her waist and held her against him. "You don't look tired," he said. "You look beautiful. I almost felt like sending everyone home early."

That was enough. She untwined his hands and turned to face him. "Don't," she said.

"Why not?" He kissed her cheek and then her neck, and she felt a rush of anger that he could be so playful.

"I know what you've been doing," she said.

He looked into her eyes, his own pale blue and unreadable like Tessa's. "What are you talking about?"

"I know you're seeing that woman again," she said. She couldn't bear to say her name, although she felt that if she did, it would make her feel stronger. "Lauralee Wicks."

He narrowed his eyes and shook his head. "You're wrong. I haven't been."

"Mack, I know. I don't want to be lied to on top of everything else."

"But you're wrong," he said, his voice rising.

She turned away from him and went back to washing, fighting back tears that were made of anger and fear for the future, and the certain conviction that she wasn't going to have the time to make any more major decisions in her life.

* * *

For two days, Tessa burned with resentment whenever she thought about Mack's offer to Gerald and Louann. How come just because she had gotten married, she was out of the picture for any sort of windfall that might come along? Once again, it was a question of the gifted versus the plain—Louann with her gray eyes and perfect skin and perfect pitch; and Tessa, beautiful but without any visible talents.

She convinced herself that if only she could come up with the perfect idea, and sooner rather than after Mack and her grandmother had begun to distribute any money, she could certainly get some of it herself. Her grandmother had seemed shocked by Mack's offer, but didn't he always get his way? And if he was going to get his way in this situation, Tessa was determined not to be left out.

She thought of the idea she had batted around during her honeymoon when she and Glenn had met Celia and William Wadlen. An antiques store had seemed so wonderful, the chosen career of a woman who could have anything. But in the time that had since passed, the idea had lost its appeal for her. Without having consciously realized it, she had let the idea fade from her mind as soon as she had returned to Lodenton and Celia Wadlen was no longer around as a comparison. Tessa's inspiration inevitably came from those in her immediate surroundings.

There was one woman she had spotted a few times in Acton whom she had hated on sight. The woman had just opened up a gift shop that sold tasteful little things people could buy for everything from housewarmings to birthdays. Tessa didn't feel the gifts were that fascinating, but the woman had caught her eye because she looked artsy and sophisticated and as if she came from New York. Whenever Tessa had passed the store, she had felt a surge of hatred.

She felt that she, too, would be perfect as the owner of some sort of store in which people deferred to her; she had excellent taste—she read all the fashion magazines, and she was always up to date, even ahead of her time. When she had worked at the dress store that summer, so many of the customers had asked her what they should buy. At the time, all it had done was make her feel superior. But now she realized that her taste was something she could use.

When she brought up the idea to Glenn, he was appalled. "You haven't even finished school yet!" he said. And when she went to her grandparents' house, her grandfather played with her like a cat with a mouse. "I knew you'd be around within a few days," he said.

They were in his workshop out in the garage, where he was making a pine box for Louann's sheet music. He was sanding it carefully and deliberately, with the same slow strokes he had showed her as a child; you could start with a rough piece of wood that looked like nothing and turn it into a rabbit or anything you wanted. "Abra Cadabra," he had said once, and she had thought it was like Aladdin's lamp, but he had told her no, it was just sandpaper and there really wasn't anything magic about it at all.

"Why?" she asked, against her better judgment.

He smiled. The cat that ate the canary. "Mention money or something Louann can have that you can't, and you'll be here. I told Amelia you'd be along any day now, but she didn't believe me."

"Where is she?" Tessa asked.

"Over at the doctor's," he said, sanding slowly and carefully. The wood looked rich and gold, and even though Tessa didn't want the box in the least, she felt a childish resentment that he was working so hard on it for Louann.

"You didn't take her?"

"She wanted to go by herself. Is that a crime? Tell me your idea as long as you've come this far."

She felt deflated, but she told him. "I want to open up a clothes store," she said. "A boutique."

He laughed and went back to sanding. "There's got to be fourteen clothes stores in Lodenton alone, Tess. And how many over in the new mall? There's got to be twenty or thirty over on the Acton line." The Acton line. He still thought about the area in terms of the mines and their shafts. "And what happens when Glenn gets a job in Palo Alto or one of those places?" he asked.

"Then I'd sell," she said.

He laughed again. "You haven't thought it through," he said, taking a rag and sprinkling some linseed oil onto it. "You haven't changed one bit since you were a child. You haven't thought it through at all."

Tessa looked down at the application and tried to concentrate. Amount of loan, the blank said. She had no idea what to write. It didn't occur to her that her lack of knowledge, her inability to even begin to fill out the loan application, was suggestive of anything at all. It merely made her resent her grandfather even more, because it was his fault that she now had to deal with complicated application forms and try to estimate how much money she was going to need.

She assumed she would get the loan because once the bank heard her ideas, they would realize that ideas were more important than the mathematical ability required to fill out the stupid application. Maybe she didn't know how much the store would cost or where she would put it, but she certainly knew about clothes. And then, in a year, when she was wildly successful, she wouldn't owe her grandfather a word of thanks. She would have done it on her own.

But her plans changed the day after she went and got her application from the bank. She had gone to the doctor— normally, she avoided them because they reminded her of her mother and weakness and the unpredictability of everything— but she had a suspicion she had to confirm.

And what the doctor told her changed everything: she was pregnant. She had suspected it for a few weeks—she had missed her period, and she was lax about birth control, changing her mind every day about whether or not she wanted a child and whether she preferred a diaphragm to foam.

At first—the first moment she had heard the news from the doctor's office—she was frightened. She wasn't meant to be a mother; she had nothing to base this feeling on, except that she wasn't happy herself.

But everything became so clear after a few hours; she decided she *was* meant to be a mother! She would be the best one in the world! The reason she hadn't been able to know what to do with her life was that the answer had been under her own nose and she just hadn't *seen* it.

Glenn was thrilled—so genuinely thrilled that she felt a tremendous flood of feeling for him. This would be the beginning of her new life; she would be reborn with her child. Everything would be new. Because even Celia Wadlen, whom she admired so tremendously, even Celia and William had taken time out to have children. And all those actresses she read about—they worked hard and had children, too. And there had just been those articles in *Time* and *Newsweek* about career women having children. She could have a child and then she could have a career. Of course. She was part of a trend!

She dropped out of school immediately, which upset Glenn until she explained. There was so much to do! She wanted to redecorate the house; they would turn the seldom-used guest room into a nursery. She wanted to read every book that had ever been published about child care. She wanted to plan.

She worried about whether it would be a boy or a girl—she desperately wanted a girl even though she knew you were supposed to say you wanted either as long as it was healthy. But a girl could be like her; a girl could be beautiful; a girl could be her best friend.

She and Glenn joined a church that was on the other side of Lodenton. The members were young and hard-working and successful, and Tessa actually found herself enjoying the work she volunteered for. She wasn't religious—she didn't for a minute believe in God—but she liked belonging to a group. She felt more secure than she had ever felt in her life. And she was beginning to make friends—girlfriends—for the first time.

There were times when it was difficult. She was so unused to making friends that she didn't always know what to say or do. Usually they went over to different couples' houses for Saturday dinner—Tessa hadn't yet invited anyone over to their house, but she intended to when she felt more comfortable. On one of the evenings, they were all playing charades after dinner, which was their usual after-dinner activity. Tessa liked the game because she was so good at it, and she liked to have everyone looking at her. That night, when she pulled out her clue, she was particularly pleased; it was "Embraceable You." She knew how she could do it by herself, somehow. But it would be easier and faster to use a man, and so much more fun. She looked at the clue a second time and then walked over to Roy Donahue, who was on her team.

She had always found him attractive—he was dark and well-built, with a body like Glenn's but a more interesting and mysterious face. He looked as if he was unpredictable, as if his dark brown eyes held all sorts of secrets. She had noticed him the first time she had ever seen him in church, and since then, every time they were in a crowd together, whether it was at church or somewhere afterward, she would notice him looking at her, eyeing her, whenever he could.

She was going to have fun acting out the clue with him. She walked around so she was standing behind his chair, and she draped herself across his shoulders. She could feel his shoulders against her breasts, and she could feel the heat that came from his body. Out of the corner of her eyes, she could see that a couple of people on her team looked as if they were more shocked than trying to guess the clue, and she enjoyed it. It was only innocent fun; she wasn't going to sleep with him or anything. She was *pregnant*; she was going to be a mother, and everyone knew it.

No one was guessing the clue, and Tessa went around in front of Roy and sat down in his lap. As she put her arms around his shoulders, she could sense he was getting excited, and she pulled back and looked into his eyes.

She was laughing—she thought it was incredibly funny—but he looked excited and angry at the same time.

For a second she turned around, and she saw Roy's wife, who was on the other team. Vera looked pale and upset, but then again, Vera always did. She was thin and quiet, and she hardly ever said a peep, and honestly, Tessa couldn't understand why a man like Roy had ever married her in the first place.

"Come on, you guys," Tessa said playfully, and she felt Roy's hands as he moved her forward on his lap. For a second she realized the truth—that if they hadn't been playing charades in front of a group of people that included her husband and his wife, they would have been making love within seconds. She had never realized how seriously attracted she was to Roy. Now her heard was pounding, and she was aching for him.

" 'Embraceable You,' " someone called out, and Tessa felt the slap of disappointment. But she supposed it was lucky. In Roy's hands as he had moved her forward, and in the way he was breathing, in the heat from his body, she knew it was lucky it had ended when it had.

"It's about time," she said with a smile as she stood up. "A few more minutes, and you guys would have seen us in divorce court!"

She had thought it was funny, and Paula Rasmussen, the hostess, was laughing, but no one else was laughing or even smiling.

Tessa went back to her seat and felt her face beginning to flush. She wasn't embarrassed that no one had thought she was funny; she was angry. Sometimes, since she and Glenn had been going to church, she had felt that one thing their new friends lacked was a sense of humor, and now she was sure of it.

Later on, when Tessa went into the kitchen with some of the empty coffee cups, Paula followed her in.

"You know, you really shouldn't have been flirting with Roy that way," Paula said, stacking the dishes in the washer.

Tessa began to help her. "I wasn't flirting. I wouldn't flirt in front of all those people."

"Tessa, what do you call it? Come on. You were in his lap."

"It was a clue. And it worked."

Paula sighed. "That isn't the point. I wouldn't have appreciated it if you had been doing that with Stan, and I'm a lot stronger than Vera is. She was practically crying."

"Well, I'm sorry," Tessa said. Although she didn't mean it.

But Tessa was shocked by the repercussions of what she had thought of as hardly even an incident. On the trip back from the dinner, Glenn was silent at first. But she felt that she was an excellent reader of people's feelings, and when his face was red, it was a good guess that he was upset.

And he was. "I'd like to think there was some sort of explanation for the way you played that charade, beyond the obvious interpretation." He was driving in his usual way—slowly, carefully, deliberately—and of course not looking at her, even for a second: he would have considered it a reckless act behind the wheel, even if they were traveling at five miles an hour.

She was interested that he had brought it up. She found his willingness to discuss every detail of their relationship both appealing and somehow repellent at the same time. He was never embarrassed to mention anything, even if there was a chance the discussion might reflect badly on him.

"It was nothing," she said. "I'm amazed over the commotion it caused, though. Paula said Vera was incredibly upset."

She could see that Glenn was considering this—digesting the information as if he were loading it into a machine to be ground up into bits. "I don't believe in telling people what to do—I think it's ineffective and inhumane, and it ignores the fact that we're human beings." He paused, and then signaled for a left both with his hand and the light signal. He never spoke while he was making a turn. "So I would never tell you, Don't do this, or Don't do that. But I wish you hadn't behaved that way, Tessa. It was embarrassing; it was humiliating for Vera, and it was humiliating for me."

She took a long, deep breath and looked out the window. "I'm sorry," she said, although she wasn't. "I can't believe the way everyone has made such a federal case of this. But if you want to know how I feel right now, and you usually do, I can tell you I'm sorry."

He didn't say anything, and she put the whole incident out of her mind. But from that day on, Tessa noticed a coolness in all of the women that she interpreted along the lines Glenn and Paula had suggested. They were jealous, it seemed, and they didn't want to associate with someone they were jealous of.

Well, she couldn't help it if she found it easier to get along with their husbands. The men in the group always seemed ready to laugh with her, to help her if she was lifting benches in the church meeting hall or putting up streamers for a party the youth commission was giving. She found it easier to get along with the men in the group, and she wasn't going to apologize for that. And the cooler the women were, the more difficult it was to approach them, so they were digging their own graves, weren't they? In more than one instance, Tessa found that when she told one of the wives to call her for something—"I have plenty of time to help out," she would always say—they would end up not calling her, and she would hear later that all of the women had gotten together without her.

The one woman who remained more than an acquaintance was Paula Rasmussen. She was definitely more sophisticated than the others.

"You know, they want to accept you," Paula said one day when Tessa was over at her house and they were making cookies for a church bake sale. "It disturbs the balance of things that you and Glenn aren't included in everything. But they don't feel comfortable inviting you."

"You mean because of my so-called flirting."

Paula hesitated. "I think it's mostly that. But there's also the feeling that you don't really have much of a desire or need to be accepted. It's as if you don't care. And everyone knows you and Glenn aren't going to be staying in Lodenton too much longer."

Tessa hoped it was true, but she couldn't be sure at all. "We may be staying longer than I want to," Tessa said.

"But see? That's exactly my point," Paula said, putting the last silvery star on a star-shaped cookie. "Most of us are here for the long haul. They feel you're looking down on them."

"I can't help it if I have other ambitions," Tessa said.

Paula claimed it wasn't Tessa's ambitions that bothered the women. But Tessa's feeling was that if they couldn't accept her as she was, she had no interest in being accepted. It was the same way she had felt in high school, and she had gotten through it, even if she hadn't had a lot of friends.

Despite the women's hesitancy to include Tessa and Glenn in every single gathering, the two were invited to most of the parties, and Tessa found that the events helped her pass the months while she waited for the baby to be born. She felt that maybe she had made a mistake dropping out of school—she could spend only so much time reading about babies and decorating—but she didn't want to admit the mistake even to herself, and she was glad when there was an event or two to focus on during the week.

Plus people in the group seemed to be consistently impressed by Glenn and his work. The men were always saying that Glenn could go anywhere in the country and be guaranteed a good salary and a good future, and it made Tessa feel good to hear that. She was proud of him.

She was vaguely aware that her feeling good about Glenn depended on other people's praise; she was impressed with him when others were. But wasn't everybody like that? She was getting tired of people who were sanctimonious about how "pure" their feelings were—there was one woman in their little group who was driving her crazy, constantly trying to make herself seem like some sort of saint. She called herself a "domestic engineer," meaning she stayed home with her children all day. "Soon you'll be one of us," Kristy would say, and Tessa would smile wanly and say nothing. She wasn't ever going to be what Kristy was; she was going to give a whole new meaning to what it meant to be a mother. But what she liked was that she had noticed that Kristy's husband, Wade, was often watching *her* rather than Kristy when they were talking. He had his eye on her. She could tell.

Not that she was interested. Their minister talked often about how marriage was work—it wasn't something you simply decided to do and then forgot about—and she was determined to follow his advice. She looked back on the evening she had flirted with Roy Donahue—and on the months following, during which she had been unable to stop fantasizing about him—as an example of how directionless and shallow she had recently been, and how she had changed. Marriage was a commitment. She could flirt, and she could feel good when she noticed men looking at her—men like Wade, and still Roy whenever she saw him—but she wasn't going to think about them.

What had changed Tessa's feelings about the power of what the minister was saying was a woman who had come into the church out of the blue one Sunday. Tessa would never forget the day. The woman looked completely out of place in Lodenton—she was perfectly groomed, and she was beautiful, and she had the most perfect skin Tessa had ever seen, and straight, almost black hair that fell perfectly gracefully to her shoulders. With her was a little girl who was so obviously her daughter it was almost heartbreaking: a round, beautiful face with the same beautiful gray eyes and soft, perfect skin.

Tessa looked at the woman all during the service, and for the first time in her life, she felt close to what she imagined a man felt like when looking at a woman. It wasn't exactly lust she felt, but it was so close. She was swept up in the woman's looks, in imagining how her skin felt and just staring and staring and staring at her. She was the most perfect-looking person Tessa had ever seen, and Tessa wanted to be everything that the woman was.

The woman and her daughter left as soon as the service was over. Tessa felt a cold panic as she saw them walk down the aisle—what if they never came back? Outside, in the parking lot, Tessa—sounding vague and casual—asked Paula Rasmussen if she had seen "that new person, that woman"in her pew.

"Oh, you must mean Katherine Larrimore." Paula smiled. "She always makes a pretty dramatic impression."

"Who is she?" Tessa asked.

"She's Reverend Travis's girlfriend." It sounded so strange, the idea that the minister would have a girlfriend, but Tessa had heard that his wife had died three years earlier. "She moved here from Illinois," Paula said.

"But he's been here for six months."

"She had to finish up her work. She has her own advertising agency, and she had to tie up all her loose ends before she moved to Acton."

"Are you telling me she used to live in Chicago?" Tessa asked, suddenly realizing what "Illinois" probably meant.

Paula nodded. "She and Reverend Travis will probably be married by the end of this year. That's what I've heard, anyway."

Tessa was taken with the story and taken with the idea that this beautiful, perfectly groomed, flawless woman had thrown over her life in Chicago for life in Lodenton with this man. Tessa desperately wanted to feel what this woman felt. She wanted to love Glenn the way this woman evidently loved Reverend Travis; she wanted to embrace the idea of marriage and commitment the way Katherine Larrimore evidently planned to. She wanted to live Katherine Larrimore's life, and she desperately wanted to have a baby girl so that when she and the girl walked into church, they would look as spectacular and flawless and beautiful as Katherine Larrimore and her little girl did.

That day, Tessa went home and revised her plans for the baby.

She would call the baby Katherine. It would be the perfect name, with the perfect number of nicknames. Tessa wanted everything to be perfect in her daughter's life—*everything*—and it all started with the name. Tessa knew because of her own name, something that had felt plodding and peasant-like until Glenn had made her read *Tess of the D'Urbervilles*. Then she had come to like her name and feel it was glamorous. But she didn't want her daughter to be unhappy in any way with her name, even from the start.

After Tessa had seen Katherine Larrimore and her daughter that first time, whenever she got an invitation from someone in their little circle of friends, she hoped Katherine and the minister would be coming, too. She always dressed perfectly in maternity clothes she had ordered from Bloomingdale's in New York, hoping that Katherine Larrimore would notice how she stood out from everyone else, how she had to be different because of the impeccable way she carried herself even in the last months of pregnancy.

But no one ever invited Katherine Larrimore and the Reverend Travis. The two seemed to travel in different circles, and Tessa felt bitterly disappointed. She had developed an idea that had germinated and grown upon itself, the idea that she and Katherine Larrimore would become the best of friends. Soulmates. Katherine would take her under her wing and teach her the advertising business, and Tessa would blossom under her guidance. They would be modern women of the 1980s, career women and mothers at the same time, perfect at being both.

10

Katherine Elizabeth Stokes was born after a twenty-two-hour labor that was far beyond anything Tessa had ever imagined in terms of pain. Because Tessa had so wanted to have the baby, she had assumed she would be different. Hers would be a perfect birth-giving; the baby would want to come into the world, and so would come without any trouble. For her part, she would welcome the moment and remember it fondly; what other women described wouldn't apply to her, because she wanted her baby more than any woman on earth ever had.

When they placed the baby girl in her arms, Tessa felt all the love she had expected to feel. It was a flood the way she had imagined, and she was crying for the first time in years. But she felt a helpless anger over how much it had hurt. Why hadn't she been different from everybody else?

Women from the circle of church friends came to visit, and Tessa's grandfather and Louann, and once Gerald, and of course Glenn whenever he had even a free five minutes. And then, before Tessa was getting ready to leave the hospital, a bouquet of flowers and a card arrived, signed by Reverend Travis and Katherine Larrimore.

"Oh, thank God," Tessa said to Glenn as she read the card. "I was wondering when I was going to hear from them."

Glenn felt that Tessa looked almost insanely elated as she handed him the card.

"Isn't this beautiful?" she cried, tearing away the wrapping. "This is the most beautiful bouquet of all the flowers I've gotten."

He thought of his own bouquet—roses and baby's breath and violets, all of Tessa's favorites. The minister and Katherine Larrimore's bouquet was nice, but it was a plain, prosaic arrangement of carnations and daisies.

"Isn't it gorgeous?" Tessa said. She looked around and pointed to a vase that held a small bouquet from Paula Rasmussen and her husband. "Put them in that vase and throw Paula's out, would you, honey?"

"But Paula said she was going to visit you tomorrow."

Tessa shrugged. "I'm sure she's not going to examine the room for her flowers. Put them in the vase, Glenn."

Glenn did what she wanted because he knew it would be easier. He couldn't concentrate on much these days now that Katherine had actually been born. A baby, his little girl, existed where before there had been no one. It was so staggering to him, such a lovely, perfect event.

Tessa laid her head back against the pillows and sighed with satisfaction. "I'm so happy," she said. "Now I really feel complete." She looked at her watch. "I wish the doctor would come and let me out of here. I want to see everyone on my own turf. I can't wait to have a luncheon to thank everyone for all the attention."

"Don't you think you should wait a bit?" he said gently. "Having Katherine at home is going to be different from having her here at the hospital, where she's in the nursery so much. I'm sure no one is going to expect you to give a luncheon right away."

"I didn't say people would expect it," she said with annoyance. "It's what I want to do. Just because I have a baby doesn't mean that's all there's going to be in my life, you know."

"I didn't say that. I just said—"

"I know what you said," she snapped, and she ran a hand through her hair. "I'm tired, all right? I need to be alone for a while."

"All right, I'll leave in a few minutes. But when I was coming in, the nurse said she was going to be bringing you Katherine any minute."

Tessa sighed and looked up at the ceiling, and then she closed her eyes. "Fine," she said with her eyes still closed. "I need to be alone, though, all right?"

He thought of leaning down and kissing her, but he decided against it. What he did instead was to say, "See you later," in a voice he hoped didn't betray his emotion. Then he left the room, closing the door behind him.

He felt bitterly disappointed and betrayed, and he was trying to fight against it. For him, the birth of Katherine was like such a miracle that he felt like telling everyone in the world about her—strangers, friends, everyone. He knew that it was a corny idea, and he was certain that most parents, particularly first-time parents, had to feel that way. He would never, for as long as he lived, forget the moment when she had first opened her eyes and looked into his: magic and love.

But he had also fantasized another vision—maybe it was too corny, maybe that was his problem—but in his mind, and especially from the moment Katherine had been born, what he had seen were pictures of him, Tessa, and Katherine together, in a little circle that was the new family, laughing and with their arms around each other, filled with joy. He remembered seeing pictures of his parents holding him when he was a baby—during the years before his father had begun drinking, and he could remember the looks on his parents' faces so well: happiness, overwhelming love, tranquility. He wanted all of Katherine's times to be good—wasn't it easier to be happy than to be unhappy?—and he couldn't understand how there could already be problems.

He walked down the hall to the nursery and looked down at Katherine through the glass. The nurse, whose name was Carol, came and picked her up and smiled, and she gestured with Katherine to ask Glenn if he wanted to take her to Tessa.

He smiled back and shook his head and walked away, overcome with feeling. What he wanted to do was take a leave of absence from Radicon and spend twenty-four hours a day with Katherine. He knew it would be crazy and that he wasn't going to do it, but he couldn't help wishing. What had hurt him was Tessa's reaction when he had first told her this was his wish.

"Are you out of your mind?" she had said. She had looked appalled and angry. "What happens to your student loan if you do that? What happens to your résumé if you leave Radicon at this point? You'd better get your priorities straight, or we're going to be in trouble, Glenn."

He hadn't ever said he was going to do it—he knew he couldn't do anything like that, especially now, with all their financial obligations. What he had said was that he *wished* he could, and what hurt him was that Tessa wasn't willing or interested in sharing his fantasy.

Amelia knew that everyone always said babies looked like angels, but to her, Katherine looked like the most perfect angel she had ever seen, with her dark pink cheeks, long, dark lashes, and spun-gold hair. Sleeping absolutely peacefully in her arms. "This is really the sleep of the just," Amelia said.

Tessa rolled her eyes. "Which of course she always does whenever anyone else is around. When it's just me, all she does is cry. I think I've gotten a total of twelve hours' sleep since she was born."

Amelia stroked her great granddaughter's hair and hoped Katherine couldn't hear Tessa's voice through her sleep. It was so strident and angry. She lowered her head for a moment and smelled the top of Katherine's head. "They all smell alike," she said. "No matter where you are and no matter when."

Tessa leaned back into her chair and blew a long, thin stream of smoke toward the ceiling. "Well, they don't all sleep alike. I feel like a frayed wire. I was watching some women on TV the other day talking about their babies, and one said she was sleeping six hours a night! I'm lucky if I get an hour's sleep at a time."

"Oh, she'll grow out of it," she said. "The breastfeeding helps, I always feel."

"Well, I'm not doing it anymore," Tessa said. "And if one more person asks me why not, I'm going to scream. It hurt, and if you're in pain, you can't be a good mother."

Amelia felt as if it were 1963 and she was talking to Dolores. "You were a difficult baby, too," she said, hoping the knowledge might soften Tessa a bit. "You really did run your mother ragged back then."

Tessa took another drag and didn't say anything.

Amelia stroked Katherine's head and let her snuggle down lower. When Katherine reached her breast, Amelia had to stop herself from crying. "I'm sorry," the doctor had told her last week. "We're going to have to go in again, Amelia."

"You sound as if you already know it's bad," she had said then, forcing herself to say words she could barely even think.

"I would be irresponsible if I told you I knew with any kind of certainty," he had said, lacing his fingers together on his desk. "But it doesn't feel promising. I can feel a mass in the lymph nodes as well, Amelia."

And so she had taken the words in and taken them home, carried them around in her heart for a day, unable to tell Mack because she was still so angry at him, and because—amazingly, to her—when she had come home from the appointment, he had begun talking about Tessa and had forgotten even to ask how the appointment had gone.

Then, when she had told him the news—"The doctor doesn't think it looks good, Mack"—he had said what she had known he would. "Ah, that doctor doesn't know everything, Mele. They say those things to scare you and so you don't sue them later. You know that."

"I don't know that," she had said, so angry she was close to tears. "And you don't know that either. I know what he said the first time and the second time, and he never looked as upset as he did yesterday. Never."

He had looked at her with pale, affectionless eyes. "Why do you want to be so negative? It's not going to help."

"Because I'm trying to be *realistic*. I'm trying to face a reality that might not be wonderful but that's the truth. I don't want to be hit with it later."

"So you're going to worry, even though when *I'm* sick, you're always telling me not to worry."

"I wouldn't worry about a cold," she had said in a voice that had become thick with anger. "You've never had anything worse than the common cold in your life."

"What about that prostate thing?"

She sighed. "I'm not going to get into an illness competition," she said. "I'm trying to make sense of it and get a feel for it."

He threw up his hands. "I just don't see the point, Amelia." And that had been the extent of the discussion—Mack at his least communicative.

And she knew it wasn't a case of his not loving her, or not being frightened. On the contrary, it was his fear that made him act as if the doctor's words were nothing to worry about. But she needed him to be supportive; she was frightened, too.

And now she wanted to tell Tessa, but she hadn't been able to find the words. She felt a support from holding the baby in her arms; at first, when Katherine had nuzzled at her breast, she had cringed involuntarily and pushed her aside—she didn't want Katherine to be near a sickness. But now she felt a strength from that warm little shape who had fitted herself against her so comfortably. There had to be some good in the world when babies like Katherine were born; maybe some good would come to her, too.

"If you want to take a nap," Amelia said, "I can watch her all afternoon, Tess."

"I don't know," Tessa said. "It's hard to take a nap when you know it's so temporary, that you'll just have to get up in an hour."

"But that's exactly what you have to learn to do," Amelia said. Katherine made a little sound against her neck, and Amelia held her tight. "You really will get used to it."

Tessa lit another cigarette. "I just feel so isolated," she said. "Maybe if I knew I could go out every afternoon for a while, like if I knew you would take her."

Amelia picked up one of Katherine's hands and held it against her palm. "I don't know if that will be possible," she said softly. There. She had begun to say it.

Tessa looked surprised. "Why not?" she asked. "You always said you would take her as much as I wanted."

"Well—" She took a deep breath, and Katherine shifted comfortably against her breast, breathing softly herself. "I have to go into the hospital again," she said. She hated the way she sounded—her voice was filled with fear, literally quavering. "They think it won't be good."

"How can they say that?" Tessa asked. "They won't know anything until they go in, Grandma. I *hate* that."

"They can feel things," Amelia said. "My doctor has spent a lifetime feeling things exactly like this."

Tessa was shaking her head. "I don't believe it. I think you should get another doctor if he's going to say things like that. Doesn't he know how important it is for you to be confident?"

"Tess, he didn't say it was certain. But he's trying to prepare me. And I'm trying to prepare you and Mack, and Louann when I tell her."

"Well, I think it's ridiculous and horrible that he would say something like that. You're going to live forever." She sounded like a child.

"Tessa."

"You are," Tessa said. "You have to."

Tessa's was a different reaction from Mack's, yet the same in that neither could face the truth. And in that way, Amelia felt the two were so alike; they wanted the world to be the way they saw it, and if it wasn't, they simply wouldn't acknowledge the truth.

"Let me hold her," Tessa suddenly said, holding out her arms.

"But she's asleep," Amelia said. "I had thought that was what you wanted."

"I need to hold her," Tessa said, standing up. She pulled Katherine out of Amelia's arms, and Katherine immediately began to cry. "Shh," Tessa said, patting her back.

She leaned back in her chair and picked up her cigarette again, and patted Katherine's back with one hand while she held the cigarette in the other.

"Watch the ash," Amelia said.

Tessa looked confused. "What?"

"Watch the ash on your cigarette. It's about to drop. I don't think you should be smoking at all around her, Tess, but if you do—"

"I'm not going to drop a flaming *ash* on her," Tessa said, her voice frayed. She stubbed out the cigarette and looked across at her grandmother, and for a moment, Amelia felt as if she were looking into eyes she hadn't seen in years. They were filled with sadness, hiding nothing at all. "I wouldn't be able to do any of this without you," Tessa said. "I don't know how else to say it except to come out and say it. I had had plans to be the best mother in the world, and I really would love to be. But it's so much harder than I had thought it would be. I can't stand to hear you talk as if you're giving up."

"I'm not going to give up," Amelia said. She looked over at the top of Katherine's sleeping head, at her pale wisps of hair, and that small, warm back that looked so vulnerable. And she knew that Tessa was telling the truth for once. Amelia had to be there for her great granddaughter, no matter what it took.

After Amelia left for the afternoon, Tessa took Katherine upstairs and put her into her crib. She listened at the bedroom door to see if the crying would start again—she was sure it would—and indeed it began, the way it almost always did: a cough, a short cry, and then the wailing would begin.

Tessa swallowed and walked away from the doorway. She went downstairs, and she made some more coffee for herself, and then she read the paper from cover to cover.

She heard the crying get louder and hoarser—there was always a point when Katherine's voice would climb to another register—and she stood up and sighed. Then she stepped outside and began to take down the laundry.

11

"How does she look?" Louann asked. She and Tessa were walking up the hospital steps, Katherine all bundled up in Tessa's arms, and Louann felt as if her knees had turned to water. The forecasters had called for snow, but so far it was just bitingly cold and gray, and Louann felt her words sounded unreal and dead in the chill air.

"She's thin," Tessa said, pulling the blanket up over Katherine's face. "And, of course, she has all those tubes."

The smell of the hospital hit Louann with a force she hadn't expected. It smelled like embalming fluid rather than medicine or disinfectant, and Louann felt the panic of stage fright as she followed Tessa along the blue line on the floor toward the Gentran Wing.

"Is Grandpa going to be here?" Louann asked.

"Who knows? This time he's been better. He's certainly been here every day, and usually for almost the whole day. But I don't know if Grandma even wants him here."

Louann didn't say anything. The problems between her grandparents had always felt unreal to her. She had even said so once to her grandmother, who had told her that she was glad. "He's still your grandfather, and he's still a good man," she had said, "and I want you always to love him no matter what."

And she did. Her childhood memories of being at their house were absolutely idyllic; her grandmother had always felt warm and soft and full of love, and her grandfather had seemed like a magician, always making toys out of things that looked like nothing. Their mother had resented him, she knew, for the same reasons Tessa did. But Louann had never been able to stop loving him.

"Does she know her great grandma yet?" Louann asked,

catching up to Tessa and putting a hand on Katherine. She still couldn't get over that she had an actual niece.

"She adores her," Tessa said. "I've never seen her eyes follow anyone as much as they follow Grandma when she walks around the room. Here we are."

Louann took a deep breath. She prepared herself for what she had visualized since Tessa had called her with the news: her grandmother would be thinner and older-looking and pale.

But her heart broke when she saw her. She was all cheekbones and white and pale blue, and her hair had thinned to almost nothing. She smiled as they all came in, and Louann couldn't help crying.

"It's all right," her grandmother said, holding out her arms. Her skin felt cool as Louann pressed her cheek against her grandmother's. "We all have to cry." Louann drew her head back, and her grandmother smiled again. "We'd be pretending if we did anything else."

Katherine began to cry, too, and Tessa laid her against Amelia's knees. "Now watch her stop crying," Tessa said. "Grandma is like the world's greatest miracle drug."

Louann saw such sharp sadness in her grandmother's eyes that she had to look away. She felt cheated and horrified and guilty, and she wished she had never left Lodenton to go to New York. It wasn't that she thought her absence had caused anything terrible—she was no longer superstitious—but she felt she had missed out. And that the absence hadn't been worth it, because the truth was that she didn't even belong at Juilliard.

"Oh, honey," Amelia said. "Or honeys." She smiled a thin, worn-out smile. "It's good to have you here."

"Are you still in pain?" Louann asked.

Her grandmother nodded and then raised a wrist. "This helps," she said softly, and she looked into Louann's eyes. "Tell me about New York. Tell me about your concerts." She reached her hand down and laid it at the top of Katherine's head, and Katherine breathed softly and contentedly.

"Oh, I haven't given any concerts," Louann said. "I'll be lucky if I make it through this year, Gran." She shook her head. "It isn't like Lodenton or even Acton up there. Everyone at Juilliard has spent their whole lives just desperate to be there, and I'm just not like that. I don't belong." She hesitated. "Somebody has to be at the bottom of every class, and that somebody is me."

"You're throwing away an incredible opportunity," Tessa said. "You have to try harder."

"I am trying. I'm just not as talented as everyone else is."

"I want to talk to you," Amelia said. "Just the two of us, since you're leaving tomorrow. Tess, do you mind?"

"Of course not," Tessa said. "Can I leave Katherine in here? You know if I take her, she'll start to cry."

Amelia nodded. "Louann will get you when we're done."

Tessa left the room, and for a moment Louann thought that her grandmother had fallen asleep. Her eyes were closed, and she seemed to be breathing slowly and evenly. But then she winced, and Louann realized she was in pain. "Should I call the nurse?"

Amelia shook her head and opened her eyes. "I'm fine," she said, and indeed her voice sounded clear. "It passes quickly when it comes." She glanced at the door. "I don't want to get maudlin or melodramatic, Louann. I have every intention of being here for a while. But there are times I think it's going to come quickly—and I've reconciled myself to it, in a way. I don't believe in an afterlife; I think that when I go, I'll be gone. But I'm sad for everyone I'll leave behind—you and Tessa, and Mack. And this one here," she said, gently combing Katherine's hair with her fingers. "This is the one I'm really worried about."

Louann didn't say anything. Her throat ached, and she was trying not to cry.

"I watched your mother bring the two of you up as well as she could," Amelia said, "which wasn't nearly good enough. I lost my first grandchild because I couldn't recognize the signs of neglect—of course I'll never know exactly what happened, and I'll never know if there was anything I could have done to prevent it." She took a long, shallow breath and closed her eyes for another moment. "I want you to swear to me that no matter where you are geographically, you'll be watching out for your niece."

Louann was stunned. As if she were reading her mind, Amelia went on, "It's not that I think she's in the same situation as Matthew was. Not at all. I know that Tessa is determined to be a good mother, and she's trying. But trying isn't always enough."

Louann felt disloyal, but she understood what her grandmother was saying. "I'll see her whenever I can," she said. "I may even move back here sooner than we both think."

Amelia shook her head. "Don't give up so soon."

"But it isn't what I want," Louann said.

"I won't ask you to promise, because I believe you know what's best for yourself. I do ask you to promise me about Katherine," she said softly.

"I promise, Grandma. Absolutely."

Amelia nodded. "Call Tessa back in."

"Whose mommy loves her more than anyone in the world?" Tessa asked.

Katherine's eyes were so bright. Tessa hoped she would start to talk soon so that they could have real conversations the way she saw other mothers having on the street.

"Hm?" she said. "Whose mommy loves her?"

Katherine made her happy sound, reaching out for Tessa, and Tessa felt her heart melting as she hoisted Katherine into her arms.

The phone rang, and Tessa answered it with Katherine against her shoulder, still cooing—was she trying to imitate the phone?—and then giggling when Tessa answered.

"Tess," a voice said. It was a man's voice, so quiet she could hardly hear.

"Hello?" she said again.

"She's passed," he said, and she realized it was her grandfather.

"What?" she said, even though she knew what he meant. She felt her knees giving way.

Katherine made a sound, and Tessa caught herself and pulled up a chair.

"I'm at the hospital," he said. "Louann's on her way. Can you come?"

"When did it happen?" Tessa asked. What did he mean, Louann was on her way? He made it sound as if her grandmother had died days ago!

"Two o'clock," he said. Which meant he hadn't called her for half an hour. She, who had loved her grandmother more than anyone else had. "Can you come?" he asked. "I don't want to be alone."

"I'll be right there," she said, and she hung up.

She began to shake, and she set Katherine down on her changing blanket. She lit a cigarette, closed her eyes, and could feel herself shaking more. Then she opened her eyes and tried to picture her grandmother when she had been healthy.

Stop, she told herself. She felt broken and wounded and out of control, raw in a way she never wanted to feel again.

Think about something else, she told herself, and she looked over at Katherine.

She could dress her in the dress Amelia had bought for her before she had gone into the hospital, with the little blue shoes that were half like socks.

You'll stop shaking when you stand up from the chair, she told herself, and she stood up and said, Think about something else, to herself.

She dressed Katherine as she had planned, and they left the house. Her hands started to shake again when she tried to put the key into the ignition, but she told herself, Think about something else, and she leaned back against the seat. She thought of a cool white blankness, and she told herself that nothing mattered, that she wouldn't cry and she wouldn't mourn because it couldn't do any good. She took another deep breath, patted Katherine on the head, and set off for the hospital as if nothing bad had happened at all.

"Will you call Grandpa every day?" Louann asked.

Tessa looked across the living room at him, dressed in funeral black and looking frail and lost. It was exactly the way he had looked that day she had gone to meet him at the hospital, and she had been shocked by the transformation; in less than an hour, he had aged and taken on a posture that was vulnerable and somehow out of date, as if with Amelia's death he had been left in some other time. She had felt a sympathy for him that day that she had crushed immediately. He hadn't ever treated her grandmother right; he deserved nothing.

Now, with friends, neighbors, and relatives gathered around him, he seemed even smaller and more frail, as if he were shrinking more as each new person commiserated with him and shook his hand or gave him a hug.

"Tess? Will you?"

"Every day sounds like a lot," Tessa said. "I'll call him as often as I can." She looked across the room at Glenn, who was sitting on the couch with Katherine in his lap, proudly showing her off to one of Mack's neighbors. For a moment, Tessa felt as if it were the last glance she would ever take of the two of them—now that her grandmother was gone, she felt there was nothing holding her in Lodenton at all. But of course that was crazy. She loved her daughter more than life itself; it was just a crazy thought.

"Just at the beginning," Louann said. "I'm sure he'll get used to being on his own."

Tessa shook her head. "Are you kidding? He won't get used to anything of the kind. I'm sure he'll have found another woman within two weeks."

"Tess."

"Maybe two months, just to make it seem more proper."

Something made her look across the room to the front door. The woman who was handing her coat to Gerald was well groomed and beautiful, and Tessa's heart began to beat more quickly as the woman entered the room. She looked as if she were usually quite confident but at that moment was tentative, touching her hands together at her waist as if she were uncertain.

Mack was still talking to a neighbor, and Tessa watched as the new woman watched Mack, obviously waiting for the right moment to go up to him.

"I'll be back," she said to Louann, and she felt as if she were flying across the room.

"Excuse me," she said to the woman, and the woman looked surprised and nervous, like a wounded deer. "Your name is—?"

"Lauralee Wicks," she said.

"That's what I thought," Tessa said. Her mother had described the woman so often; she had always said she was perfectly dressed. "You weren't a friend of my grandmother's."

"I—" Lauralee Wicks said.

"I think you should get your coat and you should go. You have no right to be here." Out of the corner of her eye, she could see a couple of people looking at her, but she didn't care.

"I wanted to extend my sympathy to the family," Lauralee Wicks said.

"I just told you, you're not welcome here. Now, please leave."

"Lauralee," a voice said. It was Mack, coming over. He moved slowly—he still looked frail—but Tessa could see the color coming back into his cheeks.

"I'm so sorry," Lauralee said, leaning over—she was taller than he was—and kissing him on the cheek.

"Well, it was a blessing in one way," he said softly, words Tessa had heard at least ten times that day. "She went quickly so she didn't have to suffer as much. God saw to that."

"That's right," Tessa said, her voice shaking. "You two are the ones who made her suffer."

She walked away—she felt as if something were going to burst inside—and she scooped Katherine out of Glenn's arms. "We're going," she said to Glenn over her shoulder.

"What?" he said, but he followed her.

She was alone with Katherine outside—Glenn would be getting their coats and saying polite good-byes all around—and she leaned against the side of the house and began to cry.

12

"My mucus is running clear," Tessa's grandfather said, looking down into his Kleenex and then folding it. "That's a good sign, according to the article I just read."

Tessa looked away from him and went back to her dusting. She felt as if she were losing her mind, as if her life had become everything she had ever feared. Her grandfather called her almost every day, sometimes more than once. "What are you doing?" he would ask, generally between ten and eleven each morning. "I thought I would come over and play with Katherine. I've got a little something I think she'd like."

The "little something" would always be something big and wooden that he had made—a toy box, a rocking horse, a baby carriage—and it would amaze Tessa that with all her grandfather's talk about his illnesses, he was able to go home each day and do the work of three or four men. Plus the toys he picked up at yard sales—a plastic pool, an old swing set he was going to fix up, everything took up room, and each thing meant one more visit from him.

And most important of all, why did he think she wanted to spend every day with him?

"Did you read the clipping I sent you?" he asked.

She didn't answer. Sometimes she liked to pretend she had spoken so that he would think he was losing his hearing even more than he was.

"Did you?" he asked.

She turned to face him. "I just asked you," she said. "Which clipping? You send me so many." Which was true: clippings on how you could tell your general health from the look of your hair, how you could improve your memory by eating fish and carrots, how she could help Katherine's future *now* by getting her to eat okra or something else that Tessa found equally unlikely.

"About the mucus," he said. "You can analyze it the way archaeologists analyze bones and remains, only it's a lot more immediate. You can tell about your health at that exact moment."

He had become obsessed with his health ever since Amelia had died. Tessa knew that he had always been concerned with himself—for him, a pimple had always seemed like cancer or at least a precancerous lesion; she could remember that every time he had had a cold or the flu, he would run her grandmother ragged. But now, ever since her grandmother had died, his health had become the entire focus of his life. And oddly, he hadn't dated anyone since Amelia had died.

"Did you read it?" he asked.

"I don't know," Tessa said, listening for Katherine. She had begun forcing Katherine to take naps when she knew her grandfather was on his way, just to spite him and possibly to discourage him from coming, but so far it hadn't seemed to make any difference at all; her grandfather was perfectly happy to sit and talk whether Katherine was around or not.

"You'd remember if you had," he said, and he blew his nose again. "See?" he said, holding out the Kleenex.

"I don't want to," she said.

He laced his fingers behind his head and leaned back in the easy chair that seemed to be becoming his permanent home. "I'm learning to cure myself," he said with satisfaction. "They say that's the key, you know. Knowledge and the concentration to do it. I cured myself of diarrhea the other day, with some bananas and a little rice; it's amazing what you can do without medicine."

"Not when it's important," she said, throwing down her dust cloth. She felt as if she were going to scream at any moment.

"What do you mean, 'important'?"

"I mean if you were *really* sick. The way Grandma was. She couldn't have cured herself—if anyone would have been able to, it would have been her. Even medicine couldn't cure her. So what you're talking about is just unimportant."

His pale blue eyes showed nothing. Sometimes she could see those eyes in her own face when she looked in the mirror, and she wondered if that was what she showed to the world. She hoped she was as unreadable as he was—to be so was to hold a certain power, she felt—but when she was on the receiving end, she found it infuriating. "When is my great granddaughter's nap going to be over?" he asked. "Or is this the pattern? When I come over, she's asleep?"

"Maybe it is," she said, lighting a cigarette. What had she ever done to deserve this—daily visits from an old man. She felt cheated because the impression she had been given of what it meant to be a mother had been so wrong. Why hadn't anyone told her how alone she would feel, how she would have to spend countless hours doing mindless tasks, and with no reward? Yet, Glenn would come home and want to spend hours with the baby—staring at her, playing with her, holding her. "You're so lucky to be able to spend all day with her," he would say, and Tessa would turn away nearly in tears.

One day when she was in the grocery store, she was wheeling her cart behind two women about her age, and they kept talking about their friends. "*One* friend of mine said I should do it," one of the women said. "But Alice and Jessica—well, you know we talk on the phone all day, so they know the whole story," she had said, and the other one had laughed and agreed. Listening to the conversation had made Tessa feel cold with loneliness. It was almost an ache she could feel.

"I don't know why you would object," he said, reaching for a Saltine. "A pleasant visit each day from your grandfather. Katherine loves it when you let her stay awake for me. And it's not as if you have anyone else you would be seeing instead."

She picked up her cigarettes and walked out of the room before she could say something she would regret forever.

"I don't understand why you don't want to go," Glenn said. When Tessa didn't want to do something, she could seem as childish as Katherine. She would refuse to look at him and usually would look in the mirror instead, for some reason reminding him of Katherine's covering her eyes and thinking that would make her invisible. "I had thought you wanted to make some new friends."

"New friends would be wonderful. The same boring church people I could do without, Glenn. They're just so conventional." She sighed and looked out the car window, and Katherine began to cry in the backseat.

He knew why Tessa was feeling frustrated. All of a sudden, Lodenton was like a new town. Radicon alone had expanded their workforce by fifty percent that year, and what had once been a grim, soot-covered, blue-collar town was quickly being transformed into a chic little village. He knew that Tessa felt left out of the new atmosphere, and he knew that she felt isolated at home with Katherine and the nearly daily visits from her grandfather. But that was why he couldn't understand why she wouldn't welcome the chance to go to the "Celebrate Spring" barbecue at the Rasmussens. Granted, the Reverend and Katherine Travis, the only two people Tessa had ever shown any interest in cultivating, never showed up at any of the gatherings; and each time, Tessa was as disappointed as a child. But Glenn felt that she hadn't given anyone else a chance.

"Looks like quite a crowd," he said as they pulled on to the Rasmussens' street. It was a warm April afternoon, and the Rasmussens' backyard was the perfect spot for a barbecue, shaded by tall willow trees, with a flawless, lush lawn that was ideal for the children to play on.

Katherine stuck close to Tessa and Glenn from the start—something Glenn knew bothered Tessa, because she wanted her to be "social," even at two and a half years old. Some of the other children were playing in among the trunks of the trees, setting up a miniature town with wooden houses and toy trucks and cars, but Glenn had the feeling Katherine would want to stick with them for most of the afternoon. The way she had fit her hand into his had a long-afternoon feel to it.

"You could go over and play with the other kids," Tessa said, straightening Katherine's collar and smoothing down her hair.

Katherine frowned and said, "Stay," and looked up hopefully at Glenn.

"You can stay with us all afternoon if you want, baby," he said, hoisting her into his arms as Tessa sat down with some of the women.

"Lord, I heard a terrible story the other day," Paula said, pouring more iced tea in all the empty and half-empty glasses. "My sister over in Highland? The one with the two twin girls? She told me the worst story I ever heard. A mother who sends her son to the same nursery school as Dora does—well, one day just last week, the mother—I think her name was Harriet something or other, Harriet Borl, I think—anyway, she let her son wander off near where they live, near some old mines no one uses anymore. She couldn't find him and she couldn't find him—he was four, I think—and after a long while she began to look for him, and she heard him crying down one of the mines—he had crawled down into one, and he couldn't get out. And instead of going down into it, she called the police and the fire department and then she went back to the mine, and by the time they got there, the boy had fallen down into one of those pools that sometimes form down in those old ones. He had been in the water for I don't know how many minutes." Glenn wanted to walk away—he felt a pain starting at the pit of his stomach, and he didn't think it was good for Katherine to hear stories like that either—but something fixed him to the spot.

"Did they revive him?" someone asked.

Paula shook her head. "They couldn't. They tried but they couldn't do it. And now the mother has to ask herself how it would have been different if she had gone in after her son instead of calling the fire department."

"But probably she *couldn't* have gone in," June Wilkerson said. "Good Lord, Paula, if a mother sees her child in some sort of danger, she's going to go in and rescue him if there's any possibility that it can be humanly done. What about all of those stories of women lifting cars and even tractors because their child is caught underneath? Those aren't old wives' tales."

"I know," Paula said. "But Harriet Borl didn't do it. That's the whole point."

"I think it's shocking," Tessa said, reaching over to stroke Katherine's hair. "There's something wrong with a mother who doesn't absolutely risk her life to save her child. It's an instinct, I think. And if you don't have it, there's something very, very wrong."

There was a silence for a moment, and Glenn could feel an awkwardness settle over the group like a heavy fog.

"I don't think anyone was questioning Harriet's *intentions*, Tessa," Paula said. "It was just that she made the wrong choice. She had thought she couldn't go down into the mine, so she called the fire department. And now she has to live with her choice. I don't think anyone is saying she wanted her son to die."

Glenn could tell from Tessa's expression that she felt slighted and uncomfortable—though he was certain no one else could tell, since Tessa always concentrated on making herself unreadable. And this, Glenn felt, was one of the reasons Tessa hadn't ever been able to make any friends. Friendship was supposed to be a two-way street, and he felt that if Tessa never shared her feelings, most women would soon tire of her company.

Later in the afternoon, after everyone had eaten, Tessa and Glenn were sitting with Paula under one of the willow trees, and Katherine was playing quietly with one of the other two-year-old girls.

"She's learned another language," Tessa said to Paula. "Did I tell you?"

"Language?" Paula asked. She glanced at June Wilkerson, and Glenn felt the exchange was an indication that they had spoken often—and unflatteringly—of Tessa.

"Listen and I'll show you," Tessa said, and she called Katherine. "Hurry, Katherine," she called out. "Come here and give me a kiss and show the women how many languages you know."

Katherine came toddling over and put her hands on her mother's knees. "I love you, je t'aime, te quiero and ti amo from now until forever," she said in her faltering, two-year-old's voice.

"Isn't that something?" Tessa said. "That's four languages so far. I'm working on having her know twelve by the time she's in nursery school. I'll show you again," she said, and she called out to Katherine. "Katherine, come quick! Hurry up, hurry up! It's an emergency! I need to be kissed and sung to!" Katherine came running over and kissed her and said the litany again.

Glenn had never seen Tessa do the routine more than once, and he felt it was wrong to repeat. Their daughter wasn't a trained seal.

After the fourth time, Katherine came slowly, and when she reached Tessa, she rubbed her eyes and looked up at the sky. "What's the matter?" Tessa asked. "Where are my languages? Where are my kisses?"

June Wilkerson stood up. "I can't stand it anymore," she said under her breath. She stood up and walked over to the barbecue area where most of the men were.

Glenn watched as Tessa looked over at Paula, but Paula looked away.

Tessa hadn't wanted to admit to Glenn how lonely she felt; she didn't want to show any signs of weakness. But with her grandfather's visits becoming daily instead of almost daily, she realized she had to do something to save her sanity, even if it only meant getting out of the house so he wouldn't be able to reach her.

She began taking Katherine in her stroller down to Echo Street, which was the location of most of the new boutiques in Lodenton. The store she went into most was the one owned by the woman she had begun to hate more than three years earlier—Great Expectations, it was called, and it sold mostly gifts and a few clothes.

She didn't want to admit to herself that she was going in a few times a week because she admired the woman who ran the store. She told herself it was because she was scouting it out and investigating it as research for when she opened her own store, which she hoped to do as soon as Katherine was old enough for preschool.

The woman who owned the store was named Gail Hendrickson. Tessa knew this because she had seen envelopes addressed to her lying on the counter, and also because she usually answered the phone in the store by saying "Gail Hendrickson" in a clipped, low voice Tessa secretly wished were hers. She was tall and thin with wavy red hair and dark brown eyes, pretty but not spectacular looking, in Tessa's view. She wore quite a bit of makeup, especially around the eyes, and Tessa thought she was probably one of those women who looked terrible in the morning until they had put on lots of mascara and eyeliner.

Tessa had been into the shop four or five times when Gail Hendrickson finally spoke to her. "Your daughter must be exactly the same age as mine," she said, coming over to Katherine. "How old are you, honey?"

Katherine pulled at Tessa's skirt and hid her face behind the fabric. "She's shy," Tessa said. "She's almost two and a half," she added.

"Amanda's just turned two," Gail Hendrickson said. She was wearing something Tessa had seen her wear before when she had looked in the windows—a beautiful sweater Tessa was sure had come from New York City or Paris or someplace far away.

"Where is she?" Tessa asked. "I never see her in here."

"I've got a wonderful woman who's been taking care of her," Gail said, straightening up and going over to the cash register. "Which, thank God, has lasted this long. It's going to turn part-time in a few weeks, and I don't know what I'm going to do, but I know I've been lucky to have her as long as I have. What do you do? Do you have someone taking care of her usually?"

"No, I've decided to stay home with her until she's in school." She didn't know whether to pretend she had a career or not.

"I wish I had done that, in a way," Gail said, settling back onto the stool behind the counter. "They grow up so fast, you know? And Amanda's having some trouble—well, it depends on who you believe, but she's not exactly doing a lot of talking, and I wonder if it would have been different if I had been home with her more. And this store is driving me crazy. I don't know whether it'll end up being worth it in the end, you know?'' She sounded as if she were from New York—she sounded like New Yorkers Tessa had seen on the news, and she felt a blaze of jealousy and resentment. ''I think you might have done the right thing, staying home with her. What's her name?''

''Katherine,'' Tessa said.

Gail smiled, ''Hi, Katie,'' she said in a baby voice.

''I'd prefer it if people called her Katherine,'' Tessa said quickly, annoyed because Amanda was a better name in that respect—people wouldn't be so quick to shorten it to Mandy. ''Are you from New York?'' Tessa asked.

Gail smiled. ''I hope I don't still have an accent. How could you tell?''

''I just guessed,'' Tessa said. ''The clothes, for one thing. Now there are a couple of more stores like this in Lodenton, but for a while, you were the only one.''

Gail made a face. ''It felt like it, too. What I discovered is it's all very well to say you're ahead of your time in a small town like this, but it certainly doesn't get you very far.'' She looked Tessa up and down. ''You must have felt that way yourself. Your taste has always seemed different from most people's around here.''

Against her will, Tessa felt herself almost glowing with pride. This woman had noticed her before. She had managed to set herself apart from other people in Lodenton, even in the eyes of someone who didn't know her. ''Well, it was hard growing up here—I mean from that point of view,'' Tessa said. ''Everyone always hated me for wanting to leave.''

''Then why haven't you? If you don't mind my asking.'' Gail opened up her purse and pulled out a cigarette, and Tessa was pleased to see it was her brand.

She lit one, too. ''My husband works over at Radicon. It's—''

''You're kidding,'' Gail said. ''Mine does, too. That's why we're here. Dave Hendrickson. Do you know him?''

Tessa shook her head. ''I haven't gone to any of their functions or anything. I never wanted Glenn to even stay on after he got his degree, but he did.''

Gail smiled. ''That's funny. It was the opposite with us. Dave was fed up with New York, and we thought it would be so great to come to a place like this.'' She took a long drag and then let it out slowly. ''I haven't made many friends, though,'' she said. ''I think this is probably the longest conversation I've had with someone besides the baby-sitter and Dave for maybe six months.''

Tessa felt as if she had found a soulmate. She had found a friend, and as she had suspected would be necessary, it was someone more sophisticated, someone not from Lodenton. A woman from New York City who thought her taste was different and interesting and sophisticated, and who had said ''come by anytime.''

Tessa didn't want to make a pest of herself, so she waited two days to go back. It was a Wednesday, a sunny October day that was perfect for the little kilt she had bought on Echo Street for Katherine, and she was just leaving the house when the phone rang.

Tessa knew it was her grandfather—who else would it be?

''Tessa,'' he said when she had answered. ''I feel a little bit funny.''

''What's the matter?'' she asked, looking at her watch.

''My throat. It's scratchy. I took the herb lozenges—the ones from Healthy Kitchens that I like—but they didn't help.''

''Mack, I have to go,'' she said. ''I'm late for an appointment.''

''Do you think if I gargled? My tongue has white spots.''

''Listen to me. Katherine is extremely ill, and we're rushing to the doctor right this minute.''

''Can I help? What's the matter?'' he asked.

''She has blinding headaches. He wants to see her immediately. Now, I'll talk to you later,'' she said, and she hung up.

In the car, Katherine was pulling at her lip and looking worried, holding onto the bear they always kept in the car for her and staring straight ahead. Tessa didn't think she would have understood what she might have overheard in the phone call—certainly she wouldn't have known what the word ''blinding'' meant.

''Honey, we're going to meet a wonderful friend today,'' Tessa said. ''She has a daughter who's almost your age, and we're going to get to know them both. Doesn't that sound like fun?''

Katherine looked at her with a squint.

''Don't squint, honey.'' She was sure Katherine's squinting came just when she was in a bad mood. Glenn had said maybe she was nearsighted, but Tessa was sure he was wrong. She hated the way young children looked in glasses—they always looked so sad, she felt, as if they would always be outcasts—and she thought that was a tough burden for a child. You had to make them look as good as they could if they were going to get along well with other kids.

"Honey? Doesn't that sound like fun?"

Katherine didn't say anything. But Tessa was sure Katherine would have a wonderful afternoon—far better than if they had stayed home and played with her great-grandfather.

The girls got along well, and Tessa was pleased. But what made her feel she would remember the day forever was that Gail told her she needed a manager for the store, and she was looking for someone who would ultimately be interested in buying into it.

Tessa couldn't wait to bring up the idea to Glenn.

Glenn paced across the living room for what felt like the five hundredth time and looked at his watch. Three-thirty. Where *were* they?

He didn't understand what was going on or what had happened—if there were something wrong with Katherine, something that hadn't just happened that day, as Mack had said, surely Tessa would have told him about it. Surely she would have discussed it with him. And certainly he would have noticed it in Katherine. He had always felt that he was a bit more observant than Tessa was in that area; in any case, if Katherine were having blinding headaches, wouldn't she have told him, and wouldn't he have noticed even if she hadn't? Plus, in his experience, Katherine, as was true with most children he had known, was anything but reticent about pain or discomfort. When she was uncomfortable, she cried. When she had burned her hand six months ago, she had screamed as if she were dying.

Which made him wonder exactly what was going on. He had called the pediatrician and been told that Tessa had had no appointment that day. He couldn't believe that Tessa would take Katherine to a specialist without telling him. And if she hadn't taken Katherine to the doctor, why had she told her grandfather that was where they were headed? Glenn would never forget the breathless fear in Mack's voice from this morning. He had called Glenn's office to find out more about what might be wrong with Katherine. Glenn knew how Tessa was with him, Mack had said. She wasn't exactly a woman of a thousand words, he had added quietly. And he just had to know: was Katherine going to be all right?

Glenn heard a car pull up outside, and he went to the door.

Tessa was getting out of the car, then helping Katherine out of her car seat and lifting her out onto the ground.

He felt almost helplessly grateful to see that she was well. He had to tell himself that there was a 99 percent chance that everything was fine, because there was that much of a probability that it was some sort of mix-up or lie.

"Daddy!" Katherine cried as he opened the door, and she came toddling up to him, holding up her arms as high as she could.

"Hello, baby," he said, lifting her up. He felt close to tears as he felt her soft skin against his cheek and smelled her hair.

Tessa had gone back to the car and had brought out two grocery bags, one of which she was carrying as she came up the walk. "I could use some help, Glenn," she said, and then she frowned. "What are you doing home?"

"Did you go to the doctor? With K-a-t-h?" he spelled, because he didn't want to alarm Katherine. He was never certain how much she understood—but in all the books he had read on child development, they always said that children understood much more than adults thought they did.

Tessa blinked. "I had lunch with a friend. That woman Gail that I told you about? Her daughter and Katherine hit it off unbelievably well."

"Why did you tell your grandfather you were taking her to the doctor?" he asked. It was difficult to control his voice, but he was managing.

Tessa sighed. "Would you help me with these bags, and then I can tell you?"

He tried to concentrate on what was good as he set Katherine down and went and got the other grocery bag. Katherine was all right. Tessa hadn't taken her to the doctor. That was what was important, above all else.

"You know how crazy my grandfather has been making me," she said in the kitchen. He glanced into the living room, where Katherine was carefully arranging some of her stuffed animals into a circle. "He called right when we were leaving for the lunch, and there was no way I was going to be able to get rid of him unless I said we had an appointment. He's been coming here almost every day and calling me at least twice every day. This isn't my idea of a great existence."

He didn't know what to say. He couldn't begin to understand why she couldn't have just been clear and direct with him. He firmly believed that when you were clear and direct, you could accomplish anything. But then, if she hadn't felt comfortable doing that, why had she hurt him by worrying him like that? And involving Katherine, which he felt was frightening, although he couldn't at that moment put his finger on the reason.

"I don't know why you look so staggered by it," Tessa said. "Why are you so upset? You look as if somebody just died."

"Your grandfather thought somebody might!" he yelled. He hadn't meant to yell—he had never yelled at Tessa in all the years of their marriage, because he didn't believe there was a purpose to it. But this time, he hadn't been able to help himself.

He turned around, and Katherine was in the doorway. "It's okay, honey. Play with your animals, okay?"

She held up her arms to be held, and he picked her up and carried her back to the living room. Feeling her weight in his arms, he felt sick to think of the story Tessa had told. He couldn't explain why—and this went against everything he believed about causation and reality—but he felt that it was unlucky, even dangerous, to tell a lie about the health of someone you loved. He didn't believe in superstition, and he tried not to believe in luck, but no amount of scientific evidence could convince him that there weren't certain things that were simply unexplainable. And he felt that what Tessa had done, aside from worrying him and her grandfather half to death, had somehow created a halo of risk around Katherine.

When he went back to the kitchen, he took the pan that Tessa was holding and set it down on the stove, and he faced her as squarely and calmly as he could. "I want you to promise me," he said slowly, because he wanted to keep his temper, "I want you to promise me that you'll never, ever involve Katherine in any kind of lie again."

She gave him a blank, unreadable look, and then she smiled. "You really are upset about this, aren't you." She shook her head. "It just didn't seem like that big a deal at the time. But if it was, then fine. I'll never do it again." She reached up and put her arms around him and brushed her lips against his. "I really am sorry," she said.

This time, when she looked into his eyes, she was what he thought of as the original Tessa, the one he had fallen in love with.

13

Glenn wasn't looking forward to the evening. He had had a hard day at work, and what he wanted to do was stay home and play with Katherine. She was growing up so fast; each day she learned new words, and he couldn't put out of his mind the fact that he had missed the first utterance of almost each of her new words. He knew his feelings were sentimental and obvious truths: that one's children grew up so fast, that they were young only once, that each day missed was a day that could never be recaptured—but he felt the weight of those truths, corny as they might have sounded to other people, like a heavy, unbearably sad weight on his spirit. Yes, certainly it was wonderful that Katherine seemed unusually verbal, and yes, it was wonderful that Tessa was "teaching" her other languages—although so far, all the phrases meant only one thing: I love you. All of these things were pleasing to him and made him feel a pride beyond anything he had ever felt. But he wanted to participate, too; his free time seemed so precious.

He had bought Katherine a new stuffed animal—Tessa had been angry because she wanted Katherine to have just educational games, but he had read that this could be counterproductive. The most important thing at this stage was to let them have fun, and he had been looking forward to the one night all week when he would get home early enough to really play with her.

But Tessa had been insistent. Gail wasn't much of a hostess, but she had invited the three of them, and didn't Glenn want to get to know Dave better, since they both worked at Radicon?

The real purpose of the evening, he knew, was to talk about Gail's store. Tessa had brought up the idea the day he had rushed home from work worried that Katherine had been taken to the doctor. She had cooked a wonderful meal, and she had pre-

146

sented the idea to him like an excited child. It would be so much fun, and it would mean so much to her! It was one of the few jobs she could have where she could bring Katherine to work every day, because she and Gail had already agreed on that; they both needed child care, and this was a solution they would both be willing to try. And Gail was the very person she had been waiting years to meet in Lodenton; Gail was already her best friend, she had told him excitedly.

"Two kids that age in a tiny little gift shop? It sounds like a joke," he had said. "Or a comedy movie."

"She has an entire back room no one even sees," Tessa had said, almost pleading. "She's already set up a playpen and all kinds of cute little games, and it's carpeted almost across the entire room. It would be wonderful. And it would get me out of the house, Glenn. It's something I really need. You go out to work every day, but I'm home, and then Mack comes over, and I'm beginning to go a little crazy."

And that was what had touched him, what had opened the door a bit in his mind. The Tessa he loved was the Tessa who was honest and vulnerable and told him how she really felt instead of pretending she was someone else. The Tessa he loved was the one who long ago had expressed, tentatively at first, and then completely honestly, that she had a terrible fear she would end up taking on her mother's personality as she grew older. "Do they know anything about that in terms of science?" she had asked him. "I mean, do you think you can inherit something like that?"

He had answered her carefully and honestly. "That's a difficult question to answer because sometimes what people think of as inherited is really learned: the child is in the presence of one or more parents and takes on his or her qualities because of learning, and it has nothing to do with genetics." She had begun to look confused and desperate, and he had decided he had to tell her simply and quickly. "But in your case, I wouldn't worry that much, Tessa. In terms of inheriting, it's mostly schizophrenia that they've targeted. And you seem to me to be so *un*depressed."

But the other night, she had brought it up tremulously. "I know you think that what happened to my mother can never happen to me," she had said. "And it's true, I think. I'm basically a happy person. But still, ever since Katherine, I've thought about it more because I've been home more. I don't want to risk it, Glenn. Being home was a terrible problem for her."

He had felt she was wrong, and he had also felt saddened, because for him, he couldn't think of anything more fun than to be home with Katherine all day. For him, the pleasure of coming home and looking into those eyes and seeing her whole face light up was limitless; he saw that what he had always hoped for was true—that the greatest pleasures in life could come from the smallest, most routine moments: for him, coming home and greeting his family was pure joy.

But he had to admit two things to himself: he hadn't actually been home all day every day for more than a few days and the occasional vacation, so he felt it was unfair to claim he would have loved it week in and week out, even though he was sure it would be true; and it didn't really matter whether Tessa's fear was realistic. What mattered was that she had it. As far as he was concerned, the mind was so powerful that it could create almost any physical manifestations if the impulse were strong enough, and he was worried now that Tessa was worried. If she was as unhappy at home as she said, naturally he would do anything to make her happier.

Tessa always wanted to appear strong to others—he was the only person in the world in whom she confided, and he was glad to hear there was a good chance she would finally have a friend, but he was convinced that because she was so consistently unwilling ever to reveal her true feelings—except to him—she was indeed likely to create the dire circumstances she had projected. He would never forget last Christmas, when his mother had visited from Utah. Tessa had insisted it was fine with her. "She's your mother, and she has a right to visit and a right to see Katherine," she had said. But from the day before his mother had arrived until the day after she had left, Tessa—who until then had never been sick even for a day since he had known her—had been bedridden with one of the worst cases of flu he had ever seen.

And he knew how important it was for her to "find" herself. He was sorry that, for her, raising Katherine wasn't fulfilling enough by itself, but he could only respect her wishes and then help her address them. In his view, it was one of the primary obligations in any good marriage.

And so he had decided that after he met Gail and talked a bit about the store, he would tell Tessa that he'd be happy to contribute her share so that she could form a partnership with Gail, as long as all of their understandings were reflected properly in writing.

"Are you really going to wear that shirt?" Tessa asked him as they were getting ready to leave the house.

He looked down at his sleeves—he never remembered what he was wearing until he had actually looked. "I was. Why? Is it dirty?"

"No," Tessa said, giving her hair a last comb through in the mirror. "It's just that I don't think it's particularly flattering. It makes you look as if you never leave your lab." She went to the closet and pulled a red L.L. Bean shirt off a hanger. "This is a thousand times nicer," she said.

He changed without a word. It depressed him when she criticized his clothes, not because he cared about his taste but because it saddened him that she could ever be embarrassed by the way he looked. The first time it had happened, he had asked himself if there were anything Tessa could ever wear that would make him wish he wasn't going to be seen with her. And the answer had been no. But he supposed maybe that that was one of the differences between men and women; he just didn't know.

Tessa began working for Gail exactly three weeks after they had first met, and Gail seemed genuinely happy to have her there. On the first day, Gail was deciding how many placemats to take on consignment from a woman who lived in Acton, and the first thing Gail had said was, "Well, Ms. Manager, what do you think?"

For Tessa, they were like words in a dream. No one but Glenn and Louann had ever asked her opinion about anything. And this was a woman from New York, someone sophisticated, someone who had chosen her as a manager and potential partner because of her good taste and her talent.

Tessa was surprised about how many people who came into the store were what she considered the "new breed" of Lodenton, women who were probably married to the new chemists and engineers at Radicon, and, of course, faculty members and even some students from Acton. These were people who were going to ask *her* opinion about what they should buy—*her* opinion even though they were generally better educated than she was.

But as the weeks passed, Tessa found that she was spending hours on end alone in the store, without Gail and without customers. It was an off period, Gail had told her; things would pick up. And on the days that Mrs. Everson, her baby-sitter, was off, couldn't Tessa watch Amanda as long as she was going to be in the store anyway, especially if she had Katherine with her? Everyone *knew* that they loved to play with each other.

Liberated by the convenience of having someone to watch the store all day every day that it was open, Gail had shed all her responsibility and interest overnight; it might have been Tessa at any point in her life, latching on with great passion to a project and dropping it without a word two weeks later. But for Tessa to be on the receiving end of this swift kind of change was intolerable. Every day, she woke up angry, and as each day wore on, she grew angrier still.

"Why don't you talk to her?" Glenn said one morning while he was making breakfast for Katherine. He had begun waking up at six so he would have more time to relax and play with her in the mornings, which was fine with Tessa. She felt so tightly wound up with anger that she could barely decide what to wear, much less get breakfast for everyone.

"I have," Tessa said. "Every time I ask her whether it's really necessary for her to leave, she either says yes, just like that, or she reminds me that I'm being paid to be the manager. Which I am. I just thought it was going to be more equal."

"But equal would mean the full partnership," Glenn said.

"That's right. And I'm not even sure I would want it at this point, the way I feel about her."

"You have to talk more to her," Glenn said. "Tell her exactly what you've told me. Communication can solve anything, Tess. If you let her know how you feel, she's going to have to respond—maybe not in the way you'd like, but she'll have to respond."

Tessa knew that Glenn was right—not that communication could solve anything, but that she should talk to Gail about the problem; maybe Gail didn't even know how angry she was. And she decided that no matter what kind of mood Gail was in that morning, she would broach the subject and get the discussion over with.

But Gail broached it first, as soon as she had walked in the door and kissed Katherine hello. "Listen," she said, pouring herself a cup of tea. "I really have to apologize to you."

Tessa swallowed and didn't say anything. She didn't want to seem vulnerable. "Why?" she finally asked.

"Oh, come on. I know I've been horrible. I told you I wanted you to come in with me on this, one way or another, and then I completely abandoned you." She had an odd, excited look in her eyes. "But it was for a reason," she said, and she paused. "I've met someone."

At the back of her mind, Tessa knew what Gail meant: she had met a man. But at first, she was unable to process the words—she found it shocking and infuriating—and she said, "What do you mean?"

"A man," Gail said, shaking a cigarette out of a pack. "The most wonderful, amazing man I've ever met in my life."

Tessa felt as if she couldn't breathe. "And that's where you've been all this time? Not out at meetings? Do you take Amanda with you when you meet him and you haven't left her here?"

"Of course not. Are you crazy? No, thank God Mrs. Everson is still around three days a week. And you a few times. Which I really appreciated."

Tessa was so angry she could hardly speak. She had so many questions, yet she felt that each one she asked made her sound stupid. Who was the man? How had Gail met him? Where did they meet when they got together?

"So anyway," Gail said, "I'm sorry. I can't say I've gotten him out of my system, because I haven't, at all, but I'm ready to be back at the store again. He has to get to work on a project so he can't see me as much as he has, and . . ." She shrugged. "It's just time."

"What sort of project?" Tessa asked, half against her will. Part of her wanted to end the discussion and never ask a single question about this man.

"He's a novelist," Gail said, with what Tessa felt was a note of triumph. "He just inherited his grandmother's house over in Acton, and he came down here to finish the book he's working on. And he says I've been so much of a distraction that he's thinking of moving back to New York."

New York. Another New Yorker. "Do you think he will?"

Gail grinned. "Not for a long, long time."

Tessa felt cold and jealous. "I hadn't realized you had serious problems with Dave," she said. "I mean, I would never consider having an affair right now. Particularly with Katherine at this age."

Gail smiled. "That's you," she said with more triumph. "And the problems aren't serious. There's nothing dramatic or awful going on. I think that's a common misconception people have, that a woman has an affair because her husband is terrible or beats her or screams at her all the time." She gave a little shiver.

"I'm with Walter because I can talk to him for hours and hours and make love to him for hours and hours and still want more."

Tessa didn't want to hear it. She had felt that she was on the same track as Gail, that she and Gail had singled themselves out as better and more complex than the other women in Lodenton; they had hopes and dreams that surpassed everyone else's. Yet now, Gail made her feel as if life were passing her by, as if Gail had identified a source of unhappiness in her life and was doing something about it, trying something new. Tessa had become the manager of a boutique, but Gail had immediately passed her by and labeled it as dull.

The phone rang and Gail answered it in her usual clipped voice. "Gail Hendrickson." She wasn't very pretty—that was what Tessa had to keep telling herself. In looks, there was just no competition. And now, her features looked twisted and unattractive. "Hold on," she said, and she thrust the receiver at Tessa. "I think it's for you. I can't understand him."

Tessa sighed and took the phone. It had to be her grandfather, to whom she should have never given the boutique's number. "Hello," she said wearily.

"Help me," he said. "They're coming, but I don't want to go alone."

"Mack? What's the matter?"

"I called the ambulance, and they're coming," he said.

Three weeks had passed since Mack had been rushed to the hospital, and Tessa felt a sharp resentment as she pulled into his driveway. She had spent the past fifteen minutes explaining to Louann all the daily chores that had to be taken care of, but she didn't feel that she had conveyed at all how tedious it was. "Oh, one more thing," she said over Katherine's crying from the backseat. "Every day, I have to hear all the details about what he ate the day before. I guess this is a substitute for all the vitamin details I got before. But, honestly, it's going to drive me crazy."

"Well, maybe some of the pressure will disappear if we can convince him to hire someone," Louann said.

Tessa got out of the car and pulled Katherine from the backseat. The smell of fall was sharp in the air, and she tried to ignore the look of the property. The lawn, always her grandfather's pride and joy, was brown and covered with newly fallen leaves, and she knew he would nag her relentlessly about getting someone to trim the shrubs along the walkway until it got done.

And, of course, it was easy for Louann to be sympathetic to him; coming up once a week from New York was easy. For a moment, walking up the path, Tessa remembered an idyllic sunny afternoon, before Louann had ever touched the piano, when her grandfather had taken her for a ride in a wagon behind the tractor—"Just you," he had said, "because you're my special girl, and you always will be." He had had eyes that made you feel you had been scooped up into his arms and that you'd be held there forever, but then one day he had just stopped telling her she was special, and the look in his eyes had changed forever.

From Tessa's arms, Katherine was knocking loudly on the door and ringing the bell. "Poppa," she was calling, her tears long gone.

"He doesn't hear us," Louann said.

"We should just go in," Tessa said. "I always do."

Louann knocked one more time and yelled out "Poppa!" and then turned the knob.

The smell was always the same inside—even after their grandmother had died, it smelled of something wonderful that had been cooked the night before, onions and something Tessa could never identify.

"Poppa?" Louann called.

He was in the living room in an easy chair, with the television on full blast.

They went over and kissed him, and Tessa felt a chill. He smelled old. He reached out for Katherine, and Tessa let him kiss her, but she almost hesitated; it was as if his oldness could somehow be catching. It seemed wrong that such old skin should touch such new.

"So," he said when they sat down. "It's a predicament, isn't it. I have a sourness in my stomach they didn't warn me about—I don't know if it comes from the stroke or not."

"I doubt it," Tessa said.

"I need to have bland food," he said, touching his abdomen. "That's what Dr. Katz told me last night."

"You called him last night?" Tessa asked.

"It wasn't late," he said. "Eleven-thirty. I couldn't sleep anyway."

"But maybe *he* was," Tessa said. "You can't call him every night."

"Then he has to give me some answers," he said, holding

his stomach and then his arm, which looked withered and ancient.

"Have they told you anything new?" Louann asked, nearly shouting.

He sighed and shook his head. "Maybe my arm and leg will get better, and maybe they won't. Maybe I'll have another heart attack and maybe I'll have another stroke, and maybe I won't. Maybe I'll live to be a hundred, and maybe I won't. That's what they know. They know what I know." He leaned forward and held up a magazine with an ad in it. "I subscribed last night to this magazine. *Prevention*, they call it. All about health. Maybe I'll learn more than the doctors." He made a face, and Tessa thought he was going senile, but then she realized he was looking at Katherine. "She looks just like you," he said, and he turned to Louann. "How about your classes? When am I going to see you at Carnegie Hall on the television?"

Louann blushed and smiled. "We'll see," she said.

"What about your finances?"

"I'm fine," Louann said. "Really."

"You'd better not be shading the truth any. You know I have more to give you if you need it."

Louann looked down at her hands. "I'm fine," she said. "But what we should talk about is how you're going to get along."

He looked confused. "Get along?"

"On your own. We should hire someone to stay with you, just so you're not alone. Just until you get better."

He shook his head with more strength than Tessa had thought was in him. "Nah," he said. "Have a stranger live with me? Never. I remember once there was a fellow named Angelmeyer. Ardis Angelmeyer, his name was, and everyone used to make fun of him when he first came to school because of his name. Of course, that's a separate story. Back then, it wasn't fashionable the way it is today to have an unusual name, something no one's ever heard before. But this Ardis, when his father was in an accident and the department of something or other—back then, there weren't as many of them departments, things like welfare that there are now, but seeing as his father was a veteran, that's right . . . it was the VA, they went and sent him some lady to take care of him. To take care of the whole family, really—"

Tessa felt the fuzziness start in her head, the feeling she always had when her grandfather started in on his long stories.

She had thought that after he got sick, at least it might quiet him down a bit, but his zeal for detail was as strong as ever. And listening to him go on and on with his endless tales always made her feel as if she were a hundred years old and that her head was about to burst—not out of pain, but out of confusion and boredom and a nearly insane restlessness.

"Anyway," her grandfather was saying, "they had this lady living there and no one liked her much, the kids said she was mean and old Ardis senior said she was giving him some kind of an evil eye, I forget what he called it—he didn't use the Italian phrase. He was Italian on his mother's side, his mother's name was—what was it? Martuccio, I think. Or, no—Martucci. But that word, I know his mother taught him, but I remember he didn't know the word. What is that? *Mal* something."

"*Malocchio*," Louann said, looking perfectly interested and alert.

Tessa couldn't stand it.

"That's right, *malocchio*. Only he used some other name for it. But anyway, he said she was giving him some kind of an evil eye all the time, and none of them trusted her, only they couldn't do anything about it, because it was some kind of requirement that he had someone watching over him. Maybe it was the bank he worked for that hired her. That's right, it was the bank—"

Tessa thought she was going to scream. She stood up and started to walk around the living room, and she could hear by her grandfather's voice that he was looking at her, that as she walked, his head was turning, and he was probably wondering why she wasn't sitting there in rapt attention the way Louann was. Even Katherine was playing quietly on the floor, perfectly content with a pinecone someone had brought in from outside.

"Will you watch her?" Tessa asked Louann, then disappeared without waiting for an answer. Tessa walked into her grandfather's den to see if there was anything new. There had been years she had never been able to come to the house without leaving with something she had wanted. She would tell him or her grandmother that she liked something—it had started when she was a child, and she had admired a little china dog they had—and they had given it to her. It had seemed miraculous at the time, being able to admire something and having it handed over to you, just like that.

But now she had something else in mind. He wasn't at all well, it was clear. You didn't have to be a doctor to know that he'd never be well again. The end of someone's life was something you could think about in many ways, but there was one thing that was clear: they wouldn't be using their possessions anymore. There were all these objects—furniture, clothing, jewelry, lawn mowers and tools and keepsakes—that would have no owner anymore unless the owner gave them away.

She knew what was in his will, and it was something she tried not to think of too often, because she knew she could become obsessed with it and because she knew that the will could change. After her grandmother died, he had changed it so that she and Louann would get everything. Everything! At first, she hadn't been able to believe it. "Everything" meant his house, which was one of the nicest houses in Lodenton, plus a considerable amount of cash. He had never believed in the stock market, so he had kept all his money in slow-growing passbook savings accounts, but even so—he had been wise in terms of spending, and he was the richest member of the family.

There was so much. What if he died tomorrow?

". . . a cheese sandwich for lunch," he was saying to Louann as Tessa drifted back into the living room. "And let's see. For dinner last night, I had one of those turkey TV dinners Tessa bought me. It wasn't bad. I can remember Amelia would never let them in the house, but it wasn't bad at all. The stuffing was better than Amelia's," he said with a laugh. "But mostly I have soup for lunch, soup and a cheese sandwich, rye bread if I can get it at Kaiser's, and for breakfast toast, tea naturally . . ."

Tessa blew a kiss at Katherine, who smiled and came toddling over. Tessa hoisted her into her arms and sat down on a recliner across from her grandfather.

"There," she said. "Now sit up and look at your great grandpa."

Her grandfather's eyes lit up, and for a moment Tessa had a pang of guilt because of what she had been thinking. But her thoughts weren't going to make him die any sooner. There was nothing to feel guilty about.

14

In Lodenton, winter always set in overnight, it seemed. One moment it was Indian summer, and the next, it was gray and bleak and bitter cold. The leaves turned brown and fell off the trees, and then it was winter, and the old brick buildings, blackened by smoke from the mill, made the streets look narrow and dark even in the winter sun.

Louann couldn't bear going to her grandfather's house on days like this. She dreaded seeing how he would have changed in the past weeks. Every time she had seen him lately, he looked older and thinner and weaker, and it broke her heart.

Louann pulled into the driveway and left room for Tessa's car, in case she decided to come. She probably wouldn't—it was hard for her to get away from the store on a Saturday, and Louann also knew that it wasn't easy for Tessa to face seeing their grandfather. Louann knew why Tessa felt so much hostility toward him, both because of his unfaithfulness to their grandmother and because he had always seemed to favor Louann. She could understand why Tessa felt as she did, but he was still their grandfather, and he always would be.

She could remember when she was little, so long ago, looking into his blue eyes and thinking how much she loved him and how he knew so many different things, how he could take a piece of wood and put it in the saw and he'd tell her to close her eyes, and when she opened them, the wood would be in the shape of a bunny, or when she got older and he showed her how he made the shapes, and then when she was older still, he let her use the saw and taught her how to cut and sand and use a drawknife and plane and a file and each kind of sandpaper.

Sometimes, when she and Tessa were at his house, she would

see a hard look in Tessa's eyes, a distance and hostility, and she wondered whether he could feel it as well.

His house looked washed out and forgotten, a bleak shell of peeling white clapboard against a gray sky, and Louann knew he would want her to rake the last of the late-fall leaves before she left. From what she had heard, the girl they had hired to live there—Ingrid Rakolsky was her name—didn't do much but watch television.

Louann braced herself so that she wouldn't look shocked or disappointed when she saw him. She knocked on the door and then let herself in, and her heart sank when she walked into the living room and she saw him. He was sitting in the recliner with his mouth open and his hair uncombed, looking weak and unaware of where he was.

There was a quiz show on—it was too loud, and the contestants were screaming. Ingrid glanced up at her and waved dully, then went back to watching. Louann's grandfather was staring at the screen—it was clear he hadn't heard her come in—but she had the feeling he wasn't watching, that he wouldn't have been able to tell her whether it was a quiz show or the news or a sitcom.

"Grandpa?"

He looked surprised as he looked around, and she could tell she had made a mistake. She should have made enough noise as she was coming in so that he would have heard her. In his eyes she could see he was upset that he hadn't known she was there.

She kissed him on the cheek, and he held her there for a second, her cheek against his, and then she drew back. "How's my girl?" he said. His voice was weak and slurry.

She smiled. "Fine, fine." She looked at Ingrid, thinking Ingrid might have something to say, but she was concentrating on the show.

"Do you want to go into the kitchen so we can talk?" Louann yelled.

He nodded, and she held out her arm. He felt lighter than he had last week, and he was more stooped over. Each step she took was small, but none seemed small enough. She helped him down onto one of the kitchen chairs, and he motioned for her to open the shades, which she did.

"She likes it dark," he said. "I never get to see the sun anymore."

"I'll tell her to keep the shades open," Louann said.

He waved a thin, bony hand. There were purple, almost black splotches on his skin. "Don't," he said. "I don't want to antagonize her."

"What's the matter? What's going on?"

He shook his head and gazed out the window, shading his eyes from the sun.

"Grandpa?"

"I don't want to talk about it," he said. His voice was hoarse, and he began to cough. It was the old-person's cough she had heard for so many years in Lodenton Park, old people in wheelchairs with their caretakers, a hacking, labored cough, and now it was coming from her grandfather.

"I want to know what you're talking about," she said.

She heard footsteps, and she looked up. Ingrid had come into the kitchen. "Is everything okay?" Ingrid asked. She was nineteen or twenty, but already she looked more than thirty. She had dirty blond hair and browning teeth, and she must have needed glasses because she always seemed to be squinting.

"He's fine," Louann said.

Ingrid nodded. "Good. I'm worried about that cough. I've been giving him that Vick's Forty-Four but it isn't doing squat for him."

"I thought he had some prescription medicine."

Ingrid shook her head. "The doctor said to forget it. It was making your granddad sick to his stomach."

"But did the doctor say the Vick's was all right?"

Ingrid got a stubborn look in her eyes. "They don't know everything there is to know."

"Wait a minute. What are you saying? That he said *not* to give him anything?"

"Louann," her grandfather said. "Relax. I take it if it doesn't bother me. It can't hurt."

Ingrid walked out and swung the kitchen door shut.

Louann looked at her grandfather. "Tell me what's going on," she said.

His eyes were watery and red, and she wished she knew whether that was from crying or the eye condition he had. He dabbed at them with a handkerchief that looked filthy, and Louann took it away from him and stood up. "I'll be right back," she said.

"Where are you going?"

"She's getting paid to keep you in clean clothes and a clean house, and this handkerchief is filthy."

"Louann, sit down."

"All right, tell me what's going on." She put on the water to make them both tea, and then she sat.

"It's nothing I can put my finger on," he said. "She's just . . . I don't want you upsetting her."

"Then you're afraid of her?"

"She's not a bad person," he said. "I'm not afraid of her. I'm not. But she's not a happy person. She's not happy to be here, and I can't say I blame her. I just don't want you doing anything to upset her."

Louann heard a car in the driveway, and she looked out the window. Tessa was getting out, and the other door flew open and Katherine jumped out. Louann was furious; had Tessa not attached the belts to her carrier again, or was it just that Katherine knew how to undo them?

"Grandpa!" Katherine screamed when the door opened. She went rushing into her great-grandfather's arms, and then flung herself into Louann's. "Lou," she said, pressing her cheek against Louann's. Louann was always amazed at how tightly Katherine could hug her. Who would have thought there could be so much strength in those tiny arms?

"Hey, sweetie," Louann said.

"Actually, you should both probably keep your distance," Tessa said. "She's getting over a horrible stomach virus and she's on all kinds of medicine. I'm amazed she even ran in here."

"Then you should have held her back," Louann said. "I don't care about myself, but Grandpa shouldn't have been exposed, Tessa."

"Ah," he said, waving a hand. "I don't care. Maybe I'll be lucky and it'll kill me."

"I didn't know she was going to come racing in here," Tessa said. "Whew, it's cold out there. Is it freezing in New York?"

"It's beautiful right now," Louann said. "I mean, it's cold, but everything looks cleaner. It's always a mess when you start getting snow and it turns black. Then it's horrible."

"Lou, play with the farm?" Katherine said, taking her by the hand and trying to pull her up from the chair. "You be the cow?"

Louann laughed. It was a game she had played with Katherine from the time Katherine was a baby and too young to understand much of what was going on, but they had both always loved it. Her grandfather had originally made the farm set for her when she was six—wooden animals and fences and barns—and these days, Katherine seemed to be obsessed with it. "I'll help you set it up," Louann said. "We can put it on the living room floor, okay?"

Katherine clapped and raced into the living room, and Louann got the set out of the cupboard her grandfather had made and started laying out the pieces. She could remember the day he had made most of the pieces in the set, when he had led her into the workshop and told her he was going to show her some magic. "We're going to start with wood, and we're going to end up with animals, and they can be whatever animals you want, no matter whether they belong on a real farm or not." She could remember she had wanted to stick to the rules. He had suggested making a giraffe and she had been furious—real farms didn't have giraffes!—and because of that, the set was pretty true to a real farm, with cows and horses and pigs and sheep and chickens. Back then he could do anything, one of the strongest men in the world, she'd thought. And she could remember how he had laughed and laughed when she had asked him if the neighbors would know the horses were just toys, or would they ask for rides? "You're a silly little girl, do you know that?" he had said, scooping her up into his arms.

"Moo," Katherine said, moving one of the cows around on the rug. "Somebody gots to come and milk me."

Louann heard Tessa in the den, and she realized their grandfather was sitting by himself in the kitchen. "Honey, I'm going to go back into the kitchen for a while and talk to Grandpa, okay?"

Katherine threw down the cow. "No one ever plays with me except in school."

"I'll play with you later. I promise."

Katherine's eyes started filling with tears. "You won't. Mommy says."

Louann knelt down to the floor again. "What do you mean, Mommy says? What did your Mommy say?"

Katherine leaned her head against Louann's shoulder and put her arms around her, and once again, Louann couldn't get over how tightly Katherine could hold on to her. "She said she's the only one that loves me." She looked up into Louann's face, and her eyes were swollen and brimming with tears. "My teacher at school, I wanted to give her a doll because it was her birthday, and Mommy said no I couldn't, because the teacher didn't love me."

"And that's when she told you she's the only one who loves you? You know that's not true, honey, because I love you and your daddy loves you and Grandpa loves you and Grandpa Gerald loves you, and probably everyone who meets you does, when they get to know you. Sometimes even the second they see you."

Katherine laid her head against Louann's shoulder again, and then she sighed and picked up the cow and made it trot along on the rug. "Moo," she said, and she picked up the woman farmer with her other hand. "My husband brang the pail so here it is," she piped in a high, thin voice.

Louann kissed the top of her head. "I'll play with you for a while more, okay?"

Louann looked at her watch. She would have to leave soon if she was going to have time to visit with her father, and get back to New York in time. "Are you sleeping all right these days, Grandpa?"

He sighed. "I can't sleep without the sleeping pills, but I think it's the pills that are making me feel funny some of the time."

"I thought the doctor said you shouldn't take them," Louann said.

"I can't lie in bed until four in the morning thinking," he said. "I don't care what the doctor says."

Tessa stood up. "I need to look for something in the garage. Louann, keep an ear out for Katherine?"

"Sure," Louann said, "she's playing with the farm set on the living room rug."

"So I guess I'm all set for dinner," he said. "I've got the TV dinners that Ingrid bought, and the soda." He touched his arm, as if he were in pain. His hand shook as he reached for a cracker, and he moved slowly and uncertainly as he brought the cracker nearer to his mouth. It made Louann ache to watch him. How had he gotten so old so fast? "Tessa's got her eye on something in the garage," he said. "It's the second time she's been in there today, I think."

"I don't think so," Louann said.

He rubbed his forehead, and he looked confused and in pain. "Maybe not today, but sometime. She's looking all through this house, I can tell. Wanting to see what'll be hers pretty soon."

"Grandpa."

He shook his head. "I don't care. It's bred into her, anyway. You should have seen her as a girl. When she'd go over to the neighbors' house—you remember the Malenkys?—and she'd see all the dolls their little Susan had." He frowned. "Got in trouble a couple of times, too, for 'borrowing' those dolls from her friend."

"I don't remember that," Louann said.

"You were too young, I imagine." His lips started to tremble, and he looked down at the table. "Sometimes it all seems like such a waste." He looked into her eyes. "You know, I never imagined it would be like this. I always thought I would go first. I never imagined I'd be as useless as a rusted-out old mower." He shook his head. "What I know now is Amelia was the lucky one, and even your mother when you look at the facts. What no one knows in this country until it's too late is that it's better to die young."

"Don't say that," she said.

"I can say it because I know it's true," he said, breaking the cracker with great effort into two smaller pieces. "I don't feel good physically. I don't like to be weak, and I know I'm not clear all the time. Ingrid tells me I'm mixing things up." He shrugged. "Maybe it's the pills, and maybe it's not." He looked down at his hands and shook his head, and for a moment he was silent. Then he said, "This is no way to live, Louann."

She tried to think of something to say, but she couldn't. Of course he was right—he was talking about the way he felt, so of course he was right. But it was so horrifying to her, thinking he would really rather die.

She got up and went into the living room, and Katherine was asleep on the rug with the farm animals gathered against her elbow. She was sleeping the way a recovering child sleeps, absolutely deeply, and Louann walked out without moving her.

When she went back into the kitchen, her grandfather looked up at her with his sad, red-rimmed eyes, and she felt she had to say something comforting. "I'm going to talk to that woman at school who was the typist for that book on geriatric health," she said. "Maybe she'll have some ideas."

He half smiled. "Geriatric health. There is no such thing. I could have typed that book in one sentence, because all you have to say about it is, 'Shoot yourself before it's too late.' "

Glenn threw the ball back to Katherine and watched as she ran across the den to pick it up. It was two weeks since her stomach virus had ended, and he felt tremendous relief that once again she was healthy. And he was happy that she was in school because it meant she was meeting new friends and that her life was really beginning, but it also broke his heart, in a certain way. She belonged to the world now, not just to them.

He knew there were some who weren't as, well, obsessed as he was (although he didn't even like to think the word). Glenn supposed there were as many differences between people in this area as in any other. Some were tall, some were short; some adored their children, some took them for granted or even ignored them.

"Daddy, quick!" Katherine yelled, and she pretended to throw the ball and then collapsed in a heap of laughter on the floor. "Fooled you," she laughed, and he got down on the floor and laughed with her.

What frightened him was thinking about Tessa.

He believed earnestly—it was the foundation of his life—that it was one's duty to analyze one's life at every moment, to not allow changes to occur unless one examined them and accepted them first. He had always tried to follow his credo, to be true to himself and to those around him by not allowing anything to slide in his life; it would be tantamount, he had always felt, to beginning an experiment in a lab and then walking away from it before you were finished.

Yet, with his marriage, he knew he had done just that.

He hadn't walked away from it. He couldn't. He loved Tessa and he adored Katherine; he could honestly say he would give his life up, without hesitation, for his daughter.

But changes were occurring—they had been occurring for years—and he hadn't allowed himself to think about them until now.

He didn't understand Tessa at all. When he had first met her that day in the math department, she had seemed like a beautiful, quiet young woman who hadn't yet explored much that life had to offer. She had been full of potential and enthusiasm and hope, like an unopened gift. Yes, full of mystery, but she had been so enthusiastic about so many things—their life together, their future, her hopes and ambitions.

But back then, she had expressed them so positively. She would finish school; she didn't know what she would become, but she would be the best at it in the world. She believed in his work because it was so promising and they could go anywhere in the country.

What he hadn't recognized was the bitterness that had been

lying beneath the surface—at least he assumed it had been there all along. He certainly hoped he hadn't caused it.

"Daddy, watch how I can make it go on the floor," Katherine said, and she batted the ball along, keeping up with it and then batting it some more. "Like a dog," she said, looking up at him and beaming.

"That's right, honey," he said, brushing the top of her head with a hand. The movement was all love—sometimes he felt he just wanted to hold her in his arms forever—but as was always the case these days, beneath the love was an aching sadness, and beneath that, a panic.

When he watched Tessa with Katherine, there were times he had to leave the room. There was something missing in the way she looked at Katherine, the way she touched Katherine. Sometimes he would think about it so much he felt as if he were losing his mind. Maybe Tessa just showed her feelings differently than he did, but that didn't change the fact that there definitely seemed to be something missing in the way she dealt with Katherine, even the way she felt about her.

Sometimes he watched other mothers, and he saw similar things with them—an exhaustion that made them careless, an irritability that made them snappish.

The phone rang, and Glenn got up off the floor and took Katherine by the hand. "Come with Daddy to get the phone," he said as she put her small hand in his. "Do you want to answer it?"

She nodded, and he hoisted her up to the wall phone, and his heart melted when he heard her say, "Hello." He knew that to anyone else it would sound pathetically corny—her voice was like all little girls' voices; she was just a little girl.

She handed the receiver to him, and she was frowning.

"Hello," he said unnaturally forcefully—he supposed to counter Katherine's tentative "Hello."

"Glenn?" It was Tessa's grandfather, and though he was yelling, his voice sounded faint.

"Grandpa Lundgren," Glenn said loudly. "Are you all right?"

"I want Tessa," he said faintly.

"She's at the store," Glenn yelled.

"The what?"

"The store," Glenn said.

"What? Can you spell it?"

"Store!" Glenn yelled. "S-t—"

"D?"

"No. T. T as in Thomas."

"What?"

Glenn sighed. "She'll be home in a few minutes," he yelled. "She said she'd call me, and she didn't."

"When was that?"

"Yesterday, today, day before yesterday," Tessa's grandfather said.

"Is everything all right?"

"I need to talk to her."

Just then Glenn saw Tessa's car in the driveway, and he told Tessa's grandfather to hold on. But Mack had already hung up.

"Call your grandfather," Glenn said as Tessa walked in the door.

"Hello to you, too," she said. She knelt down and lifted Katherine into the air. "How's my baby girl?" she said, and she rubbed noses with Katherine until Katherine started to laugh and throw her head back.

Glenn stepped back and watched. Maybe he was worried about nothing. Certainly Tessa had grown more distant to him lately, but he knew from reading books about relationships that this was inevitable; it was just one cycle that would eventually lead to another one. There were times, especially when it came to lovemaking, when relations grew distant for a time. But all the books said it was natural; you couldn't always expect to be at the apex of a relationship.

"Hon?" he said.

"I heard you," she said. She was still playing with Katherine.

"He said you had promised to call, and you didn't," Glenn said.

She was rubbing noses again with Katherine. "You're mommy's little angel, aren't you? Just a perfect little angel."

"Tess?"

Finally she set Katherine down. "What *is* your problem? I heard you the first time."

"I thought you were going to call him every day," Glenn said. "That was part of the deal you made with Louann."

"Ah. Saint Louann. I didn't know she had shared the details of our little deal with you."

"She did, and apparently you're not following through."

"My grandfather has a very poor memory," she said, running her fingers through Katherine's hair. "I call him every single day, rain or shine."

He knew she was lying, and it frightened him, because she seemed to be emotionally dumb. He could remember Tessa telling him that in her family, she had felt as a child that there was only a certain amount of love that was available; if her mother lavished affection on her one day, that would mean there would be none left for days and sometimes weeks after; when her grandfather "fell for" Louann, there was no love left for her.

And he was beginning to feel that he didn't know his wife at all.

15

There were customers in the store, so Tessa had kept the answering machine on when she had opened up. She had gotten to the point that she couldn't stand to hear either of her grandfather's voices—the falsely cheerful one ("Good morning! Isn't it a hell of a day?") or the unhappy, more sincere one ("Tess? This is your grandfather.") It was about a year since they had first hired Ingrid to look out for him, and in those months, Ingrid had become increasingly lazy, and Tessa's grandfather had come to depend on Tessa more than ever.

"Tessa?" he was now calling into the machine. "Tessa? Can you hear me?"

She would never get over it; he was an intelligent man, certainly worldly enough, but he didn't have the faintest idea how an answering machine worked or even what it was for. Every time he called, he seemed to be trying to break the sound barrier; it was as if he thought that if he yelled loudly enough, she would miraculously appear and pick up the receiver.

Which, indeed, in this case turned out to be correct, because his voice was distracting the customers. "Hello, Grandpa," she said as she shut off the machine. "What's the matter?"

"I don't like talking to that box," he said.

"Well, now you're talking to me. What's the matter?"

"I thought you would be here," he said.

"I told you I'd be there at two o'clock, when that woman is supposed to come to your house."

"Two?"

"TWO!" she yelled, and a customer turned to look at her. Tessa cupped the receiver in her hand and faced the wall. "We've been through this a dozen times. The woman is going to come at two o'clock, and I'll be there, too, so I can meet her."

"I'm all alone," he said.

"I know that," she yelled. "But it's just for today. Ingrid's day off."

"I don't feel right," he said.

Tessa sighed. She couldn't leave the store, and Gail wasn't due in for another two hours. "I'll come when I can," she yelled.

"What?"

"I'll come when I can!"

"You'll be done? I can't understand you."

"I WILL COME WHEN I CAN. BY TWO O'CLOCK. OKAY?"

"Today?"

Tessa hung up the phone. She knew he would be upset, but the fact was that she'd be there in a few hours, and whether he knew it or not at this point, she would be there eventually.

And at the back of her mind, there was another factor. She knew he would be upset by her hanging up on him, but she was glad. Sometimes she fantasized that, little by little, she was cutting his life short by actions that couldn't *really* be called evil, but that shortened his life nevertheless—things like promising to call and raising his hopes and then not calling for days, things that would inevitably hurt him physically if you could believe everything that was in the magazines these days about the effects of stress on the body. One day last weekend when she had been alone with him at his house, she had loaded up his food with real salt instead of the salt substitute he was supposed to be using. He had loved it—she had made his favorite stew, and he had been complaining lately about how tasteless Ingrid's food was—and she had felt a twinge of guilt but also happiness and hope as she had watched him eat seconds and then thirds.

He was unhappy anyway, wasn't he?

Gail came in early—breathlessly and with that annoying glow that meant she had been seeing Walter. "How were sales?" she asked.

"One candlestick and one potholder," Tessa said. "A total of seventeen dollars." It made her wonder whether it would have been smart to enter into a partnership with Gail.

Gail checked her lipstick in one of the mirrors. "It will pick up," she said.

"You always say that," Tessa said. "Here we are getting close to Christmas, and I don't see any signs, Gail."

Gail came over to the counter, and she had an odd, dreamy look in her eyes. "Do you know what? I don't even care."

"What?"

She took a long, deep breath. "I know it's crazy, but I don't even care. Something amazing happened to me this morning."

Tessa sat down on one of the stools. She was filled with dread; Gail looked so happy all of a sudden.

"Walter wants me to leave Dave," Gail said.

"Are you serious?"

Gail smiled crookedly. "Do you know I never let myself hope it could be true? I wanted to marry that man the day I met him—"

"You told me it was a fling," Tessa said, feeling betrayed.

Gail nodded. "I told myself it was a fling, too. But I know I fell in love with him the day I met him. And now he says he's finally ready."

"What do you mean, finally? You've barely known each other for a year."

Gail smiled. "Do you really think there are rules about this sort of thing? I'd expect Glenn to say something like that—not you."

Tessa was silent. How could Gail just pick up and leave? What about Amanda? What about the store? "Would you leave Lodenton?" Tessa asked.

Gail laughed. "That's a little like asking a prisoner if he would leave jail if he got the chance, isn't it? Wouldn't *you* leave Lodenton if you had the chance?"

The door opened, and an old woman walked in and pulled her shawl closer around her head. From the looks of her it was obvious that she wasn't going to buy anything, but Tessa needed to get away from Gail, and she went over to ask the woman if she needed any help.

"Just looking," she said with a hopeful, pathetic smile.

Tessa straightened out some scarves and went back to the counter, where Gail had settled in with a cup of tea.

"What does this mean in terms of the store?"

"I don't know," Gail said. "Maybe you'll be able to have the store of your dreams after all, if I leave."

Tessa didn't like the way Gail sounded so condescending. Now that she had what *she* wanted, the store had become instantaneously undesirable. "What if he changes his mind?"

Tessa asked. "I can't believe you'd plan your whole life around someone else's whims."

The dreamy look had come back into Gail's eyes. "If you had the kind of relationship I have with Walter, you'd understand. This is a man I'd do anything for, Tessa. This isn't about convention or being married to someone or committed to a man because you've agreed to some abstract idea. This is about being so in love that you don't have a choice."

Tessa looked at the old woman and watched as she ran a hand over a scarf she obviously couldn't afford. Why was the world filled with people who either had everything or had nothing? And why couldn't she be one of the ones who had everything?

"Anyway," Gail said, "I don't know when all of this is going to actually happen, so don't worry about the store. I mean, either you'll continue to have a job for a while, or you'll have a chance to buy me out. I haven't even spoken to Dave."

"What about Amanda?"

"Amanda will come with us, naturally."

"What do you mean, naturally? How can you assume Dave won't fight for her? And if he decides to, he's going to have a lot of evidence on his side if he knows that you've been with Walter, which he will if you tell him you're leaving him. How can you assume anything, Gail?"

"I know Dave," she said, sounding completely relaxed. "He works much too hard to take care of a small child, and he knows it."

"I don't think you know any of the things you think you know," Tessa said, watching the old woman leave.

Tessa looked at her watch and realized she should go to her grandfather's now that Gail was back. But she felt angry and distracted, as if there were too much energy in her body for her to go over to her grandfather's and just sit. It would make her feel insane.

"If you were in my situation, you would understand," Gail said.

"Why do you keep saying, 'If you were in my situation,' and implying that I wish I were? Or that I'm married to someone I don't even love?"

"I didn't know what love was until so recently, Tessa. I had thought I did, but I had no idea."

"Well, you're talking about your own life," Tessa said. "Not mine."

* * *

Tessa pulled into her grandfather's driveway and felt a flash of pain in her head as she got out of the car. This was going to be a bad headache, she could feel it, and it would only be made worse by her being there in that stultifying house with that hot, dry air and her grandfather.

As she began walking up the path, she realized she hadn't brought him anything. He subscribed to the *Chronicle*, but he liked being brought the *Clarion*, too, and Louann always brought some kind of treat, like a stack of magazines or the special health-store cookies he loved.

Well, too bad. Louann was different.

"Grandpa?" She didn't know why she was even calling out—some vestigial habit from the past, because he certainly wouldn't hear her. She opened the door and walked into the living room, and for a moment her head stopped hurting and her heart seemed to stop. Her grandfather was in the easy chair, his head lying back and his mouth open.

"Grandpa?"

There was a tiny movement in his face—a squinting of his eyes and a tremor—so he was alive.

But he could have been anyone walking in! He was so vulnerable!

She went into the kitchen and turned on the water to make coffee and started thinking about Gail again. What if Gail left Lodenton next week, just picked up Amanda and Walter and left? It was true that she and Gail fought, but Gail was her only friend in Lodenton. And what about the store?

"Wha?" she heard from the living room—a fearful, garbled sound.

She swung the door from the kitchen open and looked in. Her grandfather was drawn back in terror, looking in her direction. He slumped as he realized who she was. "It's you," he said, letting out a deep breath.

"Of course it's me," she said. "Who else would it be?" She liked playing that game with him, pretending she didn't know what he was worrying about. Because that was what he had done with her while she was growing up, hinting obliquely at all sorts of terrible things that might or might not happen, making her feel she wasn't loved. She would never forget how he had fastened on to her taking Susan Malenky's dolls those times—it was as if she had stolen the gold from Fort Knox! And for years afterward, he would talk about how her "tendencies" were going to get her into trouble someday. Just you wait and see.

He rubbed his eyes and looked at the television, but it was off. "I thought you were coming a long time ago. Why did you hang up on me?"

"I told you I had to work at the store. I got here as soon as I could."

He rubbed his eyes again. "I don't feel right," he said.

She came in and sat on the hassock next to the chair. "What's the matter?"

"I don't feel good." He looked into her eyes, and he was squinting. "I don't like this. Being alone. I don't like it at all."

"I know that," she said. "But there's nothing we can do about it until we can get someone to live here full-time. Maybe this woman Jean Marvin will be the one. She needs someplace to live, and she would live here without getting paid, so it could be perfect." He would be off her hands, and he wouldn't be paying someone like Ingrid anymore! Jean Marvin would do all the cooking, cleaning, and talking to him in return for having a nice place to live. It sounded so ideal!

"I don't want another stranger," he said. "I don't like having a stranger living in the house with me. I saw Ingrid looking in my desk yesterday, going through my drawers."

Tessa was shocked. It was the kind of thing she would have done if taking care of old people were her job, but it seemed surprising someone else would do it. "Did she find anything?" she asked. "What would she have been looking for?"

He squinted as if he were in pain. "I was working on my will for a few days—"

"What do you mean, working on your will? How can you work on your will without a lawyer? What are you talking about?" She tried to control herself. "What do you mean?"

He squinted again. "I was thinking of changing a few things. You never know, with Katherine—"

"What do you mean, 'you never know'? What are you talking about?"

He covered his eyes and shook his head, and when he looked up at her again his eyes were filled with tears. "I don't like this," he said. "I don't like living this way."

"It will get better," she said.

"It will get worse," he said. "If Ingrid leaves, there will be someone worse. We don't know anything about Ingrid, and we don't know anything about this woman who's coming today. What I know about Ingrid is that she can sit in the same room with me all day and say three words. Maybe ten. I have to sit here and watch quiz shows all day, and I can tell you I don't like it. I'm uncomfortable and I'm lonely and I don't like it.''

Tessa wanted to know what was in his will and why he was changing it. She had heard his feelings before. They were disturbing to her not so much because he was feeling them but because there was a chance she would feel that way, too, when she got to be his age. But she wouldn't let it happen. Either she would be dead or she would be rich, but she wouldn't let herself live the way he was living.

Tessa heard a car door slam, and she got up to look out the window. ''Well, she's early if that's her,'' she said.

Jean Marvin looked younger than Tessa had pictured. On the phone she had said she was a widow, and Tessa had pictured someone old with gray hair.

She seemed to be one of those ageless women the streets of Lodenton were filled with—women with graying but not gray hair, wearing lipstick in old-fashioned, too-dark shades, and always dressed as if they were on their way to church.

Tessa watched as Jean Marvin looked up at the house and around the yard and then adjusted her hair before ringing the bell.

''What does she look like?'' Tessa's grandfather asked, straining to change positions in the easy chair.

''Like ninety percent of the women in Lodenton,'' Tessa said, and she got up to answer the door.

''And that was how I ended up in Acton,'' Jean Marvin was saying. ''A husband who didn't know how to read a map, and here I am, forty years later.''

That made Jean Marvin sixty or so years old, but she didn't look it, and she didn't act it. What amazed Tessa most was how her grandfather had pepped up since the woman had come into the house. He had actually gotten up himself to get a glass of water, and he had walked taller than Tessa had seen him walk in months.

That night, Tessa's grandfather called her and sounded so excited that Tessa thought something terrible had happened. ''What's the matter?'' she asked.

''Nothing's the matter,'' he said. His voice sounded so strong! ''I'm just excited. Jean said she could move in next week. I gave Ingrid her notice this afternoon. I called her at her house.''

''You gave her notice? Don't you think you should think about it a little?''

"What's to think about? You saw that woman. She's attractive, she's articulate, and she's the best thing that's ever happened to me since your grandmother. I'm not letting her pass me by. So I said move in when you can, honey."

"You called her 'honey'?"

He laughed. It was the first time she had heard him laugh in months. "She loved it. And I think she likes me, Tessa, I really do."

Jean Marvin moved in exactly a week after Tessa had met her—Louann had checked her references, and each was better and more glowing than the last—and the calls from Tessa's grandfather grew less and less frequent. Where he had once called every day, sometimes twice or three times, Tessa now had to call him every few days just to be sure he was all right.

"I'm worried," Tessa said to Louann a few weeks after Jean Marvin had moved in. "He never calls anymore. It seems so odd."

"Be glad," Louann said. "What could be bad about it?"

"What if she's drugging him or doing something weird? Look at Ingrid, going through his desk. We don't know what this woman could be doing."

Louann discounted Tessa's worries, but Tessa began going there on her way to pick up Katherine from school, just to check on him. At first she couldn't articulate the source of her worry even to herself; if he had become more independent, wasn't that good? If he was happy, wasn't that good?

But with each visit, the reason for her worry—and the justification for it—became clearer to Tessa. Yes, he was less dependent on her, but only because he was becoming completely dependent on Jean Marvin. Half the time when Tessa went over there, they were just coming back from shopping or even the theater—the theater!—over at the college. Jean Marvin took him to the library to the afternoon movies they showed for senior citizens and to the art gallery at the college. She had to hold him on her arm while they walked, he would tell Tessa with a gleam in his eyes, but what was wrong with that?

One day when Tessa knew that Jean was down in Castleton, first at the doctor and then doing the week's grocery shopping, Tessa went over to see her grandfather. He was in the garage, puttering around trying to fix a broken toaster. "What brought you out today?" he asked.

"I just wanted to see you," Tessa said. "Why does there have to be a reason?"

"I mean today," he said. "It's a funny thing because we had a fight." When she had first walked in, she had felt he looked good—a month ago, she would never have imagined he'd be back in his garage, working on fixing things. But now that he was facing her, he looked ancient.

"You and Jean?" she asked, with a skip in her heartbeat. The way he had said the words made it sound as if they were lovers!

"I can't understand it," he said. He set the toaster down and held his back as he trudged slowly back toward the house. "It's too cold out here," he said. "My bones hurt. Come inside so we can talk."

She held his arm as they walked up the path and into the house, and he felt tiny and thin but also weak and therefore heavy, as if he wouldn't be able to walk on his own more than a few steps.

"I was confused about something, and she got upset," he said. "I can't understand why she was so upset."

"What happened?"

He rubbed his eyes. "I can't help it if I get confused." He looked into Tessa's eyes. "She said I was driving her crazy."

"But what happened?"

"I left the toaster oven on." He paused. "The smoke alarm started ringing at two in the morning, and I didn't hear it, and she got upset."

"I can understand why," Tessa said. "That sounds dangerous. What had you left in it?"

"A frozen turnover. I wanted to surprise Jean, and then I forgot about it and went to bed." He scratched at his chin where there was a sore. "And we argued about my pills because she hadn't checked them off on the chart, and I took double."

"Grandpa, you have to be more careful."

"I can't remember," he said helplessly. "There are twenty-three pills every day, and I can't remember. I thought she was writing them down. I was wrong."

"Well, you really don't know her very well, do you? What I mean is that, as much as you might like her, I don't think you should put your complete trust in her, Grandpa."

He began to cry. She looked up and there were tears streaming down his face. "I'm in love with her," he said quietly. "I'm an old, old man, and I'm in love with her, and now she's mad at me."

Tessa didn't know what to do. She could hardly breathe. She had to look away from her grandfather.

"What am I going to do?" he asked in an old, pathetic voice.

Tessa stood up. "I'm going to make some tea," she said, and she went into the kitchen. In love with Jean Marvin! So she had been right to fear the worst. She had been right!

She made the tea, and her hands were shaking, which frightened her—since when did she let her emotions affect her like that?—and brought the cups into the living room. She had thought her grandfather would have stopped crying, but he was sitting in his chair weeping like a young girl.

"I'm an old man," he said, wiping at his eyes. "To think a woman like that would want me. I can't be a husband to her, I'm not much of a companion . . ." He looked at her hopefully, but she didn't say anything. She wasn't going to tell him he was wrong. It couldn't happen; she wouldn't let it happen.

"Was I wrong?" he asked as if reading her mind. "Am I wrong, Tessa?"

She took a deep breath. "I think there are a lot of things to think about," she said carefully. "Of course it's not wrong to fall in love. You can't help it when it happens. But there are things to consider. You really don't know Jean very well, even if you think you do. You don't know much about her background or why she's here. And what about us? Would you really want everything you've worked for your whole life to go to someone you hardly know?"

"You mean if I die?"

If! "That's right. If something happened to you—"

"She's not like that," he said, wiping away his tears. "If something happened to me, she would leave what I left for her to you after she died."

Tessa was shocked. Would it really be all right with him that they would have to wait until Jean Marvin died before they would get anything? "Are you saying this is already done?" she asked. "Did you change your will?"

He shook his head and began to cry again. "How can I when I don't know where I stand with her?"

Tessa stood up and looked out the window. It was a bleak, bitter-gray landscape—she had always felt Sweden probably looked like Lodenton did at this time of year. According to several magazines she had read, Sweden had one of the world's highest suicide rates, and she could see why. On days like this, when the world looked so gray, she could almost feel how her mother must have felt.

She had to think. She had no way of knowing how Jean Marvin would feel about any of it. But what if he asked her to marry him and she accepted? What if Tessa had to wait twenty or thirty years to get what was rightfully hers, what she had *counted* on?

"Tess?"

She turned around. He was wiping his eyes and examining the handkerchief after each dab. "I don't feel right," he said.

"What's the matter?"

His voice was quavering. "I'm scared. I don't want to live the way I was living before Jean came here. I'd rather die."

"But she's not leaving."

"We don't know," he said. "She was so upset when she left. We don't know."

"Just relax," she said. "Drink your tea."

But he was breathing hard and suddenly his eyes were big, younger-looking, filled with panic, and he was holding his chest. "Help," he said.

"What's the matter?"

"I can feel it. You have to help me."

"What's the matter? Tell me."

His breathing was shallow and fast. "I can feel it, I know—Oh." His eyes were shut now, and he was wincing.

"I'll call an ambulance," she said, standing up. "Just stay calm, all right?"

He was doubled over then, his head down over his knees. Tessa took one last look at him and went into the kitchen.

She picked up the phone and looked at the number—her grandfather had written it on a large blue-and-white label and stuck it on the wall over the phone. "EMERGENCY! CALL: 555-1000" and then, in slightly smaller letters: "IN CASE OF DEATH, CONTACT GRANDDAUGHTER: TESSA STOKES, 555-6753." She began to dial the emergency number.

Then she put down the phone, and she waited.

16

It was a month since Tessa's grandfather had died, two weeks since Tessa and Louann had decided to put the house on the market. At first, Louann had balked—was it right just to sell something like that, the house that had been their grandfather's home for more than seventy years, so quickly? But Tessa had convinced her: Louann had left Lodenton and lived in New York now. She couldn't very well live in the house herself, even if she wanted to move back to Lodenton after graduation. He had left it to both of them, and Tessa wanted to sell it.

"I suppose it's the only thing we can do, then," Louann had said.

They had let Jean Marvin stay on until she found another place. Partly it was because the house would look better and be safer if someone were living there. Louann felt strongly that Jean Marvin had made their grandfather so happy that the least they could do was give her a place to live until the house was sold or she decided to leave on her own.

And Tessa didn't argue. The day her grandfather had died, she had been more frightened—for a few minutes—than she had ever been in her life.

At first it had seemed unreal. She had gone back into the living room when she felt enough time had passed, and there he was, dead on the floor. She had heard a clunk and assumed he had fallen to the floor, but actually seeing him there, with his knees brought up to his chest and his face wincing as if he were still alive, brought a sour panic up through her chest into her throat, and she had had to cover her mouth.

She had done it. She had listened while he had died—she had heard his labored breathing and heard him fall, she had heard

sounds she didn't ever want to think about again, and then silence. She had taken a chance. Now, when she thought about
it, it made her fingers numb with panic just to imagine—what if
she had left him there and he *hadn't* died? What she should have
done was at least to pretend to call the ambulance, so that if he
had lived, he couldn't accuse her afterward of having done what
she had, in fact, done. She didn't know if people in that much
pain, in panic for their life, were able to hear or remember
anything at all afterward. But she still shivered when she thought
of what a chance she had taken.

After several minutes had passed, and she knew he was dead,
she did call the ambulance, pretending he was still alive. And
that was another chance she had taken—what if Jean Marvin had
returned in the meantime? It made her ill to think she had been
so careless on two crucial counts, that she had probably been in
extreme panic even though she had felt as cool as a cucumber.

But luck had been with her.

She had called the ambulance, sounding appropriately panicked, she felt, and then she had made herself some fresh coffee.

The paramedics had come, and she was amazed at how
she didn't even have to plan her words. She told them that
he had died while they were on their way, that she didn't
know CPR, and could they revive him? She could remember
a questioning look in one of the paramedics' eyes, when he
saw her drinking her coffee and he glanced at the pot. Maybe
it had looked too fresh, as if she had made it while she
was waiting for them. That probably hadn't been a normal
thing to do, she had realized. Another mistake. But looking
back, she thought perhaps she had imagined the look in the
man's eyes.

What she hadn't imagined was Jean Marvin's reaction. Talking to the first aid crew, Tessa had begun to believe her own
words. She was devastated; she had done everything she could,
but it hadn't been enough. And then, hearing Jean Marvin's car,
she had felt the lie for the first time: she had listened to him
die. And when Jean Marvin came in, what Tessa saw in her eyes
and heard in her voice was horror and sadness. But then, as Jean
Marvin had looked at Tessa, suspicion and doubt that felt almost
physical, as if Jean Marvin had come up to her and held her by
the back of her neck like a mother cat.

Tessa tried to figure out why she didn't feel worse. She had
loved her grandfather when she was a child, but, honestly, she
had felt that he had lived long enough. And it was so important

that he not give his house and his money to Jean Marvin! She knew it would sound callous to say out loud, but everyone's life had to end at some point, and he hadn't had long to live anyway.

She was going to come into quite a bit of money—the real estate agent said that she and Louann would probably get a hundred and thirty thousand dollars for his house, and their grandfather had also had sixty thousand dollars in the bank. But Tessa had always imagined it would be more, and she was disappointed. She would end up with about ninety-five thousand dollars, which was a fortune, certainly, compared to the money she had had up to that point. She knew that; she told herself that at least ten times a day. But still, she was disappointed, and she felt bitter at each dollar he had spent before his death. If they hadn't hired Ingrid, there would have been thousands more; if he hadn't had the house repainted, there would have been thousands more.

She supposed that part of the problem was that she didn't know what she would do with the money. The amount was liberating—with ninety-five thousand dollars, you could leave your husband; you could run your own store without a partner; you could go to New York City. But she realized that already, she had a fear of spending all the money and ending up with nothing, back where she had started, in six or eight or ten months. Now was her chance—she could point herself in any direction she wanted. But she didn't know where to begin.

And it was hard to concentrate on vague future plans when the Christmas season had created so many complications. Katherine was off from nursery school, and Tessa had hired Mrs. Everson, Gail's part-time nanny, to baby-sit her. Luckily, Katherine adored her—she was a gray-haired grandmother with children in another state—but Glenn seemed to resent it that Tessa had to spend longer hours at the store now. He seemed to be brooding about something these days, and she had no idea what it was about.

"The brown one!" Katherine said, jumping up and down and clapping. "Daddy, look at him!"

Glenn laughed and asked the woman to give Katherine the brown puppy.

Katherine looked up at him and gripped his arm for a second, and he was sure he had never seen her so excited or so happy. The woman opened the cage and handed Katherine a squirming, squealing puppy, and Katherine began to coo until the puppy started to lick her, and then she couldn't stop laughing. "Daddy, look! He loves me!"

"He seems like a wonderful little fellow," the pound attendant said. "I think he was the last one to go because he was the runt, but I tend to think they can be the nicest ones."

"What's a runt?" Katherine asked. She had sat down on the floor and was letting the puppy lick her whole face and neck, and the puppy was acting as if it was his duty in life to be sure this little person who was holding him got completely clean.

"That's the smallest one in the family," Glenn said. "Like the baby brother." He turned to the attendant. "But he's healthy, isn't he? The fact that he's a runt doesn't mean he's sick."

She shook her head. "Not at all. He's been given a full okay by our vet. And you'll have a month's worth of free care if you adopt him."

He tried not to hear the other dogs crying or to look into their faces. He hadn't even wanted to bring Katherine inside the pound, because he was sure she would want to adopt each dog. But he was the one who was being affected most; there was a black-and-white dog who, unlike the others, wasn't even barking. He was just staring soulfully at Glenn, as if he could will him to open the cage and take him home. And Glenn had seriously considered it for a few minutes. Couldn't they get one dog and one puppy? He had read that that kind of age spread was often ideal: the older one would take the puppy on as a project, teaching him all those dog ideas that a dog could probably teach better than a human being could.

But it wasn't fair to Tessa. Even though Mrs. Everson had begun to do quite a bit of cleaning, and he certainly did his share, he knew that one dog plus one puppy was probably like three, and in any case, it wouldn't be fair to make the decision by himself.

"Daddy, look. He loves me," Katherine said.

This was the way life was supposed to be—taking your daughter to adopt a puppy and having her face light up with happiness, hearing her laugh—

But he heard her laugh too infrequently these days. And tonight, Tessa had come home from work and told him some news that was extremely upsetting. Gail was leaving Dave, and she was going to take Amanda with her, Tessa had told him almost in passing. "I don't know where that's going to leave me in terms of the store," Tessa had said. "And I really don't know if I even want to go into the business at the moment. I mean, now that I have the money, is that really what I would want to do with it?''

He had been chilled by her words, chilled by her lack of emotion, and he couldn't stop himself from comparing her response with the way she had acted after her grandfather died.

She hadn't called him that day at work. He could remember that he had come home and found Katherine playing happily on the living room floor. It was a relief because she had been over-tired and prone to crying when she was tired, and he was happy to see that she was in a good mood.

He had gone into the kitchen—Tessa was cooking dinner—and she turned to him. ''You won't believe what happened to-day,'' she had said. She had stopped slicing the green peppers, and he could remember thinking that she looked slightly pale and shaky.

His first thought was that something had happened with Kath-erine, but Katherine had looked wonderful and happy. And then Tessa said, ''My grandfather died today. When I was over there.''

''Are you serious?'' he had said. He couldn't believe that she could be telling the truth. Her grandfather had *died*, and while she was *there*? ''What happened? Tell me everything.'' His im-pulse had been to go over and touch her, put an arm around her and hold her, because that was what came naturally to him. But he stopped when he had gotten close to her.

She took a deep breath. ''I think there were signs we maybe should have noticed,'' she said. ''I don't know. But when I was over there, he started having chest pains, and I called the am-bulance, but by the time they got there, he was dead.''

''You didn't do CPR?''

''Glenn, I don't know CPR. Do you know how many people have asked me that today? I feel badly enough that he died,'' she had said.

In that moment, he had seen something he was tired of see-ing. He had seen her lying. She didn't feel bad that her grand-father had died; he knew that. He had seen her lying, and he had seen a coolness that terrified him. And he had another thought, a thought that had come back to him every day since that day, a question he couldn't quite answer: would she have helped her grandfather if she had known how?

But then this afternoon, when she had told him about Gail and Dave, he had seen the same emotional pattern: the fact that a marriage had broken up, that a child was going to lose what would seem like everything in the world, didn't matter to Tessa. What mattered was that there would be a bit of uncertainty in her life because of the store.

And he had left the house, driven Katherine over to the pound in Acton so that she would be able to have a puppy for Christmas. She missed her great-grandfather, but he also knew that she was too young to understand what it meant that he had died. Every few days, she would ask if Poppa Mack was "back" yet, and Glenn was glad she would have a puppy to make her happier all around.

Katherine was laughing again, and the puppy was back to his licking. His eyes were a glistening brown, and he was all brown except for a silly-looking white spot at the top of his head. "What are you going to name him, kid?"

"Oh, gee," she said, and he had to smile, because that was the way her baby-sitter, Mrs. Everson, started almost every sentence. "I don't even know!"

"Well, maybe your mom will have some ideas. Let's go fill out the papers and get this little guy home, baby."

"Home!" she said into the puppy's ear. "We're going home!"

The evening was better than the afternoon had been. Glenn was happy to see that Tessa was as entranced by the picture of Katherine with her new puppy as he was. She wasn't an animal lover—she had told him that at the beginning of their relationship, and he hadn't thought too much about it—but she laughed as much as anyone else in the room when the puppy began chasing his tail.

Glenn looked around at the living room, all done up for Christmas with stockings by the fireplace and the tree they had decorated the night before, and he told himself that things weren't as bad as he had made them out to be. He had been upset this afternoon when he had learned of Dave and Gail's separation, and certainly a month ago he had been upset about Poppa Lundgren, of whom he had been extremely fond. But perhaps his emotions had clouded his vision of Tessa.

Watching her now, cradling Katherine on one side and the puppy on the other as they all sat on the couch, he told himself that his life with her was good; it was unfair to expect her to have the same emotional responses that he did.

"What about Spot?" Tessa asked. She was joking with Katherine and suggesting some names that were appropriate and some that were just plain silly, like "Mr. Richardson," which was the name of the principal of Katherine's school.

Katherine shook her head. "There's already a Spot in my book. I want him to have his own name."

"I can understand that," Tessa said. "How about Higgledy-biggledy, then? There aren't too many dogs named that."

Katherine looked serious, as if she were considering it for a moment. Finally she shook her head. "I don't like it." She stood up. "He's going to make a nest with me in my bed. Maybe I'll call him Nesty."

Glenn watched as Tessa laughed and then followed Katherine and the puppy upstairs.

Later on, holding Tessa in his arms in bed, he closed his eyes and breathed in her scent for a long, long time. She was the mother of his child and he loved her, and he didn't want anything like what had happened to Gail and Dave to ever happen to them. "I'm sorry," he said quietly, into the darkness.

"About what?"

"I'm sorry if I seemed angry with you when you told me about Gail and Dave," he said. He liked talking in the darkness with Tessa; he always had. To him, it was one of the best things about marriage, that you had the whole night to lie in each other's arms and talk if you wanted to. "I know there was no reason to be angry with you," he said, stroking her hair. "It's just that when I hear stories like that, it chills me to the bone. These things shouldn't just happen out of the blue."

"It didn't," she said. "Gail had been bored and unhappy for a long time. Ever since I met her."

He closed his eyes again and fought a bile that was coming up from his stomach. The way Tessa had said "bored and unhappy" had been too knowledgeable, too smooth and knowing. "Are you bored and unhappy?" he asked.

"Don't be ridiculous. It's not going to happen to us," she said.

"But why do you say that?" He paused. "I think it would be unrealistic to bar the possibility entirely; statistically, it wouldn't make sense, when you look around us at people our age. At our own friends. That's why I think we need to work on our marriage, Tessa. Really talk."

"We can talk another time," she said, flipping on the light and looking across the pillows at him. She looked sleepy and beautiful; he adored the way she looked without makeup—she reminded him of a Botticelli with her fine, perfect features and those intense blue eyes. "All right? I'm just tired."

He thought about the money, the subject he had been afraid to bring up ever since her grandfather had died, other than to say, "So I guess you'll be getting quite a bit of money." And seeing the look in her eyes, excitement masked by something he couldn't read.

He wanted to look into her eyes and tell her he was worried. He wanted to look into her eyes and ask if she had had new thoughts since she had found out she would be inheriting all of this money, if she had had more thoughts since Gail had decided to leave Dave.

He wanted her to say he was crazy to worry, that of course she would never leave him.

He turned off the light and said "Good night," which was the only thing he felt it was safe to say.

17

The old section of Acton was the only part of town Tessa found beautiful—old brick buildings mostly painted white, huge old trees that shaded all the sidewalks, and an atmosphere that felt far removed from the mills and mines outside of town. Tessa wasn't looking forward to the morning's appointment—a meeting with her grandfather's lawyer—but she told herself it was all to the good; many bridges had to be crossed before she would get her money.

She didn't like the lawyer—he was an old man, almost as old as her grandfather, it seemed, and she felt too closely watched when she was in his presence. She wondered if he suspected anything, but then again, even if he did, how could he prove anything? No one ever had, and no one ever would. And she had to remind herself that she hadn't actually killed her grandfather, which was the way she had begun to think of it. She hadn't done that at all.

Anyway, what was more disturbing was the call she had gotten from the real estate agent that morning. When he had first seen her grandfather's house, he had raved about it, and he had told her it would sell "in a flash." But all of a sudden, there were "problems" with the house; prospective buyers had complaints, and he thought they should lower the asking price and that Tessa should make all kinds of repairs. The conversation had made her feel as if crucial details were beginning to unravel, as if everything she had been counting on was going to be removed and undone.

The lawyer was brusque and impatient, and annoying because he said it would be weeks until they could open the safe deposit box, weeks, too, until the will would be submitted for probate. Tessa had argued at first but realized there was nothing she could do about it; the lawyer as much as said so with his eyes alone.

She left with an uneasy feeling. She went out into the street and tried to decide where to go, if she had time to get a bite to eat before meeting the real estate agent out at her grandfather's house.

"Tessa."

She turned around. Roy Donahue was coming toward her, and she barely recognized him. At the church get-togethers he had always worn jeans and a T-shirt, or a flannel shirt when it was cooler outside, and casual suits in church. Now he was wearing an expensive, beautifully cut suit and tie, and was looking quite the lawyer. He was definitely a handsome man—there was something enormously appealing about how his dark brown eyes seemed to flash his intelligence. He had thick, dark hair and a great body, yet she didn't feel he was at all vain or self-conscious.

"Roy," she said. "I wouldn't have recognized you." She liked him better in his casual clothes, but she was still attracted to him—she had forgotten just how much, in fact.

"You mean these old things?" he said, spreading his hands. "Actually, I've just won an important case, so you're seeing me in my number-one Acton's-finest-lawyer suit."

"Well," she said. "Congratulations. I'm glad one of us has won something."

"What's the matter? You're not down here for legal reasons—?"

"Actually, I am," she said, and she told him about her grandfather. "It's so strange, really. Today—I don't know if it's for specific reasons or no reason at all, but I have this terrible feeling that everything is unraveling. The lawyer told me that the will is going to take longer than I had thought—not that I need the money for any particular reason, but it just makes you feel better when you actually have it—"

"Of course," he said. "But these things do take time. What else?"

"Well, the real estate agent called me this morning—the one I'm listing my grandfather's house with—and he's told me there are all sorts of things wrong with the house that I didn't know about. It upsets me because I know my grandfather was a fanatic about keeping the house in good shape, but certainly at the end he wasn't well enough."

"What sort of things? You know, you have to be careful of

these agents. They'll give you one price—a high price—so that you give them the listing, and then as soon as you do, they want to make a quick sale, so they'll start downplaying the house to you. Which means playing up its faults.''

"I don't know exactly what he's found," she said. She looked at her watch. "Actually, I have to meet him out at the house in an hour. He said it would be easier if he could show the problems to me in person and then maybe recommend a few people who could do the repair work."

"Well, I'd watch out for that, too. I know plenty of people who can fix whatever you need fixed. And Glenn must, too, I imagine."

"I haven't told Glenn about any of this yet," she said. His eyes met hers. She hadn't said anything unusual or suggestive, but she hoped she knew the leap his thoughts had taken: secrets could be kept.

He was still looking into her eyes, not saying anything, and she thought about the night of the charades. Honestly, if no one else had been there, or if she and Roy had been able to go off alone somewhere together, she knew they would have made love that night. The memory had a long-ago, intensely desirable feel to it. She had been pregnant back then. Her life had held out so many more possibilities; she had been so much freer.

"Would you like me to look at the house?" he suddenly said.

"Oh. Sure," she said. "Do you mean now?"

He hesitated. "When is the real estate agent coming?"

"I'm meeting him in about an hour."

"I see. Well, maybe it would be more helpful if I showed up afterward. That way we could go over whatever he said."

Oh God. Was he really thinking what she was thinking? "You don't have to work?" she asked.

He spread his arms. She could remember the feel of them from that night—how strong they were. "I just told you I won my case," he said. "Naturally I have some work to do back at the office, but I don't have to be back at any particular time. It's the best thing about being your own boss." He took a long, slow, deep breath, and she did, too. He *was* thinking what she was thinking. They were already in tune.

"Well, then, come whenever you think the time would be right," she said. "I can't imagine that the agent would stay more than half an hour."

"Do you have to get home at any particular time?" he asked.

"The baby-sitter can stay till five," she said, looking into his eyes.

She couldn't wait for the man to stop talking. She wasn't interested; it was all clear, what he was saying, but he was repeating himself, and twenty-five minutes had passed.

"I think I have a good picture of what needs to be done," she said, moving toward the door. If necessary, she was going to walk outside so he would have no choice but to follow her.

"You do understand I'm not telling you that you have to make these repairs," he said for the third time. "It's just that the buyer deducts five hundred here and two hundred there, and before you know it, your selling price and your asking price are way farther apart than you can accept."

"I understand," she said. "I'll have the work done, and I'll let you know when it's finished."

"You let me know if you need any names," he said. He was still lingering. She felt like pushing him out into the driveway.

She reached for her coat and began putting it on. "I will." She held out her hand. "And thank you for the advice."

"Oh, you're going out? We can lock up together," he said, pulling out his keys.

"Actually, no, I'm just going to walk outside for a minute. I'll call you, though."

Finally he left—it seemed as if he had hung around for an hour—and Tessa went back inside.

A car pulled up as soon as the agent's car left, and she looked out the kitchen window.

Roy. Tessa felt exhilarated and excited and alive for the first time in she couldn't think how long. She didn't think about Glenn except for a flash.

"Oh, God," Roy said. He was looking up at the ceiling, and he was holding the back of his hand against his forehead.

"Do you have a headache?" Tessa asked.

He looked at her. "No. I just can't believe what I've done."

She didn't like the sound of his words. "Do you mean you wish it hadn't happened?"

He didn't say anything, and she sat up. "Roy, is that what you're saying?"

"No, no, not at all. God, not at all. It's just something I had thought about for a long time, and not let myself . . . I remember that night, but that was a long time ago.'' He sighed. ''I've never done anything like this in my life.''

''I haven't, either,'' she said.

He looked amazed. ''Really?''

She smiled. ''Do you mean I strike you as the type who has? Never, Roy. Not ever, not once.''

''I suppose I should be flattered, then.''

''You should be,'' she said, and she kissed his shoulder and inhaled his scent.

She wondered if she was falling in love with him. When she thought of Glenn she thought of a big, rubbery shape with no face, someone who would be waiting for her at home like a lawn ornament. He had never made love to her the way Roy had, yet she had thought she was happy all these years. Glenn had never been that breathless; she had never felt such intense pleasure. She couldn't believe how much more exciting it was to make love with someone who was forbidden.

''When do you think we'll be able to get together again?'' she asked, her lips against his skin. She loved how soft it was, yet how masculine. It was the way a man was supposed to feel. And he was a lawyer, someone who had gone to school for all those years, someone who had built a family and a life, and now he had chosen her.

''I don't know,'' he said. ''It's going to be difficult.'' His gaze slid to hers in the most languid way, as if he were touching her with every inch of his body. ''But we'll work it out somehow. I'm not ready to give you up by a long shot.''

''Roy,'' she whispered. She kissed him and leaned him back against the pillows, and then she trailed her lips along his body, slowly across his chest and down. This time was going to be slow and drawn out. She wanted it to be an afternoon Roy would never forget. She was sure she was falling in love with him, and she didn't think she had ever been so happy.

''I'm sorry, but it's simply unacceptable,'' Glenn heard Jim Morden saying in his office. ''We've hired you to write this history in a given period of time—one of the *reasons* we hired you was that you made it clear you could produce it in the allotted time. Yet, since you contracted with us, you've done nothing but malinger and report late each day. When you report at all.''

''It isn't a question of malingering,'' the woman said. ''I've had to register my daughter in a new school, and I've had to take her there myself—I haven't been able to find anyone to take care of her yet—and she's been sick on the very few days I was unable to come in. But I made it clear to you—at least I thought I did—that on the days I was home, I was working."

"I don't have time for this," Jim said, and Glenn could hear his chair scrape against the floor. It was how he always ended his meetings; he stood up, and the meeting was over. "Our board is meeting Friday at noon, and I intend to express my dissatisfaction with your performance. If, between now and then, you exhibit sufficient improvement, I'll reconsider my plans. But I'm not going to tell you one way or another until that day comes."

Glenn heard footsteps, and he moved down the hall to the coffee machine, where he had been headed before he overheard the conversation.

He turned to look at the woman. He had seen Caroline Leighton around Radicon a few times; she was pretty in a scattered sort of way—and he knew that she was an ex-journalist who had been hired to write a history of the company.

She was in tears as she came toward him, and he set his coffee down and stepped toward her.

But she walked past him.

"Wait," he said, and she turned around. She quickly wiped at her cheek.

"I'm sorry," she said. "I can't talk right now."

He began walking with her. "I just wanted to tell you something," Glenn said. "I couldn't help overhearing. Jim's bark is worse than his bite."

She was twisting her face against tears—he could see the strain of her muscles—and she nodded slowly. "Really," she said. She rolled her eyes. "I can't believe I'm crying. Just ignore this, all right? I'm not usually like this." She stepped into her office and motioned him inside. "Sit if you want. God. What a day."

He was shocked by her office. Plants had vined their way along the windowsill and up along the venetian blind ropes, and cacti covered almost every horizontal surface.

As if reading his mind, she laughed and said, "He *can't* fire me—he wouldn't know what to do with all my plants."

"Haven't you only been here a few weeks?" Glenn asked.

"This is our traveling collection. My daughter and I started it as a small project, and it just kind of mushroomed, and now I take them with me wherever I'm working. Sort of a good luck charm gone bad, I guess." She smiled again, and he decided it was a great smile, one of those smiles that could transform a woman from pretty to beautiful. She had fine, curly, light brown hair that fell softly to her shoulders, and hazel eyes that he supposed were what most transformed when she smiled. She flopped into her desk chair and motioned for him to sit in the other. "It's just not what I needed today," she said. "I really hope you don't think I'm always crying. It's just that today is really not my day. It started with a call from my bank that my mortgage check bounced and went down from there. Whew."

"Well, what I really wanted to say was that Jim Morden likes to intimidate people, and he has an excellent sixth sense for people's moods. At least twice—no, three times—I've left here thinking I had been fired, and not only am I still here, but I've been promoted three times since then."

"Really. What do you do?"

"I'm in research and development. But I started pretty low on the totem pole, when I was still getting my doctorate. And Jim Morden—well, just don't worry too much. I'm sure the board has no intention of starting another search. It took them a long time to choose you."

She looked pleased but as if she were trying not to show it. "Well, I certainly hope that's true. My daughter and I made the decision to stay on in the area after my husband left, and I'd like to be able to keep my promise to her. She's so attached to the house and the gardens—"

"How old is she?" Glenn asked.

"Three and a half."

He smiled. "Exactly my daughter's age. They should meet."

"That would be lovely. I want to switch Julie to a new school—your daughter isn't at the Family Nursery, is she?"

He shook his head. "Masters."

"Does she like it?"

"She loves it," he said, feeling the pride in his voice was justified. He knew that for some children, school was often cause for daily temper tantrums, and he was proud and relieved that Katherine looked forward to it.

"I think it's really hard to tell when the problem is with your child or with the school. Maybe 'problem' isn't the right word. But sometimes the school can be fine—which I think ours is—but the mix just isn't right." She sighed. "And I feel awful I haven't settled it yet. That's why I've been out so much, just looking around at other places, and, of course, taking her around for interviews. But if they're the same age, don't you think they should meet? I'm dying for Julie to have a really great close friend.''

''Absolutely,'' he said. ''We should set up a play date as soon as we can.''

Her face was radiant, and for a moment, he looked at her as if he weren't married. He tried never to do this—he felt it was wrong even to fantasize about anyone else, because he believed that you could lead yourself in the wrong direction if you gave in.

''Well, at the moment,'' Caroline said, ''Julie and I are sort of living like animals—it always happens to me when I'm in the middle of a project.'' ''She loves it—eating TV dinners and making tents all through the house, that sort of thing. But if your daughter doesn't mind, we'd love to have her over.''

''That would be great,'' he said. ''Are you feeling any better, by the way?''

She looked into his eyes and half smiled. ''Yes, and thank you. You know when you have the feeling you're just fooling the world and that any minute, you'll be discovered? I felt as if today were that day.''

''Well, I certainly hope I was right,'' he said.

For the rest of the afternoon, Glenn found it difficult to concentrate on his work. It had to be difficult being a single mother and dealing with a small daughter on one's own. He wondered when Caroline's husband had left her and why, and if she had asked him to stay or not. He wondered whether she had become bored and unhappy, as Tessa claimed Gail had become, or whether Caroline's husband had simply lost interest in her, or perhaps fallen in love with another woman. He didn't understand why so many marriages were falling apart. Yet, at the same time, he could feel a window opening at the back of his mind, and he was afraid to look to see what was on the other side.

''Are you almost ready?'' Glenn asked.

Tessa looked at herself one more time in the mirror. It would be the first time they had gone to church in months, and Tessa wanted to look her best. At first she hadn't wanted to go—Glenn was insistent they get back into it, partly because it was a week before Christmas, but also because he was feeling the loss of the church in their lives, he said—and she just hadn't been interested. Those *women* and their petty, judgmental theories. She could well live without their deciding whether she knew about children or not.

But then she realized Roy would be there. He would *have* to be! Vera was as devout a churchgoer as anyone in Lodenton, and certainly they would be at today's service, since it was so close to Christmas. Tessa had dreaded the involvement she'd be sucked into again—the committees, the meetings, the get-togethers—but if she were going to see Roy, it would be so worth it. And it would be so exciting to look at Vera and the other women and know that there was *one* thing they couldn't judge her for, because they didn't even *know* about it. And what they didn't know could hurt them—because even though she felt sure she was in love with Roy now, who knew how she would feel in a year? *None* of their marriages were safe.

Tessa had dressed Katherine in her true Sunday best, and she looked down at her and adjusted her hair one more time.

She wasn't a beautiful girl. She was definitely cute, but she wasn't beautiful the way Amanda was. Her hair—dark brown with auburn highlights like Tessa's—and her soft brown eyes like Glenn's were her best features, but she didn't look like an angel the way she had when she was born. It was probably the greatest disappointment of Tessa's life, and it had taken her a long time to admit the truth—surely it was just a phase, she had said to herself earlier—Katherine's eyes would grow farther apart, and her eyebrows would grow lighter. But she had finally realized her daughter just wasn't going to be a great beauty. At three and a half, you could tell so much; she knew from looking at pictures of herself at that age that you could. At Katherine's age, she had been a beauty—she could remember the comments, and she could see it in pictures.

But she would just have to hide her feelings from Katherine. Of course, she still loved her, certainly as much as she ever had. It was just one of the many disappointments she supposed people had to learn to live with.

And anyway, she had so many exciting things to think about for the near future. Seeing Roy. Thinking about the afternoon they had spent. Knowing there would be so many more. Knowing they shared a secret that would stun those stodgy, supposedly "sophisticated" women in that prissy little group. Plus there would be so much more time in which to get together now; Gail had closed the store, and Tessa had turned down the chance to take it over. Why would she be interested in something that had been such a failure when she had such an exciting new person in her life? She wanted to keep absolutely every free minute available for Roy and only for Roy.

The one part of the affair that she genuinely felt badly about was Glenn, though this surprised her. He was still obsessed with the breakup of Gail and Dave's marriage—he compared it to a strike of lightning, wondering how things like that could happen when one of the parties hadn't had any idea it was coming—and she did feel genuinely sorry for him. He was naive enough to believe that if two people loved each other, they could work out any problems that would ever possibly come up, and Tessa had noticed that he had begun taking books on relationships out of the library.

"That isn't something you can learn the way you'd learn geometry or chemistry," she had snapped a few days earlier. Beneath the pity, she felt an almost vicious disdain for his hopeful, workmanlike approach to the issue.

"I don't believe that's true," he had said, stolidly, and she had felt a rush of anger.

But that had been before Roy. Now she merely felt sorry for Glenn and his illusory world of theories and solutions. He had always believed that if you were good, good things would happen to you; when she watched him training the new puppy, she realized that, in fact, Glenn felt that the patterns applied to people as well. If you were good, and you sat when commanded, you would get a biscuit. And she felt that it was pathetic that he could be laboring under such a hopeful, inaccurate belief. But even so, she was glad he didn't know about her and Roy; she didn't want to hurt him. And as they walked into church, she was glad she had props like church to provide a structure and constancy to their marriage.

"Let us pray."

Roy was one pew ahead of them, over to the left. Tessa had let Glenn lead them to the pew, wondering if fate would be kind, and it had been. She could study the back of Roy's head and remember what it felt like to run her hands through his hair; she could study Vera for as long as she liked.

Vera wasn't an unattractive woman; with annoyance, Tessa could see that she had beautiful bone structure, a dainty, high-cheeked face that, with the right makeup and hairdo, would be beautiful. Their children were handsome, actually patrician-looking—a blond little boy and girl with perfect, tiny features. Tessa looked away.

"—and in this season of giving, it's important that we remember those less fortunate . . ."

Tessa looked at Glenn. He had a handsome profile, and he was listening so carefully to every word. His eyes, even the way he held his face up high, everything about him seemed so positive and full of hope. He was holding Katherine's hand—he was always touching her when he was close enough—and Katherine was resting her head against her father's shoulder.

For a moment, Tessa felt a bit of guilt—the man loved her so much—but then she looked over at Roy and thought of the afternoon they had spent together.

"—and this includes honesty in each task we undertake, in each exchange between ourselves and others, no matter how small. . . .

"If we look to our left—" Glenn turned, and Tessa smiled at him.

She could feel that Roy had noticed her, that he was looking at her, and she felt an almost uncontrollable urge to go over to him at that moment and put her arms around him.

After the service, Tessa moved toward Roy with her family as if she were being drawn to him by a powerful current. It was easy and fluid and swift—one minute the church was a jumble of people, and the next, they were out in the cold winter sun, and Roy was five feet away.

"Roy and Vera," Tessa called out.

Roy and Vera had been walking away, and Tessa was certain she had seen Vera stiffen when she had called out her name. Roy turned around right away, and Tessa felt that, for at least a moment, he had looked annoyed. But why? She was only going to say hello; she wasn't going to throw her arms around him.

"Oh, hello there," Roy said casually. He shook hands with Glenn and then Tessa. "Nice to see you two back here."

"Yes, well, we had felt it was time, what with the season and all," Glenn said.

Vera was hanging back, looking at her warily. It was only then that Tessa realized Vera might actually still be harboring some sort of grudge because of the night of the charades. But how petty! It had been years earlier!

"Lovely service, wasn't it?" Tessa said. "I'm so glad we've come back."

"He's always good," Roy said, looking around. He looked frightened and nervous, and Tessa was annoyed; she didn't want Roy to show vulnerability or fear; she wanted him to feel the same pleasure of their secret that she felt. "Oh, honey, there are the Gerards. I want to catch them before they leave." He said a hurried good-bye, and he led Vera and their children away.

Tessa couldn't think of anything else for the next few days. On Christmas Eve she and Glenn wrapped their presents for Katherine—the puppy had been her early present and it was certainly her main one, but they had bought all kinds of accessories, and there was a lot to wrap. Glenn wanted to go to the Christmas Eve service, but Tessa refused. There was too much to do, she claimed, which was almost true; she knew she couldn't face seeing Roy again in that kind of setting unless he were going to be more friendly.

And she felt cheated and powerless because there was no way she could call him. She knew he would want to hear from her. What was it he had said? "I'm not ready to give you up by a long shot." You couldn't get much more definite than that.

Cristmas Day felt like a blur to Tessa. In the morning they opened their presents, and of course Katherine loved everything, and then Gerald and Louann came over for a midday Christmas dinner. It was easy for Tessa to withdraw—whenever Louann was around, Katherine was on cloud nine—and Gerald, of course, didn't care whether Tessa was in the room or not. Glenn seemed distracted and slightly disappointed—"Why are you spending so much time away from everyone else?" he kept asking, and she said she had a headache.

The best thing about the day was that Glenn's mother had called to say she wouldn't be coming for New Year's—it was a painful, every-other-year tradition Tessa despised. But her pleasure over the news wasn't enough to lighten her mood. What she wanted to do was to call Roy.

She knew his home number—she had looked it up in the phone book on the evening after they had made love, just looked at his name and felt a surge of lust. She had memorized it, and now she was so, so tempted. And with Vera so shy and timid, what were the chances the phone would be answered by Roy? It was more than likely, she felt. Maybe even much more than likely.

She closed the door to the kitchen, and she picked up the receiver. As she dialed Roy's number, her heart was pounding. Just to hear his voice . . . it was all she wanted.

It rang once, twice—"Hello?"

It was Roy. "Hi," she said.

Silence.

"It's Tessa."

There was a pause, and then, "Sorry, you have the wrong number."

"Is Vera right there?" she asked.

A loud, sudden dial tone sounded in her ear, and she slammed down the phone.

A moment later, Glenn came in. "Is something wrong?" he asked.

"No. Why?"

"I heard you slam the phone down," he said.

He was looking at her carefully, the way he always did these days.

"It was nothing," she said, walking past him. "I knocked it off and I slammed it back on; that's all."

He caught her by the shoulders and turned her to face him. "Tess?"

"What?"

She had thought he was going to grill her, ask her a long, dull list of "relationship" questions he had learned in one of his books. But instead he took her by the hand and opened the door to the living room. "I just don't want you to miss this," he said quietly.

Katherine and Louann were playing with the puppy. Katherine was holding him up so he had to march like a human being— she had named him Patrick, the name of a boy in a story Glenn liked to read to her—and he seemed to be enjoying every minute of it. Louann was taking pictures with a Polaroid, and Katherine was ordering her when to "Snap," as she put it, and when to wait.

"I don't know when she's ever looked so happy," he said, squeezing Tessa's hand.

Tessa knew it was true. Katherine was a quiet girl, and she didn't smile often. Actually, Tessa had always felt that smiling made Katherine look less attractive, since her eyes tended to squint whenever she did.

But she was laughing with Louann, rubbing her face against the puppy's and commanding Louann to take more pictures, and it was a rare moment because she seemed completely happy and completely unself-conscious at the same time.

Tessa watched for a few minutes, but then she got bored. She wanted Christmas to be over, and she wanted to see Roy.

18

"You shouldn't have called me at home," Roy said. He was getting out of his car in her grandfather's driveway.

"Hello to you, too," she said. She didn't want him to be angry at her, and she was hurt.

He took his hat off and ran a hand through his hair. "I mean it," he said. "It could have been very upsetting to Vera."

"I'm not going to discuss it out here in the cold," she said, heading into the house.

He followed her in, and she hung up their coats. It wasn't the scene she had envisioned—she had fantasized that they would be tearing off each other's clothes before they were even fully inside the door; instead they were fighting.

"Listen," she said. "I'm sorry if I upset Vera—"

"You didn't upset her," he cut in. "She doesn't even know you called. But she could have found out. It was very poor judgment on your part, Tessa."

She didn't like being chastised or listening to the lawyerly tone he was using. "I'm sorry," she said. "As I said. I just wanted to hear your voice."

"But you realize that can't always be possible."

"Of course," she said. Her voice sounded brittle and defensive, but it was the way she felt. She didn't like being the needy party in the partnership; she didn't want to be like Glenn. "Look," she said. "I assume you came here because you wanted to continue to see me. But if this is too complicated for you—"

He held a finger to his lips and then moved it to hers. "Shh," he said, and then he covered her mouth with his.

The lovemaking was better than the first time, though Tessa wouldn't have thought it was possible. It occurred to her afterward that he made love as if his life depended on it, as if, at the beginning, he had to convince her physically to be with him, and then when it was clear she was his, he took her over the brink as a reward. She had never been with anyone so passionate—she had never felt so satisfied, so completely released when it was over. As they lay in each other's arms and she ran her lips along his skin, she fantasized about what it would be like to actually live with Roy instead of stealing afternoons as they were doing.

She felt that it would be paradise, and it made her burn with anger to picture Vera going to sleep in this man's arms every night. She had decided that Roy and Vera never made love anymore, that they hadn't, in fact, made love since they had conceived their children. How could he make love with someone so pale and bony-looking? How could he be as passionate as he always was with her, if he was making love to someone who looked as if she would break if you touched her?

She asked him once, although a warning voice had told her not to—she didn't want him to be angry with her, ever, but there were some things she just couldn't resist. "Are you and Vera still pretty active? I mean, do you still make love with her?"

She would never forget the look in his eyes when she had asked the question—even when she had said the name Vera—a bitter anger that seemed close to hatred. "Don't ask me about Vera," he had said.

"I just—"

"I'm telling you, Tessa, not to mention Vera when we're together," he had warned, and she had had to accept it. It was clear he wouldn't change his mind, at least until he was deeply in love with her—and then perhaps it would still be true, since the truth would be difficult for someone like Roy to face.

But she couldn't stop fantasizing about what it would be like, just the two of them, two people so passionately in love that they didn't need anyone else in their entire worlds. She felt so helplessly in need of him physically now; she felt she couldn't live without him.

And she wondered if this was the way Gail had felt with Walter, if in fact she still felt that way now that they had gone and were in New York. At first, when Gail had closed the store, she had felt a helpless anger that Gail's life could turn out so wonderfully. Why did everything always come so easily to Gail? But then she told herself the truth, which was that she, too, had a new love. And she felt that it was ideal, almost a sign from fate, that, suddenly, she could truly keep her time free for Roy; she wouldn't have to be bored at the store anymore, and now Mrs. Everson was with them every afternoon for when Katherine got home.

They began meeting at motels outside of Acton rather than at Tessa's grandfather's house—Roy said it gave him an uncomfortable feeling to be in that house, and he was worried that the real estate agent or someone else would show up unannounced. Tessa secretly felt that it was more likely they would be discovered at a motel than at her grandfather's, which was completely isolated and at the end of a dead-end road. But also secretly, she half hoped they would be discovered. She didn't let herself think about what would happen with Katherine if the affair were discovered—she didn't find it odd that Katherine was absent from all her fantasies about the future—but what she knew was that it was frustrating to feel so passionate about someone and not have anyone else know about it.

Katherine felt her mom was driving too fast, that it was like a ride on a TV show where the people at the carnival fell all the way to the ground. Mrs. Everson, when she drove, you could see everything and even wave if you saw a dog or a cat. Mrs. Everson said Lodenton was filled with people called "speed demons," and that they were bad people.

"I don't know if it's nine or nine-thirty that the mall opens at," her mom was saying. "Did you ever notice, honey? Does the mall open at nine or nine-thirty?"

Mrs. Everson was teaching her how to tell time, how there was a big hand and a little hand, but she didn't know the numbers yet. "I don't know," she said.

"Well, I guess it doesn't really matter," her mom said. "If we're early, we'll just wait."

Katherine didn't say anything, except that she knew her mom didn't like to wait. Katherine just hoped the little dots didn't happen in her mom's cheeks, because that meant she was going to get mad.

"I'm going to take you to a wonderful toy store," her mom said, "and maybe to buy some clothes, too, if the timing is right. Would you like that?"

"Uh-huh," Katherine said, except that she didn't always like to try on clothes if it took a long time.

They got to the mall and her mom was hurrying, holding on

tight to her hand and pulling her like she was Patrick on the leash. "Wait," Katherine said.

"I just want to be sure we get to the toy store when it opens," her mom said, and she pulled rush, rush, rush.

They got to the store—"This is Lulu's Lullabye," her mom said. "You were here with Daddy once, weren't you?"

"Uh-huh," Katherine said. She thought they were going to go in, but her mom was looking through the door with her hands on the glass. "Are there good toys inside?" Katherine asked. "Aren't we going to go in?"

"Uh, not just yet," her mom said. "I want to look in the window." She squeezed Katherine's hands tight and went to the other window.

"Ooh, Mommy, can I get the donkey?"

"I don't know," her mom said. "Do you really like it?"

"It would be a present," Katherine said.

Her mom smiled. "Really. For anyone I know?"

"Uh-huh."

"Let's see. For Daddy?"

Katherine shook her head.

"For Louann?"

Katherine shook her head. She loved guessing games.

"Hm. Would it be for me?"

Katherine laughed and shook her head again.

"Then who?" her mom said, and she didn't look so happy anymore.

"Miss Pine!" Katherine said, and she clapped her hands. She loved when a grownup couldn't guess. "She loves donkeys more than anything."

"You've given your teacher enough presents," her mom said. "And the card at Christmas and Halloween. I really think that's enough. Now tell me, which do you think is the prettiest?" She was looking in the window again.

"The dolls?"

"Uh-huh. Don't you think the blond one?"

Katherine looked at one and then the other and then the other. "Um, I think the lady with the brown hair," she said.

"Are you sure? But why?"

"She looks like Miss Pine," Katherine said. "Miss Pine wears her hair just like that. Plus she lets us make braids."

Her mom pulled at her hand. "Let's go in," she said. Katherine guessed she didn't want to look at the dolls anymore.

"Mommy, look, for Patrick!" Katherine said, because they had little coats for dogs that they could wear in the wintertime.

"In a second," her mom said. "You go over and look, honey. I see someone I know."

Katherine went over to look at the jackets. Mrs. Everson said it was the silliest thing she had ever seen when they saw a dog in a coat, but Katherine thought it was the greatest. Patrick would look so cute, and she already knew he liked clothes because she sometimes made him wear a nightgown when he went to bed.

"What a coincidence," she heard her mom say, and she looked over to the doorway.

It was a man from church; Katherine had seen him before. In church he always had two children who had red cheeks.

"What are you doing here?" he asked. "When I told you I was coming here for my daughter's present, I didn't mean for you to—"

"I'm here with my daughter," her mom said quickly. "Katherine saw something in here last week with her dad, and she was begging all morning for me to bring her here, so I figured for once it might be better to give in than argue."

He looked over at Katherine, and she looked away.

"Well, you're just about my daughter's age," he said, coming over to her and bending down. "You know me from church, right? My name's Roy. And you'd probably be the best person in the world to help me choose a present for my daughter, Jennifer," he said. "What was it that you liked so much?"

Katherine looked at her mom. She didn't understand why her mom fibbed.

"Honey, you can tell him," her mom said, coming over and putting her hand on top of Katherine's head. "Didn't you like that doll in the window? The one with the brown hair?"

"I don't know," Katherine said. She wanted to run away, but she could feel her mom's hand hard on her shoulder now, like a bone.

Her mom was smiling at the man. "You know how shy they are at this age. But I can show you if you'd like. What she was *begging* for this morning at breakfast was a little stuffed donkey, but I know she also loved the brown-haired doll."

Katherine watched her mom leave the store with the man, and she moved so she could see. Mrs. Everson said you should always be able to see the grownup you were with or you could get into bad trouble.

Her mom was pointing at the doll and then she did something funny, she put her hand out and she slid it into the man's back pocket and put her hand on the man's stomach. The man jumped and pushed her back like she was an enemy, and then Katherine's mom laughed.

Katherine turned away. She felt her face was hot on fire, and she looked at the jacket for Patrick, and she tried not to think about the thing she saw her mom do.

It was close to Valentine's Day, and Tessa was determined to reach some sort of turning point; she couldn't get over the fact that she and Roy had been together for more than two months! She had bought him the cutest valentine, and she had been certain she had chosen the right one. At first, she had been planning to be perfectly romantic. Glenn always was in his choice of cards—there were always hearts and roses and beautiful old-fashioned drawings, and she always thought they were lovely—but something had told her to stay a bit light. Then the sentiment, whatever she wrote by hand, could be romantic. The card was a drawing of two penguins holding hands in a cool, snowy landscape. Inside, the printed inscription said, "Who needs central heating when I've got you? Be my Valentine forever!"

Beneath the inscription was Tessa's chance to be more personal. She had always been proud of her penmanship—she had always felt that her script looked extremely sophisticated, like script that would be written by Faye Dunaway or even Jacqueline. At the bottom of the card, she had written, "I truly do love you, Roy," with "XOX, Tessa" underneath.

For three days, she looked forward to giving him the card. On Valentine's Day, he was able to take a late two-hour lunch, and Tessa couldn't wait; she would give him his valentine, and he would give her hers.

She arrived at the Starlight Motel and pulled up around the back, their usual place, next to Roy's Pontiac. She had brought the negligee he liked best, a black teddy with bikini underpants, and she felt sure it would be one of their best times ever together. She had told him many times that she loved him, but it was always while they were making love, always in the heat of passion. This would be different—written words, and then spoken, she hoped. It would be a milestone.

When she came into the room, she felt a flash of disappointment—secretly, she had hoped he would present her with flowers. In one of her fantasies, the room had been filled with roses, and Roy had swept her into his arms and said, "Next year, we'll be together, and I mean really together. But this is a start, Tessa." What she saw instead was a flickering television set in the corner, which made her feel Roy had been bored waiting for her; whereas with her, when she knew she was going to see him on any given day, she was so excited that she barely knew what to do with herself until he arrived.

"Happy Valentine's Day," she said as he closed the door. She pulled the card out of her purse and handed it to him, and she tried to read his face as he looked at the card.

"Thanks," he said, and he set it down on one of the bureaus. "Happy Valentine's Day to you, too." He took her in his arms and drew her into a long, deep kiss. She felt herself melting in his arms and needing to make love—it was always that way with Roy, it was just one of those attractions you couldn't fight. But now, she forced herself to pull back from him.

"Did you get me anything?" she asked.

"I'm not big on holidays, Tessa. Particularly if someone's not family."

She felt as if her heart were beating against the edges of her chest. "That means you didn't get me anything?" She knew what the answer was—he had made it perfectly clear—but she felt as if she were stuck on the question, as if she couldn't move on until she heard the word "No."

"I think being together is a lot better than a card," he said, brushing his lips against her neck. He held her against him, and she had to fight herself to stay clear; she wanted him, but he hadn't brought her a card! She just couldn't get over it.

"Don't," she said, turning her head. She moved away and looked into his eyes. "What about my card?" she asked. "What did you think of it?"

He shrugged. "It was nice. I told you. But this isn't that big a holiday for me, Tessa."

"What about what it said?"

He looked kind of pained, but then he took her in his arms again. "I didn't come here to fight," he said, and he took a deep breath. "I love you, too," he said, so softly she almost hadn't heard it. "All right?" he asked. "Is that what's bothering you?"

She was so happy she felt as if she were exploding, as if her body wasn't even her own anymore. "Let's not talk anymore," she whispered, and she kissed him on his neck and then lowered her lips down his chest as she unbuttoned his shirt.

19

"Happy birthday to you, Happy birthday to you—" Glenn felt like a huge cornball, what Tessa had once called him when she had seen tears in his eyes at a movie. It was Katherine's fourth birthday, and they had decided to celebrate just with the three of them and Patrick, Katherine's puppy. "Happy birthday, dear Katherine, happy birthday to you."

Patrick had been squealing during the song, but now he threw his head back and howled, and Katherine clapped her hands together and laughed and then hugged him. "You're so silly," she said. Her eyes were shining with happiness, and Glenn felt as he always did these days when he saw Katherine and Patrick together—almost pathetically grateful to Patrick for existing, because he seemed to be the happiest part of Katherine's life.

The party had been a compromise between Glenn and Tessa, one of the delicate balancing acts that made Glenn feel as if their relationship were made of glass. For years, Tessa had talked about how she was going to give Katherine the greatest birthday parties the world had ever seen. She had told him about her first party, which had been a disaster because her mother hadn't been able to face it and had left Tessa and Louann to fend for themselves. "I think birthdays are incredibly important," he remembered Tessa saying, and he had felt that now that Katherine was four, she would be old enough to choose the friends she wanted to invite from her school.

"I'd like Katherine to have a real party this year," he had said to Tessa three weeks ago. At first she had agreed, and she had said she would start planning the party. She had also agreed that she would call Caroline Leighton to invite Julie to the party. But every few days, when Glenn would ask if she had called, Tessa would say no. One night when he was talking about the party to Katherine as he was tucking her in, she had looked confused and said, "Mommy didn't say about a party," and he had realized Tessa hadn't even begun to plan it.

"She didn't ask you who you wanted to invite?"

Katherine had shaken her head, and he had felt the sinking of his heart that was too familiar these days, the edges of suspicions he didn't want to voice to himself.

Tessa was gone during the day at least a few times a week—he often called from work just to say hello, and these days to check. Certainly she had to do the shopping, and he hardly expected her to stay home and clean the house all day; now that she didn't have the store *or* Katherine, she would want to fill her time somehow.

But he felt his mind shut down when he asked himself the obvious questions. There were too many things going on anyway. He was worried about Katherine because she never asked to have play dates at anyone else's house, or if she could bring any friends home from school. He hadn't ever given it a thought until lately, actually; he had always been so happy to find her home every evening that he hadn't even questioned why she was always there.

But a colleague of his at Radicon had been talking the other day about how he and his wife were going out of their minds now that the visiting had begun. "Our house looks like an explosion at a toy store when I come home," he had said. "I'm so used to having two or three kids in the living room every day, I feel like we're running a nursery school." And it had struck Glenn then, and he had felt like a terrible father. Their house was too quiet; Katherine didn't have friends.

And the fact remained that Katherine was sick too often, indeed that she had been sick off and on for months. At first he had assumed that this was normal—in his reading about children, he had always concentrated on the psychological rather than the physical, assuming that this was the area in which he could make the most difference.

But lately it had become obvious that something was wrong—each week, Katherine would have a different complaint, sometimes even twice a week. After running various tests, the doctor had said that there was nothing he could find; he felt it was a phase that would pass. Glenn felt a rush of sadness when he heard the words. Katherine wasn't even quite four yet; she wasn't supposed to have phases like that.

On the issue of the birthday party and her friends, he didn't want to confront Katherine or question her; he didn't want to make her feel she was doing anything wrong, or that she was at fault. But he had questioned Tessa: why hadn't she said anything? How could they have a party for Katherine if she didn't have any friends? Why hadn't she begun planning the party?

Tessa had seemed calm and relaxed. "I really wouldn't worry," she had said. "*You've* picked her up at school. You've seen her playing."

It was true; he had. But she always seemed to be off on the sidelines. And he couldn't understand why, after all her unhappy memories of her own isolated childhood, Tessa wasn't making an effort to fill Katherine's life with at least a few friends.

"I think Katherine might not have felt comfortable asking Mrs. Everson if she could have friends over," Tessa had said. "Since I wasn't home in the afternoons. But now that I am . . ." She had shrugged, and he had tried to read the look in her eyes. She *wasn't* home in the afternoons, or was he losing his mind? "I really wouldn't worry, Glenn."

He had asked Katherine what she wanted to do. If she wanted a big party, they would invite anyone she wanted. Did that seem like a good idea? She was holding on to Patrick, her body wrapped around his at the end of her bed, where he had his "nest," a collection of old blankets and towels he liked to sleep against. "Maybe just us," she had said in a quiet voice. "And Louann if she can come."

"You don't want to invite anybody from school?" he had asked gently, trying not to let his voice show too much concern; he didn't want her to think she had done anything wrong.

She had shrugged and then shaken her head. "Just us," she said again quietly.

"Do you want to invite just one little girl?" Because he had heard her mention names—Marlie and Jennifer and Kristy. He hadn't been lax or asleep, had he? "What about that girl Marlie you sometimes mention? Or a little girl who's the daughter of a lady I work with? Her name's Julie, and her mom said she'd like to meet you."

She had shaken her head and then laid it down against Patrick's neck. "Just us," she had said.

And so that was how it had ended up, and Louann hadn't been able to come because of a concert she was helping with in New York. "Open this one first," Tessa said, handing Katherine a small pink-wrapped box tied with a purple ribbon.

He watched Tessa and tried to imagine what for him was

almost unimaginable. Was hers the face of someone who was having an affair?

"Oh, Mommy, I love it," Katherine said. She held it up to Glenn—it was a silver necklace with an amethyst heart—and then she draped it over Patrick's forehead. "Patrick loves it, too," she said.

"Let me help you put it on," Tessa said, and Katherine turned as Tessa fastened the clasp behind her daughter's neck.

There could have been a thousand reasons Tessa was gone so much, he told himself. He had asked her some of the times, when he had gotten home from work, and they were innocent enough questions, completely natural. "So what'd you do today? Did you do much shopping?"

And she hadn't seemed nervous or suspicious or hesitant. And he had to ask himself why he was suspicious, both as a husband and as a scientist. If you had a theory, what were the reasons behind it? Was it instinct, which he questioned as a valid starting point, or were there facts that had led you to pose the questions?

He was afraid and unable to answer his own questions. Sometimes, he wondered whether he was even half hoping that she *was* having an affair, because that would be something specific, something that could be corrected. The thought was terribly painful to him, but the other possibilities sometimes seemed worse. When had she changed from the young woman with so many dreams to someone who seemed bitter and angry so much of the time? When had she changed into a woman who didn't seem to love him?

"Daddy, look!" Katherine cried, and he smiled. They had bought her three complete outfits for her dolls, and she seemed staggered that there were so many.

He looked at Tessa, and she turned as if she could feel his gaze. For a second, she looked distant and secretive. But then she melted into a smile, and he told himself he was wrong.

He went into the kitchen for a glass of water and sat down for a moment. A few seconds later, he heard the clicking of dog nails, and Patrick came in and immediately sat at his feet—he had learned that sitting was always his best chance for getting praised.

"What do you think?" Glenn asked, looking down at the dog. Patrick was gazing up at him hopefully. "Do you think I'm being paranoid or not?"

Patrick looked up at him with liquid brown eyes and thumped his tail, and Glenn put his head in his hands.

It was May 1, and Tessa felt good. The real estate agent for her grandfather's house had finally gotten a good offer, and it was a beautiful day, and she was in the arms of the man she loved. She had been nervous for a week after Katherine's birthday, tearing her hair out, really, because Roy had said he couldn't see her. But this morning he had called her and said he had time free at lunch, and she was certain that his lovemaking had proven she had been wrong in her fears. "Sometimes I just feel so good," she said, stretching like a cat. Glenn had once said it was one of her sexiest moves, and she had made it a point always to do it in front of Roy. "I was worried when we couldn't get together. But then there are afternoons like this, and I realize that what we have is something that can go on for a long, long time—that it almost has to because it's so good."

Silence.

"Roy?" She moved so the length of her body was up against his, and she looked into his eyes, but they were closed. "What's the matter?" she asked.

He rubbed a hand across his forehead and then opened his eyes. "I'm just not sure how much longer I can continue to lie to my wife," he said. For a moment, she had a leap of hope; he was going to tell Vera that he was in love with someone else. He was going to leave her, and he was going to ask Tessa to marry him. But then he said, "I see myself distancing myself from the marriage much more than I ever thought I would. I don't like lying to my wife."

"But you're not really lying," she said. "You're not telling her about it, but you don't tell her every little thing that happens during the day."

He shifted so he could look into her eyes. "You're not serious. You can't possibly see this as a 'little thing.' "

"I don't," she said. "But if we don't tell anyone about it, I don't see how anyone can be hurt."

He swallowed again, and she could tell that his throat was dry. "My wife is being hurt by my withdrawal. I can see it, and I can feel it. You can't possibly argue that that isn't hurtful, Tessa."

"If it were a perfect marriage . . ." She hesitated. "What I think is that if it were a perfect marriage and everyone was doing the absolutely perfect thing, and then one person stepped out, I would say that was wrong. But obviously we don't have perfect marriages. If we did, I don't think either one of us would be here.''

He didn't say anything for a few moments. Then he got out of bed and said he had to get back to work.

''We still have fifteen minutes,'' she said.

He shook his head. ''I have to get back.'' He wasn't looking at her. He was pulling on his pants, avoiding her eyes, avoiding her. She could feel it. It was the beginning of the end.

''Roy?''

''What is it?'' He was stringing on his tie, and at least now he had glanced back at her, if only in the mirror.

''Are you trying to say you feel our relationship is coming to an end?''

He was avoiding her again. He had swung around, and he was pretending to look for his jacket, even though he had to know it was under her clothes; it almost always was. ''I just think we should slow down,'' he said. ''For me the guilt is starting to outweigh the pleasure.''

''You certainly didn't sound that way half an hour ago,'' she said.

His face darkened. ''I have to go,'' he said. He brushed his lips against hers. ''Are you all right here?''

''Fine,'' she said, although she wished she had gotten dressed with him. But she had been so upset over what he was saying.

For the rest of the week, Tessa felt as if she were going out of her mind. The buyer for her grandfather's house had backed out at the last minute, so they were back to square one with that; and Katherine came down with a nasty flu and had to stay home from school, which meant that Tessa couldn't see Roy, since Katherine was home all day every day. She felt trapped and angry and restless.

''But I don't feel good,'' Katherine was saying. She was almost crying, but Tessa was sure Katherine simply didn't want to go back to school.

''You just sit by the sidelines if you don't feel like playing,'' Tessa said, tucking a lock of Katherine's hair behind her ear. Katherine looked pale and thin, but Tessa was certain she was fine. She hadn't had a fever in two days, and she had to be careful about catering to Katherine's fears. You didn't become popular by staying home; she could tell Katherine all the details about that if she wanted.

"There," she said when she had finished tucking Katherine's hair back. "Now it looks like I'm riding in the car with a beautiful little girl instead of a kitchen mop. Did you know that you look like a kitchen mop when your hair's not back behind your ears?"

Tessa thought there was the beginning of a smile on Katherine's face, but it was hard to tell. Sometimes it was so hard to tell what she was thinking; she always seemed to be watching and thinking, watching and thinking. It reminded Tessa of her own childhood; looking back, she could remember knowing more than she should have at her age, and she didn't want that ever to be true of Katherine's life. She wanted Katherine's life to be perfect, to be filled only with happiness and the most wonderful memories in the world.

She pulled up to Katherine's school and got out of the car.

"Mommy loves you," she said when it was almost time to go in. She was kneeling on the gravel, which was cutting into her bare knees, but what did she care about her knees or pain when it meant she could be close to her daughter, rubbing noses with Katherine and trying to make her laugh? "Patrick said you'd better stay un-sick so you can go swimming with him this weekend. Would you like that?"

"He said it? Really?"

"Absolutely. This morning while I was getting dressed."

Katherine was frowning. "I want to hear him talk."

"One of these days you will, I promise." She looked at her watch. It was time for them to go in. "Now, do you love your mommy?"

Katherine nodded.

"Tell me, honey."

"I love you," she said in her squeaky little voice.

"Do you love me a lot?"

She nodded and looked around, which annoyed Tessa. Katherine never wanted to have a long conversation about love.

"In how many languages, honey?"

"My teacher's going in," Katherine said.

"But how much? You haven't *told* me."

"I love you, je t'aime, te quiero, ti amo forever and ever and in a thousand ways," Katherine said, and Tessa relaxed. There was nothing more rewarding than having your child look up into your eyes and tell you how much she loved you.

* * *

Roy looked different when he opened the door, and she tried not to think about what it meant. "Come on in," he said quietly.

Don't let him say he wants us to stop seeing each other. It just wouldn't be fair; she wouldn't allow him to do it.

"Listen," he said after he had closed the door.

She knew her eyes were wide with fear, and she felt like a child.

"I'm afraid I wasn't completely honest with you the other day. Come on and let's sit down."

"I don't want to sit down," she said. "Just tell me how you weren't honest."

He took a deep breath. "I think we have to stop seeing each other," he said.

"You think?"

He sighed. "All right, I know. We have to stop seeing each other."

"Would you care to tell me why?" She was amazed that she was able to control her voice, able to stop herself from hitting him.

He swallowed, and the fact that he seemed nervous made her more so; he was going to mean it this time. No sidestepping. "I just can't go on like this," he said. "It was fun at the beginning, and it seemed easy. I didn't think we'd be caught, and I didn't think my feelings would enter into it much at all." He paused. "I liked you, certainly, but it seemed as if we were both interested in an uninvolved affair—something that wouldn't ever lead to anything else."

"I've never told you I wanted anything else," she said. Which was absolutely true—she had been so careful.

"I realize that," he said. "But I find it impossible to maintain the kind of family life that I realize I want to maintain. I can't do it and see you. And I've come to care about you too much. It's just something that has to come to an end."

She was careful not to say anything. She was concentrating on the words he had said—I've come to care about you too much. If he cared so much for her, how could he want it to end?

"If neither of us wants any more out of it," she finally said, "I don't see why we can't just keep seeing each other."

He shook his head. "I've made up my mind, Tess. It had to end sometime. Do you know that a friend of mine saw me driving out here the other day? He wanted to know if I had been on my way up to Philadelphia."

"And?"

"And that makes me nervous. I don't want people to see me out on the highway all the time. We're going to get caught."

"We were never caught," she said. "Don't confuse your fears with reality, Roy."

He moved toward her, and he put his hands at her waist. She refused to believe this would be the last time she'd ever feel his touch. "Roy," she whispered, and she tried to kiss him.

He moved away.

"Fine," she said. She picked up her purse, and she walked to the door. "If that's the way you want it, fine. I'm not going to stand here and beg."

"Tessa, I care a lot about you."

She slammed the door and got into her car and began to drive. She drove past Whittington and Bellclare and East Plainview. She drove until the clouds burst and she could barely see through the windshield. She turned around at a gas station and began to head back, and she turned on the radio to see if she could get the weather.

"—at three-fifteen in Acton, we have rainy skies and—"

She looked at her watch and nearly ran off the road. Three-fifteen. That meant Katherine had been let out of school forty-five minutes earlier.

She checked her watch again. But the radio had said it, too. It was three-fifteen, and her daughter was either waiting for her at school in tears, or they had called Glenn to come and get her.

Tessa sped up, but she could go only so fast. The roads were slick, and the rain was coming down in buckets, and she realized Glenn couldn't have picked up Katherine because today was the day he and his co-workers were going to tour some factory that used parts manufactured by Radicon. So the school wouldn't have been able to reach him.

There were a few cars in the lot at the school, and Tessa felt a flood of relief—one of Katherine's teachers had stayed with her.

But when she went inside, her footsteps were the only sound. She couldn't find anybody around.

Finally, at the end of a hall, she heard something, and she went running. A man was swabbing down the floor with a mop.

"Excuse me," she said. "Isn't anybody else here?"

"Nope," he said. "You looking for someone?"

"Yes, my daughter. Has Miss Pine gone?"

"Everybody's gone," he said. "Friday the place cleans out like an earthquake's hit."

Now she felt a cold panic starting at her fingertips. She began looking for a phone—maybe they had reached Glenn somehow?—and she heard footsteps.

"Excuse me," the porter said, running toward her. "Is your name Stokes?"

"Yes."

"I found this note," he said. "One of the men was supposed to give it to you, only he went home early. It was taped to the door, and I didn't see it."

She tore it open and read it. Another mother, Laura Celenko, had taken Katherine home with her daughter. The teacher had tried everything and hadn't been able to reach Tessa or Glenn, and she hoped everything was all right.

Tessa was so relieved she almost began to cry. "Thank you," she said to the man. "Thank you so much. Have a good weekend."

She drove to Laura Celenko's house, which wasn't far from theirs, although in a much more working-class section of town. The door opened as soon as Tessa pulled into the driveway, and Laura Celenko came out, holding Katherine's hand.

"She was very, very upset," she said, looking down at Katherine. Tessa could see that Katherine had been crying. "But she knows Tracey pretty well, so once we all got home and had some hot chocolate, everything was just fine, wasn't it, Kathy?"

"It's Katherine," Tessa said, following her in. The house was furnished simply, but it was the most spotless house Tessa had ever seen in her life. "I appreciate what you did, though. I hope I can return the favor in some way someday."

"Oh, not at all," Laura said. "I just hope that your emergency or whatever it was has been resolved."

"Emergency?"

Laura Celenko looked surprised. "The reason you couldn't come pick your daughter up."

"Oh, right. Well, you know flat tires. They always hit at exactly the wrong time."

Laura Celenko nodded, and Tessa wondered if she believed her. But why wouldn't she? Why wouldn't anyone? She wasn't going to worry about it, because it could have been true even if it wasn't.

"Tracey let me play with her dog today," Katherine said. "She said our dogs could play together when Patrick gets old enough. She said they go together because Patrick's brown and white and Lucy is white and brown." She leaned down and kissed the top of Patrick's head, and Patrick gazed proudly at Glenn as if to say, See how much she loves me? Even if I turned the garbage upside down yesterday, I'm still a good dog.

"Not while you're at the table," Tessa said sharply. "You have no idea where that dog's nose has been, Katherine."

"You went to a friend's house after school today?" Glenn asked.

He looked over at Tessa and was surprised to see her looking angrily at her daughter.

"Whoops," Katherine suddenly said, covering her mouth.

"What's the matter?" Glenn asked.

"It was a secret," Katherine said. She looked terrified.

"It's okay, honey. You can tell him," Tessa said. She looked at Glenn. "I had a flat tire today so Katherine had to go home with Tracey's mother."

He looked confused. "Why would that be a secret? What's going on?"

"Nothing," Tessa said, shrugging. "It was just a game."

"What are you talking about?" Glenn asked. He felt a hollow sourness in the pit of his stomach and anger beneath. What did she mean, a game?

"Nothing," Tessa said. "I said to forget it. I don't know why you're making such a big deal about it. I had a flat. I called the school and told them to send Katherine home with Tracey's mom—"

Katherine jumped up and ran out of the room.

Glenn looked at Tessa and stood up. "I'm going to get to the bottom of this," he said, and he walked out.

Katherine was in her room, on the bed with Patrick. She was facing the wall with her arms wrapped around the dog, and her chin resting on his head.

"Honey?"

She didn't answer, but he saw her hand move, slowly stroking Patrick's forehead.

He knew he had to be careful. Something had happened, and he couldn't expect her to speak against her mother. She had looked absolutely terrified when she'd realized she'd revealed a "secret."

"Are you feeling bad?" he asked, sitting down at the edge of the bed. He reached down and slowly stroked her forehead. "Does that make you feel better?"

She nodded her head. "Patrick loves it, too," she said in a small, high voice; she was fighting tears.

"Is there anything you want to tell me?" he asked. "You know that when you're feeling bad, I like to know why, because sometimes I can make you feel better just if we talk about it," he said. "Even when bad things happen," he added.

Silence.

"Honey?"

"I can't," she said quietly, and she wrapped herself tighter around Patrick.

"Did you get my card?" Tessa asked.

There was silence at the other end of the line.

"Roy? Is this not a good time?" Because it always had been before; if she wanted to call him at the office, she could call before nine or after five, and chances were he'd pick up.

"Tessa, would be better if you didn't call."

She closed her eyes. That wasn't what he was supposed to say.

"Did you hear me?" he asked.

"Of course I heard you. I'm just sorry you feel that way," she said. "You said you cared a lot for me, and this is your birthday. I wanted you to know that I care for you, too."

"Well, thank you," he said. "But you really shouldn't have sent it here."

"Would you rather I had sent it to your house? I marked it 'personal,' Roy."

"That isn't the point," he said. "I don't want to get any more mail from you, Tessa."

"It was just a card," she said. "It's not as if I've been sending you notes every day."

"I know," he said. He was using his patient voice, the one she had heard him use on his wife once after church. "But I'd appreciate it if it stopped right here. There was a reason I said we should stop seeing each other."

"I realize that," she said. "You're making an awfully big deal about a birthday card, though."

She heard him sigh. "All right," he said. "Well then, good-bye."

"Good-bye? That's it?"

Silence.

"I love you," she said. She hadn't meant to say it—it had just slipped out.

"Good-bye," he said, and he hung up.

She stared at the phone, and she wanted to scream.

20

"She's mine and you can't touch her," Katherine said, and she burst into tears.

Glenn ran over and knelt beside his daughter. "Katherine, that isn't very nice to Julie. She's letting you play with all of her dolls, and you brought just one. You can let her play with Rebecca."

"She's mine," Katherine said with narrowed eyes. "She's mine, and that girl can't touch her."

Glenn looked up at Caroline, who smiled and motioned for him to come back.

"I'm sorry," he said when he got to her. "I thought they'd really hit it off."

"Oh, don't worry about it," she said, sipping at her tea. They were sitting on a wonderful old bench that had been built around a huge oak tree in her backyard, and Glenn felt as if he were in another part of the world. It was quiet out here, far from any other houses, and he felt more relaxed than he had in months. "It always happens this way—parents try to choose their children's friends, *swearing* they've made the perfect choice, and half the time it goes over like a lead balloon." She looked out at Katherine and Julie, sitting far apart on the lawn, each with a small, determined-looking collection of dolls and doll clothes. "But I have the feeling they'll hit it off eventually." She smiled her dazzling smile at him, the one he tried not to think about. "And it's not the end of the world if they don't. We can still be friends."

"Yes, of course," he said. He knew he sounded stilted and awkward; it was because he felt stilted and awkward. "Friends," Caroline had said, and he considered her a friend. Since that day he had warned her about Jim Morden at Radicon, they had spoken often at the office—at first every few days, and then somehow it had slipped into an everyday routine. Her office was near the coffee machine; his was near one of the Xeroxes. She often asked him about products the company had developed, things she needed to know for her project. And he always asked her things in a roundabout way, never quite coming out and completing the *real* discussion because he felt it was wrong. When he and Tessa were planning Katherine's birthday party, and he found out that Tessa had done nothing to plan the party, he asked Caroline many questions about how she handled Julie's birthdays. Yet he had never come out and asked the most important question of all: did she think it was wrong of a mother to let something like that slide? Did she think it meant anything that Tessa seemed to be gone a lot? Did she think . . .

Then he had realized he had to take things into his own hands more. If he was worried about Katherine's not having friends, he could help her on his own; it was Tessa's responsibility only because she was home more; but if she couldn't take it on, he would take it on himself.

"Oh Lord, look at them now," Caroline said.

Julie, a wiry-looking little girl with dark hair and nearly coal-black eyes, was pulling at a doll's sweater or dress—Glenn couldn't quite see—and Katherine was pulling back for all she was worth.

"Girls," Caroline called out. "Julie, is that Emily's sweater?"

"It's mine," Julie called out. "Emily is my doll, so it's my sweater."

"It's going to be your rag if you don't stop pulling on it," she said, walking over to them. "Now, listen, you two. I have some material in the house, and Julie, you know how to make tunics for your dolls. If I bring the material out, will you show Katherine how to make them?"

Glenn smiled as he watched Julie shrug. She was reluctant—why pass on a good piece of information to a girl she didn't like?—but it was also clear that she was proud to know how to make something, and that she saw it would be a chance to show off.

Caroline was already walking into the house, and when she came back, it was with a shopping bag full of colorful pieces of material. Glenn watched as she threaded two needles and handed one carefully to each little girl, and he watched Katherine's face as she listened wide-eyed to Caroline as if she were in the presence of a wizard.

"There," Caroline said, smiling as she came back and sat down. "Julie's always happy when she can lecture someone—I had never heard a lecture in such a tiny, piping-high voice until I heard her the other day absolutely *lecturing* another little girl about the mysteries of cloud formations. It was the most ridiculous thing I had ever heard."

He loved the way she looked when she was talking about her daughter. And he realized suddenly that she spoke about Julie in a way that he had never heard Tessa speak about Katherine—with a sense of humor. With Tessa, it always had to be a compliment or a statement of disappointment about their daughter. Of *course* Katherine would be the best at something in her class, eventually; she would *have* to be. But then, ten minutes later, she would be eyeing her daughter critically, warning her not to frown or boys wouldn't want to date her when she got older.

He felt he was realizing and seeing too much by spending this time with Caroline. He was seeing Tessa's flaws too clearly; he was seeing things in Caroline he wished he saw in his own wife.

"Look at that," Caroline said, setting down her tea. "They may end up being friends yet."

Julie was leaning over and showing something to Katherine, their cheeks close as they huddled together over the small, colorful scraps.

"That girl just loves to be in charge," Caroline said.

"I think my wife is having an affair," he said. He had said it into the air . . . to the clear, blue sky, to the oak tree, to the lawn. The words had come out on their own, and he felt more surprised than Caroline looked now that he had said them.

She was looking more thoughtful than surprised. "What makes you think that?" she asked.

He told her of his suspicions, of Tessa's absences and her odd "secret" with Katherine.

"How would you feel if it were true?" she asked.

"I don't really know," he answered truthfully. "It's almost funny, because I feel I've worked so hard—I don't want to sound self-righteous, but I believe in marriage, and I believe in making it work, and that means certain disciplines—you just don't even look at another woman." He felt he was lying as he said those last words, because he had begun to look at Caroline in that way, hadn't he? "But suddenly I feel I've been working for something I'm not even sure about anymore. I feel that Tessa's looking to get out in the same way that she's always been looking to get out of Lodenton. I lost sight of that somewhere along the way—"

"Lost sight of what?" Caroline asked.

"Maybe I lost sight of what she saw in me," he said. "When I first met her and we decided to get married, it was all so quick. I had fallen in love with her, and it didn't occur to me that she might see me as some sort of ticket away from home. But looking back, I remember how excited she was by the idea that we might move to Palo Alto or Phoenix or New York." He sighed. "Maybe I was unfair not to move more quickly, but I didn't feel I had finished at Radicon." He stopped and didn't say anything for a few moments. He knew he was looking at the problem at its edges because it was all he could face. But he knew what the real problem was; he could feel it. "I think the problem is that she doesn't love me anymore," he said quietly.

"Right this way, please."

Tessa walked past Roy's secretary as she opened the door to Roy's office, and she girded herself for what Roy's reaction might be. She had felt triumphant when the secretary had made the appointment for her—using a false name had been easy, and Roy had had no idea. She knew that if she could just see him in person, she would be able to change his mind. She just had to get past his first, inevitable anger, and everything would be all right again.

He looked astonished and angry as the secretary showed Tessa in.

"Miss DeLaFrance," the secretary said, and Tessa swept into the room as if she really were French.

"Thank you," Roy said hoarsely.

"Would you like some coffee or tea, Miss DeLaFrance?" the secretary asked.

"Coffee would be wonderful," Tessa said. "With cream if you have it."

"We have milk. Is that all right?"

"Fine."

Tessa sat back in the chair across from Roy and smiled.

"We'll wait until Judy comes back with the coffee," he said in a tight, controlled voice.

"Fine." She looked around at the shelves of books on the walls, the beautiful mahogany paneling and brown leather furniture. It was what a lawyer's office was supposed to look like, and she was impressed. "I like your furniture," she said.

He just looked at her.

"I assume that's real leather?"

He didn't say anything. The secretary brought Tessa's coffee in, and Roy told her to hold all calls.

Tessa was starting to get a bad feeling.

Roy leaned forward and folded his hands the way the principal at Tessa's school had always done. He looked as if he were preparing to talk to a child. "I don't want you to come here," he said in the same newly hoarse voice.

"Do you have a cold?"

"I don't know," he said. "We're not talking about me."

"Vera should take better care of you," she said.

"I don't need taking care of," he said. "I need to be left alone, Tessa."

She swallowed. She didn't like the conversation at all. She looked down at her hands for a minute, and she pictured how only weeks earlier they had rubbed Roy's shoulders, run through his hair, touched him everywhere. "I really don't see how you can just turn off your feelings and pretend that you didn't say all those things to me," she said. She looked into his eyes. "I don't see how you can tell someone you love her, and then the next week you don't even want to see her."

He shifted in his chair, and she could see he was nervous. "I've told you," he said in that overly patient voice. "I've told you that I made a decision to concentrate on my marriage." He narrowed his eyes. "I don't understand what you think I owe you."

"I don't think you *owe* me anything," she said. "It's not that. I'd just appreciate it if we could be friendly. I'd like to talk to you once in a while." She shrugged. "That's all."

"Come on." He put his hands flat on the table. "I think we both have to agree that, for at least a while, we can't see each other."

"We see each other at church every week."

"You know that's not what I'm talking about."

"But how long a period are you talking about?" she asked. "Are you saying we can be friends after a month or two? It would help me to know."

"Not a month or two." Now he was sounding impatient. "Tessa, it's over," he said harshly. "You're going to have to realize that at some point, sooner or later. And the sooner you see it, the happier we're both going to be."

She didn't say anything. She couldn't say anything. He sounded so definite, as if his mind were so permanently made up.

"I don't love you," he said suddenly. "I never loved you. I said it on Valentine's Day because I felt pressured, and if I said it at other times"—he looked embarrassed, and she hated him—"sometimes people say things in the heat of the moment. But I never loved you. And at the moment, I can't say I like you very much, either."

She stood up. She didn't say anything. She wasn't going to make a scene. She was going to leave quietly so she could preserve her dignity. That was what someone with a perfect background would do, and that was what she was going to do.

She walked out and shut the door quietly, and she walked outside to her car and tried to calm herself before starting the engine.

But her hands were shaking. It wasn't fair. He had said he loved her, and now he was saying he didn't . . . that he never had. That he didn't even like her.

She drove away from his office and was tempted to drive to Katherine's school and take her out for the afternoon. What she wanted was someone who loved her completely, and she knew she would feel better if she felt Katherine's arms around her neck. But it was so unusual for Katherine to be in school for three days in a row—it was always something, usually her stomach, and Tessa knew that Glenn would be furious and suspicious if she went and picked Katherine up.

But when she pulled into her driveway at home, she felt a rush of anger at the house and at Glenn, and beneath that, a sadness that made her suddenly think of her mother. It was at times like this when she wished she were anywhere other than Lodenton, that she was certain she was touching at the edges of what her mother had felt all those years. And it frightened her. She was strong; her mother had been weak. Her life had nothing to do with her mother's; it was silly to even think about.

When she let herself into the kitchen, the dog jumped up on her, and she pushed him away savagely. "Leave me alone," she said. The dog sat down, but the minute she looked down at him, he thumped his tail and looked at her as if he expected some sort of praise.

"Stop staring at me," she said.

And then she had a brainstorm. She felt almost as if her body were on fire as she took out her writing paper and her best pen. Her hands were filled with energy, and she wrote as quickly as she could, almost breathlessly.

Ten minutes later, she had finished. Oddly, she felt physically relaxed now that she was finished, as if she had just run ten miles, or had just made love.

Dear Vera,

I realize this letter might possibly come as something of a shock to you—I don't know—but Glenn and I are preparing to join Reverend Travis's encounter group for married couples, and I've heard that one of the prerequisites for joining the group is total honesty in one's personal relationships.

I thought long and hard about writing this letter, but I feel that in the end, it will help us both.

Your husband and I had an affair, which has just ended. It was physically passionate, but what I feel is important for you to know is that your husband decided to end it because he loves you very much. He has told me on many occasions how much he loves you, and although I assume there are problems in your marriage—why else would he have come to me for his physical satisfaction?—it is clear that these problems must be repairable, or Roy wouldn't have broken off the affair.

I should tell you that I'm writing this letter in an emotional state—perhaps tomorrow I'll regret having written it—but doesn't Reverend Travis always talk about the importance of honesty? And truly, I feel that no marriage can be rebuilt unless it is examined down to its foundations; with the knowledge I have given you, you can work to repair the obviously promising relationship that has remained.

I love my own husband, and that's why we're hoping to join the Reverend's marriage group. I hope that this will help you—I don't know—but I felt I had to write it, whatever the cost.

Sincerely,
Tessa Stokes

"Now, honey, we're going to go to the doctor, and you're going to tell him what's wrong, all right?"

Katherine nodded. She was afraid, sometimes, to tell the doctor, because sometimes his eyes looked like he didn't believe her. But it was the truth; her stomach felt funny almost all the time, like she was going to throw up all over everything.

"Do you still feel sick to your stomach?"

Katherine nodded again. Patrick was licking her hand so she was almost laughing, except for her stomach. "It hurts a lot," she said, and she held it because Mrs. Everson said sometimes that would make you feel better. What helped the most was if Patrick lay down with his head on her stomach, but he couldn't when she was standing up on the floor. Then second was if Mrs. Everson made her cambric tea and read stories to her, or if her dad did.

"You look so cute with your little hat and that little purse," Katherine's mom said. She reached out and tucked Katherine's hair behind her ear, and Katherine closed her eyes for a minute. She liked it when her mom touched her like that. "Just like a little doll," she said.

Katherine thought about the dolls at Julie's house and the things they had made called "tunics." It was like magic how Julie's mom knew how to make so many things.

"After the doctor's we'll go right to your school, all right? Unless he says you have to go to the hospital."

Katherine felt more pain in her stomach. "The hospital?"

"I'm sure he won't," Tessa said. "But if he needs to take more tests, he might have to send you. If he still can't figure out what's wrong with you."

Katherine thought about how she had seen hospitals on the TV, all white plus sick people and lots of doctors. "I don't want to go," she said.

"Well, you might have to," her mom said. She was looking at herself in the mirror, and Katherine felt she looked like a fairy princess.

"But would you come?"

"Of course. How could I not go with you?"

"What about Patrick?"

"Patrick wouldn't be able to come," Tessa said, putting her coat on. Patrick started to bark. "Not now!" Katherine's mom yelled. "Not *now!*"

But Katherine saw why he was barking, at the door.

"Mommy, there's that man," she said. "The one at the store." The one her mom had put her hand into his pocket.

Her mom went to the window. "Roy," she said in a funny voice, like she thought Katherine wasn't even there.

"Wait here," she said. "Mommy just has to go to talk to a

friend of hers." She looked at her face in the mirror again. "Be *quiet,*" she yelled, and she picked up a book and threw it at Patrick. It missed, but he ran away.

"Just a minute," she called. "You," she said, and she grabbed Patrick by the collar and put him in the cellar and shut the door. "You stay in the living room, honey, okay?" she said. Then she ran to the door, and Katherine walked to the hallway to see.

She opened the door and said, "Whew. Sorry you had to wait. As you can see, we have rather a crazy dog."

"If you ever do anything like that again, I'm going to sue you for harassment," the man said, stepping in.

Katherine saw her mom's mouth open in a funny way. "Do you mean the letter?"

"Do I mean the letter? Hell, yes, I mean the letter. What the Christ was in your head when you wrote that, Tessa?"

Katherine knew it was bad to say "Christ" like that, and she felt a pain in her stomach that was sharp like a knife.

"I don't know what you mean," her mom said.

"Did you think that was going to get me back?" the man yelled. "Did you think it was going to make me *like* you? How did you think it was going to make my wife feel?"

"I don't care how your wife feels," Katherine's mom said.

The man made a face. "That's pretty obvious. Although I loved the way you pretended you were only writing the letter in the interests of honesty. Nobody's as stupid as you think they are, Tessa."

"Well. I'm happy to hear that. Is that why you came over here?" Her mom's voice sounded funny, like she was maybe about to cry.

"I came over here to tell you that if you ever write or speak to my wife again, I will personally sue you until you'll wish you had never been born. Do you understand?"

Katherine dropped her purse on the floor and said, "Whoops," and looked up.

"Oh," the man said. He was looking right at her all of a sudden. "Sorry. I didn't realize your daughter was home."

"Get out," Katherine's mom said.

"I'll get out but you've been warned," he said. "I meant every word, Tessa."

"You'd better get out of here now," she said. Then the door made a big banging sound, and the man was gone.

* * *

"What did the doctor say?" Glenn asked. He was amazed that his voice had come out normally, indeed that it had come out at all.

He had never imagined that he would have a day like today, that he would wake up as if the morning were going to be like any other morning, and then be confronted with a letter like the one that Roy Donahue had brought over to Radicon.

And it was strange, he felt, but somehow good that today was also the day he had had to call Katherine's doctor to find out what was going on, because together, the two pieces of news had enabled him to think much more clearly than if he had gotten either one by itself.

He would never forget Katherine's doctor's words—"At this point, Glenn, as I told your wife, I think there's genuine cause for concern. I feel that Katherine is crying out for attention she might not be finding at home."

He had calmly told himself that the two events had acted as catalysts, creating a reaction that he hadn't allowed himself to contemplate seriously until that afternoon. He had had so many days and nights of doubts about Tessa, questions and fears he hadn't been able to answer definitively.

Then this afternoon, he had told himself that it was good the truth had come out, because now he could base his decisions and feelings on the truth rather than on suspicions and doubts. Now he knew answers to questions he had asked himself for months. Knowing the truth was always a good thing.

But here, looking at Tessa, he felt heartbroken. She was the mother of his child.

"It's the usual," Tessa said, unwrapping frozen manicotti and putting it in the microwave. "He said there's nothing wrong that he can see." From the back, he could tell she was hesitating, debating whether to tell him more or not.

"Interesting," Glenn said. "Is that all he said?"

"Pretty much." Tessa punched in the timing instructions and turned around, but she still wouldn't look at him.

"Funny, that's not what he said to me," Glenn said.

Tessa looked at him, and she looked genuinely surprised. "You spoke to him?"

"I called at eleven to see what had happened. He told me everything he said to you." He paused. "It's very upsetting to think that Katherine likes to go to the doctor because it's a place where she can feel loved. I'm surprised you don't feel that's unusual enough or important enough to tell me."

Now she looked guilty, and he took a small bit of pleasure in that, but he also found it sad beyond words. It was all over.

She shrugged. "I don't tell you everything he says," she said, trying to sound casual. "And I don't happen to agree with what he said. The *essence* of what he said, in my opinion, is that he doesn't think there's anything organically wrong with her. Which is what he's always said. It's a phase."

Glenn shook his head and looked down at the table. He didn't know where to begin, where to end. "I think it's very sad," he finally said.

"I think it's sad that you would trust the word of a doctor you barely know over my word and my opinion," Tessa said. "And I find it amazing and infuriating that you would suggest or even think that somehow it's my fault, when there's *nothing* I wouldn't do to make Katherine better. Nothing."

He looked into her eyes. "Roy Donahue showed me a letter today," he said. Again, he was amazed that he could get the words out. In the car on the way home, he had choked at even the thought. But now he felt strangely calm.

She looked surprised again. She walked over to the table and picked up a cigarette, put it down, and then picked it up again and lit it. "Well, then," she said. She took a long, deep breath and leaned back against the sink. She shrugged. "Sorry."

He shook his head again. "You know that I always try—I don't always *succeed*, but certainly I always try—to find the best approach to everything," he said. "If there's a problem, there has to be a solution, and if you try hard enough, you'll be able to find it." He swallowed. "If there's a problem in a marriage, it should be fixable.

"But I don't think that's true anymore," he said. "I read the letter, and I don't see how it could be true, and I don't see how I can continue to live with you anymore." He had said it, and in a strange way, he felt relieved. "The person who wrote that letter, which was so obviously designed to hurt, isn't the person I want to have raising Katherine."

Tessa looked amazed. "She's my daughter, too, Glenn."

"Then I don't see how you could have done what you did. I just don't see it. What I see is someone so unhappy—I see all of your railings against Lodenton, against life, against everyone you know—they're suddenly more important than ever, because it's obvious to me that you're so unhappy that you *have* to leave. You've created a situation that calls for your leaving, Tessa. It's as simple as that."

She opened her mouth and then closed it. "I would never give Katherine up," she said. They were words he had feared, the words he most feared in the world, but her voice was hollow and weak. It was clear she was afraid.

"This would be a trial separation," he said calmly, as he had planned. "There would be no reason to jump into anything. But obviously, if you moved somewhere else—if you moved to New York, say—it would make sense for her to stay here with me, since you wouldn't be settled." He heard a thump upstairs—the sound of Patrick jumping off Katherine's bed—and then footsteps in the hallway and on the stairs.

He went around to the stairway, feeling somehow that he had to head Katherine and Patrick off, that Katherine would be able to feel the tension in the kitchen just by walking in.

He watched her come down the stairs next to Patrick. She had put one of her doll's caps on his head and tied it under his chin, and he had the pleased, proud look that was always in his eyes when Katherine was paying even more attention to him than usual.

"Daddy, Patrick's pretending to be a doll," she said. "His new name is Kathy."

Glenn started to laugh, and he held out his hand. But as she put her hand in his, he began to cry, and he wiped a tear away before they turned the corner and all went into the kitchen together.

BOOK TWO

21

Tessa had been in New York for three weeks, and they had seemed like the longest three weeks of her life.

It had been easy to leave Lodenton, easy to walk out of that house, except for saying good-bye to Katherine. But she hadn't even cried when she had done that, because she had told herself that the separation would be extremely temporary, and she had told Katherine the same thing.

It was a dream come true—she told herself this every day, that she was finally living in the city of her dreams. But what she hadn't been prepared for was how settled everyone else was, and how out of place she would feel. She was staying with Gail and Walter. Louann and Gail had both offered—although neither had been very enthusiastic—their apartments as temporary places for Tessa to stay, but the fact that they both had apartments only made Tessa feel even more out of place.

Yes, Tessa had known that her little sister was no longer all that little, that she had graduated from Juilliard and was now working for a record company—but Tessa hadn't been prepared for how pretty or polished Louann would look in what was now her home city. After seeing Louann, Tessa had gone and gotten her hair done and bought an entire new wardrobe, but this was yet another thing to worry about. She was racing through the cash portion of the settlement—her share was almost thirty thousand dollars—and at least two nights a week, she woke up drenched in sweat after dreams in which she had spent every cent and ended up with nothing.

When she thought about the money, she felt the same spiraling, helpless feeling—a sickening combination of ambition and confusion—she always felt when she thought about the future. This was the chance she had dreamed of; she had finally left

Lodenton, something her mother had never been able to do; she had a nest egg of money; she was ready.

Yet, three weeks after she had arrived, almost nothing had gone right. Tessa's one hope was that the appointment she had set up for that afternoon would be the turning point—she felt it with the same instinctive sense that had told her she should write the letter to Vera: true, no one had reacted as she had hoped, but the letter had set into motion a chain of events she would never regret.

And the appointment's secrecy, she felt, would give it strength, the way sex with Roy had been so amazingly pleasurable because it was secret and against the rules. Secrets were her specialty; secrets were where you had a chance to succeed.

The odd part, to her, was the fact that her new, brilliant idea had stemmed from a fight she had had with Gail last week. She had gotten up early and was reading the *Times* classifieds and making coffee for herself—dressed perfectly reasonably, she felt, in a T-shirt and underpants—when Gail had come into the kitchen.

"Don't you have a bathrobe?" Gail had snapped. Tessa hated it when people snapped that way, and she knew for a fact that Gail considered herself to be so well brought up.

"As a matter of fact, I don't," Tessa said. She had brought almost nothing with her from Lodenton, because she didn't want to look as if she came from anywhere but Manhattan.

"You'd better get one if you plan on staying here," Gail had said, in a voice that Tessa felt was just shockingly tense given what they were talking about. It wasn't as if she was standing there nude!

"This is more than a bathing suit, what I'm wearing," Tessa had said.

"Look, Tessa, I'm not going to argue about it. If you're going to stay at this apartment, I won't have you walking around half-dressed, especially when Walter spends so much time at home here. I'm not even going to discuss it anymore," she had said, and stormed out as if Tessa had committed some sort of terrible crime.

And that was the turning point, the moment when the whole course of what Tessa hoped would be her future in New York City had suddenly become so clear. She would work where Gail worked! Gail handled publicity for restaurants and stores and would probably soon graduate to handling some actors' and actresses' accounts as well.

Tessa felt as if a bolt of lightning had hit her. Suddenly it was so clear: through the business Gail was involved in, wasn't there a good chance, even an excellent chance, that Tessa would meet wealthy and successful people every day?

Initially, Tessa had resisted asking Gail questions about her job. She had preferred to remain ignorant rather than to seem less sophisticated or knowledgeable than Gail. But once the idea had struck, she swallowed her pride and began asking Gail all the questions she had wondered about.

Gail was vague at first. She was getting back into her work gradually, she said, part-time; Dale Sylvan, the owner of the agency, was letting her work that way because they were old friends and because she had been "damn good," she said immodestly. What did a person need to break into the field? Well, she couldn't really say. It was harder these days than it had been back when she had started.

"But people must start every day," Tessa had persisted. "They must have some sort of talent or skill the agencies are looking for."

Gail had shrugged. "With me it was that I could type, and I could think on my feet. I started as an assistant, but I worked my way up pretty quickly, because when you work with Dale, you either rise very quickly or you're fired in a week."

"Why?"

"Because he's a little crazy," Gail said. "He's extremely demanding and difficult, and he's also exceptionally dishonest. I've never met anyone who lies as much as he does, just for the sake of lying. Some people end up quitting because they can't work in that kind of atmosphere. But he happens to be excellent at what he does, and he's rolling in money. But there aren't any openings," Gail had said flatly, "so don't get any ideas about working there, Tessa."

Tessa hadn't liked that, at all. Gail had said it the way girls in eighth grade had said things to shut Tessa out. We don't need any more cheerleaders.

"But you could find out," Tessa had pressed. "You could ask. You could tell Dale about me so that if there *are* any openings in the next few weeks—something you might not even know about—he would call me."

Gail had shaken her head. "There's nothing," she had said. "I know it, Tessa."

"But you just said that people get fired all the time."

The look in Gail's eyes had said it all; she wasn't going to ask if there were any jobs, because she didn't want Tessa to work there. And that look had made Tessa want to work there more than anything in the world. It didn't seem strange to her, as it might have to someone else, that this was a career she had never considered before in her life, yet suddenly it was an obsession. It didn't matter that she barely knew what the job involved. She wanted to work there; if Gail felt so protective of her position, there had to be something wonderful there. And if Gail minded, well, so what? Once Tessa got a job, she wouldn't need to stay at Gail and Walter's apartment anymore anyway.

And so, she had written what she felt was the best letter of her life—addressed personally to Dale Sylvan and filled with references to her admiration of him and her lifelong dream of working in public relations. Yesterday, she had gotten a call from someone named Margery O'Connor, his personal assistant, and she was on her way to an interview there at one o'clock.

She knew Gail would be at the office today, but she didn't care. Gail didn't own Sylvan Associates.

The office, in a high-rise tower off Third Avenue, looked exactly the way Tessa would have designed it in her fantasies—salmon and chrome and black leather, everything sleek and modern and corporate-looking, but with a twist. Where other companies probably had photographs of their chairmen on the walls, Sylvan had pictures of all kinds of movie stars, politicians, even artists whose faces Tessa recognized. She announced herself to the receptionist and sat down, and she took out her résumé to be sure she had memorized all of the "facts"— manager of a boutique in Lodenton, which was true; and then the embellishments—publicity assistant for the *Lodenton Chronicle* (she had no idea whether they even had a publicity department), floor manager at Main's Department Store (it would show she had management potential, even at such a young age), assistant to the dean of students at Acton College (to show that she could deal well with all kinds of people).

"Miss Stokes?"

The receptionist led Tessa down a hall that had small offices on either side. Tessa looked at each one as she passed, and in one she saw Gail at a desk, talking on the phone. Gail looked up as she passed, and Tessa just had time to catch the expression on her face: surprise and annoyance. Well, too bad.

"Mr. Sylvan will be right with you," the receptionist said, and she left Tessa alone in the office.

It was a room Tessa wanted to own someday. The basic decor

was the same as the reception area—black leather couches and
chairs, a chrome and glass table, a glass-covered entertainment
center with some TVs and VCRs. And covering the walls were
more pictures of famous people, pictures of events Tessa could
recognize even from across the room—the Miss Universe pag-
eant, the Macy's parade, a group of actors from the soap opera
"Coronado."

She heard the door open, and she turned around.

"Have a seat," Dale Sylvan said, walking past her. "I have
to make one call, and then I'm all yours."

He sat down behind his desk, and Tessa studied him as he
made his phone call. He was very tan, with light brown, full
hair; he was probably in his mid-forties, but he had a strangely
smooth face that looked as if it had come out of a Jello mold.
His suit was expensive—it was the kind of suit she had seen on
the so-called "Dapper Don," John Gotti, on the news—and he
was wearing a ring on each pinky.

"Arno, it's Dale," he was saying. "My girl said you didn't
have the tickets. . . . No, you get them. . . . Uh-uh, Tuesday's
no good. It's tonight or that's it. . . . *Right.* We understand each
other." He hung up without saying good-bye, and then he swiv-
eled to face Tessa. He glanced at her and then picked up a piece
of paper she could see was the résumé she had sent in the mail.
"So. You saw our ad on Friday?"

"No," she said, surprised. "I wrote to you because I wanted
to work here. I didn't even see an ad."

He smiled. "Assistant at PR agency, late hours, no shrinking
violets, let me see, what else did we say?"

"I would remember it if I had seen it," she said. And Gail
hadn't told her about it.

He leaned back in his chair and studied her. "You're a very
pretty girl," he said. "Beautiful, actually."

"Thank you."

"Don't let anyone ever tell you that doesn't help you in the
business—in this business or any other."

"All right, I won't," she said, smiling. She liked the way he
looked as if he could be a singer in Las Vegas, or even a gang-
ster. He was so different from anyone she had ever met in Lodenton.

He was looking down at her résumé. "So, let's see. You
managed a store—" He stopped. "Lodenton? Do you know
Gail Hendrickson?"

Tessa nodded. "She owned the store, actually."

He looked interested. "She know you're here?"

"Actually, no. She had told me about this place—that's why I'm here—but she didn't seem to think there would be any jobs."

"But you wrote to me anyway."

"That's right."

He nodded and went back to looking at the résumé. Then he tossed it onto the desk. "So tell me which of these things are true. You were at the store, and what else?"

"It's all true," she said.

He smiled. "I can pick up the phone and call your friend. Is it still all true?"

She swallowed. She wanted the job. She wanted to meet actors like Arlen McGinnis and Jake Rodino and Pete Scanlon. "Why don't you tell me what the job will involve," she said. "Maybe it's something I won't even want, and we can both save ourselves some time."

"You'd want it," he said. "I can tell from a mile off that you'd want it. It's scutwork and it's glamour, and if you're any good at all, you'll get a lot less scut and a lot more glamour before you even know it's happened. You type, I assume."

"Eighty words a minute," she said. Which was stretching it, but she could practice.

He leaned back and laced his fingers behind his head. "Let me tell you something about this business. We stretch the truth a little bit, sometimes more than a little bit, every day of the week, twenty-four hours a day. It's the nature of the business; it's the nature of the beast. I like an employee who's not too hung up on the absolute truth, who knows how to get a client's name into the paper however he or she can do it. I like an employee who's not intimidated by people just because they're famous. We're all human beings, you know? If you're afraid of someone because they're famous, or you're afraid to call up a newspaper, you can forget it. What I *don't* like is for anyone who works for me to lie to me, Dale Sylvan." He set his hands down, and he leaned forward. "So now you tell me how much on that résumé is true."

She swallowed again. She was going to do anything she could to get the job; it sounded so *easy*. "All right, none of it, actually, except the part about the store."

He looked blank. "None of it. You're sitting here wasting my time, and you don't even type?" He picked up the phone and started to buzz the receptionist.

"I type," Tessa said. "I thought you meant the jobs."

He put down the phone. "Look," he said. "It's crazy around here right now—I'm trying to juggle ten things at once, we're down one assistant, I can't think straight. But I'll tell you what— come back at, say, six, six-thirty, and we'll talk about it some more."

"Six-thirty this evening?"

"Sure. Why not? Are you busy? There's a lot of working late in this job. Two, three times a week at least."

"I could come back," she said.

"Great. We'll talk some more, and I'll see how you do."

She looked into his eyes. She supposed it was obvious; why would you have to come back for an interview, except for one purpose? She tried to imagine what it would be like to sleep with him, and she had to admit that the idea was pretty unap- pealing. The closer you got to him, the more he looked like a mannequin. His hair seemed to be a toupee; his skin looked as if it had been stretched and then sanded; his tan looked half like a salon job and half like makeup; and even his hands looked false—she had never seen such elaborately manicured hands on a man.

"I can introduce you to Flip Casey," he said. "You ever hear of him?"

She shook her head, wishing she had.

"Yeah, well, you will soon enough. He's going to be the next Shandling, the next Leno. He's opening over at the Comedy Club tonight. You can catch his act."

"Great," she said. So maybe it wasn't what she had imag- ined.

"Yeah, I always need more people to handle the press—you know, the kits and everything. You'd be good at that. Everyone likes a pretty girl." He looked at his watch. "So you come back then, and I'll get you all set up. We'll see how you do in a crowd."

"Great. I'll see you then," she said.

She walked down the hall and looked as she got to Gail's office. Gail motioned her in.

"What are you doing here?" she asked. She reached out with her toe and swung the door shut.

"I'm interviewing for a job," Tessa said.

"I told you there wasn't anything."

"Well, you were wrong. I'm going to help out tonight at the Comedy Club"

"Are you serious? Do you mean you got the job?"

"I don't know. He wasn't that clear."

Gail threw her pen onto the desk. "I'd really rather you didn't work here, Tessa."

"Why not?"

"Because it's where *I* work. I've established myself here. It's too much to have you living at my apartment and then working here, too."

"Look. You never came out directly and said don't come."

"I didn't think I had to. Anyone else would have sensed it."

"Well, it's too bad. I'm going to work here if I get the job, Gail. It's the best offer I've had since I've gotten to New York. I mean, it's the *only* offer, but so far it's the only thing I'd even want. And if Dale wants to hire me, he'll hire me."

"Dale? You call him Dale?"

"He likes me," Tessa said with a shrug. "I really think I have the job."

Gail didn't look happy about it, but what could she do? And Tessa intended to start looking for an apartment immediately if she got the job.

She left the office and went to Bloomingdale's and then to Sak's and Lord and Taylor. At the end of the day, when she went into a coffee shop and totaled up how much she had spent, she was stunned: almost eighteen hundred dollars. But she would need the clothes more than ever now, if she were going to have to go to nightclubs and restaurants and different places at night. The clothes were going to be as necessary for her as Glenn's stupid white lab coat was for him.

When she got back to the Sylvan office, she was surprised when Dale opened the door himself. She had thought there would be other people there, getting ready to go to the club.

"What's all this?" he asked as he followed her back to his office.

"Oh, I just had to do a little shopping," she said. "I'm going to need a lot of new clothes if I'll be going to nightclubs and things like that."

He half smiled, but she couldn't read him. His skin and features were so oddly smooth—he had obviously had some sort of plastic surgery—that they didn't move in any kind of natural way. "Sit down," he said, motioning for the couch. "What can I get you to drink?" He pressed a button, and the wall unit opened up to a bar. Tessa had never seen anything like it except on TV. She wanted one for herself.

"What are you having?" she asked.

"Scotch," he said.

"Then I'll have the same," she said.

He brought the glasses back to the couch, and when he sat down, she realized he had put on a lot of aftershave, something she hated because it was what Gerald had always worn. She tried not to think about it as he made a toast.

"To your future in New York City," he said, "whatever it may be."

She drank a sip and set down her glass. "So what about tonight?" she asked. "I assume I can leave all my bags here, by the way."

"No problem," he said. "But what *about* tonight?"

"Well, what will I be doing? Maybe it would help if I saw a tape of Flip Casey, or . . . I don't know."

"This is what would help," he said, taking her hand and putting it on his thigh. He set down his glass and pulled her into his arms, and she tried to think about how much she wanted the job—how Louann had lived in New York for years and Gail already worked for Dale, how everyone had an exciting life but her—as he pushed her down against the cushions of the sofa.

22

The tears were streaming from Katherine's eyes, and Glenn held her head against his chest and stroked her hair. "But it's just a splinter," he said. "We'll take it out and everything will be all right. Hold out your hand."

"I can't," she said into his chest. She had made her right hand into a fist and pushed it under her left arm. "I want Patrick," she said.

"Patrick is right here," Glenn said. Katherine's best friend was sitting in front of them, amazingly calm because he knew that something was wrong. He was looking at Katherine with such concentrated seriousness that Glenn would have laughed under other circumstances. How could a dog who was still a puppy be so earnest at times? When he was trying to look serious and be an important part of the family, he always looked more comical than ever, Glenn felt: a brown-faced dog with a too-wide forehead and an alert, aren't-I-good sitting posture that made Glenn smile every time. Ever since Tessa had gone, it was as if Patrick had known he had to turn over a new leaf and grow up. He still followed Katherine almost constantly—literally dogging her—but Glenn had even noticed a change in Patrick's gait. He seemed to be guarding her rather than wanting to play. He was looking out for her constantly. "Patrick thinks you should let me look at it," Glenn said. "Okay?"

Katherine squeezed her eyes shut tight and then opened one of them a crack. "How can you tell?" she asked.

"Look at the way he's looking at you," Glenn said.

With two pairs of eyes directed his way, Patrick couldn't stay serious for too much longer; he began shaking his shoulders and licking his chops, and Katherine started to laugh.

"Silly," she said, and Patrick leaped up and licked her face.

242

"So we'll all look together," Glenn said, directing a warning look at Patrick, who immediately dropped to the floor. Glenn held Katherine's fingers in his hand and looked down. "I don't see it," he said, gently edging the only spot that was red. He moved the lampshade so light fell more strongly on Katherine's finger, but he couldn't see the splinter. "It was there, where I'm touching?"

Tears sprang from her eyes again as she nodded her head. "But it's not black anymore because it's gone."

"Then we don't have to take it out," Glenn said, holding her against his chest and stroking her hair. "Honey? What's the matter?"

She was sobbing now and she turned and cried into his chest. "Rickie Vallen at school said that if you gots a splinter and it goes inside your body, it goes to your heart and you die. He hitted Chris Sweeney with a board and then he said it, that Chris Sweeney was going to die."

"Oh, sweetie, that isn't true." She was crying so hard now that he didn't know if she was even hearing him. "Katherine, listen to me." He stroked her hair again and then pushed her back so he could look into her eyes. She rubbed them with her fists and then finally set her gaze on him, those pale blue eyes that made him melt every time. "I can remember hearing the very same thing when I was your age, and I can remember being afraid that a splinter would travel to my heart," he said, because it was true. How easy it was to forget those childhood fears, until you were confronted with them again. "I can even remember who told me the story. It was a girl named Rebecca, and do you know that for as long as I knew her, she was always telling people things that weren't true?"

Katherine squinted up at him. "How come?" she asked, putting her thumb in her mouth. He knew it was something Tessa hated—she said it would make Katherine bucktoothed, and that it made her look "slow." Maybe it was true that she was old to be sucking her thumb, but she only did it when she was upset. He didn't think it was the end of the world.

"Some people are just like that," he said as she leaned back against his chest. "Sometimes people just want to upset other people, to see if they can scare you. And sometimes they really believe those things themselves. But that doesn't make what they're telling you true. And the story about the splinters is very old, and very untrue."

"But what if it's true and you just don't know it?" she asked, kicking against his leg for a moment. "What if it's true and I'm going to die and never see you again or Patrick or Mommy?"

He couldn't help noticing the order of worry, and he couldn't help being pleased. He had forced himself to be fair to Tessa when he was talking to Katherine: no cheating, no suggesting that Tessa was anything less than wonderful. When he read or heard about parents who tried to poison their children's minds against the other parent, his heart ached for those children. "I promise you, you don't have to worry," he said. "I promise, Katherine."

She was silent for a while, but it was a silence of tension; he could feel it in the way she was sitting. "Also, Rickie Vallen, he said that his cousins got hurted in a fire, and that you never know if you'll wake up and smell smoke and you won't even be able to get out. He said his cousins almost died."

Glenn wanted to kill this Rickie Vallen, whoever he was. From the class list, he had been able to tell that he was new, but that was all. "There isn't going to be a fire, and there isn't going to be a splinter, and everything's going to be okay," he said. "I know that that might seem easy to say, but I know what I'm talking about, Katherine. Those aren't things you have to be afraid of, ever. There's no reason to be." He looked at his watch and gave Katherine a pat on her hip. "But if we don't start getting rustled up and ready, you're going to be late again for school."

She climbed off his lap and marched across the room in her nightgown, a small slip of cloth that made her look like a street waif. It was torn, and he had tried to throw it out the other day—it wasn't worth mending or having Mrs. Everson fix it—but Katherine had found it and had pleaded to keep it. "It's Patrick's favorite," she said, and he had had to stop himself from smiling. He had learned that when she was afraid to say something about herself, she would say that it was Patrick's wish or idea or dream. And he had realized right then that so much of her world was uncertain with Tessa having left that even something as seemingly insignificant as throwing out a nightgown could loom far more largely than he had imagined in Katherine's heart.

He watched as she gathered her socks and underwear from the drawer of her small bureau. "Patrick brang me my socks yesterday when Mrs. Everson said we were going out," she said, tearing off her nightgown and throwing it on the rocking chair he and Tessa had bought at an antiques store when Tessa was still pregnant with her. "Mrs. Everson said maybe she could teach Patrick to sort the socks during the day when I'm at school. Do you think?'' she asked, looking sidelong at him in a shy way that told him she knew it was a silly idea.

He smiled. ''What do you think?'' he asked.

She stepped into her underpants, and he felt his heart turn over as he had a flash of the future. ''He seems so smart,'' she said, looking over at the round dog bed that Patrick lay on only when Katherine was up and out of bed. Patrick thumped his tail, and Katherine smiled. ''But I don't know.''

She had stopped being a baby years ago—she was four, and he knew it hadn't happened overnight. But her shape seemed to change every day, and sometimes when he looked at her, or when he bathed her, at expected times and also the most unexpected, he could see her as a woman, dark-haired and probably beautiful like her mother, and he was filled with pain and dread and fear. He was supposed to want her to grow up and be happy and successful, and certainly he did. But realistically, he had to admit that he didn't really want her to grow up. She was his in a way that would lessen every day and every year.

''Daddy, could I wear the pink instead?''

''Which pink?'' he asked. ''You mean the pullover?''

She nodded and opened the bureau drawer. ''Julie Leighton has the same shirt, I saw it at her house, and we said we're going to dress like twins if she comes to my school.''

He smiled. She finally had a real friend. Last week when he had gone to pick her up at school and had watched her through the classroom door, he had seen a shy girl who hung back when the other girls gathered in the corner to play with the dolls, a girl who raised her hand so tentatively that the teacher couldn't even see it. But now she had a friend, and he knew it would make all the difference in her life.

''Her dad lives in California,'' Katherine said, squirming when he buttoned the top button of her blouse. ''Not that one or I'm choking,'' she said.

He unbuttoned it and stepped back. ''So you were talking about her dad?'' he asked.

Katherine nodded and then looked down at the floor. ''Do you think Mommy will call today?''

''I don't know,'' he said. ''We'll try to call her tonight when

I get home from work. And you tell Mrs. Everson that if she calls before I'm home, to be sure to tell Tessa to call back."

Katherine nodded. "Do you think she's going to come home in four days?"

He frowned. "I don't think so, no. That would surprise me. Why would you think four days?"

"She said maybe on the weekends she would come, and Mrs. Everson said that was in four days."

"Well, that's something we'll have to ask her," Glenn said.

"Do you think she found a fun job yet?" she asked.

"I don't know," Glenn said. "That's another thing we'll have to ask her." He tried to sound unemotional and unconfused when he answered Katherine's questions about her mother, but he couldn't understand anything Tessa had done, from the contact she had had with Roy Donahue to her leaving. He couldn't understand how she had left the small person he would give his life for, and he couldn't understand how, after promising to call every night, she had simply stopped. "It's too expensive to keep calling," she had told him. "And I'll be there to see her as soon as I can on the weekend."

That first night after she had left, getting into the bed and feeling the cold pillow at his side gave him a feeling he couldn't explain even to himself; he guessed it was panic and sadness and anger all rolled into one. And fear, because he felt he could never trust his feelings again. The woman he had felt that he loved, the woman he had married, had apparently never even existed.

"Daddy?"

"Yes, honey."

Katherine had pulled on her sweatpants and was looking at herself in the mirror. "If Mommy wants me to come to New York are you going to go, too? And Patrick?"

"I don't know," he said, feeling as incapable and confused as he always did when the subject of her visiting came up. There was something about the idea and all the attendant truths underneath that made him feel like a small, helpless boy. He and Tessa had spared Katherine, if only by some sort of default, the screaming arguments he had been forced to listen to as a child. But now that they were living quietly and separately, two hundred fifty miles apart, was the end result going to be the same for Katherine? Did she feel the way he had when he would pull the covers over his head so he didn't have to hear his father yelling at his mother, or hear her crying? Did she feel she had to choose between them? "We'll do whatever we have to to make it easiest for you," he said.

She looked confused, and Patrick got up from his bed and wagged hopefully. "Can I take him out before we leave, just for a second? He told me and Mrs. Everson it makes him feel better."

"If you bring him right back when your breakfast is ready," he said.

She clapped her hands and then put a hand in his as they all headed downstairs. He didn't want to think about her going up to New York. But he did want Tessa to feel reassured and secure that she would always be able to see her daughter, because he was positive that she wouldn't ask for custody, despite the fact that she had said she would "never" give up Katherine. Tessa said what she wanted to believe rather than what was true. And he knew that for Katherine's sake, as well, it would be important for her to see her mother regularly. She would have to go to New York often, whether he thought it was a great idea or not.

But as he watched Katherine run out into the front yard with Patrick, he felt what he always did when she left the house, even when she left his arms; he wished he could hold on to her and protect her from everything bad in the world forever.

"Get this typed immediately and give it to me for corrections before you run it off."

Tessa refused to even glance up from her typewriter until Courtney Ardmore had walked away. Unfortunately, she was the one Tessa was working for—she had barely seen Dale Sylvan all day—and it was like Tessa's worst nightmare. Courtney Ardmore had been born and raised in Manhattan; she was beautiful—tall and blond and one of those women who could look perfect even with no makeup at all; and she was younger than Tessa was—Tessa figured probably twenty-two or twenty-three.

Tessa looked around at the other assistants, and they were both writing things of their own—Dale was very big on having everyone contribute, Gail had said. It was cheap and easy for him to have brilliant assistants and interns helping the account executives, and the competition managed to shake out most people who didn't belong.

But Tessa didn't seem to be getting a chance to do anything other than type.

"Silverton Publishing, may I help you?"

Tessa looked over at Margery, the office manager, who so far seemed to be the only person Tessa could trust at the office. Tessa estimated that Margery was in her fifties—strangely, she looked a bit as if she had come from Lodenton, one of those ageless, gray-haired women with out-of-date makeup and clothes she had probably worn for twenty years. She had a throaty, cigarette-and-whiskey-soaked laugh and deep crow's feet around her eyes when she smiled, and she seemed to know more than anyone else about Dale; she had been working for him for six years, for five as both his personal assistant and office manager.

When Courtney left for lunch, Tessa went over to Margery's desk, which was at the end of the row of assistants' desks.

"Why do you sometimes say 'Silverton Publishing' when you answer the phone?" Tessa asked.

"Oh my God," Margery said. "I don't know where my head is these days. All right, look, you have five lines on your phone, and the first four are for Sylvan. You know how to answer the phone, and you know what to do. If the fifth line rings, say that it's Silverton Publishing, and just take a message."

"But what is it?"

Margery smiled. "One of Dale's little games," she said, lighting a cigarette. She reached behind her chair to the bookshelf and tossed a magazine at Tessa. "I'm sure you've seen the ads for these," she said.

Tessa nodded. She had, for years. It was a magazine called *Pursuits*. She smiled and took a long drag on her cigarette. "I can remember how mad Dale was five or six years ago, when we were the agency for a new cruise line, and we were sending out hundreds of passes to media people for familiarization trips—those are the free passes you always send out so that reporters will write about whatever it is you're representing—theater tickets, cruise tickets, anything. And it made Dale so angry that we were on the 'wrong end,' as he put it." She shrugged. "He decided he wanted to be a media person, too. So that was how *Pursuits* was born."

"So he could get free tickets?" Tessa asked. It seemed like an awful lot of trouble to go to for a few free passes.

"It's the essence of Dale," Margery said. "He loves to get freebies under what are essentially false pretenses."

It seemed incredible to Tessa, who had always felt that the world of magazines was almost sacred. Growing up, she had gleaned all her "important" information from magazines, and she had always pictured their staffs as sophisticated, knowledgeable, perfect people.

The knowledge shook her confidence a bit—she wanted to understand everything about the place she worked—and later that day, back at Gail's, her confidence was shaken further.

"Courtney's a piece of work, isn't she?" Gail said. "She's the type who drives Dale crazy every time."

"What do you mean?" Tessa asked.

Gail smiled, and Tessa decided that Gail had a mean, lizard-like mouth. "Sometimes he makes sleeping with him a requirement of the job—can you imagine?—but what usually happens to the ones he sleeps with is that he ignores them completely after that. I guess for Dale it's just a matter of the old one-time conquest. And then there are people like Courtney who realize that sleeping with him would be a fate worse than death, and Dale just goes crazy trying to change their minds. And giving them better and better assignments to try to change their minds."

Tessa felt a wave of panic and nausea—it couldn't have been for nothing, what she had done. She had gotten the job, hadn't she?

"Oh, did I tell you?" Gail said with another lizardish smile. "My daughter and I met with an agent yesterday, and I'm going to start taking her around on auditions."

"For what?" Tessa asked, although she knew for what—as a model, an actress, anything Amanda wanted, because she was as outgoing as Katherine was shy.

"As a model to start," Gail said. "The agent said directors go absolutely crazy for red-haired kids. Isn't that wonderful?"

"That's great," Tessa said, standing up. "But that reminds me, I want to call Katherine before she goes to sleep." Just hearing her voice, she knew, would put everything into perspective. Katherine was the jewel of her life, and no one could tell her otherwise.

Glenn answered on the first ring. "We were just about to call you," he said. "Why haven't you called us back? I've spoken to Gail twice a night for days."

She knew it was true, because Gail had told her. "Well, I called *you* this time, so that evens it out," she said. "I want to speak to Katherine."

He sighed, and she was instantly annoyed. Glenn's sighs seemed to carry the weight of an ocean when he wanted them to. "I'd like to have a few words with you first, if you don't mind," he said.

"About anything in particular? I promised Gail I wouldn't

stay on long. I want to tell Katherine about my new job. I'm an account executive at a PR firm. Isn't that wonderful?''

"Congratulations," he said. "But would you mind if I told you about Katherine first? I think it's a little more important, Tess."

"Is anything wrong?"

"Everything's fine," he said. "Mrs. Everson's new schedule is finally working out, and Katherine has a new friend—the daughter of that woman I work with. I think it's making an enormous difference, Tess."

Tessa was annoyed that it was happening without her. "How are her stomachaches and headaches?" she asked.

"Almost gone," he said. He paused, and she was hoping he was going to pass the phone to Katherine, but then he said, "You know, we're going to have to talk seriously at some point. We haven't resolved anything. I don't even know if you're coming back to Lodenton—"

"Back?" she said. "Why would I come back?"

Silence again, and she realized she had made a mistake. She wanted to keep things vague so that Glenn didn't press anything until she was ready. "I'm sorry," she said quickly. "I didn't mean that the way it sounded. It's just that I'm really getting settled in here. It's wonderful. I have a job, and I'm going to get an apartment, and it's going to be wonderful."

He didn't say anything, and she finally said, "Are you there?"

"I'll put Katherine on," he said quietly, and a moment later, a high-pitched voice said, "Mommy?"

"Hi, honey," Tessa said. "Guess what happened to Mommy a few days ago?"

"Something bad?" Katherine asked.

"No, no, silly. Something wonderful. Mommy got a wonderful new job. Isn't that great?"

"Does that mean you can come home now?"

"No. It means I have a job, and I'm making money, and I'm going to be happy the way you're happy with Patrick."

"Oh," Katherine said.

"But you're going to come up and see me soon, maybe even in my own apartment. Won't that be great?"

"With Patrick and Daddy?"

"We'll see, honey. But maybe—" She stopped. She so wanted to tell Katherine her plans—she would get settled and on her feet financially, and then she would bring Katherine to New York to live—but she couldn't trust her with the secret. Katherine would tell Glenn, or that nosy Mrs. Everson.

"Maybe what?" Katherine asked.

"Oh, nothing just yet," Tessa said. "But I wanted to tell you right away about the job, because I promised you that I'd call you as soon as I got one, and I always keep my promises, honey."

"Okay," Katherine said.

"Mommy loves you," she said, and she closed her eyes for a moment and tried to picture Katherine. The picture wasn't clear—her face wouldn't quite come into focus—and she opened her eyes. "Do you love me, too?"

"Uh-huh."

"More than anything?"

"Okay," Katherine said.

"Okay? What does that mean? That doesn't mean yes or no, honey."

"I mean yes," Katherine said.

"Then say the words. It's been so long," she said.

Katherine went through the litany—"Je t'aime, te quiero, ti amo in a thousand ways and forever and ever," she said in her small, high voice, and Tessa felt better than she had all day. She would settle in—getting the job had been the first step—and then she would bring her daughter up to New York, enroll her in the best private schools, hire a *real* nanny, and live the way they were both meant to live.

23

Tessa sealed the letter to Roy without rereading it. She felt an aching loneliness, but she felt sure that because she had written the perfect letter, Roy would soon call her.

"Mommy?" she heard Amanda call, and a second later, Amanda came running into the kitchen. Tessa could see why the agent had been enthusiastic about Amanda's looks—she had bright red hair, which Tessa had read was always in demand for children's commercials, and a beautiful, pixie face.

"I think she's in the bathroom," Tessa said.

"Can you tie this?" Amanda was holding up a ribbon, and she held up her braid. "It keeps falling off when I do it."

"Come here," Tessa said. "Turn around. Why are you so dressed up?"

"Didn't Mommy tell you? We have an audition."

"This morning?"

Amanda nodded.

"Don't move. For what?"

"Orange juice."

Tessa let go of the braid, and Amanda turned to face her again. "Do you like the dress?"

"It's beautiful," Tessa said, and it was. She remembered the exact day she and Gail had picked it out. It was when they had first met, and at the time it had looked as if it would take forever for Amanda to grow big enough to wear it. "Is it an orange juice commercial or a print ad?" Tessa asked.

"Commercial," Amanda said, opening the refrigerator door.

"Are you nervous?" Tessa asked.

Amanda slammed the door shut and frowned. "About what?"

252

About what? Tessa tried to imagine taking Katherine to an audition, but the thought was absurd. You couldn't take a child who was afraid of her own shadow.

Tessa heard Gail's high heels as she came down the hall, and a second later, she came into the kitchen. "Oh, there you are. Are you ready?"

"Aren't you going to work today?" Tessa asked.

Gail shook her head. "Dale knows. He's the one who told me about the audition."

"Really? How would he know?"

"He knows a million producers," Gail said with a shrug. "He's produced all sorts of things himself—not commercials, but he used to do plays and concerts." She put her hand on Amanda's shoulder. "And he thinks this kid here's got a huge future ahead of her."

Tessa felt sick with jealousy. It seemed as if every day, every step she took, Gail was ahead of her. And the most infuriating part was that it seemed as if Gail were waging some secret little war, because Tessa didn't even know what Gail was going to do until she was halfway there.

"Gail told me you used to be a producer," Tessa said later that day in the office.

Dale smiled. "Used to be? What, I quit for a year and I'm already a has-been?"

Tessa laughed. She really didn't mind Dale as long as she wasn't sleeping with him. "Tell me what you've produced," she said. "If you have time." She was putting together press kits on Sylvan for new clients at the front desk while the receptionist was at lunch.

"Oh, hell. There were so many different things. Everything from records to movies to commercials, Tessa. You have to understand—when you don't believe in the rules that say you need this kind of experience and that kind of money and this kind of help, if you just do what you believe in and run with it, you can do anything. I mean, who was I? A kid from Brooklyn. What did I know about making a record? I knew zip. But I made it a point to buddy up with a couple of guys who knew a lot more than zip, we found a good artist . . . named Susie Arnell—"

"You're kidding."

He was grinning. "Her first record. We produced her first four, and then she stabbed us in the back, which was *another* learning experience. But we made a hell of a lot of money off of a hunch. A hell of a lot.''

''It sounds really interesting,'' she said. ''Do you think you'll ever get back into it?''

''You never know,'' he said. ''I'm involved in so much right now—too much—but you never know. I loved producing; that's how I met Ray Nicks.''

''Really?'' Ray Nicks had been hosting his own morning talk show for years, and she knew that he and Dale had once been partners, but she had never known in what.

''Yeah, he and I go way back.'' He smiled. ''You'd never guess how far back, in fact.''

''What do you mean?''

''Ray and I—and this is a little-known fact, *not* to be put in any of our releases on Ray unless I tell you to—but Ray and I met when we were both all of three years old at the Our Lady of Mercy Orphanage in Brooklyn.''

''You were an orphan?''

''No, I was the cook. Yeah, I was an orphan. Until my parents—who I consider my parents absolutely—until they adopted me when I was eleven.''

''You were in there for eight years?''

''Hey, Ray was in there longer than that. No one ever came for him.''

Tessa was stunned. She had always found Ray Nicks to be an odd sort of a man, especially to be a daytime talk-show host. He was almost albino in coloring—pale blue eyes, pale, white-pink skin that often looked as if it were burning under the hot studio lights of his show, thinning blond hair that was almost white. He looked translucent at times, and his features weren't particularly attractive. They all seemed to be too small, dwarfed in a moon face that always seemed to be not quite there.

But Tessa had always been interested in the fact that a man who looked like Ray Nicks could have had a talk show for such a long time. Somehow he had gotten where he was without great looks, and she supposed it was because people enjoyed his unpredictability; with many of his guests he was perfectly charming—usually, when they were so-called ''real people'' who were on his show not because they were actors or actresses but because they had done something unusual—the man who saved his neighbors from a raging fire, for example. But with other people he could be scathing.

Tessa would never have guessed he had spent his childhood

in an orphanage—in her unwavering formula, people who were successful had been born into rich and successful families. But now that she felt she was beginning to overcome her unfortunate and cloistered past, she constantly looked for confirmation that this was possible. And Ray Nicks was another good example. He had developed a thick skin, and then he had used it. He wasn't afraid of anyone.

"What do you think that did to him?" she asked. "Having to spend his first eighteen years there, I mean."

Dale shook his head. "Ray left when he was fifteen. He couldn't take it anymore."

The front door opened and a man came in with a huge carton on a hand truck. "Package for Don Silverman," he mumbled.

"Don Silverman?" Tessa said.

"Sign for it," Dale said quietly, standing up.

"But—"

"Just sign for it, please, and bring it into my office."

Tessa signed, and the man unloaded the package and left.

Dale was already on the phone when Tessa knocked, but he waved her in. "Stu, I can tell you one thing and one thing only: it's the best idea I've come up with in ten years, and the timing is perfect. I can feel it in my bones." He laughed. "I know I've said it before, but it's a hundred percent true. Listen to Dale Sylvan." He laughed. "Okay, so I'll see you at the Four Seasons at one tomorrow." He hung up. "Tell Margery to make a reservation for me and Stu Benson tomorrow at the Four Seasons at one, will you?"

"Sure," Tessa said.

He swung his feet off the desk and handed her two folders. "Let's see, and give these pictures of Rafaella Borso to Margery, will you? Tell her to be sure to use the new release because I reworded it, and she doesn't know that."

Tessa let the cover flip back on the folder and looked down at the pictures. Rafaella Borso was an actress Tessa had never heard of until she had begun working at Sylvan. She was young and beautiful, and Tessa hated her. In the pictures Dale had just handed over, she was half-dressed, and she had a body that Tessa angrily recognized was better than hers—just that much more shapely without being fat.

But there was something odd about the pictures. They weren't posed at all. Rafaella Borso was changing clothes in them, and she looked completely unself-conscious, as if she were thoroughly unaware that her photograph was being taken.

"What do you think?" he asked. "Nice, huh?"

"She's very pretty," Tessa said.

"But looking at them, you'd think they were some kind of candid shots, right? Shots she didn't even know were being taken?"

"That's what it looks like, yes." She looked up at him, and he was grinning.

He spread his hands. "And they say I'm not a genius. You know Dion Ranieri, he comes in two or three times a week? The photographer. He's our client, she's our client, they both need some publicity. So *now* what we have in the press release is that we—as Rafaella's authorized representatives—we're suing Ranieri because he took these pictures unauthorized. And suddenly everyone in the whole goddamn country is going to want the pictures Rafaella doesn't want anyone to see. And what we say is, 'Here, *these* are the ones you can see,' and they're sexy enough that everyone wants to show them and think about what the *real* ones must look like. Ranieri gets his name all over the place as another nosy paparazzo—which is what he wants, the rep he wants—and suddenly Rafaella is on every news show in the country. Nice, huh?"

"And it works?"

He smiled again. "Like a charm," he said.

When Margery came back from lunch, Tessa asked her about the package that had been addressed to Don Silverman.

"You're seeing another of Dale's games," Margery said with a wink. "It's just another amusement for Dale, one of his more minor ones. He orders things under false names and checks 'bill me' on the order forms, and then he doesn't pay."

"How can he get away with that?" Tessa asked. "It came to this address."

"*He* didn't sign for it," Margery said, lighting a cigarette. "You can go to lunch if you want, by the way. I can take over until Rae comes back."

"But I still don't understand," Tessa said. "Doesn't Dale have a lot of money?"

"You have a lot to learn," Margery said, leaning back in her chair. "The wealthiest clients are always the slowest to pay, if they pay at all. It's not an ironclad rule, of course. But a lot of them find it difficult to part with their money. Dale takes that to an extreme, It's just another amusement for him."

"Has he ever gotten into any kind of trouble?"

Margery smiled. "Dale is very good at everything he does, Tessa, and that includes his games."

"The rent is twenty-one hundred a month," the woman was saying. "As you can see, there's a magnificent view of the river—it's to die for—and you can see, if you'll follow me, that even from the bathroom there's a view that's worth twenty-one hundred a month all by itself."

Tessa could hardly breathe. She hadn't let herself imagine that an apartment this nice could exist in the world, and she hadn't let herself think that she could possibly spend this much. She had already spent more than seven thousand of the thirty thousand from the cash part of her grandfather's estate, and her dreaded fantasy of watching helplessly as the money disappeared seemed to be coming true.

But yesterday, when she had told Dale she was looking for an apartment, he had mentioned that there was one available in his building—in fact, it had belonged to an ex-girlfriend of his who had moved out—and Tessa had been unable to stop herself from going to see it. Living in midtown Manhattan only a few blocks from the office was what successful people did; she felt it was an omen, that it meant something that Dale was willing to have her live in his building. And now that she had seen the apartment, she had to have it.

She loved the view. It was the view she had seen in dozens of movies that took place in New York, the view that had always said to her, Your life is nothing, when she had been back in Lodenton. It was a view seen only by successful people, available only to those with money and the taste to search out the best.

But what she loved even more was the apartment itself. It wasn't large—it had a tiny bedroom, and the kitchen was just a galley kitchen partitioned off from the living room. But the living room was huge, with polished wood floors and a modern chandelier and built-in bookcases below the huge picture window. What Tessa knew was that she could give parties in that apartment, that she could begin courting people the way she knew Courtney sometimes did, and the way she knew Dale did every day of his life.

She had promised herself that even if she liked the apartment, she would go to a coffee shop and think about it for at least five minutes before signing the lease—it was so much money!—but now that she had seen it, she knew she couldn't let it slip through her fingers. So she signed on the spot and wrote out a check with shaking fingers for six thousand three hundred dollars. Two years' rent in Lodenton, she figured; three months' rent in New York. But it would be worth it; she knew it because of the same instinct that had led her to work for Dale Sylvan, despite the fact Gail had asked her to stay away. There were certain events and people and places you were destined to involve yourself with, and this apartment, she knew, was one of those places for her.

24

The lady, Julie's mom, was the nicest lady Katherine ever met. "When you two finish planting those flowers, you can come in for cookies and milk," Julie's mom called out, and Katherine hurried to plant the last flower.

"These are my favorites," Julie said, sniffing the green part that smelled like something sharp. "Marigolds."

Katherine sniffed the green parts, too, and closed her eyes. She lay down on the ground where the sun came down, and she felt warm and happy. She missed Patrick because he always wanted to be with him when she was outside, and Julie's mom had said she could even bring him next time, because he sounded so nice. Julie's mom said they were going to get a dog, too, and that Katherine could come help pick him out, that they'd pick the friendliest one in the litter.

"What's litter?" Katherine could remember asking, even though it felt like a long time ago now. She felt like she had known Julie's mom forever. But when she asked, she had felt a little scared, because Julie had started to laugh, and it was like the time in school when Amy Grausler didn't know what the word "lavatory" meant and everyone had started to laugh, and Katherine had felt sick like she was going to throw up. But Julie's mom didn't ever laugh at you or make you feel scared. She had said all about what "litter" was and how it was a family of animals, like kittens or puppies, and she said didn't Patrick have brothers and sisters when they picked him? And then Katherine had felt good because she remembered, and she got to say what "runt" was. Plus Julie's mom looked like Glinda in the *Wizard of Oz*, with her long light brown hair that was curly and in waves, and beautiful light brownish-green eyes. Once she had even dreamed about her, and she had a crown just like Glinda's in the dream.

259

"Let's go to my clubhouse," Julie said, grabbing Katherine's arm. "We can take the cookies and hide."

Katherine felt so happy because Julie had said it was a secret and how she didn't know if she wanted to show it to Katherine ever, because she had never shown it to anyone. That day when she had said it, Julie's mom had been standing there in the kitchen, and she had said, "You're not even going to show it to your best friend?"

And Katherine had felt so happy, because it meant they were best friends. Julie had looked shy and funny and said, "I don't know," real quietly. She said her dad had helped her make it and told her to keep it secret from everyone in the whole world. Julie's mom said she hadn't even seen it, but she thought it was the "perfect place" for Julie and Katherine. And right then, Katherine had felt like hugging her, because it was such a great thing to say, and she always knew the greatest thing to say.

And so today they were going, and Katherine felt like she was going to a faraway place the way her mom had done. They went running into the kitchen and took as many cookies as they could carry, and then they ran down the hill that was the yard. The yard was all green grass with sweepy, swoopy trees that Julie said were "weeping willows," plus a stream and a pond at the bottom they were supposed to stay far away from.

And then Katherine saw it, you could tell it was something different, and Julie said, "Here it is."

There were big branchy things hanging down with all leaves, that Julie said were branches from the willows, and then wood in a little fence, with a roof that was all leaves and stringy willow and some boards. It looked like where an animal lived, like the doorway to Mrs. Tittlemouse's house in the book her dad liked to read. All kinds of animals could live there, only it was Julie's! Katherine thought it was the best thing she had ever seen in her life.

"I'm starved," Julie said, plopping down on the ground and starting to eat.

Katherine ate, too. The cookies were great that Julie's mom had made, oatmeal with raisins and nuts, and Katherine felt happier than she had ever felt in her life, she thought, because now she really had a best friend and there was a secret that Julie had showed her.

"Maybe tomorrow I could go to your house," Julie said. She was lying on her back with her feet up against some of the wood, and Katherine lay down, too.

Katherine didn't say anything. She couldn't say why she didn't want Julie to come over to her house, exactly. She wanted her to come so she could meet Patrick, because she was so proud he was like her brother and so great, plus he was *hers*. But there was something funny, not having a mom, like she didn't want to show anyone even if it was her best friend. And Mrs. Everson was so great—Katherine loved the way she held her in her arms when she read stories, it was like the nurse at the doctor's office who always held her if the doctor was taking blood, and she smelled sweet like flowers. She loved the way Mrs. Everson had these crinkly brown eyes, and she always smelled like vanilla and cookies. But she still wasn't a mom. And Katherine wanted to tell Julie that her mom didn't live with her, but she didn't know what to say.

And it was funny, because at the beginning when she and Julie were friendly, Julie had said, "My dad lives all the way in California, so I hardly ever see him." And right then, she had said, "Does your dad live at home?" And Katherine knew that right then, she could say, Uh-huh, but my mom doesn't. But all she did was nod her head. And then once she went to Julie's and Julie's mom said, "I want to call your mother to see if you can stay for dinner." All Katherine had been able to say was, "Um, you can call Mrs. Everson. She's the housekeeper." And Julie's mom had said, "Oh, does your mother work?" And Katherine had just said yes, even though what she wanted to say was, "I don't know. She lives in New York."

And now it seemed like it was too late. She couldn't find the words.

"So I can tell you something right now," Julie said, which was something she said a lot, and Katherine had the feeling she had heard on TV or something. Katherine thought it made Julie sound like she knew everything in the world. "I know all about how to make a playhouse because I built this thing almost all by myself when my dad was here, and I could build one at your house in your yard. We could build it together."

Katherine wanted to so much. And Patrick could maybe even help, because he was always trying to do whatever you were doing, like if Mrs. Everson was bringing in the wash, he tried to pull the long, hangy things off the line, the ones he could reach, and then Mrs. Everson would yell at him, but she'd always be laughing, too.

"I don't know," Katherine said. "I have to check with Mrs. Everson." She put her feet up on the rock that Julie had her feet on, too. "It'd probably be okay, but I have to check."

"I have some new ideas," Julie said, brushing her bangs back from her face in a way that Katherine wanted to start doing. She thought it looked great and like something a lady would do. "I could maybe do them on this clubhouse, too, but maybe we could start them on yours if you have curtains. My mom says all the bedspreads we use for tents are in the laundry, but if your mom has something like that, we could make a tent inside the clubhouse."

"I could ask," Katherine said. She wanted to say, but she couldn't. Because didn't it mean there was something bad about her if her mom had left?

She had a sick feeling in her stomach, but she forgot about it while they were in the clubhouse, until they went back to Julie's house, and Julie's mom said, "Your father called and said he'd pick you up at six." And then her voice got all soft as she said, "I hadn't realized your mother was in New York, Katherine," and she had a soft, velvety look in her eyes that made Katherine want to climb into her arms.

Katherine looked down at the floor, and she could feel her face get hot. She didn't want to cry or act like a baby.

"Come over here," Julie's mom said, and she held out her arms.

Katherine felt like she was going to throw up, but she went over, and Julie's mom made her climb into her lap. "I'm not trying to make you feel bad," she said, putting her arms around Katherine. "I just wish you had told me. I wouldn't have kept asking you to have your mother call me, Katherine."

Katherine put her head down on Julie's mom's shoulder, and she felt happy and sad at the same time, and there was a lump in her throat. "It isn't something you should be embarrassed about," Julie's mom said. "It isn't your fault, you know."

Katherine closed her eyes because she could feel tears coming.

"I'm sure that Julie won't mind my telling you that she felt the same way when her dad left," she said, stroking Katherine's hair. It felt good, and Katherine felt almost like she was falling down a waterfall. "I think it's something that's true of all kids and probably of everyone. When someone leaves, you think it's your fault, but it's not. Usually it isn't anyone's fault. But it's never the child's fault. Ever, Katherine."

She wished for a second that Julie's mom could be her mom, too, but then she blotted it out because it was a bad thing to think. Her mom was the greatest in the world, and it was wrong to even think.

And she thought about her mom in the place called New York

and how she had said, "Sooner than you think, you're going to be visiting me in my brand-new apartment, Katherine," and she tried to be happy about that thought.

Glenn hung up the phone and looked across the living room at Katherine. She was playing happily with her stuffed animals, making a house for them under the couch and the table with overhanging linen napkins and a tablecloth. "This is what the secret house looks like," she said. "No one in the whole world knows about it except Julie's mom and Julie and me."

"It looks wonderful," Glenn said. "It's at the bottom of their lawn?"

"You can't tell anyone," she said, looking up at him with serious eyes. "I swore on an oath."

"Then I swear, too," he said.

The change had been dramatic since she had begun spending time with Julie. Not once had she asked to stay home from school; not once had she gone to the nurse at school and asked to go home. Julie and Caroline were all that Katherine talked about these days—how they had played so many games, how they had both named their dolls Jennifer and wasn't that incredible, how Julie's mom said that Katherine could bring Patrick over whenever she wanted. According to Katherine, Caroline had helped them "invent" new clothes by taking them berry picking and then boiling the berries and dipping the clothes in the "brew." Each time Katherine had gone over there, she had learned something and had a wonderful time—what being four and a half years old was supposed to be like, as far as Glenn was concerned. And he felt that Katherine was finally getting the kind of life he wanted her to have.

But the call he had just gotten had shaken him. It was the second call he had gotten from a headhunter in as many weeks, and it was the second job offer that had sounded truly interesting. The first had been for a plastics firm out in Texas, and although the job had sounded good—he would be chief of research and development—he had ruled it out immediately. He felt that moving to Texas would be much too drastic a step to take at this point in Katherine's life, and it would mean facing what he hadn't been able to face—putting everything in writing, a possible court battle, and God only knew what end result.

But the call he had just gotten was different. Whitmere Industries, a company in northern New Jersey, was extremely interested in seeing him, according to the search firm. They wanted to fly him up for a few days, put him up wherever he wanted to stay, and talk seriously to him about a job that sounded like what he had worked his whole life for. Again, he would be chief of research and development. But Whitmere was a much more diversified company than Radicon was. And they were close to New York, which would mean Katherine could see her mother more often.

There were so many unresolved issues. Possibly unwisely, he had accepted Tessa's refusal to discuss custody possibilities, because he had Katherine. He had physical custody, and he was doing a good job, and these factors could do nothing but help if Tessa ended up fighting him. And he couldn't do anything but assume that if she had wanted Katherine with her, she would have taken her or at least laid the plans. From what he had heard, her life was such that it would be difficult now to fit a young child into it. She had a full-time job, no household help, and no place to live. These things wouldn't dispose a judge in her direction, as far as he could see. And he felt that she was finally facing a truth he had known even before she had; her ambitions were stronger than her desire to see Katherine.

But the phone call had made him realize there were possibilities he had never considered. If he were living close to New York City, then maybe he and Tessa really could share custody to an extent he had not considered.

FOR IMMEDIATE RELEASE

Child actors and their mothers: the facts and the fantasies. Do the children love their work, as their mothers claim? How does one begin in the business? Ray Nicks will explore the truths and the fictions surrounding this explosive issue in his own inimitable way on his Friday morning show.

Tessa stopped outside Dale's door and read the press release again. "Dale?" she said.

He looked up with annoyance. "What is it?"

"Is the cast all set for this? The mothers and their kids, I mean?"

"I don't know. Probably. Why?"

"I'd like to be on it," she said. "With my daughter."

He threw down his pencil. "What is it around here? Gail's all over me about it, now you—"

"Gail is going to be on the show?"

He tilted his head. She had the feeling he had dyed his hair again the night before, because suddenly, with the sun behind him, his hair looked unnaturally and unattractively red. "She asked me, and I said I'd run it past Ray."

Tessa walked into the office and closed the door.

"What are you closing the door for? Tessa, I'm busy."

"I know. But listen to me: Ray Nicks needs someone who's just starting out—a girl who doesn't even know if she wants to be a model or an actress, a mother who doesn't know much about the business but wants to find out about it. It would be the best part, Dale. It would be from the perspective of the audience. It would balance the show."

He put his head in his hands. She noticed again how beautifully manicured his nails were. "And you want to be that mother, of course."

She moved closer to the desk. "Dale, I'd do anything."

He raised his head and looked at her with unreadable eyes. "I'll run it past Ray," he said quietly.

Back at her desk, she felt as if there were a storm inside her body. The show was scheduled for the next Friday. She could have Glenn send Katherine—maybe she could even go and get her if it were necessary—and she would put Katherine on the show. There were some instincts you just had to follow—the way an animal knew how to find its way home, the way great thinkers knew to take the unexpected path—and she knew this was one of those times.

"Do you ever get afraid?" Katherine asked. She was looking up at the sky, and it looked so pretty, all blue with lots of the puffy white clouds that she liked to draw.

"I get afraid of the dark," Julie said. She had a piece of grass in her mouth, and Katherine picked a piece of grass and put it in hers, too. "And my neighbor has a dog that's kind of scary. Not like Patrick." She laughed. "He's so silly."

Katherine thought about Patrick and felt like there was an ache inside her mind. Her mom was going to come take her to New York, and Patrick was going to have to stay home, and her dad was, too. "I'm moving into my new apartment, and you'll get to stay there with me," her mom had said. "It won't have much furniture in it yet, so it will be a little like camping out. Won't that be fun?"

"Did you ever go to New York?" Katherine asked. Up in the sky there was a cloud like a dog, and she felt bad even more.

"Uh-uh," Julie said. "My mom hates it." Julie put her legs up in the air till they hooked onto the branches in the roof. "My dad wanted to move there, and my mom said she never would, no matter what.''

"And then your dad went to California?''

"Uh-huh.''

It was the scariest idea, and Katherine tried to think about something else. One day she was listening while Mrs. Everson was talking on the phone, and Mrs. Everson had said, "You can never tell what will happen in these divorces when there's a child involved. You remember Becky Quilman and her daughter? She was the one who drank and her husband put her up at that farm to dry out that time? *She* ended up with the daughter and Andy Quilman's still out looking for them. Becky just got in a car one day, picked up her daughter like a hawk with a rabbit, and disappeared them both off the face of the earth.''

And Katherine had felt cold and scared when she had heard the story, because what if? She loved her mom and she missed her, but there were times she felt something different—more like *afraid*. And when she thought about her mom maybe stealing her away, taking her way far away, it felt like something that could happen. Disappearing off the face of the earth.

"Did you ever visit your dad out there by yourself?'' Katherine asked.

Julie shook her head and swung her legs down from the branches. She sat up and crossed her legs, and Katherine did, too. "My mom always goes with me,'' she said, and she shrugged. "It's only been twice.'' She pulled up another piece of grass and put it in her mouth.

"Was it fun?''

Julie looked down. "It made me feel bad. I miss him a lot.'' She started patting down the moss. She and Katherine had brought in a bunch from near the pond, and it was going to be their rug that maybe they could even sleep on when it got warmer, Julie's mom had said.

Katherine patted the moss, too. Sometimes she felt like a copycat because everything that Julie did, she wanted to do, too, but she felt so happy being with Julie, and everything they did together was so fun. "My mom's coming to get me on Thursday night to take me to New York,'' Katherine said. She felt funny when she said it, like she was saying something that was supposed to be a secret. "We're going up to stay in her new apartment. And then my dad said the next week, he's going to take me, because he has a job interview.'' She pulled at some moss by mistake and then patted it down again.

"So you might be moving far away?" Julie asked.

"I don't know." She lay down on the moss with her head in the ferns, and she closed her eyes and breathed them in. She wished she could stay like that forever, in a way, except that Patrick would be there, too, and her dad, and her mom as long as she promised not to steal her away.

"Julie?"

"Hm?"

"If I have to move to New York, do you think you can come to visit me?"

"I don't know," Julie said. "Since my mom hates it so much. I think you'd have to come back here to Lodenton."

Katherine closed her eyes again and breathed in the ferns and wished it was next year and that nothing would have changed.

Tessa was exhausted. The lights from the oncoming cars seemed too bright, and seeing Glenn had exhausted her. She was irritated at the neatness of the house, at Glenn's cheerfulness, at the pathetic plainness of Lodenton and of the house she had lived in for so many years. She knew she would have to go back again soon, for the closing on her grandfather's house, and she wanted to see Roy when she did. But after that, she wanted never to return. Ever.

"Are you excited?" she said into the darkness.

Katherine was awake again and looking out the window, although there really wasn't much to see in the dark. Tessa felt that Katherine looked frightened, and she felt somewhat hurt. "I guess," Katherine said in a small voice. "I wish we could've brang Patrick."

"You can bring Patrick the next time you come," Tessa said. "But don't forget, Mommy just moved into a new apartment. I wouldn't want Patrick to pee on any of the floors."

"He wouldn't go in the house. He's trained."

"If he is, that's certainly a new development." She glanced over and saw Katherine squeeze her eyes shut.

"Do you love me?" Tessa asked.

Katherine kept her eyes shut, but she nodded her head.

"I love you," Tessa said. "I hope when you're home in Lodenton that your daddy tells you that, too. Does he tell you he loves you?"

Katherine opened her eyes and shrugged. "Sure." She was looking down at her hands and picking at her nails.

"Does he say he loves you more than I do?"

"Uh-uh," Katherine said in a small voice.

"I love you more than he does," Tessa said. "Did you know that?"

Katherine didn't say anything.

"It's true," Tessa said. "And do you know, sometimes you might not realize that. You might think about me and think, Gee, she left us at home, and she moved all the way to New York, so that must mean Daddy loves me more. But, Katherine, I have big plans for us. It's all a secret right now, so secret I can't even tell you, but I want you to know I have very big plans. And I love you more than anyone on earth does. More than anyone."

Katherine was squeezing her eyes shut again, and Tessa decided to try to let her sleep. They would have to get up at four the following morning to be at the show on time, and, well, if Katherine wanted to pretend to go to sleep, Tessa supposed it was her privilege.

She was just glad—and surprised—that Glenn had even let Katherine come. On the phone when Tessa had first brought it up, Glenn had said no, that there was a possibility he and Katherine would want to come up at some point quite soon anyway, and wasn't that enough?

And Tessa had exploded. She *needed* Katherine; she hadn't seen her in over a month! She felt she would lose her mind if she didn't see her, and if she waited until Friday, it would be too much driving over the course of the two days. Couldn't she pick her up on Thursday night and keep her until Sunday?

Glenn had deliberated and hesitated, as he always did about everything. She could practically hear him weighing the pros and cons, weighing his wishes against the reality that without a formal agreement, Tessa did have the right to see Katherine. "I think it's the least you can do, Glenn, considering that you have her all the time. I think it's in your interests, if you want to keep her in Lodenton, to let me see her when I'm able to," she had said, knowing her words would have to have an impact.

"Mommy?"

"What is it, honey?"

"Are you going to stay home from work tomorrow?"

"Not exactly," Tessa said.

Katherine was squinting at her in the darkness. "Do I have to have a baby-sitter?"

"You're going to have something better than a baby-sitter," Tessa said. "But it's a surprise. Mommy has a special project to take care of tomorrow, and you can come along with me and be my assistant."

She wasn't going to say any more than that. If she told Katherine the truth, it would frighten her. Katherine would claim to be sick, and then the whole thing would be ruined. And, of course, she hadn't told Glenn, because Glenn never would have allowed it. Life with Glenn would mean a limited, monotonous landscape for Katherine; it was something Tessa would have worried about if she felt for even a moment that Katherine would end up spending the rest of her childhood with him.

But even the fact that she had managed to plan this one tiny little secret, that she had actually gotten Katherine into the car and on her way up to New York, gave Tessa confidence. One step at a time was all it took.

Everyone had said yes to the dinner party—Tessa had decided not to invite Gail and Walter, so it would just be Louann and her new beau and the Wadlens, and possibly Dale. But it was exciting to think about. Amazing, really, because six months earlier, she had been bored out of her mind in Lodenton, and in exactly one week, she was going to have a world-famous producer, an antiques dealer, and a successful entertainment lawyer to her house for dinner. Less than two months earlier, she had been living in a dull, one-family house in Lodenton, and now she lived on the twentieth floor of a modern skyscraper in the middle of Manhattan. Last night, her first night in the apartment, she had slept on the floor in the living room and gone to sleep looking at the sky. It was a new beginning, the first manifestation of what her new life would be, and she had loved it.

Katherine fell asleep around Patterson, New Jersey, and Tessa played the radio softly for the rest of the trip. There was a gossip report on one of the all-news stations, a five-minute collection of little snippets from here and there, and Tessa felt pleased and condescendingly smug when two of Dale's clients were mentioned. The reporter announced with great excitement that spokesmen for both Arlette Pierce and Johnny Roper denied the two had secretly gotten married. Tessa knew the truth: Arlette Pierce and Johnny Roper barely knew each other, and no one was wondering whether they had secretly gotten married or not. No one was even asking about either of them. But Dale had written his press releases as if the world had been beating at his door, trying to find out the truth about these two actors, and now everyone was talking about them again. What fools everyone was to believe all that they read! Tessa felt good that she had had a hand in the story, if only in terms of knowing the truth; soon she would be one of the people *in* the stories, she just knew.

25

"Why do I have to wear that dress?"

"Because everyone who's part of the surprise has to dress up," Tessa said. "Amanda's going to dress up, and she's part of the surprise. Do you know, Amanda got a part in a commercial? Isn't that exciting?"

"Do you mean she's going to be on TV?" Katherine raised her arms over her head, and Tessa fitted the sleeves over her hands and down over her shoulders.

"That's right. Probably you'll see her every day on TV. Isn't that amazing?"

Katherine nodded, but she was biting her lip and looking distracted. "Doesn't she have to go to school?"

"She's going to go to a special school for kids like her who are actors and singers and dancers. They go to school, but the school knows that the kids need to take time out for auditions and performances. Doesn't that sound wonderful?"

Katherine shrugged. "I don't know."

Tessa knew she would have to tell Katherine what she would be doing and where they would be going, or there was a chance Katherine would have some sort of tantrum when they got there. And Katherine also had to be told what her responses should be on the show, or she was going to look like a dull, uninterested child.

Tessa knelt behind Katherine and began to brush her hair. In the mirror Katherine already looked nervous, so Tessa took her time. "You look absolutely beautiful this morning," she said, brushing her hair slowly and gently. It was Katherine's best feature—thick and glowing and burnished mahogany-red the way Tessa's was, but even shinier. "That shampoo I bought is obviously perfect for your hair."

Katherine didn't say anything. She was looking everywhere but at Tessa in the mirror.

"So don't you think it's fun camping out in such a fancy apartment? It's such an adventure."

"What about today?" Katherine asked with squinty eyes. "Where are we going to go?"

Tessa came around and sat Katherine down in her lap so they were both facing the mirror. "See how pretty you look today? Mommy thought it would be nice if you showed everyone how pretty you look when you dress up."

"I don't understand."

Tessa brushed Katherine's bangs back from her forehead and kissed the top of her head. She loved looking at herself in the mirror when Katherine was in her lap. Mother and child. Nothing could compare. "Mommy found a way for you to go on a TV show where we can find out all about girls who are models and actresses. Amanda's going to be on, too, so you can say hello."

Katherine looked stunned. "I don't want to be on TV." She twisted so she was looking up into Tessa's eyes. "I don't want to be on TV. I don't want to go."

"Shh." She stroked Katherine's hair and tried to stay calm. She had known Katherine wouldn't want to do it; this wasn't a misstep, because it was expected. "It will be fun, and it will help Mommy in her job a lot."

Katherine looked down at her hands. "Why?" she asked without looking up. "How could it help?"

"It just would," Tessa said. "It's something I want a lot, Katherine, and I think you would have fun once we got there."

Katherine kicked her feet against Tessa's legs. "I can't."

"Of course you can."

"No, I can't. I don't want to go."

"You're going to have to go," Tessa said, and she saw Katherine's eyes in the mirror. Like a scared rabbit again. Tessa sighed and made Katherine look into her eyes. "Do it for me," she said. "Don't you love me?"

"Yes."

"Don't you do things for people you love? When someone you love wants you to do a favor for them, something they know will be good for you, too, then you do it, even if you're afraid."

"Do I have to sing?"

Tessa laughed. "Of course not. What on earth would make you think you'd have to sing?"

"You said Amanda goes to school with singers. I don't want to have to sing."

"You won't," Tessa said, feeling immensely relieved. If that was all that Katherine was afraid of, she had nothing to worry about. "And afterward, tonight after work, you can see your aunt Louann and tell her all about it. Don't forget that when she was your age, she was already performing in front of an audience."

Katherine didn't say anything, and Tessa suddenly wished she hadn't mentioned Louann's early performances. They were unpleasant memories for Louann, a source of anxiety even now. But Katherine didn't seem to have heard; she looked paralyzed with fear.

They hailed a cab to the studio, and Katherine said she didn't understand why it was so dark. "Because it's early," Tessa said, stroking her hair. "With these morning shows, people have to get up very early. Don't try to understand absolutely everything, Katherine, or it will make your head swim."

Katherine leaned her head against her mom's shoulder and closed her eyes. She wished she was back home and that she was leaning on Mrs. Everson's shoulder, because then it would mean when she got up, it wouldn't be something scary. Or that she was at Julie's house and Julie's mom was making them cookies and telling them stories, or saying that everything was going to be okay, because it was never your fault if you were a kid.

She felt sick to her stomach, and she had told her mom, but her mom had said it was "just nerves," and not to worry about it. Then she had given her two of those pink things, the Pepto Bismols, and brushed her hair some more.

"Just remember, honey, if the man asks you any questions, you always try to smile and say the right thing."

Katherine couldn't feel the ends of her fingers anymore, and she knew she was going to throw up. When she looked out the car window, everything looked swirly and like a blur. "Mommy, I don't feel good," she said. She could feel it coming up, she felt all fuzzy, and she knew it was going to come—

"Here. Take another one of these—"

She felt black spots in front of her eyes, floaty, and then it came up, and she vomited on the floor, and she was crying.

"Oh, Katherine."

"What's going on back there?" a man's voice said. "Did she throw up back there? Jesus Christ." The car made a big jerky turn and then it stopped, and Katherine felt the door whip open.

She had her head down but she could see a man through a crack, the driver, looking down on the floor. "Jesus Christ, lady, *now* what am I supposed to do? Ride around with puke all day so the passengers can give me bigger tips?"

"This can't possibly be the first time this has ever happened," Katherine heard her mom say. "Just clean it up when we get where we're going."

The man looked like a man in a story that Mrs. Everson had read to Katherine, a man with smoke coming out of his ears. His arms were crossed, and his eyebrows had made one giant line.

"I'll make it worth your while," Katherine's mom said, "if you get us there quickly. We're late as it is."

"You'd better mean that," he said, and he slammed the door and got back in.

When the taxi started to move, Katherine felt like throwing up again, but she closed her eyes as tight as she could and tried to think about something happy, the way Mrs. Everson always said she should. She thought about Julie and Patrick and her dad, but thinking about them just made her feel sadder, so she tried to make her mind into a blank, and she held her breath.

"How do you feel?" her mom asked, rubbing her shoulders. "Now that you've gotten it out, I'm sure you'll feel better. Here we are now."

Katherine swallowed and tried not to think about what was happening, that she would have to meet all kinds of people she didn't know and then be on TV. She didn't understand why it would help her mom if she did it, but she knew it was important, so she was going to try.

The man started to yell when her mom paid him, all about how she hadn't given him enough money and what was he going to do, but her mom grabbed her hand and pulled her into the building, where it was still all dark except for a guard and a light in this lobby-type thing.

They went up in an elevator, and then it was all fancy, like a living room with big lights, and a lady who was dressed up like for a party, who shook Katherine's mom's hand and then looked down at Katherine and smiled. "Well, aren't you pretty? Are you excited about being on the show?"

Katherine didn't know if she smelled like throw-up anymore, and she was afraid to open her mouth.

"She was a bit sick on the way over here," her mom said to the lady. "But I think she's feeling all right now."

The lady looked confused. "Are you sure? If she's not feeling well—"

"She's feeling fine. Aren't you, honey?"

Katherine nodded because her mom had said to say the right things.

The lady led them back to a room that looked like school because there were so many kids. The girls were wearing party dresses fancier than Katherine's, and Katherine saw one lady putting lipstick on her daughter's lips. That part looked like fun, and Katherine started to feel better.

"Amanda," she said. There was Amanda at the end of the long mirror with lights in it, and Amanda's mom, Gail.

"I don't think she heard you," her mom said. "Let's go say hello." She took Katherine's hand and led her over, and Katherine saw one of the girls look at her in the mirror. She had eye makeup on, too, and Katherine thought, Maybe it'll be like dressing up.

"Katherine!" Amanda screamed when she saw her, and she put her arms around her, and they hugged for a long time. "I can't believe we're both on the same show. Are you nervous? Ew, what smells?"

Katherine looked up at her mom and felt like she was going to cry.

"We'll find a bathroom," her mom said, and she took her hand again.

After that, everything was like a big jumbly dream, with everyone saying things had to be done quick, quick, quick, and put this dress on, and take this dress off, and suddenly Katherine felt her mom's hand on her shoulder. A lady was saying, "Girls in the blue dresses go out on stage now," and she was in a line like in school, but she was holding hands with girls she didn't know. She walked in the line, and there were bright lights when they got out onto the stage. People in a crowd behind the lights were clapping, and Katherine had a funny feeling, and her knees felt like jelly.

"Welcome, welcome," a man was saying. He was pink and yellow, and he had tiny little light-colored eyes. He was standing up and clapping, and then he pointed to a row of seats. "Now why don't you all sit down, and we'll have a word with you and learn what it's like to be a child model. In a few minutes we'll bring out your moms and find out if it's true what they say about stage mothers, but right now I want to talk to all of you and find out *your* thoughts."

Katherine sat because the other girls sat, but she was terrified. What did he mean when he said "child models," because she *wasn't* one! What was she supposed to say? And what had her mom said . . . that it was important for her work, that she had to do it to help her out.

"Let's start with the little girl down at the end. Your name is Carla Randazzo and you've been a model since you were nine months old. Is that right?"

"Uh-huh," Carla Randazzo said in a voice that sounded like a chipmunk on a cartoon. "I've been a model and an actress. I was the baby in the Pampers commercial six years ago."

"So I guess we can assume it wasn't your choice to go into show business," the man said, and some people in the audience laughed. "Did you ever begin to regret it—that is, when you were old enough to know what was going on?"

"Oh, absolutely not," the girl said. "I love every minute of it, and I've already made enough money to pay for my whole college education. My parents are thrilled about that part, of course, but it makes me feel good, too."

Katherine felt a shock. The girl said she had made so much money, enough for college! She wondered was that why her mom wanted her to do it? Was she supposed to make a lot of money so she could pay for her school?

All of a sudden, the man was talking to the girl next to Katherine, and Katherine felt a blur and a sickness because the time was getting so close, and what would she say? What would he ask her? She wished more than anything else on earth that Mrs. Everson was there to hold her hand, plus her dad, and maybe Patrick in her lap, except here she was, and they were way far away.

"And your name is Katherine Stokes?" the man said. He was looking down at his pad, but then he looked right into her eyes, and she had a funny feeling.

"Um, uh-huh," she said. She couldn't stop looking into his eyes, because it was like he was forcing her to. She couldn't even explain it, and she couldn't even think.

"And you're the member of our little panel who's modeling for the first time. Can you tell us how you like it?"

She couldn't stop looking into his eyes. She felt like she was underwater and he was talking to her from above.

"Are you all right?" the man asked. He looked away for a second, and Katherine felt like she had been let go. "Uh, Cindy, get her some water," he said, moving his hand like the lady was a waitress. He leaned forward, and he touched Katherine's knee, and then her eyes were in the lock again, and it felt like she couldn't get out. "It'll be okay," he said. "This is your first time, and it's natural to be nervous. Isn't that right?" he said, and Katherine heard some people clap from behind the lights, and voices.

"Why don't I just go on to . . . let's see, your name is Mindy Quinn, and you've been modeling for seven years?"

"That's right," Mindy Quinn said. "Ever since I was a year old and my parents thought I was cuter than the Gerber baby on the jars of baby food."

It sounded to Katherine like the voices were underwater again, blibs and bubbles and sounds that didn't matter as much, except it was funny. Every few seconds the man would look at her, she guessed to see if she was feeling better, and she had the same funny feeling like there was a secret between them, only she didn't know what it was. His eyes were so blue, and they looked like tiny pieces of sky.

When the show was over, Katherine was standing looking at her mom, but then she heard a voice. "Are you all right?" and of course it was the man, now she knew his voice no matter what.

She looked up at him and nodded.

He was smiling, but it was a funny smile, like he wasn't really happy. "You're not much of a chatterbox, are you?"

"Oh, she can be," Katherine heard, and it was her mom coming over. She held out her hand. "I'm Tessa Stokes. I work with Dale; I don't know if you know that."

"I didn't," he said. "Nice to meet you. You've got a nice kid here. Most of them know everything there is to know when they come on a show like this. I hope I didn't scare you," he said. He was looking down at her again, and she swallowed.

"Katherine, speak to him or he's going to think you can't talk."

I talked before, she felt like saying, but she couldn't.

"Did I scare you?" he asked. He got down on the floor, and his eyes were only a little bit higher than hers.

"Uh-uh," she said.

"Did you like coming on the show?"

"I don't know."

He smiled and stood up. "At least she's honest. Tell me something, Katherine. Would you like to have a souvenir?

Something you can take home so you can remember how you appeared on the show with a man named Ray Nicks?''

Katherine shrugged. "Sure. I guess."

Ray Nicks the man smiled. "Hey, this kid's doing wonders for my ego." He looked around. "Helen? Get me a picture for the kid here, will you?"

Katherine looked around at how almost everyone else was leaving. Amanda and Gail were gone, and there were men cleaning up, so she hoped it was good that she and her mom were still there talking to the man.

A lady brought over a picture and handed it to the man Ray Nicks, and then he bent down and handed it to her. The funny part was that when he gave it to her, it felt like he squeezed her hand for a real long time underneath the picture.

"Thanks," she said. She tried not to look into his eyes, but she couldn't help it, and there they were, and she was stuck.

He straightened up and then he shook Katherine's mom's hand. "If you work with Dale, you know we're like this"—he put two of his fingers together so they were touching. "If you need any advice, any help, if you want to avoid the kind of thing those other mothers were talking about on the show today, you give me a call. You've got a sweet kid, and I wouldn't want to see her hurt."

"Thank you," Tessa said. "I'll probably take you up on that."

"Any time," he said.

He bent down and picked up Katherine's hand and then he kissed it the way she once saw someone do on TV to a princess. "Don't you worry about how quiet you were on the show today. You were the nicest girl on the stage."

She was stuck again, she couldn't say anything, but luckily he left and then her mom grabbed her hand and pulled her out to the lobby-type place. "What a morning!" she said. "Now we can have breakfast, and we can talk, and we can relive the entire show. Wasn't that amazing? Wasn't he wonderful? The way he seemed to *take* to you like that. I was worried when you weren't saying anything—that was just at first, of course—but even backstage, everyone was saying how charming and natural you were. Not like the other girls. They were too confident! No one likes to see a smug eight-year-old girl."

Katherine tried to swallow, but her throat was too dry. She felt scared but she didn't know why, and she wished so much that she was home.

"Oh, I'm so thrilled," her mom was saying. She hugged Katherine when they got out onto the street, and she looked into her eyes in a shiny way, almost with tears. "I'm so proud of you, honey. I don't think I've ever been prouder. And *Ray* was so wonderful! Didn't you love him?"

Katherine didn't know how she felt about him, except she knew she didn't love him. "He made me feel funny," she said. "He touched my hand."

Her mom gave her a funny look. "When did he touch your hand?"

"When he gave me the picture. His hand came under the picture, and he touched me in a funny way."

"Oh, don't be silly. He was handing you a picture."

"So did you see yourself on the show afterward?" Louann asked. "Did they give you a tape?"

Katherine sipped at her ice-cream soda and shook her head. "Uh-uh, but they said I was so good, I was the best," she said, in an eager, sweet voice. "The man said he liked me so much." She looked around the restaurant then, and Louann could feel her kicking the table leg.

"What's the matter?" Louann asked.

Katherine looked down into her soda. "Do I have to make a lot of money and go on TV all the time, do you think?"

"Honey, no. What would give you that idea?" she asked, although she could imagine—not that Tessa would ever go so far as to say Katherine had to, but she had the feeling Tessa had let her know, somehow, that it would be an excellent idea.

"One girl on the show, she said she was going to pay for her college," Katherine said.

"Well, that was her. You don't have to pay for your college or even go to college if you don't want to. And you don't ever have to go on a show again if you don't want, either. But it sounds as if you liked it."

Katherine was looking down into her soda again. "I was sick before the show," she said quietly. "I was scared." She was hesitating, but Louann could tell she wanted to say more. "Mommy said it would help her in her job."

"Do you mean if you went on the show?"

Katherine nodded, and Louann was furious. She hadn't had to insist on seeing Katherine by herself—Tessa had "things to do" in her apartment, and she was happy to have Katherine off her hands. But now Louann *would* have to insist on talking to

Tessa. And she could just imagine how productive it would be. She would tell Tessa it wasn't fair to pressure Katherine; she would tell Tessa that she knew all about it, because of her own experiences; and Tessa would get that glassy, stubborn look in her eyes and tell Louann that she knew nothing about it because she wasn't a mother.

"I want you to make me a promise," Louann said, and she held out her hand across the table. "Hold my hand while you give me your answer, okay?"

Katherine looked excited, and the fear had gone from her eyes. "Okay," she said, and she put her hand in Louann's.

"First of all, when we finish our ice cream, we're going to go to a stationery store and I'm going to buy you a little address book that's going to be all yours, okay? So that you can write to me and write to your mom from home. And you're going to have my phone number in it, and whenever you're coming to New York, you ask your father to tell me in advance, okay? He has my number, but I want you to, also. Do you promise?"

Katherine nodded solemnly and squeezed Louann's hand.

"And the big promise is that you always call me if you're wondering about things like whether you have to go somewhere or do something new or special. Because a lot of times, people will think something is fun for you and it may not be. I can remember when everyone thought it was so wonderful that I had to give these recitals—"

"What's a recital?"

"It's where someone gets up and plays the piano or sings or plays another instrument. And when I was your age, that's what I had to do, and everyone thought it was wonderful except me. I wanted to stay home and play with dolls and with other kids, but I had to do that instead. And I was afraid to say that. And I can remember getting sick, too, and even pretending to be sick, sometimes, to get out of it."

Katherine seemed hungry to hear more. She made a little jump on the banquette and said, "Really really? You're telling the truth? You swear on your best friend's life?"

Louann smiled. "Absolutely. Is that what they say now? That you swear on your best friend's life? When I was growing up, everyone took blood vows."

"Blood?"

"You know, where they pricked themselves with a pin and then touched their blood to their friend's." .

"You did that?"

"I never did that, no. I really didn't have a best friend," Louann said.

Katherine looked extremely serious. "I have a best friend, finally," she said with an exaggerated sigh. "I'm going to tell her about the blood because we're best best best friends now, and I think we could do that. I wouldn't even be afraid. Because once when Patrick, he just made a tiny mistake, but he jumped up and his tooth came down on my cheek, and there was blood. I wasn't even afraid. I didn't even cry one bit."

Louann smiled. "That's good. Because you knew he didn't mean it."

Katherine nodded. "Because you know what? Because Daddy said that dogs, they never hurt anyone on purpose, because if they love you, they never even want you to do anything you don't want to do. Like they wouldn't even want you to take them for a walk except if you wanted to."

"Oh, I don't know about that," Louann said. "But we have a pact, okay? That's like a promise between two people."

"Okay," Katherine said quietly, squeezing her hand.

Later, when Louann brought Katherine back to Tessa's apartment, she was shocked by what she saw—an amazing luxury, really staggering when you considered that Tessa had moved to New York only a few weeks earlier.

"This view, of course, is what everyone will go crazy over," Tessa said as she led Louann to the picture window. "I mean, you forget it's a one-bedroom apartment when you see a view like this. Dale has the same one, you know. And I heard Ray Nicks say that he'd like to have a view like that someday—can you imagine? A man like Ray Nicks, who can afford anything? But apparently he has some incredible mansion up in Dutchess County and has the same apartment he's had for twenty years in New York."

"Mommy, I have to go to the bathroom," Katherine said.

Tessa blinked. "You know where it is," she said. "Go ahead."

Katherine looked uncertain. "But the window."

"What about it?"

"It's in front of the toilet."

"Honey, no one's going to see you. We're twenty stories up."

Katherine still looked uncertain, and she was shifting from one foot to the other. She bit her lip, and she looked at Louann. "What if I fall?"

Tessa laughed. "You're not going to fall! Don't be silly. Just go in and sit down, and I promise you that you won't fall."

"I'll go in with you," Louann said, holding out her hand.

"No," Tessa said quickly. "She has to learn to get used to things like this if she's going to grow up. Just go in and sit down, Katherine."

Katherine looked as if she was going to decide against the whole thing, but Tessa said, "Go on," again, and finally she left.

"I think that's a legitimate fear," Louann said. "Twenty stories up is a lot for anyone to get used to, Tessa."

"Well, she's going to have to start someday. And if everyone coddles her for the rest of her life, she's not going to get anywhere."

"She was afraid of the show," Louann said. "She told me she was afraid, and I know exactly how she felt, Tessa. I told her she doesn't have to do that sort of thing if she doesn't want."

"You don't have the right to say *anything* like that to my daughter," Tessa said. "I can't *believe* that you did that. First of all, it was an opportunity any mother would have taken." She reached for a cigarette. "You can't understand that because you don't have a child, but believe me: when you see an opportunity, you take it." She shook her head and exhaled a long stream of smoke. "What people don't seem to realize is that I'm making an entirely new life for myself, and it's going to be everything I've always wanted. I can *see* that you think this apartment is too luxurious—I can see it in your eyes—but why is it too luxurious for me but not for Ray Nicks or for Dale?"

Louann heard footsteps, and Katherine came running back into the room.

"It was scary," she said, wiping her hands on her skirt. "But I did it. And I looked out the window before I left, and the people looked like little ants." She looked exhilarated and proud of herself.

Tessa held out her arms. "Come here," she said, and Katherine went over and put her arms around Tessa. "There are so many things I know you can do, honey," Tessa said, cradling her in her arms. "Never listen to people who tell you you can't do things, all right? I want you to promise me that," she said, looking into Louann's eyes. "Do you promise?"

"I promise," Katherine said.

26

"I'd like you to type this up before you work on anything else today," Dale said.

It was eight forty-five, and they were the only two people in the office. Tessa was glad she wasn't the only person there, and that perhaps Dale would be able to steer her thoughts from the crazy thing she had done the night before.

She knew it wasn't instinct she had followed; at this point in her life, she was positive she was able to distinguish between following her instincts and blindly following whatever path fate threw out ahead of her. Except that last night, she had made a mistake.

She had been looking through the phone book, working late at the office, and she had been in the Ms when she had finally let herself look up her father's name: Edward Madrewski.

There was no way she could have known he would be in the book—her mother had never said he had moved to New York, and not everyone who lived in New York was listed in the phone book—but something at the back of her mind had told her he would be there.

She hadn't been able to tell anything from the address—she didn't know New York well enough to know whether West Forty-sixth Street was a good or bad address—but she found it interesting and almost amazing that she lived in virtually a straight line across from him—daughter on the east side and father on the west.

What she had planned to do was to go look at the building and leave it at that, at least for a while. She had no interest in the man, no desire to know him. She merely wanted to connect in a marginal way, just to see where he lived.

The building was a crowded, broken-down tenement with fire escapes laden with broken flower pots, clothes, and pieces of lawn furniture. And Tessa was devastated by the sight. She knew it was unimportant: What did it matter where the man lived, when in fact she wanted nothing to do with him in any case? But now that she saw the squalor in which he lived, she realized she had had visions of a modern luxury building much like hers, with a doorman and a successful father somewhere inside.

And then she had done the thing she now felt had been most stupid and rash. She had gone in and pressed his buzzer— although the door inside was broken and open—and said, "It's me," when a gruff, angry voice had answered.

She had told herself this wasn't one of her good spur-of-the-moment acts—it reminded her of visiting Jim Herrick's room all those years ago—but she had climbed the stairs, four flights, up to the fifth floor. There had been sounds from televisions and stereos on each floor, and different food smells—garlic and something sweet, then something burning—but on the fifth floor, Tessa didn't notice any of the sounds or smells because her father was standing in the doorway at the top of the stairs, an older-middle-aged man, unshaven, in an undershirt and nylon pants that were too short. She knew it was him because of his eyes— the same sharp blue that had been in the pictures.

"Who the hell are you?" he said, and she had turned and run down the stairs.

"Anybody asks what you're doing," Dale said, "you tell them it's for Dale Sylvan and that's all. Don't let anyone even look over your shoulder."

Tessa was glad for the distraction. She didn't want to think about the squalor she had seen; she didn't want to feel that it could have anything to do with her life. "Fine," she said, trying to focus on reading the title. "Working Proposal: The Source," it said. "For Eyes Only."

"Just type it up as quickly as you can, please," Dale said. He walked over to the coffee machine, and Tessa felt he looked nervous, that his movements were jumpy. He was a strange bird, someone she never felt she could quite second-guess. He was certainly a man of the world, someone who knew people from every walk of life, yet he seemed almost childishly impressed by certain people. "If I could handle the publicity for even one of those astronauts, I'd do it for free," she had heard him say one day. And now, looking down at his childish script— he wrote all of his proposals in longhand—she felt as if she were looking at the work of a boy rather than a man. He put so much pressure on the pen that his words were embossed on the back of each page, and each "i" was absolutely perfectly dotted, each "t" crossed with the precision of a machine.

She wondered if her father had ever had any kind of real job, and if not, how he managed to live in Manhattan. Although it looked as if it wasn't much of an achievement in his case; she would rather have lived in Lodenton than in the building he had probably spent years in.

It has nothing to do with you, she told herself. You're going to be as successful as Dale someday. Maybe even more so.

She began to read and type.

"The idea of the Source is an idea whose time is come," she typed. "In this day and age, when the bar scene is no longer the most desirable way to meet people of the opposite sex, the Source is destined to take the place of this once-important venue.

"Today's working men and women are constantly on the go. They travel from city to city, often knowing no one except their colleagues, often knowing no one at all. The Source will provide a place for today's sophisticated singles to meet one another and relax in a sophisticated yet informal atmosphere in which membership will be the ticket to meeting similar, like-minded people in every major city across the United States.

When Tessa first began typing the proposal, she thought the idea sounded silly. She didn't like the name, and she didn't like the way Dale led off with such a long introduction before getting to the actual idea of what the clubs would be. But the more she read as she typed, the more she thought it was an excellent idea. If she were traveling on business, she knew she would like the idea of going to a club in Chicago or New Orleans or Los Angeles, where there would be other people like her who were either just visiting or who knew the city and could possibly show her around. She liked the idea that the club would provide services—travel, money, the kinds of things credit-card companies did—again, for people who were traveling to whatever city the club was in. And mostly, she liked the idea that the club would be restricted to people of a certain income, because that meant that if you went to the bar or restaurant of any of the clubs, you would know that the people you met in that club were successful. You could trust them more, and you could network with them, as the proposal suggested.

Dale had written the proposal for investors; people or corporations could invest a minimum of fifty-thousand dollars into the limited partnership, up to a maximum of two million dollars.

Tessa felt the hint of an inspiration as she typed, but she tried to ignore it; certainly she was about to inherit enough money that she could invest, but the money would be her nest egg. She was going through the first chunk of her inheritance staggeringly quickly, and the idea of parting with the second chunk was frightening, sickening even to consider.

But what if it was a wonderful idea and she could be in on the ground floor? Dale had been involved in so many different kinds of business deals over the years—restaurants, health clubs, record distributorships, production companies—and from what Tessa could see, they had all been successful.

What if this were her chance to be in on something other than the sidelines? Ever since her grandfather had died, she had known that yes, she was soon going to have more money than she had ever had in her life, but on the other hand, it wasn't so much that she could change her life completely, or live in the style in which she wanted to live. And when she had gotten the job with Dale, she had felt sure that she would soon meet all sorts of wealthy people, successful people, who could somehow change her life. She had even begun to consider moving into personal management—she felt she would be excellent acting as an adviser, and she knew that Dale had contacts who could make it happen. But she wasn't sure she wanted to be behind the scenes, acting merely on someone else's behalf.

The other day she had helped one of the account executives at a pasta-eating contest at a restaurant Sylvan represented. The cast and crew of "Coronado" were the pasta eaters, and more than three hundred fans had shown up to get photographs and peeks of their favorite soap-opera stars. At first Tessa had loved it; her job was to keep the fans back and in line, and she had loved telling them they had to wait their turn and feeling as if she were part of something important. One middle-aged woman had been sobbing—"I *have* to see Troy Wingate. My lunch hour is ending, and I haven't even gotten his autograph!" And Tessa had taken great pleasure in telling the woman she would just have to wait her turn. "*Everyone*'s here because they're a fan," she had said. "You'll have to wait in line like everyone else."

But halfway into the afternoon, her feelings had begun to change. Sure, she had met some of the actors and actresses, and yes, she was behind the velvet ropes with the "important" people. But she *wasn't* one of the important people; anyone could have served as her substitute. She was a body performing a function; the other people were the stars. And as for meeting someone wealthy, perhaps someone she could marry, she wasn't sure she wanted to deal with another relationship. She loved being on her own. If there was a way she could turn a small amount of money into a large amount, she would be able to live as she wanted, and she would have to answer to no one.

She thought about her father in his undershirt and too-short pants, and she had a vision of herself at that age. She refused to let it happen.

"Tessa, are you almost finished with that?"

"Almost," she said, "but actually, I have a question."

"Is this the road your mom took when you went last week?"

"I don't know," Katherine said, looking out the window.

They were on their way to New York. He was going to interview for the job on Saturday—the plant ran seven days a week, three hundred sixty-five days a year, and most of the managers operated on flexible schedules. The job sounded good, and he was glad to get out of Lodenton.

But he was feeling uncertain. The last time he had been over at Caroline's, together they had watched as Julie and Katherine worked on a dollhouse they were building. It had started as a small project, just a fruit box Caroline had lined with some old wallpaper. She had shown the girls how to make furniture from old cereal boxes and small scraps of wood, and the project had grown and become more elaborate every day.

"We're going to make one for Katherine after we finish with this one," Caroline had said. "You can't have just *one* mouse house, anyway, because the family has to have neighbors."

"But mine are going to be chipmunks," Katherine had piped up. "Because Dad, remember the chipmunk that's up in my closet? He would fit so perfect in one of these houses."

There was something so easy about watching the girls play and talking with Caroline. There was no tension in that house; nothing was impossible or frustrating or unfair; nothing was irritating because why why why was the world so unjust?

The contrast grew even clearer when he called Tessa that night to tell her that he was coming to New York and thought it would be nice if Katherine could spend the weekend with her again.

"What do you mean, this weekend?" she had practically

shrieked. "Why didn't you call me earlier? Why are *you* coming, too? Why did you *tell* me, Glenn?"

"Because I wasn't sure whether I was going to do it or not. It's for a job interview in New Jersey. I'm going to be staying at a hotel, but I wouldn't want Katherine to spend the weekend in a hotel room. What's the problem?"

"The problem is that I'm having a dinner party Saturday night. The problem is that I have a barely furnished apartment—I have a dining room table now, and chairs, and some living room furniture, but I'm having the entire party catered, and I can't afford to have a—"

She had stopped then, and Katherine had known what she had been about to say. She couldn't afford to have a child mess it up.

"Fine," he had said. "I'll just bring Katherine with me. Maybe Louann—"

"Louann is coming to the party!"

"All right, then maybe she can go over to Gail's. It would just be for four or five hours, while I'm at the interview."

"Why can't you leave her with Mrs. Everson?"

He had sighed then. "I could have, but I thought you would want to see her, so I gave Mrs. Everson the weekend off. I could leave her with your stepfather, or with a friend, Caroline Leighton—"

"Who?"

"The woman I told you about," he said. "The mother of Katherine's new best friend. But I thought you'd want to see her."

"Well, I do. Of course I do, Glenn. God. Look. Just . . . I'm sure I can have her stay with Gail that night, and it will be no big deal."

"All right. But look. We're going to have to bring Patrick too—"

"Patrick! Why? You're going to bring a *dog* to New York?"

He had tried to explain it, but he had explained it badly. The truth was that Katherine had come back from her last visit to New York in a strange mood, a mood he couldn't quite even describe. She had been proud and excited to tell him she had been on a television show. His first reaction had been one of anger—how could Tessa have planned something like that without consulting him?—but Katherine had picked up his feelings and almost pleaded with him. Her mom had been so happy! And she had had a fun time, she swore on a blood vow. It had been fun, and she had been a model with Amanda, and she had seen Aunt Louann, who told her she could call her any time. And she had looked out a window that was twenty stories up, and wasn't that great?

When he had heard that Amanda had been part of it, he felt better. It was the Ray Nicks show, a show he had actually heard of—not the cable nightmare that had flashed through his mind when Katherine had first told him. But she had still acted quieter than what he had become used to lately. And when he brought up the possibility of their going to New York again, she had looked frightened and asked if he could come, too.

And that was how he had come up with the idea of Patrick. If he, Glenn, couldn't be in Tessa's apartment with Katherine, at least the dog could be, and he could provide a good feeling of security for her. And Patrick had calmed down enormously in the time Tessa had been gone.

"I think it's important for Katherine to have something secure with her on these visits," he had said.

"What do you mean, 'secure'? What are you talking about?"

He knew he had to tread delicately, and he had tried to explain: New York was a large, strange city for Katherine. She needed help adjusting, and Patrick would serve as that help.

They had argued, and she had finally given in before hanging up. He suspected that Tessa was treading delicately these days, so that when they finalized Katherine's custody arrangements, he wouldn't object to the idea of Katherine's visiting her frequently.

"Daddy?"

"Yes, Kath."

"Ask Mommy if Patrick can sleep on my cot?"

He glanced at her quickly. She had her thumb in her mouth, so she must be sleepy. "I can ask her if you want, but you could ask her, too."

She didn't say anything. Then: "Daddy? Does Mommy have to go to work when I'm there like last time? In a special way like for the show?"

"Nope. It's going to be Saturday tomorrow, so she won't have to work. And you'll go see Amanda."

"Did Mommy say about the TV show some more?"

"Well, she told me about it. Is that what you mean?"

She was looking out the window. Finally she said, without looking at him, "Is there another TV show?"

"Do you mean that you have to be on? Absolutely not. I thought you were happy you had gone on the show."

Silence.

"Do you know—you must know this, honey, because I've explained it to you so many times—if you don't want to do something like that, you don't have to."

She looked down at her hands. "Mrs. Everson says there's things I gots to do every day even when I don't want to. Mrs. Everson says I gots to go to school even when I don't want to, and she says even Patrick gots to do things he doesn't want to."

"Those things are different," Glenn said. "You don't have to do *new* things—you don't have to do those strange, new things like going on a TV show if you don't want to." He felt he was unable to make himself clear, and he felt a panic over the need to explain any of it to her. She was so young; her world was supposed to be perfect. He found it unspeakably wrong that Katherine's world was filled with dangers that had not existed when he was growing up. Just the other day, she had asked if one day she could walk home from Julie's house—she had a child's conception of the distance, the fact that it was "five minutes away" because the drive was five minutes long—and he had said no, absolutely not, it was much too far. Later he had realized that, in fact, when he had been growing up, he and his friends had walked that distance all the time. But times had changed.

He glanced over at Katherine. She had fallen asleep with her head against the window and her mouth open, and she was breathing slowly and deeply. They were getting close to New York now, passing seedy-looking motels and auto-repair shops and tire stores, and he felt a sickening bolt of fear as he thought of Katherine getting lost in a city as big and impersonal and dangerous as New York. It had been years since he had been to New York—since senior year in high school, when his class had come on a trip—and now that he was seeing the city, even seeing its outskirts, he realized he wouldn't have been so quick to let Katherine come last week if he had had a good picture in his mind of how rough it all was.

Tessa's apartment was in midtown, she had said, and he went across town on Forty-fourth Street. Even when he got to Fifth Avenue, none of it looked glamorous to him. The lights seemed too bright, and the cars were all honking, cutting each other off and going much too quickly, given that there were so many of them in such a small space. And it was so unresidential. It was clearly a city to work in, not to live in. He found the garage she had told him about—she had said it was on the corner of her block, so this was where she lived—and he pulled in and woke Katherine up. The place was filled with fumes, and as he and Katherine and Patrick walked up from underground, Glenn had the feeling they were entering another world. He didn't like it.

"So what do you think?"

Tessa was twirling around the room like a girl, and Patrick thought it was a game and began to jump on her.

"Down!" she yelled.

"Patrick, come here," Glenn said, and he patted his thigh. Patrick came, but he was obviously wound up and overexcited. Because there were no rugs on the floor, the sound of every step he took seemed magnified. Somehow he seemed bigger and stronger than he did back home, his head wider and sillier-looking than in his own house, his tail obviously a potential destroyer of everything within three feet of the floor. Had Tessa had more than a few things in the apartment, it would have been a disaster.

"It's pretty nice," Glenn said. "Nice view."

"Nice view? Do you know what a view like this is *worth*? It's unbelievable that I have a view like this from my first apartment. Gail and Walter live in a *cave*."

Glenn swallowed and looked around. It was so stark. He had seen apartments like this on television, on the shows Tessa had watched, in which there were always rich, angry women living in them.

Katherine came out of the bedroom. "You got a big bed," she said.

"That's right," Tessa said, putting her arm around Katherine's shoulder. "So you and Mommy can sleep in the bed tonight instead of on the cot and the floor. Won't that be better?"

Katherine nodded and went to the window. "Daddy, I looked out the window in the bathroom before all by myself, and I wasn't scared. On the toilet."

"That's wonderful," he said in a weak-sounding voice that he knew was going to betray his fears. He knew it was irrational—millions of children lived perfectly happy lives in New York, and had for years. And his daughter was merely visiting for a weekend. But it sickened him even to think of her spending forty-eight hours in this stark, sophisticated apartment.

"Mommy?"

"Yes, honey."

"Does the window open?"

"Not this one," Tessa said. "That one over there does, and the one in the bathroom. Why?"

Katherine had a funny look on her face as she turned around. "Don't open it till we're home in Lodenton, because what if Patrick jumps out? What if he sees a cat down in the street, and he jumps out?"

"He wouldn't jump out, but if you're worried about it, I'll keep the window closed—all the windows closed—until you leave. How's that?"

Katherine nodded, and then she walked over to Glenn and put her hand in his. "Will you be way far away?"

He forced himself to smile. He didn't want to leave her even for the night. "Not way far away, just over in New Jersey, which is across the river. The river called the Hudson River." He felt he was babbling helplessly, but he couldn't stop or he would betray his feelings, his irrational panic over leaving his daughter with the woman who, after all, was her mother, leaving her in a city where millions of people were just fine every day. "It's really not far at all," he said, as much to himself as to Katherine.

"What is this job, anyway?" Tessa asked. "Do you think you'll take it if they offer it to you?"

"I don't know," Glenn said. "There's a lot it depends on."

"Well, I have a lot to do," Tessa said, "and I'm sure you still have quite a drive ahead of you. Where are you staying, anyway?"

He reached into his pocket. "Here's the phone number and the address, and also the number of the man I'm seeing in case there's an emergency. You can call that number any time—he has a beeper so he'll get the message and get in touch with me."

She was looking down at the piece of paper. "They're putting you up at a Days Inn? That's the best they could do?"

"It happens to be right next to the plant," he said. "It's convenient."

She shook her head. "Very bad PR. They should hire me as a consultant. Half the feelings you're going to have about the job will be formed by things they obviously haven't even thought of—how good a night's sleep you get the night before, how good your food is, how well you think the company is going to treat you."

"They're going to treat me very well if I accept the job," he said. "I don't have any doubts about that."

"But they should be putting you up at the *Plaza*."

"Tessa, the plant is in New Jersey."

He swept Katherine up into his arms and twirled her around. "So are you going to be okay? You're all set for the weekend? Tomorrow you'll go over to Amanda's, and then I'll pick you up on Sunday?"

She nodded. She squirmed out of his arms and knelt down on the floor with Patrick, rubbing her cheek against his. He looked thrilled and immediately began licking her face, and Katherine laughed and screamed and rolled back on the floor. "Bye, Daddy," she said happily.

Glenn said good-bye to Katherine and Tessa and left before he could change his mind.

Tessa had hardly slept. She was exhausted and she felt edgy and ill at ease—what if the caterer didn't show up? What if everyone canceled at the last minute? What if she had invited the wrong people? She felt as if she were nine years old again and about to have the most disastrous party of her life, and she could remember the same sharp, specific fear: what if everyone discovered she had no friends?

"Hurry up or we're going to be late," she called out to Katherine.

"Okay," Katherine called from the bathroom.

The idea of having the evening had come to her because of Dale Sylvan, actually. When they were discussing the Source, he had mentioned that he often connected with investors at dinner parties, and that naturally, if Tessa were having something like that, he'd be interested in coming. She had wanted to invite Louann and her new boyfriend, a man named Alexander Bollin, a producer at the record company where Louann worked.

But three people didn't seem like enough, and she hadn't wanted to invite Gail and Walter. And then suddenly she had remembered the Wadlens, who seemed perfect on all counts. They were rich and successful and probably had money to invest; they would be handy to know for general reasons; and they would make her look successful to Louann and this new boyfriend.

But Tessa kept feeling she would be exposed as a fraud; the party had been cobbed together with strangers.

"I didn't pack my pajamas," Katherine said, running back to the bedroom.

Tessa sighed and looked at her watch. They were on a tight

schedule—she had to get Katherine over to Gail and Walter's and be back at the apartment by five o'clock, and it was already nearly three. "Hurry up," she called.

"I can't find them!"

Patrick went tearing into the bedroom, and Tessa heard a shriek and then, "Down! Patrick, sit down."

Tessa followed him in. He had turned into an enormous dog, an enormous, undisciplined, clownish monster. "They have to be somewhere," Tessa said.

"I can't find them! Just the tops."

"Well, that's enough. Come on. We're going to be late."

"It isn't enough," Katherine shrieked. "I need the bottoms."

"I'm sure Amanda has an extra set."

Katherine began to cry, and Tessa grabbed her wrist. "It's nothing to cry about. Come on. Patrick, we'll be back soon, so relax. Katherine, stop crying."

"But Mommy," she was wailing.

Tessa dragged her out of the apartment and rang for the elevator. "Katherine, I want you to stop crying."

"But I didn't say good-bye to Patrick," she wailed.

"You can kiss him a special hello when you see him again."

"But I *can't*," she screamed. "I can't go to sleep without saying *good-bye*. And I don't want to sleep without a *bottom*," she wailed.

"You're going to have to," Tessa said, wishing the afternoon were already over.

They got into the elevator, joining a man Tessa had noticed a few times before. Katherine was sobbing, and the man seemed concerned but was also obviously trying not to interfere.

"I want to go back," Katherine wailed. "Mommy, please. *Please.*"

"No," Tessa said. "We're late as it is, and he'll be fine, and you'll be fine." She looked at the man in a conspiratorial way, as if to say, Children can be so difficult at times, but he gave her a cold glance and looked away.

Katherine was still crying on the street, and there were no taxis anywhere. This was the New York Tessa detested and couldn't get used to. When you wanted to get somewhere fast, there was never a taxi and you couldn't drive, because anyone who lived in New York would be insane to keep a car.

In her last letter to Roy she had talked about it, because she knew he was interested in issues like city planning and transportation. He still hadn't answered her first letter. She wasn't going to let herself be depressed about that, but she felt more vulnerable than ever now that she was alone.

She dropped Katherine off as quickly as she could at Gail and Walter's. Katherine seemed hesitant at first—Amanda had another friend there, and Katherine could be so shy. But Tessa had whispered to Katherine that she was the prettiest girl in the room to make her feel better, and then she had left.

When she got back to the apartment, she hurried upstairs so she could start getting ready.

She heard a high-pitched shrieking as she got out of the elevator, and for a minute she thought it was a child. But then she realized—Patrick!—and her fingers went cold as she hurried to unlock the door.

He was scratching wildly—it sounded like a machine that was tearing at the door—and when she opened the door, he threw himself into her arms, a ball of white and brown fur that whimpered and pushed at her so hard she fell back against the wall.

And then she saw what he had done. The apartment had been destroyed. He had dug holes in every cushion of the couch. He had peed in the center of the one small rug she owned. He had gone into her bedroom and dragged out the clothes she had laid out on the bed, and he had ripped the dress in two places. He had chewed one of the heels of her shoes off.

"You bastard!" she screamed. "What's the matter with you? You've ruined my *life*!"

He looked at her and sat down and wagged his tail hopefully, as if she were about to forgive him, his brown eyes full of affection.

"I can't *believe* you! How could you do this to me?"

He began to squeal, and he ran to the door.

"You want to go out? All right, we're going to go out."

She tried not to look at him as he gratefully wagged his tail and leaped into the air against his leash as they waited for the elevator. He sniffed at the doorman and wagged some more, and he gave a little leap as the spring air reached his nose.

Heading into the park, it was as if he had his own secret plan: his nose was down, his tail was high and alert, and he lunged and pulled as if he knew exactly where he was going.

Tessa saw a group of dogs and people in a fenced-in enclosure half a block away, and Patrick seemed to see it at the same moment. He lunged more strongly, and she let him pull her along. She was thinking about her torn dress and the heelless shoe, but she was also thinking about something else.

She unhooked Patrick's collar and leash and watched as Patrick ran and played with the other dogs in the enclosure. It was as if he was so happy he didn't know who to sniff or run with first—he would go from one to another and then leap into the air as if to express his happiness, and then he'd look for new dogs and start all over again.

Tessa looked around, and no one seemed to be looking at her or paying any attention. It looked like a cliquish group—she could remember similar people in Lodenton, pathetic people who thought more about their dogs than their own families, if they had any.

She opened the gate and took one look back—Patrick was leaping into the air with some kind of spaniel. Both their mouths were hanging open, and Patrick's eyes were bugged out in a sort of amazed joy.

She walked away from the enclosure and out onto Fifth Avenue. She threw Patrick's leash and collar into a trash can and then headed back to her apartment to get ready for the party.

27

"What do you think I should do?" Glenn asked.

Caroline took another sip of coffee and glanced out the window where the girls were playing.

He would not forget the past Sunday afternoon for as long as he lived. He had picked Katherine up at Gail and Walter's, where she had obviously had a good time with Amanda, dressing up and making pancakes, and generally creating chaos. Katherine was happy they were going to go back to Lodenton, though. She told him in the car on the way to Tessa's that even though she had had a good time, she was happier back home, and she liked Julie better. It was fun to have a best friend, and Julie was hers.

Glenn was glad that Katherine had volunteered her feelings about Lodenton without his asking. It made his decision about the job that much easier—they had offered it to him—because it was clear it would be too soon to change Katherine's circumstances again. Let her adjust to the separation and the impending divorce, and then he would think about changing jobs.

They had gone up to Tessa's apartment, and right away he had known something was wrong. Tessa had looked worried—something you didn't often see with her—and frightened as she pulled Glenn aside.

"What's the matter?" he asked.

"Where's Patrick?" Katherine asked.

"Just a minute," she said to Katherine, and she pulled Glenn into the bedroom. "Patrick's gone," she said.

"What? What do you mean? What happened?"

She took a deep breath and let it out. "I took him to the park, and I had him on his leash—I wouldn't have let him loose since it's so unfamiliar—and I was walking along and a squirrel jumped out. He jerked and somehow got loose. I ran after him, but he

296

took off across the park before I could get him. It was as if he was so happy being loose that he just didn't want to come back. He wasn't even running after the squirrel at that point. He was just running for the joy of running.''

He would never forget the feeling of horror. How could they tell Katherine?

"Why didn't you call me?" he asked. "I don't understand why you didn't call me. How many hours ago did it happen?''

She had given him the oddest look in the world then, a look he would also never forget. "Yesterday,'' she had said.

"Mommy, where'd Patrick go?'' Katherine called out. She came into the room, and Glenn saw in her eyes that she was wondering, but she had no idea that he was really gone. In her child's mind she probably thought he was out for a special walk with someone else for a Sunday treat.

And he could honestly say that telling her that Patrick was gone was the worst thing he had ever had to do. Tessa had tried to make it seem more positive—"Don't forget, he has his tags on, and he had his leash,'' she had said. "So when you get back home to Lodenton, someone will probably call and tell you they found him.''

"They *won't* call,'' Katherine had cried. "They'll want to keep him for themselves, and we'll never see him again.''

On the way back to Lodenton, Glenn had stopped at the ASPCA and found out an awful, unexpected fact. Because Patrick didn't have a New York City license, if he were found and turned in to the ASPCA in the city, they would keep him for a shorter time than if he were licensed in New York. It would be important to check every day, they told him, or Patrick would be put up for adoption or put to sleep.

Driving back to Lodenton, he had found himself nearly out of control. He had always prided himself on his careful driving, on his adherence to the rules everyone else ignored after a few weeks behind the wheel. He always kept his eyes on the road or on the rearview mirror—you could look at your passenger after the ride was over—but that night, he had driven wildly and with revenge on his mind.

It turned out that Tessa had given the party after Patrick had been lost—"I had already done everything I could do,'' she had told him calmly—and he couldn't help thinking what had already occurred to him, involuntarily, when she had first told him the news: she had let it happen on purpose.

It was obvious that something had gone wrong. Patrick had

been upset; anyone could see that from the dug-up couch and Tessa's ruined shoes on her bedroom floor. He knew how Tessa felt about her possessions, and certainly she had to feel intensely about the new possessions that were such an important part of her new life.

What stopped the thought was that he couldn't imagine anyone doing what she had done—certainly not to one's daughter's dog.

But now, Caroline told him it wasn't that difficult to imagine.

"Things like that happen all the time. My father shot my dog when I was eight," she said, looking down at her hands for a moment. "Jack had gotten into the chickens one too many times, and there was no question about what 'had to be done,' according to my father."

"Couldn't he have given the dog away?"

She shook her head quickly, and for a moment he could see her as a child—not quite beautiful but with an exotic, spirited face and flashing, angry eyes. "I asked him the same question, and he said it wouldn't be fair, that Jack would just do the same thing to the next person's chickens that he had done to ours. It was a different situation, but it happens all the time, Glenn."

"But Patrick was so important to Katherine—and now of all times."

"Do you think you'll get another?"

"Eventually, if she wants. But I think it's too soon. And maybe he'll still be found." Although it was looking pretty grim. If someone had found him, wouldn't they have already called?

"What about the job?" Caroline asked.

"I would never take it," he said. "Not now. I think her friendship with Julie is too important." He looked into her eyes. "And I hope you know how important you've become to me, too," he said.

She looked up at him and smiled.

"You're not going to regret this, I can promise you that," Dale said. "People who invest with Dale Sylvan never regret it. Never."

Tessa felt a thrill as she put her signature to the papers above the word *Investor*, and she tried to set aside the feelings of doubt that had gnawed away at her ever since the dinner party.

Looking back, she realized she had been too anxious about too many details of the party. One of the reasons she had hired a caterer was that she had no pots or pans and very few dishes, so it was virtually a necessity.

But when the Wadlens had arrived, Tessa had felt immediately uncomfortable. Celia had seemed shocked when she saw the uniformed waiter, and right away, Tessa had felt her plans had been much too elaborate. She had been furious that Patrick had ruined her nicest dress, and she had worn her second favorite, a low-cut royal blue silk dress that was almost exactly the color of her eyes. But Celia Wadlen was dressed much more casually, in a linen skirt and silk blouse and pearls. Tessa felt as if she were in a ball gown, and the fact that it was her party didn't give her any confidence or make her feel any better. These were the people who knew how to live.

The evening had been a failure. And it infuriated her that Louann seemed to be on the other side; she had crossed over into the world of the rich and successful, she and her rich and famous new boyfriend, Alexander Bollin.

But Dale Sylvan was successful, and Tessa had just signed the agreement with him. All she had to do was get Dale the money within a week—the closing on her grandfather's house was this Friday, so that was no problem—and she would be in at the ground floor of the Source.

She was ninety percent sure she was doing the right thing, ninety percent sure that she was once again following her best instincts. Wasn't it instinct that had led her to Sylvan Associates in the first place? Wasn't it instinct that had told her to tell Roy her concerns about her grandfather's house that day so that he would ''investigate'' and ultimately be drawn to her? And Dale had told her that Rag Nicks was going to be the Sources major investor, so wasn't that encouragement enough?

But a small voice of doubt told her the plan was a fantasy, that it was something her mother would have loved because of its ambitiousness. The voice told her she was unable to distinguish between real, achievable plans and unrealistic ambitions, because she was her mother's daughter and had never learned how to tell the difference.

Tessa looked down at the check for fifty-nine thousand dollars and felt like dancing. It had all been worth it: the day she rarely looked back on—''the day of her grandfather''' was as specific as she ever got in her mind—and the move to New York. The life she had always wanted was getting closer and closer to the life she was living. And now, with the rest of the money, it would come that much more quickly.

"God, I feel so sad," Louann said when they were out in the fresh air. "It feels so final."

"Oh, come on. Grandpa was an unhappy man, and he died before he became completely miserable. He was lucky. And now we're lucky."

"It just feels odd," Louann said.

"If you feel so uncomfortable with the money," Tessa said, "then give your share to me."

Louann gave her a long, intense look. "I have no reason to feel uncomfortable," she said. "I'm just sad, which I think is understandable."

Tessa shrugged it off and headed off on her own.

"Katherine isn't here," Mrs. Everson said. She had the same bovine, stubborn look in her eyes that Tessa remembered. You could ask her all the questions in the world, but if she didn't want to answer you, you'd learn absolutely nothing. And her hair was an absurd-looking silver that was nearly blue. Didn't she know how obvious it was that she dyed her hair?

"You've already said that," Tessa said. "Now, if you tell me where she is, I can go and get her."

"She's having a performance at school," Mrs. Everson said. "A dress rehearsal for the play she's going to be in. I don't think she would want to be disturbed."

Tessa had to laugh. "I've come all the way from New York to see her, and you're telling me she wouldn't want to be disturbed? I should fire you on the spot."

Mrs. Everson blinked her dull blue eyes. "Mr. Stokes is the one who pays me," she said. Then she shrugged. "You can watch the rehearsal if you want. See her that way."

"Don't you tell me what I can and can't do. Mr. Stokes is going to hear about this, and he's going to be very upset about it. *Very* upset."

She flew out of the house and drove quickly to the school. What she wanted was to hold Katherine in her arms, to feel those small, thin arms around her neck and feel the soft skin of her cheeks against her own. She wanted to feel her flesh and blood, she wanted to hear that little voice.

"They're in the auditorium," the school receptionist said. It was late afternoon, and the school lobby was empty and quiet. "It's the class play for the end of the year they're rehearsing. I don't think they've actually begun the rehearsal, so you can see the whole thing if you go in now.''

Tessa felt betrayed and disappointed that Katherine hadn't mentioned the play when she had been in New York. Surely Katherine had known she would be in a play! Tessa went inside and immediately felt as if she were back in school herself. The auditorium smelled the same, and there was the same blankety silence in the back of the room. She had been such a loner back then, and she was thrilled that Katherine was participating more than she had at that age; for her, anything where she would have to stay after school was always too complicated for her mother, something she could do the next year if the chance came up again.

''All right, kids, now take your places,'' came an echoey voice from inside the wings.

A stream of kids came out onto the stage, and Tessa spotted Katherine right away. She was dressed up as a flower, with a green shirt and pink petals strapped to her head, and she was holding hands with another girl who was also dressed as a flower.

For a moment, Tessa was tempted to let Katherine go on with the rehearsal. She looked so sweet, and she looked happy and unself-conscious.

But she needed to see her. She wanted to be back in the city by tonight, and she wanted to see Katherine without Glenn.

She walked to the front of the auditorium—she had to fight the feeling that she, too, was five years old, since the smell-memory was overpowering—and she called out Katherine's name.

Katherine froze and squinted out into the darkness.

''Katherine, it's me. Look in the aisle.''

''Mommy?'' Katherine said quietly, almost in a whisper.

Katherine's teacher—Tessa had never liked her, a pretty young woman named Miss Pine—came out to the edge of the stage. ''Mrs. Stokes? Oh, there you are. We're trying to have a re- hearsal, but if you'd like to watch, you could just sit down.''

''I've come to pick Katherine up,'' Tessa said. ''Katherine, come over and give me a kiss!''

What happened next infuriated Tessa: Katherine looked over at Miss Pine, as if she were the one to listen to. How could she look to her teacher over her own mother? But then she came running to the edge of the stage and started to climb down. ''Hi, Mommy,'' she said, running into Tessa's arms.

Miss Pine was looking at her watch. "Mrs. Stokes, we have to get started. Would you mind just waiting until we're done?"

Tessa took Katherine's hand. "We're leaving." She gave a little wave. "Good-bye."

"But this is her rehearsal. We're having the performance tomorrow night."

"It doesn't look as if there's much to rehearse. How much can she have to do as a flower?"

"She's the star of the play!"

Tessa looked down at Katherine, and Katherine looked embarrassed and afraid.

"The star of the play?" Tessa said. Her voice had come out threateningly, even though she certainly hadn't intended that. But why had Katherine been so frightened and shy on Ray Nicks's show when she was also capable of being the star of a play? It was something she would have to ask Katherine while they were having a long, long talk.

She led Katherine out of the auditorium by the hand, and she could feel resistance as she pulled Katherine along. When they got out into the lobby, Katherine stopped—she felt more like a dog on a leash—and Tessa looked down at her. Tears were streaming down her face.

"What on earth is the matter? I thought you would be happy to see me."

"I'm going to be in the play tomorrow night, and I won't know my lines!"

"Oh, don't be silly. Of course you will. We can rehearse them together if you'd like. We'll go to the mall, and we'll have chocolate sundaes. You'll tell me all about the play, and then we'll practice the lines."

She was still crying. "I won't know where to go," she wailed. The receptionist was staring at them from across the lobby, and Tessa led Katherine outside.

"Now, come on. Don't be a silly. You'll know where to go. Haven't you ever rehearsed the play before?"

"Once."

"And did you make any mistakes?"

Katherine shook her head.

"See? No daughter of mine ever would. And I'm so happy you're in the play, because when I was your age, my mother wouldn't let me do anything like that. I had to go to school and then go straight home, and that was it. And now you've been on television, and you're going to be the star of the play. I'm so proud of you, Katherine.'' She had her hand on Katherine's shoulder, and she squeezed it. Katherine felt thin and small, and Tessa suddenly missed her so much. ''I really miss you,'' she said. She looked down at her daughter, but Katherine was looking down at the ground. ''Honey? Don't you miss me, too?''

''Sure,'' Katherine said.

''Do you love me?''

''Uh-huh.''

''But do you love me a lot? The most in the whole world?''

Katherine sighed. ''After we get ice cream can I go over to Julie's?''

''Honey, you didn't answer me. Do you love me the most in the whole world?''

Katherine nodded and looked around the parking lot. ''But can we go to Julie's?''

''I don't think so,'' Tessa said. ''I've come all the way from New York just to see you, so I don't think it's right you would want to go over to Julie's. You can see Julie all the time.''

Katherine was biting her lip. ''Daddy's going to pick me up there later.''

''Well, then, we'll just have to call your Daddy and tell him you're with me.''

Katherine swallowed and looked down at the ground. ''But he—he'd be going there,'' she said. ''He has dinner sometimes.''

Tessa had to think about that. He had dinner there sometimes. Hadn't Katherine said in New York that her friend Julie had a mom but that her dad lived in California? ''Come on. Let's get in the car and get some ice cream, and then we can talk about this,'' Tessa said.

''But Mommy.''

''Katherine, if you don't start acting happier to see your mom, I'm going to be the saddest person in the world when I go back to New York tonight.''

The mall was crowded, and Tessa was thankful it wasn't part of her daily routine. The ice-cream place she had wanted to go to had disappeared, but Katherine said there was a new one— Julie's mom had taken them two weeks earlier. Tessa felt her mood getting darker. Every other sentence out of Katherine's mouth was about Julie's mother! Tessa knew life had to go on— when she had left Lodenton, she couldn't have expected everyone just to stop living—but she felt a growing rage listening to the happy little details of Katherine's new life. Glenn apparently had had dinner with Caroline Leighton two or three times that week. Katherine thought it was fun because they were all together, and it was like having a sister even more than having a best friend.

"What else?" Tessa asked when the sundaes arrived. "Does Daddy stay a long time at Julie's mom's house after dinner?"

"Um, I don't know."

"Do you mean you go home, and he stays?" Tessa was outraged.

"No. Um, but me and Julie go to her room after dinner. Sometimes we go to sleep."

Tessa felt as if she could hardly breathe. Glenn was setting up a happy domestic life without her. She had been so sure he would wither away and suffer on his own. She hadn't imagined he would ever even meet another woman, much less actually like her.

"Does Julie's mom work?" she asked.

"She works where Daddy works," Katherine said.

Tessa picked at the ice cream, but it tasted foul. "Have you seen Daddy kiss Julie's mother?"

Katherine's cheeks turned dark red, and Tessa realized she had never seen her blush before. "Um, I don't know."

"What do you mean, you don't know? If they kissed, you must have seen it."

"One time," she said quietly, almost inaudibly.

Tessa pulled out a cigarette, and the waitress came toward her from nowhere. "There's no smoking here. I'm sorry."

"In this entire restaurant?"

"In the whole mall, actually."

Tessa looked down at Katherine's bowl. She had barely touched her ice cream, either. "Are you finished?"

Katherine nodded. "I don't feel good."

"Well, we're going to get out of here and you'll feel better. We'll go see a movie. I saw there were children's movies on the marquee at the theater over there."

"But Daddy."

"Daddy can wait," Tessa said. Katherine was dragging at her, actually dragging her feet along the floors of the mall walkway. "Katherine, would you walk like an adult, please?"

Katherine pulled up short. "I think I have to throw up," she said. She was holding her stomach, and she had her old, desperate, frightened look back in her eyes.

"Oh, honey. Do you really?"

"Hurry! Mommy, help me!" Katherine sank to the floor and started to heave, and Tessa held her forehead with one hand and braced her chest with the other. *No one* but a mother was supposed to do things like this; she couldn't bear the thought that Katherine was involved to such an extent with another woman, another mother.

A mall security guard came over, and Tessa could feel Katherine's muscles tense and then relax. She began to cry and Tessa pulled her back into her arms, and Tessa said "Shh" and stroked her forehead. "See? You weren't really sick after all," Tessa said. She looked up at the guard. "Everything's okay. You can leave us alone."

Katherine needed her. That was the problem. She needed to be with her every day instead of with Glenn and this other woman. That was what was upsetting her so much.

"Are you feeling better?"

"I want to go home," Katherine murmured. "Mrs. Everson'll be there, and she can call Daddy."

It was so clear. Poor Katherine was tense because her life was confused; Tessa honestly didn't understand how Glenn could put her through so much. Didn't he understand it was crucial that neither of them see anyone else until Katherine was adjusted to the separation? Tessa had felt that it was so obvious—she had known it instinctively—that she hadn't thought it was necessary to actually discuss it with Glenn.

But now, it was so clear. And she felt it was more important than ever that she get herself in shape financially so that she could actually file for divorce and get physical custody of Katherine.

28

Tessa hadn't been able to decide what to wear. She had never been to a fund raiser before—tonight it was a gala at the Waldorf to benefit an orphanage, organized by Dale Sylvan himself—and Tessa had wanted to look her best. Basic black was always good, she knew, but did she stand out enough?

"Hi. I'm Tessa Stokes. I'm with Sylvan Associates—"

The man smiled a brittle smile, said, "Nice to meet you," and moved on.

Tessa told herself not to take the rejection personally, even though it was at least the tenth one of the night. The room was filled with famous people, and those who weren't famous had no desire to meet someone like her.

"Tough crowd," she heard someone say, and she turned around. It was Ray Nicks, lifting two drinks off a tray. He handed her one and moved off toward a corner. "I remember what that was like, when I was first starting out."

"You?" she asked. "That's hard to believe."

"Hard to believe I was ever just starting out or hard to believe I can remember?" She laughed, and he sipped his drink. "If I told you the shit I had to put up with to get where I am today, you'd never believe it. But you have to realize I started from nothing, literally. There wasn't *one* person I knew who was in show business, not one person who even knew someone who knew someone *else* who was in show business."

"So then where did you start?" she asked. "How did you do it?"

He shook his head. "I bombed in ten thousand hole-in-the-wall clubs and then another ten thousand hole-in-the-wall clubs, only these ones had bathrooms, and on up from there." He touched her shoulder. "But you're different with your little girl. You've got Dale, and you've got me."

"Well, I don't know that I'm necessarily going to go in that direction right away," she said, although she suddenly felt an almost pathological energy, as if there were too much blood in her veins: Ray Nicks had been thinking about Katherine, and he assumed she would be going into show business! "I'm not sure she's quite ready," she said, thinking about Katherine's collapsing on the floor at the mall. If she was going to vomit or almost vomit every time she was under stress, it would take time before she was ready to go out on stage again. But then again, hadn't she just *starred* in her school play? "Do you really think she has a future?"

He was smiling. "You know, it's funny. I have mothers ask me that question all the time. And ninety-nine—no, ninety-nine point nine nine nine nine nine percent of the time, the answer is hell no, only you say it a little more politely to the nice ones. The nasty ones, you stick them with the truth. But it's funny, that day on the show when we had all those professional little girls, those pretty faces the modeling agencies love—and I'm not saying your girl isn't pretty, because she is, she's a hell of a cute kid—but I'll tell you: she was the only one who really caught my eye. There was a vulnerability there that I—I can't really put my finger on it—but she could go far, Tessa. She could go damn far."

Tessa wanted to run out of the room and leap through the air. She wanted to get on the first train down to Lodenton, or rent a car and drive all night so she could bring Katherine back right away. "She's coming back up to New York next weekend," Tessa said. "I wonder—" She stopped. What was she thinking? She had just told herself that Katherine would need time before she could appear before an audience. But then again, there was so much groundwork to be laid! Maybe they could just meet with Ray Nicks, and he could advise them on directions and contacts. It wouldn't mean that Katherine would be appearing before an audience.

"Are *you* interested in the business?" he suddenly asked. "I mean you yourself, not your daughter."

"Oh no, not really," she said. She felt flustered, although she didn't know why. "It's really—no, it's not something I'm interested in in terms of being out in front of any cameras or anything. I see myself as more of a behind-the-scenes person. After I get enough experience with Dale, I think I'd like to work as a personal assistant to a star—you know, someone's right hand—and then move into management. I think that's more where my talents lie.'' In fact, she had decided that working for someone else would make her seethe with annoyance and envy, but she didn't want to jinx the high hopes she had for her investment in the Source.

He nodded. ''Could be a good idea. You just seemed so gung ho there, I thought you might have your own designs there, so to speak.''

''No, not for myself. Uh-uh.''

''You were saying a minute ago, and I interrupted—you wonder what?''

''Oh. Well, I was wondering . . . I know you're busy and everything, but I was wondering if when my daughter was here we could talk to you—you know, about career directions and that sort of thing.''

He was smiling a smile she didn't understand. ''Hm. It's an interesting idea. I'll tell you what.'' He hesitated, and then he said, ''Ah, what the hell. I was going to go up by myself, but I guess the right kind of company is better than none at all. Why don't you come up to my place in Dutchess County? I've got a kind of zoo your kid would flip over, and we could talk. You need talking to, you know.''

''I do?'' she asked.

''Aren't you talking about investing in Dale's new idea?''

Her heart stopped for a moment. ''I already did. Aren't you?''

There was a commotion by the orchestra pit, and Dale was suddenly up on the stage behind a microphone. He was wearing a white suit with white shoes and a red tie, and his hair was now a deep, rich brown—in his latest dye job, he had gotten rid of the red highlights, and he had deepened his tan in the past day as well. For a moment, Tessa had a sickening vision, a moment in which she viewed him objectively, as if for the first time: he was her enemy.

''Ladies and gentlemen,'' he said. ''We're proud to begin the twentieth annual dinner and auction for Our Lady of Mercy Orphanage. As you know—''

Ray Nicks's arm had slid from Tessa's shoulder to her waist. He turned to speak. ''I've got to get up on that stage in three seconds.'' When she looked into his eyes, she felt the oddest sensation. It was close to what she felt when she was attracted to a man, when there was a mutual attraction and the moment came when she was looking into his eyes and she could feel how it would be to make love with him. It was close to that, but she couldn't honestly say she was attracted to Ray Nicks; the feeling was one shade removed, as if she *wanted* to feel an attraction for him. They were being drawn together by the look; something had shifted.

He went up on stage and told some jokes and stories, and Tessa tried to look at him objectively. He wasn't an attractive man physically—his paleness was off-putting, almost upsetting to her. But she liked him. It was amazing to her that only a few months earlier, he had been a shadowy figure on television, someone whose show she never watched but who always seemed to be there.

And now, she knew him. And there seemed to be a chance he was attracted to her. Even more than a chance, because why else had he singled her out?

There was a huge crowd around Dale and Ray, and Tessa couldn't get close to either one of them. She had been at edges all evening—the edge of the ballroom during the auction, and now the edge of the only circle she had a chance of breaking into.

Suddenly Ray was breaking through the knot of people, saying he had to get some air, and Tessa decided to latch on to him. Either he would reject her as everyone else had, or not, but at least she had a chance with him.

Without even looking at him, she could feel him noticing her at his side. When she finally looked, he was smiling crookedly but not looking at her. "*Some* of these people are going to think we're together," he said as they stepped out into the cool night air.

He took her arm, and she felt the moment was a turning point: Ray was going to be an important man in her life, in some way. "Maybe we could be," she said softly.

He looked down at her and smiled. In the light of the streetlights he looked strange—the shadows of his face were exaggerated, and his smile seemed to be contorted. "You're very ambitious, aren't you?"

"Well, yes, but I hope that isn't why you think I said that."

"Darling, I've had more offers from women like you than you can imagine. Women and men. We all have. And I don't expect you to separate me from my image. Why should you when no one else does? God, what a bore these charity auctions are. How'd you like to go out and get truly smashed with yours truly?"

"I'd love to," she said, feeling as if she were crossing an invisible line.

His stories about his childhood stunned her. Life in the orphanage—not Our Lady of Mercy—was tough, grueling, and violent, both sexually and otherwise. He had stolen to survive when he had left, and he had even hustled when he was fifteen and sixteen.

She was shocked he was telling her the details. As far as she knew, he had never gone public with any of it.

"Christ," he said after his fourth drink, holding his head in his hands. "I'm a wreck."

"Are you sorry you told me? I mean about your childhood?"

He lifted his head. "Ah, I've been thinking of talking about it in public . . . everybody's doing it these days. I guess I'm just testing you out." He turned his head slowly, as if it hurt, and looked into her eyes for a long time. "You don't have to come this weekend if you don't want," he said. "If you think I'm pushing you into it."

"You? Not at all. Why would you feel you were pushing me into it?"

He waved a hand and put his head in his hands again. "Ah, I'm drunk. I don't know. Sometimes . . ." His voice trailed off, and he was just sitting there then, a drunken man at a nearly empty bar holding his head in his hands.

29

"I wish I wasn't going," Katherine said. She and Julie were in Julie's playhouse with the toy horses Julie's mom had given them. Katherine's was the baby colt, and Julie's was the mom that was called a mare. Katherine loved the horses, but she didn't feel like playing.

"Couldn't you say you don't want to?" Julie asked. She made her horse jump over the little fence they had made out of sticks, and then she made the horse whinny.

"I told my dad," Katherine said.

"What'd he say?"

Katherine shrugged and looked down at her horse. "He said I didn't have to if I didn't want to, but that I'd have to go sometimes, so maybe it was the best time." She made her horse leap over the fence like Julie's did, but it didn't feel like any fun. "If I don't go, my mom'll start crying and asking do I love her and why won't I come."

"She cries in front of you?" Julie asked.

"Sometimes. Maybe her eyes are dry, but her voice is all sobby."

"My mom cried all the time when my dad and her got divorced," Julie said. She was crawling on the ground out to the outside.

Katherine followed her out onto the lawn. The grass smelled so green and like dirt, and she put her cheek down on it and closed her eyes. The funny thing was how it was never soft like it looked, not like cotton when you touched it, but she still loved the way it felt, like she was settled and she wasn't going to have to go anywhere.

Her dad was coming to pick her up the way he did almost every night most of the time, and she was so happy, she couldn't even explain it. At the beginning when her mom left she had felt so bad, and all she could think was, When will they get back together and I can be happy?

But it was a funny thing, and Julie had said the same thing: what if her dad and Julie's mom could get married? Katherine had thought the thought maybe twice, but she couldn't say anything out loud, but then Julie was the one: "And we'd be sisters!" they both yelled at the same time, and the dog next door started to bark because he thought they were in trouble.

She had even dreamed it one night, and it was such a happy dream, Katherine and her dad, and they were laughing at Julie's mom's house, only they *all* lived there. It gave her a pain inside when she thought of how her mom would look, and right away she could feel her stomach get that feeling, and she'd have to think about something else. "You married that *woman*?" she could hear her mom screaming, even when she was trying not to think about it. "I'm going to take Katherine, and I'm going to take her as far away as we can go, and you'll never find us again, ever ever ever!"

And she guessed that was the thing she was afraid of, that what if she went to New York, and her mom wouldn't let her come back? Sometimes when she was in New York before, her mom would talk about "when we're together," and Katherine couldn't stop thinking about the story. What if she bundled them into a car and they started to drive and they didn't stop until they were way far away?

Sometimes Katherine felt like she was a balloon that was about to burst with so many worries. Today in school she was thinking about what if her mom stole her away, and she had to run out of the room because she thought she was going to throw up, and Timmy Graves said "There goes Kathy Throw-up." And then in a high voice like hers, "Uh-oh, I think I'm going to throw up!"

It had made her feel so bad because it wasn't like she did it on purpose, sometimes she just got scared. And it had only happened two times in school, so she couldn't see why he was making so much fun of her.

The night before she was supposed to leave with her mom, Mrs. Everson was tucking her into bed, and Katherine pulled her down so her ear was right down where she could talk into it real quietly. "I have a secret question," Katherine whispered.

"Tell me the secret question," Mrs. Everson whispered back.

"If my mom said she was keeping me for the weekend, only

she didn't bring me back, would you and Daddy and Julie's mom be able to find me?''

Mrs. Everson made her head go back like an animal, and even in the dark Katherine could see she was surprised. ''What on earth would give you an idea like that, Katherine? Your mom isn't going to kidnap you and take you away.''

Kidnap. It was the word Katherine had forgotten.

''But if she did,'' Katherine said.

Mrs. Everson put her hand behind Katherine's head, and Katherine could see she was looking down at her like she felt sorry for her. ''Honey, if you only knew . . . your mother is the very last person on earth who's interested in taking care of a child, and if she took it into her head to kidnap you and keep you, I'd say that the world was coming to an end.''

Katherine didn't understand. Did she mean it would be the end of the world because it would be so terrible? ''But what if she did?'' she asked. Because that was the important part of the question. Would they find her?

''If she did, we would drive up to New York and bring you back.''

Katherine kicked at the blanket. ''No! If she took me far away! Would you find us if she took me far *away*?''

Mrs. Everson patted her forehead. ''Of course we would find you. No matter what it took.'' She stood up. ''Now, go to sleep. The weekend will fly by, and you'll be back home safe in your bed, and in a few weeks you'll have the whole summer to play with Julie.''

Katherine closed her eyes tight, but she had scary thoughts right away, a car door slamming that she couldn't get out of, and Patrick barking on the other side. She was afraid, and it felt like no one understood why.

''Hello, is this Mr. Masterson's secretary?'' Tessa asked. ''Good. Hi. My name is Tessa Stokes, and I work with Dale Sylvan at Sylvan Associates. We represent a restaurant called Borelio's . . . I don't know if you've heard of it.''

''No, I haven't,'' the woman said coolly.

''Oh. Well. It's really wonderful. I know Mr. Masterson is in town, shooting a film; I saw him the other night at the Our Lady of Mercy fund raiser, and we were calling to offer him lunch at Borelio's. Or dinner, if he'd prefer.''

''He's leaving for L.A. tomorrow morning,'' the woman said.

''Well, he could go today,'' Tessa said.

"I'm afraid not. But thank you."

Tessa hung up. She felt ill at ease and afraid. First thing on the Monday morning after the orphanage fund raiser, Dale had told her he wanted her to begin taking on more responsibility. "I can't have one of my investors be one of my secretaries," he had said. "If you're going to stay on at Sylvan, I want you to take on more responsibility. Get more of a feel for it. Start working your way up."

She had asked him right then and there, in his office. "Is Ray Nicks one of your investors or not?"

He had been sitting at his desk with the morning sun streaming in at his back, and he was searching through his in box as she asked. He didn't stop riffling through the papers, or even look up at her, as he said, "When it's all signed, sealed, and delivered, you'll have the name and address of every other partner. That's New York State law."

"But what about now? I thought you told me Ray was going to be the Source's major investor."

Finally he stopped looking through his papers. "Tell me what's bothering you," he said. "What difference does it make whether Ray Nicks is going to invest in the Source or not? He doesn't invest in everything I do."

"It gave me confidence," she said. "I'm getting worried."

He leaned back in his chair and put his feet up on his desk. "There's nothing to worry about. The project is a gold mine, Tessa."

She didn't say anything. She wished she had asked Ray more about what he meant. Maybe it didn't mean anything that he hadn't invested in it.

"Listen," he said, swinging his feet down to the floor. "If you're that worried, I'll have my lawyer draw up papers for you. You can withdraw, and we can be done with it. I didn't ask you to invest with me. *You* came to Dale Sylvan, remember?"

She swallowed. He was letting her withdraw.

He shrugged his shoulders and went on looking through his papers. "It's entirely up to you what you want to do, but I need to know by the end of the afternoon. It's not exactly standard procedure to let people back out like this, and I don't want to waste a lot of my lawyer's time on it. If you want to withdraw, fine. But tell me by this afternoon."

She finally decided to stay in, feeling that since Dale had offered her an out, he couldn't be thoroughly dishonest. She couldn't ignore the fact that he had a tremendous amount of experience in just this sort of venture; if he had started restaurants and clubs and produced records and even a movie, why not something like the Source?

She had slept badly, with nightmares about the deal waking her up every few hours. In her dreams, her mother kept saying how wonderful the idea was, and how this was the project that would cement Tessa's wonderful future. "I even think the idea would appeal to Jacqueline," she said, moments before Tessa woke up in a cold sweat.

And then this morning Dale had handed her a new project—it was another side venture, something that didn't have anything directly to do with public relations. It was an art contest sponsored by the Drake Silver Art School. Right away, Tessa had thought of the obvious—Dale Sylvan, Drake Silver.

"Do you have a few minutes?" Tessa had asked Margery. Again Tessa felt that Margery was the only one she could trust.

"This Drake Silver Art Award," Tessa had said. "Is there something strange about it?"

"How much have you read?"

"Just that this is the third year they're giving it."

Margery smiled and drew hard on her cigarette. "It's vintage Dale. Absolutely vintage. But there's absolutely no way he's going to get away with it three years in a row." She leaned back in her chair and took another long drag. "Dale buys mailing lists of all sorts of people—so-called opportunity seekers, who are known to be ripe for this sort of thing, subscribers to certain magazines, anything he can think of.

"He announces a contest—you draw your dream landscape was what it was one year—this year it's what?"

"A realistic drawing of a person," Tessa said.

"Whatever," Margery said. "It really doesn't matter. Now, just for entering, you get a prize, and of course it's something cheap, but it's an incentive and an encouragement; it keeps people interested. Little old Miss Smith, the retired art teacher who taught for sixty years, enters the contest, and amazingly, a month later, she's told that she's the winner of the Drake Silver Art Award. This is her dream come true—all her life she's considered herself an unsung portrait painter, and now she's actually won an award! She's invited to the ceremony, and naturally she buys the so-called limited-edition 'awards book' at thirty dollars a copy.

"Our Little Miss Art Teacher arrives at the ceremony just thrilled, and maybe she even brings her family along. And then, at the actual ceremony, the truth comes out: everyone who entered—everyone!—has 'won' the contest. People have traveled from Louisiana and Alabama and Ohio and Pennsylvania because this is the first prize they think they've ever gotten for an actual achievement. Only it's not; it's . . . well, Dale and I go back an awfully long way. Most of his games don't bother me, because they don't hurt anyone directly. But this lonely old widow thing bothers me; I've never had anything to do with it, and I never will."

Tessa felt the blood leave her fingers and toes. "Have you ever invested in any of Dale's ideas? Any of his productions or anything like that?"

Margery grinned. "Nope, and I haven't been to the moon either."

"This is going to be absolutely wonderful," her mom said, rolling down the window to pay the toll. "I've fixed up the apartment quite a bit since you were here last. I think you're really going to like it. And I have a special surprise for you for tomorrow."

Katherine shut her eyes and started to pray. Her dad had been taking her to church almost every Sunday, and there were parts she thought were so creepy, like the smell of the incense, because sometimes it made her sick, plus sometimes when she closed her eyes to pray, she saw a witch. But she liked the idea of talking up to God, with his white hair and everything, like a wise old man.

So right now, she prayed it wasn't going to be, We're going to take a long, long trip and go way far away. Anything but that.

"Do you remember that time your father and I took you to that castle outside of Lodenton, where there was a big lake and a dock and a garden like a zoo?"

"Uh-huh," Katherine said, because it had been one of the funnest days, and she could still remember how she had walked holding her mom's and dad's hands with her feet up in the air and she swang like a monkey.

"Well, we're going to go to a place like that tomorrow. How does that sound?"

"You mean to the zoo?"

"To a place like the zoo," her mom said. "It's a place where a man lives, and he loves all kinds of wild animals, so he has all kinds of wild animals at his private estate. He told me he has peacocks and snakes and llamas, and that it's better than the children's zoo in New York. Sometimes he even lets school kids come to his castle, but this time it's just going to be the two of us.''

"Why?" Katherine asked.

"What do you mean, why? Because he invited us. Because he's your mom's friend.''

Katherine felt sick. She wished she could leave a trail of breadcrumbs or tie a string, but she had the feeling this place would be way far away, too far for a string. What if no one could ever find them?

She shut her eyes even tighter and tried to make up a prayer that would be special just for tomorrow. The minister sometimes said that if you wanted something bad enough, and you had been a good person, you would probably get it if you prayed to God. Although she had prayed for Patrick to be found, and he still hadn't come back yet.

Her mom's apartment felt scary and like a doctor's office. She went around the apartment showing Katherine the new things she had bought, like a home entertainment center with a TV and a VCR, because it was important for her work, and new covering for the couch that Patrick had dug up, plus a whole new rug for the bedroom. Katherine looked at it all but she couldn't speak.

"Isn't it amazing what I've done in only a few weeks?" her mom said, and then she held out her arms like an eagle and knelt down on the floor. "Come here and give me a kiss. You look so beautiful, Katherine.''

Katherine walked over to her and climbed into her arms.

"Do you love me?"

"Uh-huh," Katherine said.

"I love you more than anyone on earth," her mom said. "And you know what? Tomorrow is going to be such a wonderful day, it will be such a wonderful place, you'll probably never want to leave.''

"Honey, are you almost finished with your cereal?" her mom called out from the bathroom.

"I'm trying." Katherine forced the food into her mouth and then swallowed it like a machine. In and then down and then more in and down her throat.

Her mom came out into the living room, and she looked different.

"What's different?" Katherine asked, because she couldn't say.

"Oh, just a little makeup. A new kind of eye shadow I decided to try. Do you like it?"

Katherine nodded. She thought her mom was always beautiful no matter what, even if she just woke up from a nap.

Her mom was looking at her watch. "Ray said the car should be downstairs at nine-thirty, so we should be out of here in a couple of minutes. I don't want to keep him waiting."

"Ray?"

Katherine's mom smiled. "You know Ray, from the television show," she said. "He's the man who owns the castle."

Katherine could feel her stomach start to jump around, and she bit her lip so she could think about something else.

Ray was the man who owned the castle. Ray was the man that had made her feel so funny when he looked at her.

"Mommy?" They were out by the elevator now.

"Yes, honey."

"I don't want to go."

Her mom gave her a look like the one that meant, Don't be silly. "Of course you want to go. Any little girl would want to go see a castle and a zoo, where it would all be yours for the whole day and no other little kids would be around to bother you."

Katherine felt her heart beating fast. "I wish there *was* other kids. I don't mind the other kids when Daddy takes me to the zoo near home."

"Well, that's different."

They got into the elevator, and it sounded like the doors were banging shut too hard.

Katherine tried to swallow, but her spit caught in her throat and she started to cough.

"Are you all right?"

"I feel sick," Katherine said.

Her mom gave her a fierce look, like, You'd better not. "Now, I'm not going to hear any of that nonsense about feeling sick. If I thought you were really sick, then of course we wouldn't go. But honestly, I've heard it too many times. That day at the mall, and you didn't even throw up—you're going to have to realize someday that people will stop responding if you're always threatening, Katherine. You remember the story of the boy who cried wolf."

It was one of the scariest stories Katherine had ever heard, but she couldn't see how she was like the boy, because she *did* get sick; she really did!

"And you're also going to have to realize that it isn't an attractive quality," her mom said. She took her hand and led her out through the lobby.

Katherine looked up at the doorman and he put a hand on his hat and smiled.

"You know there's no one in the world who loves you more than I do," her mom said. She was looking up and down the street and Katherine did, too, but luckily she didn't see any Ray in any car. "No one loves you more than I do, no matter what anyone might tell you. And that's why I want so many things for you, honey. But those things don't happen to girls who get sick all the time. People don't like to be around little girls who get sick all the time."

A giant black car came down the street so quiet you couldn't hardly hear a sound, and a man with a hat came out. Katherine felt happy for a second because he had a hat like the doorman, and he touched it the way the doorman did, and it seemed like a friendly thing to do. Maybe he was going to come and take them away before Ray came to get them! Maybe Mrs. Everson had even gotten nervous about all the questions Katherine had asked her, and she had sent a man to save her.

"Mrs. Stokes? I'm Quinn, your driver. I'll be taking you up to the estate whenever you're ready."

"Isn't Ray coming?"

"Mr. Nicks is already up there. I took him up last night."

"Oh. Well, we're ready."

Katherine couldn't tell what it meant that the man didn't say anything to her, but then Katherine didn't think about that anymore when she saw the car more close up. It was big and black, like the car they took her great-grandfather away in that time, when Louann was crying so much and said that he was dead. And "dead" meant he wasn't coming back to see them ever again, that he had gone to live with the angels.

Katherine took hold of her mom's hand when they got into the car, and she squeezed her eyes shut tight.

30

It was like a fairyland Katherine saw once in a movie. The castle was built of giant stones, and there was even a little guard's house in front of it. The trees were tall tall tall, and if you stood underneath them it was like being in the bird place at the zoo, because the birds were chirping and flying all over the place, more than Katherine had ever seen.

There was a lake behind the castle—you could see it behind if you looked through the trees, and the lawn even when you got over to it was like green velvet, the softest grass Katherine had ever felt.

"There you are!" came a voice, and Katherine looked up.

"Ray, how are you," her mom said, and she went up and kissed him on the cheek.

Ray Nicks looked over her mom's shoulder right into her eyes. "Glad you could come," he said. "Glad you could come."

He unhugged from her mom and came over to her, and he got down half-bent and took her hand again like the last time, and kissed it like the last time.

When he let go of it she could feel his spit still on it, and she wanted to wipe it off, but she had the feeling that it would be a rude thing to do.

"So," he said, and he straightened up. "What would you all like to do first today? Tessa, naturally you and I have to get together to talk. But first, how about some Bloody Marys and a little Virgin Mary for our little virgin Katherine?"

Katherine looked up at him even though she didn't want to. She didn't know what he meant, but she knew that the minister talked about Virgin Mary all the time.

"That sounds wonderful," Tessa said. "Honey, maybe a little tomato juice would make you feel better."

"Tomato juice!" Ray Nicks said. "Give me a little more credit than that, Tessa. This is the famous Ray Nicks secret blend, famous from Katmandu to Kalamazoo. Haven't you ever heard me talk about it on my show?"

"Sorry," she said.

"Ah. Confessing you don't watch my solid week of shows on New Year's Eve and New Year's Day celebrations? Shame on you, Tessa. Shame on you."

There was something funny in the way he talked, like he was nervous, too, Katherine felt. They went into the castle, and it was echoey and just like a real castle, with stone floors. There was even a knight in armor near the front door. The kitchen was like in a fairy tale, with a giant old wooden table and a stove you could put wood in, all black and old-looking, and Katherine thought about Hansel and Gretel, because it was just like the stove the witch put them into. It was exactly big enough, and Katherine looked up at her mom.

"Oh, Ray, this is amazing," she was saying. She was running her hand along the table and looking up at the ceiling, and Katherine guessed maybe she shouldn't be scared about the stove, because her mom wasn't scared at all.

"Yeah, this is it for me," he said. He was taking two giant pitchers of the juice mixture out of the refrigerator. "When I get fed up with my producer or agent or the show, and I wonder why I don't just throw in the towel, I come up here and realize this is why. This is what keeps me going."

"It's really amazing," Katherine's mom said.

Ray Nicks set up a tray with glasses and the pitchers and said they should all go outside, where they could sit and relax. They walked through a narrowish stone hallway and then through a room that was like a storeroom, and then suddenly out into the sun where it was like a park. The lake was right there, all sparkling in the sun, and there were ducks on it and geese, and Ray Nicks said sometimes swans were there, but they had died. There were benches like in a park, and stone walls, and yellow flowers that smelled so sweet almost everywhere you looked, and there were more birds singing, even, than there had been under the big giant pines in front.

"We can go in the gazebo to have our drinks," Ray said, "unless you'd like to go sit by the lake. Katherine, would you like to go see the ducks?"

"Sure," she said.

"In that little shed over there, go in and look for a little brown box," Ray Nicks said. "It's a surprise for you."

Katherine ran down along the grass to the shed and opened the door, and right away she saw a brown wood box, mixed in with tools and things, but on a shelf by itself. She opened it up, but all that was inside was crumbs.

She went out into the sunlight, and her mom called out, "What is it?"

"Um, crumbs," she said, because it felt like a joke.

"It's to feed the ducks with," Ray Nicks called out. He and her mom were sitting on a bench, but Ray Nicks came walking down the grass to the lake and took the box from Katherine's hands. "Here. See? If you just throw the bread, the ducks will come right in."

She was afraid to, but she looked up at him while he was throwing the bread at the ducks. She liked the way they were coming in, like friends. From the side, Ray Nicks didn't look so scary. When she couldn't see his pale blue eyes, he looked more like a regular person, only almost like a ghost.

"See?" he said. He put the box in her hands, and she looked up at him by mistake.

She meant to say thank you, but she couldn't open her mouth. The way he looked at her—it was for a long time and it was like a message, like before at the TV show—and she held on to the box and couldn't speak.

"Did you know that ducks marry each other for their whole lives?" Ray Nicks said. He reached into the box and picked out some crumbs, and he looked into her eyes while he was doing it. "Hm? Did you know that, Katherine?"

She shook her head.

"Do you know what that means when I say 'marry'? Because, of course, they don't actually go to a church and stand in front of a minister. It means when they mate together, when they make babies, they make babies with only one other duck."

Katherine looked up to see where her mom was, but she was walking around in the thing that was called a gazebo and sipping at her drink.

"Do you know how they make babies?" Mr. Nicks asked.

Katherine had a funny feeling. She didn't want to say the answer. Her dad had told her about it on the day they got Patrick, plus her and Julie looked at a book once that Julie's mom had read to them.

"Hm? Do you?" Ray Nicks asked.

Katherine knew she was supposed to be polite and answer what he asked, because her mom said you always had to do what adults wanted, plus even when she didn't want to kiss somebody hi or good-bye, she had to when her mom said.

But then she remembered her dad saying she didn't have to ever talk about things she didn't want to talk about, and she didn't never have to talk to a stranger, not ever. Only she guessed Mr. Nicks wasn't a stranger, because she knew him.

"Are you always this shy?" Mr. Nicks asked. He was smiling down at her, and she didn't know what to say, and then he put his hand on her shoulder, and it felt hot. "Well, we can talk about all kinds of things later on, when it's just the two of us."

He walked away, back up the lawn, and Katherine watched while he went up to her mom and then sat down on a bench.

She saw her mom sipping her drink and laughing, and then taking another sip and laughing some more.

"I'm not saying it was necessarily a mistake," Ray Nicks was saying. "Dale has made a tremendous amount of money in the past. A tremendous amount. But he's in some serious trouble with the IRS. I mean *serious*. And it wouldn't be the first time Dale has borrowed from Peter to pay Paul. He missed going to jail by that much once ten years ago," he said, gesturing with his fingers, "and it was hushed up pretty well. But I'd never invest with him again. Unless I wanted to lose a carload of money," he said with a laugh.

Tessa felt as if the lawn and the willows and the gazebo were swirling before her eyes. "What kind of trouble with the IRS?" she asked. Her voice was thin and weak, and she could barely breathe. How could she have been such a fool?

"He owes them, basically. He's always hidden behind so many corporate names. He's always thought they'd never catch up to him. But he was kind of a challenge to them is my guess. And they've got him. Three weeks ago he was almost crying when he was telling me, I swear."

"What am I going to do?" Tessa said. "That's all the money I had in the world. I'm paying twenty-one hundred dollars a month in rent alone, and I was counting on getting money back."

"Look. Don't panic. The investment may be completely legit; maybe he's come up with some other way to pay the IRS. You never know."

She looked around for a moment at the world Ray had created for himself. A hundred miles from New York, he had made his

own paradise, a landscape of deep greens and quiet and manicured luxury that was his and his alone. He owned a castle and
acres of deep green lawns, a topiary garden, a children's zoo, a
private lake—probably everything he had wanted as a young boy
just barely scraping by on the streets. And what had she been
dreaming of for herself and for Katherine? She had honestly
thought that she was on her way to creating a wildly successful
future, but it looked as if she had been completely wrong.

She sipped at her drink and leaned back against the bench
and looked out at Katherine. *She* was the one Tessa had wanted
to create the perfect world for. She looked so happy feeding the
ducks, such a perfectly happy-looking girl at that moment. "I
want so much for her," Tessa said. "It's amazing how when
you have a child you just refocus all your energies. There's so
much you want that you had never wanted before." They were
words she had heard other people say so many times; in her case
she felt they weren't quite true, because she had *always* wanted
the world. But she also truly did want so much for Katherine;
she wanted to have her in New York, to put her in an atmosphere
in which she could thrive. The idea that Katherine might have
to grow up in Lodenton was just horrifying.

"Well, we've talked about that a bit," Ray said. "And I've
told you I think she has real potential. I remember feeling that
way about Cory Whitson—do you know who that is?"

"Of course," Tessa said, setting down her drink. Cory Whitson was a young teen star who had recently been on the cover
of *People* magazine.

"Well, I got together with him and his mom when he was, oh,
actually, I think he was exactly Katherine's age. And it was very
similar to Katherine's situation—he wasn't the handsomest little
boy I had ever seen; he wasn't model perfect. But he had a spark."

A spark. Tessa had felt herself bristling when he had implied
that Katherine wasn't the prettiest girl in the world. But she had
already faced that fact; she had already adjusted to it. And Ray
was saying Katherine had a spark!

"There are so many people I can call," Ray said. "What we
have to do—the three of us—is to decide what direction would
be right for her at this point in her life."

"What would you recommend?" Tessa asked. She was beginning to feel drunk—she had been too nervous to eat breakfast
back in New York, and the Bloody Mary was going to her head.
But she had the feeling she would have felt drunk anyway: Ray
talking about "directions" for Katherine! There Glenn was, back

in Lodenton, plodding along with his life, too stuck to even consider a dream job near New York, and here *she* was, talking to Ray Nicks and arranging the next five years of Katherine's life!

"It's hard to say," Ray said. He finished his drink and set his glass down, then changed his mind and poured another for himself. "Help me out, here, or we're both going to be sorry," he said, and he filled her glass to the top. "Is it great or is it great, by the way?"

"It's really amazing," Tessa said. "I don't even usually like Bloody Marys that much, but this is delicious."

He raised his glass and took another long sip. "I think the best thing for me to do is talk to Katherine and get a feel for what kinds of situations she'd feel comfortable with. Sometimes mothers and fathers can't get as much information as outsiders can. Or maybe it's an instinct with me. I remember that with Cory Whitson, his mother thought he'd be perfect for commercials because he was so outgoing at home. But when I talked it over with him and playacted a few of the situations—what it would be like to be in front of a camera with a crew, that sort of thing—he was scared out of his wits. He wasn't ready. And if we had forced him into something he hadn't wanted to do at that young an age, he might have been turned off from the profession forever. So it has to be right for Katherine and where she is now. We can't decide for her."

Tessa nodded. She was definitely getting drunk.

"Are you feeling all right?"

"I'm fine," she said, touching her head. Of all times, she could feel a headache coming on! "I just feel a little dizzy. Probably if I take some aspirin I'll be okay."

"Why don't you lie down right here in the gazebo?" he said. "The mosquitoes won't be able to get you, and you can still be outside in the fresh air. I want to talk to Katherine by myself anyway. Take her over to see the animals and get a sense of what she'd feel comfortable with."

Tessa was looking in her purse for aspirin, and luckily she found them. She took two and stood up and felt a wave of dizziness. She braced herself, and Ray caught her.

"Maybe you should go inside," he said.

"Actually, I think I would feel better if I lie down for a few minutes," she said. She had been silly to have two drinks; if you hardly drank, two was a lot, and she had the feeling Ray had made them strong. For a moment, a voice told her that Ray had made her drunk on purpose. For a moment, the voice said that she shouldn't lie down, that if Ray had anything to say to her daughter, or anything to ask, he could say it in front of both of them.

"Of course you can come with us if you'd like," Ray suddenly said. "I happen to think kids open up better sometimes when they're without their parents, but it's up to you."

"I think I will just lie down for a bit," she said.

"Honey?" she called out. Katherine looked so perfect down by the lake, a charming little girl feeding a charming little group of ducks. "I'm going to go inside to lie down for a little while. Mr. Nicks is going to show you the animals."

"What?" Katherine called out. She was squinting the way she always did when she couldn't hear.

"I'll be right back," Tessa called out. "She'll be fine," she said to Ray as he followed her up toward the house. "She knows not to go too near the water."

"Good," he said. "You can never train kids early enough, I always say. Safety first." He led her through the entryway, which was stone cool and instantly soothing, and up the stairs. The walls of the stairway were covered with prints of amazing beauty. Tessa couldn't tell when they had been made or in what country, but they were achingly beautiful engravings of flowers and animals. "Up here there's a guest room where you can lie down."

It was a lovely room—Ray opened the windows and the scent of daffodils and new-mown grass wafted in. Tessa sat down on the four-poster bed and immediately felt better. If she could just lie down for one minute, she knew her headache wouldn't even have a chance to begin.

He smiled, blew her a kiss, and left the room.

"Are you enjoying the ducks?" Ray Nicks called out.

Katherine turned around. "Sure," she said. "Where's my mom?"

"She went to lie down," he said. "She has a headache."

She felt herself blinking at him, trying to concentrate. "She said she was coming right back."

He put his hand on her shoulder. "She will, in a few minutes. She'll come back outside as soon as she feels better. But she wanted us to have a little talk before she comes back out."

Katherine swallowed and turned back toward the lake. "Little talk" was what you had when you were in trouble, she knew from school.

"I didn't do anything bad," she said.

He smiled and knelt down so he was as short as she was. "I

didn't think you did. Is that what you think it means when someone wants to talk to you?''

She shrugged. She didn't want him to be asking her questions. She looked up at the castle, but she couldn't see her mom
in any of the windows. ''Is she upstairs, my mom?''

''She's resting,'' he said. He touched her shoulder again, and
she looked at him by mistake. ''She'll be fine. But I do want to
talk to you. And it's only about good things, Katherine. Nothing
bad at all.''

He was looking at her in the funny way, and she felt she
couldn't breathe.

''Would you like that?'' he asked. ''We could go to the zoo to
see the animals if you'd like. And I have a miniature castle up by
the zoo that could be yours to play in all afternoon, and inside the
castle, if you're lucky, you might even get to see Felix.''

''Who's Felix?''

''Felix the Cat. Haven't you ever heard of Felix the Cat?''
She nodded.

''He lives way up in the castle, and if you're lucky, you'll be
able to see him.''

''Is it far away?'' she asked. She wanted to see the animals.

''Not at all,'' he said. He stood up and held out his hand.
''Come along with me. It's just down this path. See how it's red
stones? Kind of like the yellow brick road, only they're red.''

She didn't want to hold his hand, but she didn't want to be
rude, so she put her hand in his, and he began to walk with her.

Tessa got up from the bed and felt a flash of pain behind her
eyes as she walked over to the window.

At first she thought they had gone. Out the window it was all
green treetops and lawn, manicured but somehow wild-looking
at the same time. She saw the pond and the gazebo beyond the
lush, full tops of the trees, and then she saw Katherine, walking
with Ray, holding his hand.

For a moment she saw herself as a young girl—she remembered a picture of herself at that age, walking hand-in-hand with
her grandmother up the hill behind her grandparents' house.
She remembered feeling totally safe and wishing she could be
with her grandmother all the time.

She walked out of the room and down the cold stone steps
and out into the sunlight that was suddenly somehow painful,
and then she began to run.

She saw them around a turn in the stone path, and she felt as if her heart had stopped for a moment. Katherine had heard her and turned around, and Tessa couldn't lie to herself: what she saw in Katherine's eyes was helpless, boundless relief—and fear.

Ray let go of Katherine's hand and turned around. She saw anger in his eyes, and hatred. "Tessa," he said.

"I think we're going to leave," she said, and she held out her hand.

Ray Nicks looked confused. "Why? What are you talking about?"

"Katherine, come here," Tessa said. "Come to Mommy."

Katherine came running, and she held Tessa's hand tightly when she reached her.

"I'm going to go back to the house and call a taxi," she said to Ray, "and I'd appreciate it if you waited out here until we left."

"You really are out of your mind. Do you know that?" he said, and for a moment she wondered if she had made an awful, irrevocable mistake. She had damaged Katherine's future forever! She had insulted an important, famous man!

But she knew.

It didn't occur to her that if she was right about Ray Nicks, this meant that she had brought Katherine to him with the same knowledge. She saw herself as heroic and valiant and honorable, and in the taxi on the way to the train station, she clung to Katherine with a feeling of joy. She had been a good mother today; with instinct and intelligence, she had rescued her daughter.

Tessa had a thousand questions for Dale. She knew it was early—only eight-forty, and a Monday as well—but Dale was usually in by eight-thirty at the latest. And she wanted to talk to him alone.

Her first questions were going to be about the Source and Dale's general financial health. She would be calm but forceful; if he felt there was any danger of any kind of collapse, she, as a small investor, had a right to her money. She wasn't like some of the corporations that had invested, or some of the small limited partnerships that had formed to become part of his larger one. Without the Source, she had nothing.

She walked down the hall and felt an odd sense of quiet—odd because the hallway was carpeted, and the other suites were always quiet at this hour. There was nothing wrong with quiet, nothing unusual about it. Yet it *felt* different.

As she rounded the corner of the hall, she saw something bright—neon green—on the door of Sylvan Associates' suite.

She had a sinking, panicked feeling—but maybe it was some sort of announcement?

"SEIZED," the label said in huge black letters. And underneath, "BY ORDER OF THE INTERNAL REVENUE SERVICE."

Tessa tried the door, but it was locked.

She looked around the hallway, and there was no one around. She tried the door again and then went downstairs to the coffee shop on the corner and called Gail. "I'm down at Sylvan, and the office is locked," Tessa said. "It's all been seized, Gail. By the IRS."

"I know," Gail said quietly. "I tried to call you on Saturday. Margery called me at six in the morning."

"But where's Dale? I would think he'd be there, sorting things out."

"What things? They're not his anymore. It all belongs to the government. And anyway, no one even knows where he is. If anyone did, it would be Margery, but she says she has no idea. She remembered that he was asking about South America a few weeks ago, but she has no idea if that was because he was planning to go there or if he was just trying to get a free trip."

Tessa hung up and headed back for the office. Maybe there would be IRS agents there, and she could talk to them?

But when she went back upstairs, the only people in the hallway were going to other offices. They stopped to look at the bright green labels on the door and talked among themselves, but no one knew anything.

Tessa thought about the money and tried to imagine telling anyone what had happened. She had invested fifty thousand dollars. How had she ever thought that was a small, unsatisfying sum? It seemed like a king's ransom now, like a fortune.

She thought about her grandfather and what she had done on that last afternoon of his life. She could see him lying on the living room floor and she could hear his labored breathing and his fear, and she wondered, in a way that hadn't occurred to her before, if he would have lived had she called for help. She had a sudden picture of him making a play-face at Katherine one day at his house, and she felt a burning, aching sadness.

She had lost everything. It was all over.

31

Katherine held out her hands. "Throw it the same way, low like that."

Glenn watched Caroline as she threw another pitch with the ratty old baseball the girls had found in the street. She was so good with Katherine—she had never forced herself into her life, indeed had never forced herself into his, either. "I don't think you're ready for me," she kept telling him. And he had been afraid for a while that she was right. He had been wrong with his first fiancée and wrong with Tessa, so what could lead him to believe that he would ever be right about falling in love?

"I caught it again!" Katherine yelled.

Caroline gave Glenn a sidelong glance and the smile that had been the first thing that had made him fall in love with her.

He had been lucky. The letter he had gotten three days ago had brought him more than he had allowed himself to hope for. Tessa had written:

Dear Glenn,

I've been doing a lot of thinking, and I realize that I've made a few wrong turns lately—nothing that can't be fixed, but a few mistakes that have cost me a lot of money. I never told you about a certain investment I made . . . it's gone bad, so there's no point in going through the details at this point. What this means is that I'm not nearly as far along with my plans as I had hoped to be at this point.

I'm thinking of moving to California, to L.A., where Gail has a friend who's looking for a roommate. The woman works in personal management, which is something I've always been interested in, and I think I'm going to follow my instincts and go out there.

Glenn, what I want to tell you is that Katherine is my priority—she always has been and always will be absolutely number one in my life—and because of that, I'm realistic enough to know that at this point, she would be better off with you now that my life has become unsettled.

I write this with the hope that when I'm ready to see more of her, you'll be open-minded enough to realize what I did—that I'm thinking more of Katherine than of myself—and that you'll be as generous as I'm being now.

Her letter had continued with specifics about her lawyer and arrangements, and he had felt the greatest relief of his life, realizing she wasn't going to fight for Katherine at all.

Louann had come back to Lodenton to pick up some things she had left at her grandfather's house, and she had made him feel even more confident. "I don't think Tessa's thought her plans through at all," Louann had said. "But I think she's changed a lot. When I asked about Katherine, I could see it. I brought up all the plans Tessa had had in terms of show business, and she just cut me off. 'That's over,' she said really quickly. And she said she had made a mistake. Which I've never heard her admit in her life."

He heard laughter, and he looked out to where Caroline and Katherine were playing on the lawn. Julie had finished her bath and gone running out to join them, and the three of them were racing across the lawn. He set down his coffee and began walking across the lawn to join his new family.

About the Author

Nell Kincaid was born into a literary family in New York City and has been writing books ever since she was eight.

She has published fourteen romance novels, which are still selling in translation all over the world.

But she is happiest writing suspense and is currently working on her second suspense novel.

Kincaid divides her time between New York City, where she works part-time for a financial magazine, and upstate New York, where she lives a semirustic life with her dog, Peach.